AiB

BIG IN JAPAN

Book II: Power

SANDY
ありがとう！
THANK YOU SO MUCH!!

Book II: Power

A NOVEL

by

TIMOTHY PRICE

WITH ILLUSTRATIONS BY
ALAN OW BARNES

Big In Japan
Book II: Power

Text copyright © 2016 by Timothy Price
Illustrations © 2016 by Alan OW Barnes

Additional Creative Input

Alan OW Barnes, Benny Boynton, Robert Scott Field, Alyce Price

Special Thanks

Martin Arlt, Alan OW Barnes, Benny Boynton, Mark Butler,
Robert Scott Field, Buddy Finethy, Michael Gordon, Jeff Horne,
Yutaka Ichimura, Jas Ingram, Gary Johnson, J.D. Lees,
Sean Linkenback, Bambi Lynn, Jerry Moore, Shane Morton,
David Mott, J.R. Mounts, Bobby Nash,
Nicholas (Nick Adams) Poling, Neil Riebe, Jess Rosen,
Paul Shane, Akira Takarada, Jon Waterhouse, Ricky Zero

A very special thanks to my three wonderful kids:
Kayla, Jeffrey and Daniel, and also to my awesome mom,
Joan Nims. I'd also like to thank Kathy Trantham
and Loraine VandenBosch, and last but not least, the love of
my life, Alyce, who (still) never ceases to amaze me.

This book is dedicated to Big In Japan fans worldwide! It is also
dedicated to the loving memory of my all-time horror and
sci-fi partner in crime, Jeff Woolard.

But most of all, this book is dedicated to my dad, who passed away
while I was in the process of writing it. Your sobriety will always
be the inspiration for mine. Love and miss you, Pop.

Chapter I

I have been witness to this marvel and it is indeed magnificent. It is that of an endless river, ever flowing as it circulates through an elaborate labyrinth of veins. It is like blood: precious and powerful, sweet, yet poisonous. It fuels, but yet, it does not burn. A small amount (no larger than a mustard seed) has enough energy to light a city. A dollop can sustain an entire aircraft carrier for months at sea, and a stream has the means to breathe the very life into a towering, two-hundred-forty-foot battle-bot. With a substantial amount you could rule the planet, with a little bit more, destroy it. It is, without a doubt, the future of man. This new form of energy is what both dreams and nightmares are made of, especially for the puny men who gain access to its unlimited possibilities. And this is what terrifies me so, because when you get right down to the heart of the matter, it is bloody well what this is truly all about, power. It is not about you and it is not about me, as we, as mere men, do not have the means to dictate or write history. As soldiers we can only protect it, and with energy of this nature we must accept its reality before we can accept its existence.

I note that splitting the atom was merely another evolutionary rung on the so-called stepladder of life. This is what I believe to be man's first "true" endeavor, tampering with the fires of the very gods themselves. It was indeed inevitable, and in the dying days of the second world war, man put his new discovery to the test. He unleashed his hideous new creation, brutally wiping out thousands upon thousands of lives in a shroud of black and white. And that, as they say, was only the beginning, the beginning of a journey that would lead the human race down a dark path through a thick forest, riddled with monsters just waiting to strike. May I also state that in my career I have seen far more of my share of these monsters than I care to admit, be they manmade or not. I must go on record as saying that even as beneficial as dissecting atoms, exploding hydrogen bombs and delving into hit-or-miss

1

nuclear energy has proven to be, it is still (after all of these years) dangerously unstable, and when misused can yield terrifying results. I have seen these results. I have fought these results.

Another dilemma we are forced to examine is that fossil-based fuel is now an archaic energy source. It is becoming ridiculously more and more like the decaying bones of the dinosaurs that created it, extinct. With ever-growing demands and never-growing resources, this modern world will soon find itself either utilizing alternatives, or bowing down to those who have. As a realist, I know we need extraordinary amounts of energy in order for the Earth Intelligence Organization to uphold its sacred duty of protecting the planet. But as a dreamer, I wish it were not this way. However, it is.

The simple fact is that the oil is almost gone and atomic energy continues to outsmart those who try to harness its unpredictable power. So, it would seem now is the time for an altogether new nightmare, a new abomination to spread fear, create monsters and show the world just who that proverbial king of the hill is. I believe organic thorium to be that source as it answers all of my proposed thoughts and concerns. I also believe that for power of this nature, a man would kill, destroy and compromise every belief he holds true. It will indeed change his heart to a dismal, black void and his body to an empty, soulless vessel, as the cost of ultimate power is indeed high. In my encounters, I have seen this time after time, and I fear I will see it again very soon.

Commander's Private Log
Brigadier Sir Jonathon Winston
Earth Intelligence Organization (E.I.O.)

THREE YEARS AGO

Sir Jack, commanding officer of the Earth Intelligence Organization, gave the order to evacuate London headquarters while there was still time enough to do so. The subterranean base was buried far beneath the earth, and even though it was built like freakin' Fort Knox, it shook and trembled as it began to give way. This was a crucial moment, we're talking Cuban Missile Crisis crucial, as the hidden facility protected something far beyond top secret and far beyond powerful. Something that, if it were ever to get into the wrong hands, would change the fate of the entire planet, hence the over-the-top, Area 51-type security and secrecy. Still, no fortress (even that strong or that concealed) could withstand the constant barrage of 60,000 tons colliding against its surface, which was bringing it one step closer to becoming one with the dirt with each pummeling crash from above.

London had been declared a disaster zone and was crumbling to the ground as the two mighty behemoths brawled their way towards the heart of the city. One creature had a mission, while the other, as odd as it sounds, was placed there quite intentionally. The idea being that maybe these monsters, these daikaiju, would fight it out and hopefully kill each other in the process.

Sir Jonathon (or Sir Jack as he was sometimes known) had remained calm and cool for the most part during the entire crisis. He scrutinized the screens, and his eyes narrowed into tiny slits that peered through the glass of his round, wired spectacles. Back and forth, they shifted between two live video feeds from almost 4000 miles away. He glared first to the bunker located beneath Westminster Palace, then to his birds-eye view of London, courtesy of an E.I.O. F.U. series fighter jet. He could see debris scatter and panic ensue every time one of the beasties from above slammed into the ground. Jack wished he was in London and felt helpless as he watched from the command center located in Japan, deep within the mighty Mount Fuji-san. His helplessness soon turned to frustration. Then his frustration turned to anger, and soon any traces of "calm and cool" were nowhere to be found. A bead of sweat rolled down Sir Jack's forehead, finding its way into his eye, and the sting of the small droplet seemed to set him off. He gnashed his teeth and barked into the comm. system,

"Send a bloody recon team to the surface in order to retrieve as many Glaucusidious skin samples as humanly possible! Make sure to seal the organic thorium, then promptly get your asses out of there!"

The feed crackled and the signal was interrupted by brief moments of static, and all systems began to fail.

ZZZPPPPTTTTT!! SKECHEEEEEE!! ZZPPTTT!!

"Are you ruddy well receiving this?" Jack yelled. The moment seemed to last an eternity, but through the darkness, sharp snaps and pops, a faint voice uttered through the digital feed.

ZZZZZPPTT!!

3

"... ell recon team sent ... cuation in proc ..."
SSSPPPTTT!!
"... Repeat ... evac in process ... organic thorium chamber being ..."
ZZPPTT!!
"... Repeat ..."
SSSSPPTTTT!!
"... chamber being sealed."

The green spheres of power illuminated and hovered as opposing magnetic forces kept the spinning globes suspended in the air. When the alarm bellowed, twelve-inch-thick cylinders slammed together, each concealing one of the two floating elements. Once encased, robotic welders arose from the floor and sealed the capsules tight with a line of hot liquid metal. The ceiling opened up and a flood of dense cement poured in like day-old oatmeal, filling the room and creating an impenetrable concrete tomb. For now, it seemed both orbs of regenerating radioactive element were safe, not only from the oncoming war of the kaiju above, but from the likes of an organic-thorium Chernobyl as well.

Up to this point the organic thorium (or O.T.) was still unstable and experimental, however that was all about to change. Soon the glowing, green gold would be used in a liquid form to power a magnificent, new secret weapon. It had been proven by its creator, Dr. Kyoshi Takarada, that this new source of power was not only self-sustaining, but infinite, as demonstrated in an android he had developed. The great doctor knew, without a shadow of a doubt, that his idea could *and would* work. He just needed something tangible to prove to the E.I.O. that his hypothesis was absolute and correct. Takarada called his experimental creation *Sophisticated & Complex Organic Thorium Tackle*, or SCOTT for short. This verified that he could substitute a brain with an elaborate set of computer microchips. It also proved he could pump organic thorium through the veins of a synthetic body for blood, the life force needed to make it mobile.

What gave organic thorium its remarkable regenerating ability were cells from a monster who, at that very moment, was on its way to the London base. Takarada had found, through the study of skin samples, that the cellules of this demon could constantly regrow themselves. Not reproduce, just sustain what it already had. When combined with thorium, the Glaucusidious cells had the ability to regenerate the radioactive element before it could exhaust itself. The sinister cells were the magic ingredient that not only gave the element eternal life, but the E.I.O. an endless power supply. However, Glaucusidious, a freakin' twenty-four-story, walking bag of slime, was created by the blackest of Yokai magic and by the evilest of witches. It was a mixture of both reality and nightmare, something super-science wasn't quite ready to grasp as of yet, however Takarada was. He had seen his beloved homeland destroyed numerous times by daikaiju as well as other outside forces. He had lost many loved ones over the years, and *this* is what fueled his determination. He was loyal beyond words to both Sir Jack and the Earth Intelligence Organization, as they gave this brilliant man something he needed desperately, the means to fight back.

Jack and Takarada both knew why the creature was on its way to the E.I.O. compound that resided directly beneath Westminster Palace. Its mission was clear: retrieve the organic thorium and bring it back to public enemy number one, Oko Rikoku. Each of the men held their breath as the Saturday-night smack-down broadcasted "LIVE" from London-town. They, and many others, nervously watched from their ringside HD monitors of the eastern E.I.O. base known as the FUJI. Their hopes being that by strategically placing another monster in the middle of its path, it would keep tall, dark and slimy, aka Glaucusidious, from ever getting its weird, tentacle-type fingers on the element. Yup, the ol' lesser-of-two-evils ploy, and when its opponent (a lovely, 300-foot, damn spider crab) spread Glaucusidious all over London, it looked like their plan was going to work. After all, the giant crab was just a "rogue," an atomic freak with no agenda, a simple radioactive abomination cursed to walk the planet for an eternity. And compared to Glaucusidious, well, let's just say it was a complete no-brainer.

A cheer filled the air in the FUJI control center, and Jack gave Dr. Takarada's back a triumphant WHACK!

"Take that, you dinosaur … or whatever the ruddy hell you are!" he yelled while he shook his fist at the monitor.

The FUJI Flunkies in the control room began to ease up, and Sir Jack reminded them that it wasn't time to break out the bubbly quite yet and to "Stay focused, damn it!" And sure as shit, just like a bad movie, or worse yet, a crummy book, a cowering voice advised Jack to look back up to the viewing screen.

Sir Jonathon's giant walrus 'stache lowered about an inch as the smile on his face turned quickly to a frown. "God blind me," he whispered to himself. It was Zargatron, (another one of Rikoku's nasty daikaiju) showing up to claim the glowing-green prize after Glaucusidious had failed to do so. The gargantuan red demanoid looked as though he had been run through a giant meat grinder. The once-magnificent beast was missing one of its four arms, and its large gargoyle wings could barely keep it in the air. But nevertheless, being Rikoku's "Number One," Zargatron began wiping up the streets of London with the giant rogue, pulling off its legs and hurling chunks of its bloodied cretaceous exoskeleton into the air.

The once-great city lay in ruins, the rogue spider-crab was dead and the ancient kaiju dropped to his knees from within the wreckage of the Palace of Westminster.

BOOM!

In his dying gasps for air, the great winged demon reached deep down into the earth, breaking through the E.I.O.'s impenetrable cement-and-steel enclosure that concealed the organic thorium. He crushed the metal cylinder like an aluminum can in his massive claw and retrieved the green-glowing orb of power. But what the demon beast and his captor were unaware of was that there were two cylinders protecting *two* orbs of organic thorium. Had the other been there, Zargatron would've surely taken that as well, but he couldn't very well steal what had already been stolen.

Chapter II

THE NOW

Upon the conclusion of their mandatory morning meeting, a small group of desperate men and women stood up, then assembled into an awkward circle. Each person reached out and clutched the hand of the next in order to affix the chain. It was a symbol, a bond that demonstrated strength and hope, something that at the moment was foreign to them all. Instead, most only gazed down upon the floor, probably lost in their thoughts of the trouble they had caused to themselves and to the ones they loved. For some, understanding the significance along with the power that the ring represented would come. But for others, they would never be so lucky, and Nathan Fox at that moment, was definitely of the latter.

Just before the group adjourned, one led them in a closing prayer, and even though Nathan may have mumbled the words, he in reality did not get it, not at all. And while *The Serenity Prayer* attempted to pound its way in through the thick stone of his cranium, its ass was kicked by the thundering voice in his head.

"Jesus H. Christ! The courage to accept the freakin' serenity to change the wisdom and know the effing difference? What the hell does that even mean?"

So by the time his angry inner ramblings had subsided, the brief prayer was over, and once again that elusive "moment of clarity" had slipped on by and right out the back door. He groaned out an "amen," then loosened his grip, severing the link that held the small circle of alcoholics and addicts together. Nathan, always quick to bail, hightailed it towards the door, and just as one foot stepped into the hallway, he heard his name.

"Hey Fox!"

Nathan stopped and sighed. "Here it comes again," he thought just

8

before trudging back to his counselor who was still seated from where he'd chaired the meeting. He had heard Nathan state over and over during his stay that he didn't really think he had a problem, he just needed a break. Hell, he'd already been here for a few months and still hadn't died of the DT's or anything yet, so maybe there never *was* a problem. Nathan figured if he could go that long without a drink, maybe he didn't need it after all.

His counselor laughed, "You don't even have to say a word. I can tell what you're thinking by the smug look on your face. You're so textbook, you're like most people who come through these doors. But as we've discussed again and again, maybe you don't have a problem. Only *you* can decide that."

Nathan didn't even bother to sit down, he only groaned and then asked Doctor Freud if he was finished yet.

His counselor shook his head because he hadn't even started, but simply said, "Of course." As Nathan walked back towards the door, he let him in on a little secret. "It's always there Nathan, you can't get away from it, not after two days, two weeks or even two hundred years. It's patient, like a hungry spider hiding in the darkness, sharpening its pincers … waiting."

"Yeah thanks, I'll remember that," Nathan said with his back to his counselor as he walked out the door, followed by a slight mumble of "ya freakin' psycho."

He hated it here, some days more than others, and today was one of them. "This is such bullshit," consumed his mind, like it had so often in the days of late, and the thought of, "What the hell am I doing here?" replayed in his head over and over like a broken record - broken record - broken record. Nathan, without a doubt, had no idea and sincerely thought he'd been sucker punched from behind by his so-called "friends." Even during his intervention, as superiors, colleagues and bandmates read him the riot act, Nathan couldn't help feel a little like Stevie Wonder, cuz he just couldn't see it. It's funny though, how some people seem to be immune from regret, and Nathan Fox was obviously one of them. He could say or do anything he wanted without a trace of any internal repercussions. However, *external* repercussions were a different story. As a result he soon found his narrow ass here, this lousy place filled with addicts and drunks, not to mention the brainwashing shrinks constantly touting you with crummy clichés

9

like, "Keep it simple" and "One day at a time."

At least there was one good thing about being in rehab though: all of the food with which to fatten up all those skinny meth heads and coke addicts. Plus, there was a virtual cornucopia of high-calorie desserts to get those alcoholics their much needed sugar fix. Nathan had already gained a few pounds during his stay at the Casa De' Crocked, as eating was the only freakin' thing to do, well, that and smoking. It was like some throwback to the seventies or something where nobody gave a frog's fat ass about when and where they lit up, making it impossible to escape the freakin' foul stench! Nathan hated cigarettes, but even he knew better than to say anything to a drunk who was drying out or to an addict who practically convulsed with every reassuring drag. Nope, he'd keep his big mouth shut and let it go this time. Besides, it seemed there were two things for these people you didn't want to screw with unless you yearned to be lynched from the tallest of trees. Coming in first (and foremost) were their smokes, and, in a close second, their coffee. Nathan had even grown fond of it and was becoming accustomed to always having a tall, strong cup of joe on hand. Plenty of sugar, a little cinnamon and filled about halfway with hazelnut creamer, it was just what the coffee doctor ordered, strong and only slightly feminine. Nathan loved it (even though he'd never admit it), and as he clenched the cup with both hands, he blew away the hot cloud of sweet steam that hovered over it.

He began to think how Tommy'd feel right at home here with all the cigs, psychobabble, gay coffee and the stale daily rigmarole...

Wake up, have a smoke, eat some breakfast, go to group, have another smoke, lunch, followed by another smoke, afternoon group, take a smoke break, then have a cigarette, eat a massive dinner with a huge dessert, group, AA meeting, after-AA-meeting smoke and coffee, have a smoke, eat a snack, one last smoke, go to bed, repeat.

He knew Tommy was a creature of habit, plus being the little girly-man he was, Nathan knew he liked talking through his "witto-fee-wings." "Yeah," he thought, "this place was perfect for freakin' O.C.D.T.L.T." (a nickname he had given Tommy a long, long time ago).

Nathan groaned as he thought about all of the things that were wrong with Tommy and, becoming aware of what he was doing, stopped in his tracks, caressed the back of his neck and sighed. He hated it when Tommy took up residence in his mind, and every time he caught himself thinking about him, he became furious. Problem was, that was about twenty-three out of twenty-four hours a day. Nathan shook his head, then did his best to shake it off. He stopped by the cafeteria and grabbed a honkin'-sized piece of strawberry-glazed cheesecake to go with his not-quite-feminine, but a little less than manly, cup of coffee. Carrying one in each hand, Nathan then made his way through the smoke-infested hallway toward his room. He had a few minutes to kill before group and decided to hide out on his bed, hoping that maybe (completely by accident of course) he'd fall asleep and miss it. Nathan balanced the plate in one hand, bit down on the rim of the cup in order to secure it in his mouth and fumbled to open his door. As the cup began to slip between his clenched teeth, the knob turned all by itself, the door opened inward and the cheesecake hit the ground.

CRASH!!

Nathan never looked down (he probably didn't even notice the crash), and as he sneered, the coffee soon joined the cheesecake on the floor.

Tommy gave Nathan a soft, gentle smile, then held out his right hand and Nathan couldn't believe what he was seeing. He didn't move and only stood there, glaring at Tommy's stupid, extended mitt. He began to boil on the inside as the hate of a thousand lifetimes festered deep within him. Then, with his empty hand still reaching out to Nathan, Tommy let him have it with those big puppy-dog eyes of his. Nathan groaned and shook his head as this (even for Tommy) way surpassed pitiful. Nathan took a deep breath in order to reduce his bubbling insides to a nice, warm simmer, and when he finally felt calm, he smiled back. With that, Tommy couldn't help but gasp in total relief, he then offered humble salutations.

"How ya doin', Lizard King?" and Nathan answered Tommy with a solid right hook to the face.

CRACK!

"Better now," he said, "thanks for asking."

Just behind the space that Tommy had previously occupied (before joining the cheesecake and coffee on the floor) stood Olivia, who, like

11

Tommy and Nathan, was an agent for the E.I.O. She was also the bass player in their band, Vinyl Crush, the wildly successful group that was assembled by the secret organization as a front. After all, who would ever suspect a blithering rock star of being an undercover spy, capable of piloting a 60-meter, kaiju-fighting mech? Nobody, that's who.

She observed Tommy, who was flat on his ass in a puddle of joe as he wiggled his jaw back and forth. She then looked up at Nathan, who was shaking off the pain that consumed his hand after making impact with Tommy's chin.

"Well, it seems some things will never change," she said, and as she stepped over Tommy, she opened her arms in Nathan's general direction. Nathan sighed. He hated that he had become so attached to Olivia, but accepted the hug anyhow.

"So, they ah, treating you all right?" she asked.

Nathan didn't say a word as he broke his grip from Olivia and backed up. The silence made her nervous, and she proceeded to do what most people do when a room is booming with the sounds of silence, she said something stupid (which for Olivia was pretty rare).

"You look like you've gained some weight."

Nathan winced. He hated hearing that, more so than he'd care to admit, and the small-talk comment only seemed to piss him off more. Nathan looked down and watched Tommy groan while he pushed himself up from the floor. He looked gravely concerned, not for Tommy, but for the pummeled piece of coffee-drenched cheesecake that lay in ruins at his feet.

"What the hell are you guys doing here, Olivia?" he asked while still eyeing the mess.

Olivia shrugged, "We just wanted to stop by and see how you were getting along."

Nathan smirked and shook his head. He wasn't buying it.

"Stop by huh? Waddya guys catch a redeye out of Tokyo just to *stop on by*? Yeah, that makes sense. I don't know exactly *where* I am, but I do know where I'm not, and that's Japan. The only thing that's remotely Japanese here is the fact that everybody freakin' smokes like he does."

Nathan glared over towards Tommy, who was now preoccupied with trying to pat dry his coffee-drenched ass. Nathan stepped a few feet over to the small bathroom in his temporary flat, reached in, grabbed a towel and chucked it at Tommy.

"Really, I'll ask you guys again, what the hell are you doing here?"

Tommy was straining to look behind himself as he did the butt mambo in an attempt to dry off the back of his pants with the towel.

"Something's coming," he said as he yanked the towel from side to side. Nathan watched on and thought about punching him again, when finally Tommy turned his head from his ass and looked Nathan square in the eye, "something big."

"God," Nathan said in that louder than a whisper kind of voice, "always such a damn drama queen, and what makes you think that, your highness?"

Olivia interjected, "Well, for starters, seismic activity in Utah is extremely irregular, not to mention off the charts."

"So what's that have to do with me?" Nathan hissed. "Besides, aren't you morons long overdue for a big one anyhow?"

Nathan knew Olivia was from Utah. He also knew she had lost her entire family in the great Salt Lake City atomic blast a few short years ago. He felt a little funny after making his cold comment, which was something quite new for Nathan Fox. He wasn't exactly sure what the uneasiness in his stomach meant, so he chalked it up to too much coffee and was suddenly grateful he didn't eat the cheesecake.

Olivia sneered at Nathan, took a deep breath and nudged her glasses up a little higher on her nose.

"True, there have been cases of minute tremors in the past, especially at the Wasatch Fault, but there has not been any major movement or shifting in thousands of years."

Nathan had completely forgotten about the uneasiness in his stomach, and again his mouth took over.

"So, like I said, sounds like Utah's long overdue, Tootz, and speaking of major movement, maybe it's time for you to move on as well."

Olivia was having a hard time dealing with Nathan. Usually she could just brush him *and* his bullshit off, but the thought of her family frying in that nuclear nightmare kept permeating her brain, and her emotions began to get the best of her.

"Look, you little dipshit, the problem is NOT coming from the traditional faults, it's coming from directly under Salt Lake City. You know, where the big bomb went boom! And these are not little tremors, this is major seismic activity, and it is absolutely unheard of!"

Between breaths, Olivia thought to herself how funny it was that whenever she was away from Nathan, she'd get down on herself for always being so short with him. She also vowed that the next time she saw him, she would try to have more patience. Well, now that it was "next time," Olivia was once again finding it pretty damn hard to keep that promise. It only took a few short sentences from Nathan before it all came flooding back to her, and she remembered why. It wasn't a lack of patience on her part, it was the simple fact that the majority of conversations with Nathan were nothing shy of pulling teeth. She also concluded that it was positively a case of absence making the heart grow fonder, because it was a formulated impossibility to have a rational conversation with Nathan freakin' Fox.

Olivia gave Tommy a "how about a little help here" kind of look, and Tommy thought long and hard.

"Look dude, I'm tellin' ya, something big is coming … I can feel it."

Nathan sat down on the edge of his bed.

"Okay … so something *BIG* is coming." (Nathan rolled his eyes at the same time he said "big.") "You're obviously here because you need me for who-the-hell-knows what, so I'll try a new approach."

Nathan pretended to clear his throat.

"Ahem … Attention! May I have your attention, please! I - Don't - Give - A - Shit! I don't care about Utah, I don't care about you guys, and while we're at it, I couldn't care less if the whole damn planet blew up into a million, microscopic, stupid-ass pieces."

Nathan paused. "How's that for an answer?" he asked, and while he waited for a response that uneasy feeling crept back into his gut. Once again the silence got real loud, so he filled the room up with a little backpedaling.

"Besides … you're talking the possibility of a major quake. Big deal, it happens every day in California. Why don't you look on the bright side? At least nobody's there; it's a freakin' wasteland. I think you guys need to relax." Nathan looked down. "Actually, I think you guys just need to leave."

Tommy shook his head and sighed. "C'mon Olivia, I knew this was a waste of time."

Olivia put her hand on Nathan's shoulder and sat next to him on the bed. "Obviously there's more, Nathan. Dr. Takarada has informed us that a very large amount of organic thorium may have found its way into the wrong hands. If this is indeed the case, we're not only looking at the threat of war, we are looking at possible extermination."

Nathan jerked a bit but held in his reaction for the most part.

"*That's* the big deal," Olivia said. "We wouldn't have come all the way here for the threat of an earthquake. We also have reason to believe these events may be linked together somehow, and if something is going to happen, I thought we should be ready."

Nathan couldn't look Olivia in the eye, and as he continued to glare at the floor he asked her, "Why?" He didn't need to elaborate, she knew exactly what he was talking about.

"You were spiraling out of control, Nathan. Hell, the road crew had ongoing bets about what kind of stupid, drunk stunt you would pull at that night's concert and if you would live or not. It was scary just watching you, not to mention the king-sized ass you'd become when you were loaded. You were like a Jekyll and Hyde or something. Everybody was worried we were going to have to cancel the rest of the tour, and some of us were just plain worried! Worried about getting a call from the police, the hospital or the morgue! We thought for sure you'd kill yourself before the tour even ended."

"Well, I didn't!" Nathan defended.

"No, at least you waited until after the tour before you lost *ALL* control. You're here, Nathan, because we love you and we want to see you get better. Everybody wants to see you get better, even the E.I.O. Hell, they wanted you locked up following the Tokyo incident after the countless damage you caused in a drunken stupor. I still don't know how Sir Jack talked them out of it, and it never ceases to amaze me that we didn't kill anybody."

Nathan began to boil again. "Ya know, OCD Boy should have had more sense than to put me in that giant freakin' cowboy robot. I mean I was, after all, passed out! Nobody's ever said a damn thing to him about strapping an inebriated pilot into the cockpit of an effing battle bot! What the hell did he expect with an operating system that functions off of the subconscious? As drunk as I was, he should've left me. He woulda' saved both of us a lot of headaches! But *NOBODY* ever seems to hear about that, nothing about the great Tommy Lynn Taylor and his bonehead decision! Nope, just freakin' Nathan Fox and the

16

trouble his dumb, drunk ass caused!"

Olivia didn't say anything, she just listened. Tommy was about to get his two cents in when Olivia sneered at him with her eyes, telling him to just keep quiet for now and let Nathan go on.

"You know, Tommy, I've told you this before. You're freakin' charmed, man. You just have your head lodged so far up your butt, you can't see it. As always, you're the hero, and *you* got to figure out exactly what it was that *you* wanted! *You* got the pats on the back and *you* got to ride off into the sunset in the end with the girl. I mean that's cool and all, but God you're such a little dink! You and your freakin' committee. Let it go, man. If it barks like a duck, it's a freakin' duck! What's the big effing deal? And now, according to you guys, I'm here because you love me, but you're also here to get me to come with you because the world may be in trouble again. So I guess if you want me to leave, that sorta cancels out that whole 'I'm here cuz you love me' thing. Please, explain *that* nonsense to me. Actually ... don't, if the world goes to hell, or even if it doesn't, I don't give a crap. I've got a 'Plan B,' and it involves the Florida Keys, naked women and a shitload of Tequila. I don't wanna fight monsters, and I don't wanna be an agent for the lame-ass E.I.E.I.O. anymore. I just wanna go home, wherever the hell that is."

Tommy looked over to the little alarm clock that was perched upon Nathan's night stand. Time was running short, and he had a million things he needed to say to him. "We gotta go Olivia, this is a total dead end."

She hesitated but agreed and joined Tommy at the doorway. "Sure you won't change your mind?" she asked one more time, and Nathan just sat there in his shit, staring deep into the abyss. Olivia walked out of the room, and as Tommy gripped the doorknob to leave, he said one final thing.

"I don't know the last time you talked to your dad, but he's really sick. Just another dumb reason we came all this way to see you. I wanted to let you know myself so we could go see him if you wanted. Hope you enjoy your 'Plan B' and the rest of your miserable little existence. Good news is, it won't last very long," and Tommy closed the door behind him.

Chapter III

It had been well over a week since Tommy had closed the door on Nathan, leaving him to his spiraling thoughts. After Tommy and Olivia took off, he just sat there on the edge of his bed, zoning out as the darkness consumed him. Usually, and mostly due to his "I don't give a shit" rocker 'tude, Nathan was pretty good about taking life's crap in stride, and whenever things would get a little *too* real he always had his friend, Jack Daniels, to confide in. However, this latest onslaught of shit was mind-blowingly bad and messing with Nathan's leopard spots. It forced him to resort to drastic measures, such as thinking, followed by (heaven forbid!) taking action. He never had a problem when it came down to doing the "right" thing, but on the other hand, he never seemed to struggle much when it came down to doing the "wrong" thing either. He was just used to doing the "Nathan" thing, which meant doing whatever it was that worked best for him, no matter what it happened to be. It wasn't necessarily about right, wrong, good or evil, it just was. And as of a few days ago, the "Nathan" thing started leaning heavily towards, "This whole rehab trip is a freakin' monumental waste of time, and I - Am - Outa- Here!" The more he thought about it, the more it made sense. It worked. It was something he could easily justify, and nobody could ever blame him for cutting out to go see his dying father one last time.

Nathan figured he was about halfway to L.A. when he stopped just outside of Needles for the night. He took off his shirt, kicked off his shoes and positioned himself on the motel's lumpy bed with his back up against the headboard. He looked around his room, then down at his protruding stomach, then thought about Olivia's little "weight gain" comment. He pinched about an inch of flab and made his belly button talk in a high-pitched, stupid voice. It was both funny and a little creepy all at the same time.

"Gee, Nathan, it's sure nice to see you, and you're getting soooo fat! You're gonna look juuuuust like your ol' pal, Sir Jack, pretty soon."

The Lizard King scowled and snapped back at his stomach, or himself, or freakin' whatever, saying, "So what's a few extra pounds anyhow. It's not like I'm trying to win a damn beauty contest or anything. I don't need to impress anybody. Besides, I can't even remember the last time I got laid, so ..."

Nathan stopped dead in his tracks when he realized he really *couldn't* remember the last time he got laid. Not because it was that long ago, but because he was in such a drunken stupor, he literally couldn't remember. Nathan started to go bye-bye, but the mere thought of him acting all crazy (like his old pal Tommy) snapped him right back to reality. Nathan looked down and sighed, when he realized he was still holding the rolled-up layer of fat and skin in his hands. He let go and his little tummy buddy succumbed to gravity and took its rightful place back around Nathan's waist. He felt as though he'd just dodged a bullet and grabbed the TV remote from the other side of the bed. He turned on the old television that was perched on a cheesy, laminate dresser right in front of him, and the dull room lit up in a glorious UHF-burst of gray and white. As Nathan scrolled through all five of the local channels, he reached down with his other hand into a cooler that just happened to be next to the bed. He rummaged his fingers through the ice, digging through the thousand or so miniature bricks of frozen water. It was then he found what he was looking for.

"A-ha, there you are my little beauty!" he said after scoring the frosty, ice-cold beverage. Little streams of cold condensation rolled down the side of the bottle, and Nathan felt a sharp little twinge under his tongue as he eyed it. He cracked open the tomb from which the sinful liquid was held and let it escape straight down his throat. After slamming half of it in the first swallow, he then let out a big, wet "Ahhhhh" and screwed the cap back on tight. He clicked the remote a few more times and stopped when he heard the opening theme song to *Entertainment! NOW*. He set the remote down, loosened the cap on the bottle and finished the rest of its contents.

Nathan let out a massive, "BUUUUUURP," and aimed it in the direction of the TV. He hated *Entertainment! NOW*. It seemed every time he got drunk and did something stupid, those parasites always just happened to be there with their freakin' cameras! They'd follow

him around for days at a time, peering out from behind cracks and concealed corners. Sometimes those stinkin' *E! NOW* rats would even hide in the bushes, and sooner, rather than later, you'd see Nathan Fox on national television, once again making a gigantic ass out of himself. He couldn't decide which he hated more, the root beer he'd just devoured or *Entertainment! NOW*. He looked back down at his stomach and could've sworn he heard it tell him in that funny, yet creepy, voice which one *it* hated worse. This time, he ignored the strong impulse to converse with his tummy, deciding he hated both *Entertainment! NOW* AND root beer about the same (as he cracked open another bottle and settled in to watch the show).

"Coming to you 'live' from Hollywood, USA, it's time for *Entertainment! NOW!*, your up-to-the-moment news source surrounding all of the glitz and glam of your favorite stars! If it's happening now and it's entertainment, it's entertainment NOW!"

"And now your hosts of *E.N.*, Glenn Glenn and Susan Watson!"

"Thanks, Charlie, and welcome to another edition of *Entertainment! Now*. Well, Susan, tonight on the show, we get down to the nitty-gritty concerning all of those rumors circulating about another Vinyl Crush world tour!"

"Ooooh, that's right, Glenn, and if there's gonna be a tour, we can probably count on another triple-platinum-selling album as well! Hopefully lead vocalist and front man, Nathan Fox, will be sober enough to remember the words to his own songs this time! But I guess *no* words would still be better than that world-wide F-Bomb he dropped a few years ago at the simulcast Concert For Earth!"

"Ha-ha! You got that right Susan! My ears are still ringing from that one!"

"Speaking of Nathan Fox, it seems there could be a bit of trouble in paradise, and *nobody* will have to worry about him or his all-too-well-known drunken shenanigans ever again, at least not with Vinyl Crush! According to *E! NOW* sources, Fox has left the band for the serene, green landscapes of Clean and Soberville!"

"Well, Glenn, that's all right with me as long as Tommy Lynn and those lightning fast fingers keep right on — "

"Jesus Christ, Ritchie, will you shut that crap off, I'm trying to eat."

From behind the shoddy diner's long, lonely counter, a scrawny man in a ketchup-stained T-shirt walked over to the hundred-year-old television that was mounted to the ceiling. He stretched up and looked over his shoulder as he balanced on his tippy toes to shut it off.

"Guess you're not a music lover," Ritchie stated to the gruff old guy on the stool who was now shoveling in a heaping portion of his blue-plate special.

"Music? That's not music, that's a joke. Why they're nothin' but a bunch of untalented little pukes! And I'll bet you dollars to donuts, they're probably high on dope or speed or maybe even both," the old curmudgeon growled.

Ritchie just laughed, "Untalented pukes or not, I still say their bass player's smokin' hot!"

"What's his name?" the old guy perched at the counter remarked as mashed potatoes and a small piece of mystery meat slipped through the corner of his mouth. Ritchie gave the older gentleman a smile, then promptly followed it up with half a peace sign. He then grabbed a dish towel from an overflowing bus pan that sat behind the counter. He shook the dinner debris from the towel and was about to go back to his diner duties when he stopped dead in his tracks. Like an animal sensing a bad storm on the horizon, Ritchie looked around the restaurant. He wasn't sure, but whatever it was, he could tell it was something big ... something bad, just like Tommy had said.

The old goat started griping about the diner being way too hot and his dinner being way too cold when Ritchie shushed him quiet. The guy on the stool looked up, and his plate crashed to the floor. He grabbed Ritchie's arm and screamed, "Quake! It's a damn quake!" The lights started to flicker, and the walls began to shed loose anything that hung from them as the diner began to shake. Both men made their way to the exit (as though it would help), and even though it wasn't funny, it was impossible for them not to look like a couple of clumsy clods as they fought their way to safety.

BOOSH! CRACK! SNAP!

A large section of the ceiling broke free, and as it fell on Ritchie's head, it blocked the exit.

"RITCHIE!" the old codger screamed as they both lost their footing and fell. The diner went dark, and with the exception of a burst of sparks from above, all was black. From the floor, the old man held

Ritchie's blood-soaked head in his lap.

"It's so damn hot," he complained, staring into the nothingness for an answer. He tried to wipe away the soot and sweat that had merged with the wound, but due to his trembling hands, he only made it worse. It was then that the ear-shattering thunder had come to an abrupt and peculiar stop, but neither man had noticed the silence. Ritchie opened his eyes and reached up to grab the guy's arm.

"Stop it, Gus, you're not helping. I'm all right, for God's sake." The old guy finally smiled, revealing his lack of teeth, and he hugged Ritchie's neck.

"Thank Go—"

KABOOSH!!!

In one split second, everything was gone: the men, the diner and the very ground from which it stood. All that remained was a thousand tons of sinking debris that settled to the floor of the mammoth crater left by the quake.

When Tommy and Olivia tried to re-recruit Nathan, he reminded them that Salt Lake City was nothing more than a freakin' radioactive ghost town, and he was absolutely right. Only a handful of locals on the outskirts of the city and in the surrounding burbs had held their ground, refusing to leave even after the blast. In a little under two seconds, about a hundred-thousand people lost their lives. In a little over two years, cancer had consumed most of the others to where now only a few remained. Sick with the disease, nobody dared to force these "incasts" out, so they were avoided like the plague. It was far better than any government-issued quarantine, because the fools wanted to stay, and the powers-that-be couldn't ask for a better means of containment, sheer stubbornness. Now the number had dropped by two more. Soon there would be none at all, and the problem, along with the cancer, could be swept under the rug, nice and tidy-like. Yup, a convenient end to the last remaining colony of forgotten lepers.

The world was such a different place now. It was scary, diseased and completely effed up. In the aftermath of not only Salt Lake City, but London and Tokyo as well, humanity seemed to take yet another nosedive headfirst into the deep, swirling sea of de-evolution. Sure, everybody went through the motions. They went to work, attended school, listened to their favorite music, watched their reality shows and pretended like everything was okay, but in all reality, it wasn't. Just ask the sick and dying survivors of Salt Lake City, or ask their kids, or ask Olivia. Recent events made people long for simpler times, maybe the good ol' days of a post 9/11, pre-Oko-Rikoku era. What appeared to be such desperate times back then seemed like some sort of paradise now. The fact being, times were bad, really bad, and most were convinced things were gonna get worse, a whole lot worse, before they got any better.

The monstrous crater lay dormant for a few moments, while thick streams of fire and smoke ascended from it. The rising vapor cast an eerie likeness to that of a towering mushroom cloud, while the dark, crumbling silhouette of Salt Lake City painted the perfect, yet disturbing backdrop on the edge of the purple horizon. It was a sick reminder, and though it only lasted for a couple of seconds, it could be seen for hundreds of miles, thus breathing new life into an old nightmare. A strong, lonely wind moaned, forcing the demon cloud to dissipate, and the earth began to settle into the silence, as short-lived as it was.

Upon the gasp of relief that the storm had passed, the barren land once again started to seethe and boil, only this time from the bottom of the giant pit. The ground cried in pain as a blanket of dirt, debris and fire churned its way up to the top of the crater towards some sort of inevitable eruption. Tons of thick, rising dust camouflaged what the dim light of the moon was trying so desperately to seek out. The land was horrifically sick, choking and spewing up the atomic poison that was forced down its throat in the great explosion not too long ago. The desert wasn't only sick though, it was furious and on the verge of spitting up a living, breathing abomination. Something was coming, something that would rival even the worst world wars, while giving solid evidence to that "things are gonna get a whole lot worse" theory.

KAAARAAAAAMMMMMM!!!!!

Chapter IV

Nathan continued to haul ass towards Palmdale in the gaudy, candy-apple red convertible he had rented after bailing from rehab. The E.I.O., in their infinite wisdom, thought a court order demanding him to stay in treatment wouldn't be necessary. They thought it would more than likely diminish any opportunity to work with Mr. Fox in the future. Meaning, Sir Jack and the powers that be opted for the family approach with Nathan, deciding it would be best for both parties if they just "trusted" him to do the right thing. Big mistake. Oh, and nothing quite says trust like blindfolding someone and dragging them to detox in a remote facility somewhere in the middle of nowhere. So, with that being said, and Nathan not legally forced to stay, he could leave whenever he wanted. They (being Them) also seemed to have a need to remind Nathan of every time he became frustrated in his recovery. It was just as one of his counselors would always tell him, "The only thing keeping you here, Nathan, is yourself." Then he'd add, "That, and the fact that you're a million miles away from anybody or anything, smack dab in the center of the Mojave Desert." One thing's for sure though, if you've got cash, it doesn't matter where you are, or what time it is, somebody will come get your ass. They'll also drop you off at the closest rent-a-car place as well!

Nathan loved the hundred-mile-per-hour wind blowing through his hair, and while he drove his left arm hung out of the convertible's open window. He'd never admit it, but he was a bit scared, after all he hadn't seen his dad in a few years and they didn't part on the best of terms. But he was enjoying his freedom and the combined feelings turned to a brisk and nervous exhilaration that pulsed through his veins.

He pounded the outside of the car door to the beat of "Roadhouse Blues" as it blasted through the rental's crappy stereo. It was his second day out since leaving the "Winehouse Clinic," and so far he'd made it ... one day. One whole day clean and sober out in the real world, and by his choice, because he could've bought a bottle of JD just as easily as he bought that case of root beer (which he'd almost completely downed already). Maybe rehab somehow managed to infiltrate that thick, stone head of his, or maybe it had something to do with going to see his dad. Maybe he'd had enough of the bullshit and was sick and tired of being sick and tired. Or maybe (and more than likely) his newfound sobriety simply wouldn't last.

The local news just outside of L.A. interrupted Nathan's dose of music medication to broadcast that another quake had hit outside of old Salt Lake City. They also stated that tremors had been reported from Utah all the way to the borders of Los Angeles. Nathan didn't think much of it and groaned at the radio announcer for interrupting his tunage over something as lame as an earthquake. He hit search, and every time the radio found a home it was the same thing: earthquake this, earthquake that, lives lost, property damage already in the millions, blah-blah-blah. Nathan, becoming concerned, stopped the station search and opted for the rental's satellite radio instead.

When he finally pulled into Palmdale, he decided that it still looked exactly the same. He also concluded that the few years he'd been away hadn't accounted for a damn thing. Nope, not in this godforsaken place.

"Nothing changes here," he thought to himself, not knowing that eventually he'd miss the familiarity of that "same old, same old."

Nathan tuned in to an all-KISS satellite station and cranked up the volume in order to let everybody know that Palmdale's prodigal son had indeed returned. The dirtier the looks, the louder he turned it up.

He pulled up to a stoplight, and the jam that thundered from the 1974 Monte Carlo next to him far exceeded his little factory-installed radio. He lowered his shades showing his distaste, and then retaliated by turning "Detroit Rock City" up to eleven on his measly stock stereo. Which, of course, became nothing but obnoxious as his speakers couldn't handle the volume. He looked over to the "Monte Carlos" (as was proudly displayed on the car's ancient bug visor with shiny, yellowish-green, stick-on letters) and grinned. He couldn't see in through the tinted window, but he knew they were watching, because the low end of their subsonic subwoofers soon engulfed any sound

26

within a five-mile radius. The glimmer of a gold tooth from the neighboring car's passenger's seat revealed to Nathan that they must be laughing at him *and* his piece-of-shit radio. After becoming a mega-giant superstar with gobs of cash, Nathan had something like fourteen cars and now knew a few things about high-end convertibles, even the ones with junkie stock sound systems. So he knew this one sucked royally. (After all, beggars can't be choosers, especially when it comes to renting a car from Big Al's Discount Auto just outside of the middle of nowhere.) He also knew there was no way he could top their billion-watt sound system, so he opened his car door as hard and fast as he could and slammed it smack into the side of the "Monte Carlos."

BAM!

Both cars were now the proud owners of two lovely king-sized dents on their doors, one of which abruptly kicked open.

"Hey, pendejo, you gotta death weesh or sometheem?"

Nathan waited for the driver to jump out, and when he did, he slammed down on the accelerator. His tires spun fiercely against the pavement and the smell of burning rubber permeated throughout the cloud of smoke. For about two seconds his car didn't move but only vibrated as it reached for the point of takeoff. And when it did, Nathan was gone.

SHOOOM!

His pop (as Nathan used to call him) lived in a small, run-down shack on the outskirts of town, and if that wasn't cliché enough, the house also stood just opposite the wrong side of the tracks. Since the accident, his dad spent most of his time buried deep in a bottle while surviving off of government-funded cheese. At least that's the way it was back when Tommy and Nathan packed up and took off for L.A. As a matter of fact, it was more than likely a major component involved in pushing Nathan right out the door. It was also the last time he had spoken to his father.

He pulled up and parked across the street, staring as an onslaught of memories (mostly bad) infiltrated his mind. He hated the fact that, contrary to how he pictured this moment, the house wasn't quite as bad as he remembered. There was a nice rosebush stemming up from beneath the living-room window, and the green, lush lawn was neatly tailored. Nathan scowled at the old-fashioned sprinkler that showered the grass with water, first to the left, then to the right. The hood wasn't looking too bad either, and he almost didn't recognize his quaint little slice of Palmdale (you know, that godforsaken place where nothing changes). There was something else he didn't recognize either, and that was the big SUV that was parked in the driveway. He did, however, have a good idea. It was a jet-black Tahoe with tinted windows that had "E.I.O. issue" written all over it. Nathan shook his head and whispered under his breath, "Freakin Tommy."

Out of instinct, he reached into the cooler that was buried in the back and felt around through the thick water, scouring for a little liquid courage. For a brief second, not even quite the tick of a clock, Nathan forgot, forgot the fact that he was now clean. Unfortunately though, that small interlude in time is all it takes, and in less than a heartbeat, the enemy can infiltrate your lips, undoing a lifetime's worth of hard work. Even if that lifetime happens to only be one day long. Cuz that's how it works. It's a lot like that spider, the one that's waiting patiently in the darkness. Only now it's biding its time, waiting for you to forget, which seems to be the number one cause of relapses everywhere. Maybe if you had a clue as to what was waiting for you in the shadows, maybe you'd work harder at not forgetting. Because the second you do...

Nathan's head sunk ever so slightly when he glared at the perspiring, ice-cold can of root beer he'd pulled from the freezing depths of the cooler. As he held it in his grasp, it reminded him of the precious victory of the last twenty-four hours, and everything came rushing back to him. He ripped the top off, slammed yet another soda (thus proving it to be no match for the mighty Nathan Fox) and made his way across the street towards the front door. The spider retreated back to its web, but it had a hunch that it wouldn't be long now.

Before Nathan could even knock, his dad burst through the front door, bending a bit at the waist in order to bury his face deep into his son's shoulder. Nathan almost resisted, but something inside told him not to, so instead of recoiling, he hugged his dad back. Brandon Fox was a surprisingly big man with thin, sandy-brown hair, and given Nathan's smaller build along with his curly, jet-black locks, you'd never know they were father and son. That is until they started talking, then it became obvious that the apple indeed did not fall far from the tree.

"So what, are ya' too damn famous now to pick up a phone to give your old man a call?"

Nathan broke his grip from his father, backed up and was absolutely floored that his dad had the freakin' gall to say something so way off base. His mind went back in time to when his dad "lost it" in a drunken rage that night he and Tommy left. It's funny how the biggest and oldest of scars can still sting when they come rushing back in that sudden flash of pain. More often than not, that seems to be how it goes, and the whole, long, painful memory raced through Nathan's head in less than a millisecond. But before he could ruin the moment by opening his mouth, he caught a quick glimpse of Tommy and Olivia who were already sitting comfortably on the sofa.

"Tommy ... Olivia ... My, my, what a pleasant surprise. So good to see you guys!"

Nathan's sentence could barely sustain itself as the weight of the attached sarcasm pulled every word down, deep into the shag, disco carpeting. They both jumped up from the couch and went into full character, offering phony salutations and hugs, probably in an effort to conceal the last few months of Nathan's life from his dad.

"It's great to see you Nathan, whatcha been up to?" Tommy lied.

Brandon Fox looked concerned and blurted out, "He's been in rehab."

Tommy and Olivia tried to look shocked, but it was obvious they weren't fooling anybody. They still, however, looked a little stunned that Mr. Fox knew.

"What?" he stated. "Don't you guys watch *Entertainment! Now?*"

Nathan turned beet red, not because he was embarrassed, because he wasn't, but because he couldn't stand freakin' *Entertainment! Now* and their bullshit take on his life. It always pissed him off to no end how other people seemed to know more about him than he did.

Nathan took a deep breath and thought about his next set of words very carefully, something he wasn't quite used to yet.

"Yeah dad, you're right, I've been in long-term rehab. I was there for almost three months until yesterday."

He didn't really know what else to add to that, so Nathan stopped talking and just waited. His pop sighed and shook his lowering head, while Nathan braced for some sort of impact. Brandon Fox, while still looking down, reached deep into the right pocket of his loose-fitting khakis. You could see the outline of his large hand as it felt around the inside of the baggy pants, and when he stopped, he pulled out one of his greatest treasures. Nathan knew what it was and felt a bolt of lightning shoot down the back of his neck. Tommy and Olivia, however, had no idea.

It was a shiny, bronze medallion that Brandon held up to his son pinched between his thumb and index finger. Nathan took it from his dad and read it to himself out loud. "To Thine Own Self Be True." He flipped it over and the words "Unity," "Service" and "Recovery" outlined a triangle forged in the middle of the coin, and within the triangle, a smaller circle bordered a Roman numeral III. Nathan gazed over at his pop who hadn't uttered a word, because like his son, he had decided just to wait. As Nathan stood there, he forgot about his ill feelings towards Tommy, welled up and handed the medallion over to him.

Nathan held his arms out to hug his dad again, only this time when they embraced the water main freakin' broke wide open, and both men began to sob as they held each other tight. Tommy watched on and his lower lip began to quiver. Olivia still wasn't quite sure what to think

of all of this. Tommy handed her the medallion and eased towards Nathan and his dad. Brandon Fox lifted his right arm in order to let Tommy join in, and all three men wept as they hugged each other. Olivia nudged up her glasses, and when she read the medallion, she soon figured out that Nathan's dad had accumulated three years of sobriety himself. She thought about Nathan and his demons, then about Mr. Fox who apparently had the same struggles. Then Olivia thought about how she always strived to get a better understanding of why Nathan Fox was always such a freakin' Nathan Fox, and in the blink of an eye it all hit her. She took off her glasses and wiped her eyes in an attempt to mask her own watery emotions. Nathan reached over and tugged on Olivia's arm, pulling her into the community hug-a-thon. For those few brief seconds, everything seemed fine. For those few brief seconds, it seemed like everything was gonna be all right.

Chapter V

Nathan had a very long, not to mention overdue, day of reuniting with his dad. Both Brandon Fox and his son spent hours spinning yarns and telling timely tales of the past, many of which included Tommy. Olivia felt as though she had just learned the true meaning of "dysfunctional," listening to these three idiots go on and on about concerts, bands and growing up in Palmdale. Brandon was not only a great story-teller, but also a seasoned pro at evading any yarn that included Nathan's mom. This was undoubtedly the demon that drove the final nails into his and Nathan's relationship. It was also what had pushed Brandon Fox over the edge a few years back. But even though he was a pro at avoiding the stories that included Pamela (Nathan's mother), it wasn't for reasons you would think. It was for the simple fact that nobody in the room knew how the other would react, so the topic was just avoided. Brandon Fox decided he would talk to his son alone about his mother the first chance he had, and there was no doubt he would, but now was not the time. Dealing with the bitterness and tragic loss of Pamela was something Fox had to work through, and he knew he needed to pass along that same wisdom to Nathan. Besides, this way he could tap dance around his own little ailments as well. Or so he hoped. Regardless, it could wait until tomorrow, as this very long day had slipped deep into the night.

It was almost one a.m. by the time everybody had settled in for the night at Nathan's childhood home on Lockheed Avenue. He lay back in his creaky, old bed, folded his prized, foam-rubber pillow under his head and stared at the posters that still decorated the walls. It was quite the collection, but his favorites were, hands down, a Kiss "Farewell Tour" poster from the first concert he and Tommy ever went to, a Doors "Live at the Whiskey" psychedelic repro print and next to that, an authentic 1979 Jim Morrison "American Poet" 24 x 36 he'd snagged off of eBay. And finally, for his crème de la crème, he had a big-ass Led

Zeppelin collage from their 1975 world tour that hung right above him, taped to the ceiling. Nathan had stumbled upon it when a guy he knew from school needed a little bread for a dime bag. Nathan's pal claimed to have scored the "holy grail" of Zep posters from some kid who had stolen it from his cousin's neighbor's dad … or something like that. Either way, Nathan always figured it was the best ten bucks he'd ever spent.

It was funny how most of the musicians taped and tacked to Nathan's walls had one particular thing in common, the fact that they were all dead. Jim Morrison, Jimi Hendrix and Curt Cobain, to name a few, were not only dead though, they were also part of a very exclusive society known as The 27 Club. A group in which you needed two very important qualifications to join: first, achieve groundbreaking, mega-superstar status in popular music and second, die. Yup, that was all there was to it, just as long as you croaked at 27. And back when Nathan splattered their images on his wall, it gave him about a decade until he hit that definitive rock-star retirement age. Which was plenty of time, because he believed his destiny was already written in stone anyhow. A destiny where he was indeed one of those groundbreaking mega-superstars. One that would not only make him worthy of wielding the hammer of the rock gods themselves, but one that would also gain him admittance into the elusive club. At least that's what he had convinced himself of, and when you're a seventeen-year-old know-it-all like Nathan Fox, you'll believe anything you tell yourself. This had always been the driving force behind much of his persona, and the young Lizard King simply acted accordingly. No big deal, it was just a plan, one he'd need to stick to if he wanted to become that stereotypical, brilliant-yet-troubled, rock-god type. And you can bet your ass it was, without a doubt, what he wanted.

Seriously though, it was a tough job, something not cut out for everybody. Employment responsibilities included the ability to drink like a fish, assemble words into sentences (for both lyrics and talking) and show up to work once in a while. It was perfect. Nathan saw this as the ultimate plan for his life, and at a very young age he began to hone his skills. The Doors were always his favorite band. They were also his dad's, and as a result, he couldn't remember a time when they weren't the soundtrack to his life. He had access to all of their CD's through his dad's huge classic rock collection, so it was an absolute no-brainer that Nathan (intentionally or not) patterned himself after his idol, Jim Morrison. It could've also stemmed from one of Nathan's earliest and fondest memories.

Around the age of five or six, while peeking through the staircase railings of this very house, Nathan watched on as his dad and mom enjoyed a bit of much-needed alone time. The TV was off, and as far as they knew, Nathan was upstairs fast asleep, dreaming his little rock-star dreams. Brandon Fox smirked at his wife, tinkled the ice cubes in his glass and winked at Pamela in an attempt (a very poor one at that) at being sexy. He eased himself over to the stereo, put on *The Doors Greatest Hits* and immediately hit track 2 (because he knew Pamela was a sucker for "Light My Fire.")

From the seclusion of his seventh-stair hideout, a young Nathan giggled as he spied on his mom and dad. They were doing all sorts of yucky adult kinda' things, talking mushy, hugging, kissing and smoking this weird, smelly stuff. "Ugh!" Nathan thought to himself as Brandon was now doing some sort of secret jungle dance while singing like Jim Morrison into his drink. Pamela Fox gazed at him like an enamored, star-struck groupie and Nathan did a six-year-old face palm. He couldn't help but giggle a tiny bit and continued to watch through the cracks of his fingers. It may have been one of the only times that Nathan ever truly felt part of something, and he loved his mommy and daddy dearly. He continued to secretly watch from his hidden balcony seat, but when Brandon Fox dove down and started tickling Pamela on the couch, their uncontrollable laughter finally made Nathan laugh out loud as well.

Brandon Fox looked up through the lingering smoke of the smelly stuff and shrieked. Both he and Pamela jumped from the couch and started waving their arms about like they were being attacked by a swarm of killer bees. Nathan's dad cleared his throat and told his young son he needed to climb into bed and that mommy would come tuck him back in. They were both still laughing and Pamela made her way toward her little boy. She swooped him up as she ascended the stairs and rubbed her nose into his tummy, and for a certain six-year-old boy, all was right with the world.

Nathan never forgot that. He also never forgot the smell that accompanied it, and to this day, whenever he got a whiff of that *weird, smelly stuff,* he always remembered his parents, the Doors and that space in time. Maybe that was the defining moment that started all of this rock-star stuff for Nathan. Maybe not, but Brandon Fox always did say that his son could belt out any Doors song even before he was out of diapers. Maybe it was a coincidence, but it was only a few short years later that Tommy came into his life.

Something that resembled the rumblings of Nathan's stomach snapped him back to the now. He thought about getting up and grabbing something to eat when he noticed his prized, foam-rubber pillow wasn't what it used to be. He attempted to get a little more life out of it by punching it a few times, and upon placing it back behind his head, he forgot all about grabbing a snack. It didn't take long and he immediately slipped back to the then.

The master plan that bubbled in the head of this eleven-year-old kid first consisted of putting together a band, or at least finding a guitar player, a partner in crime so to speak. After all, Jim Morrison had his Robby Krieger just as Robert Plant had his Jimmy Page, so it only made sense that Nathan Fox found *himself* a guitarist as well. After all, there were plenty of junior, rock-star wannabes at school who already knew how to play both "Smoke on the Water" and "Come As You Are," so it shouldn't be too hard to find some doofus guitar player he could boss around. However, the more he talked to his fellow rock-stars-in-training, the more he realized (even at eleven) they were nothing more than mere posers, kids with expensive toys that couldn't play a freakin' lick. At least the good news was that, being his first year at junior high, Nathan had a ton of hopefuls from a load of schools to choose from. The bad news however, was that Nathan tended to be a jerk, and none of the ton of hopefuls wanted to play with him. It must be some inbred, singer mentality or something to naturally be an egotistical ass. And Nathan was no exception to the rule. But sometimes, the rock-and-roll gods, with their keen skills of observation, create a stir in the cosmos and shake the very pillars of Earth itself. And sometimes there's a fat kid in the corner of one of your classes who's just beggin' for it.

In silence, Thomas Len Taylor sat at his desk submerged in his artwork. He had flipped over his math assignment and was taking full advantage of a nice, blank, glorious white sheet of paper.

While the other kids tackled their problems, Tom sketched away at a fierce, fire-breathing dragon: one donning shades, a baseball hat and a Led Zeppelin T-shirt. Nathan had noticed the kid before but didn't think too much of him, probably because he was so quiet.

Mr. Biggles closed his gradebook and announced to the class that he needed to step out and would be right back. Nathan decided this was his chance, and just as soon as the back of Biggles' heel cleared the doorway, he crept over in order to see what this kid was up to. As he peered over Tom's shoulder, Nathan was secretly impressed with his drawing skills and a little floored that this chunky kid knew how to accurately draw the Zeppelin logo. After all, when looking at a picture of a fierce, fire-breathing dragon that's wearing shades, a baseball cap and a Led Zeppelin T-shirt, that's what you notice. As Nathan looked on, he wondered why this kid hadn't noticed him looming from behind, when he spotted a pair of mini headphones hidden beneath his bushy, blonde hair. Nathan got a big, shitty grin on his face when he figured this kid had probably been tuning out since day one. He then heard the faint rumble of Kashmir coming from the hidden phones, and he couldn't hold back any longer.

Now Nathan's ability to be a jerk was only surpassed by his inability to make friends. He simply wasn't good at it, not because he was shy or apprehensive, but because he was that kid in school who craved attention at any cost. He wasn't a bully, but he was a freakin' smartass and seemed to have a need to prove to others (and maybe himself) that he was better than they were. You know, like someone who plays jazz. It's how he was wired, his nature so to speak, and since you can't go against nature, Nathan simply acted accordingly by promptly yanking the phones from Tom's ears.

Thomas erupted from his seat and fired out a loud "Hey man!" at Nathan, and if anybody hadn't noticed him in the corner before, they sure as shit did now. Nathan dangled the buds in front of Tom's face and started singing N'Syncs "Bye Bye Bye" at the top of his lungs. Tom turned beat red and screamed, "That's not even what I'm listening to!" in an unsuccessful attempt at defending himself.

However, the damage was already done, and the roar of the classroom's laughter engulfed any puny statements of explanation. It was then that Nathan (like a good front man in training) turned towards the class, stuck out his butt and went into his own version of his pop's secret jungle dance all while still singing. This was indeed a nightmare come true for Tom, a guy who suffered from ADHD and OCD, not to mention a huge dose of low self-esteem.

In his little life, Tom had always opted for the seclusion of his art and music in an attempt to escape the chasms of his own mind. But as Nathan went on, Tom saw himself shrinking in front of the class's very eyes. He didn't know how to react, and that adolescent, middle-school, icy chill of fear shot down his spine, the one that makes your hairs stand up on end. Obviously he wasn't of the same smartass caliber as this jerk, Nathan, was, but he had to do something. So when Nathan turned to Tom for one final, "Bye Bye Bye," Thomas Len Taylor laid the Lizard King out with one mighty left hook to the head!

BWAP!

Neither would ever again hear thundering applause of this nature until playing in Osaka many years down the road. While still on his ass, Nathan scratched his head, gathered his bearings and raised up a peace offering, the dangling headphones. Tom reached out his hand

and apologized for decking him as he helped him to his feet. Nathan simply replied with, "It's okay man, I know I'm a jerk." Upon the admission, the entire class once again applauded, especially the rock-star posers Nathan had previously dissed.

"So you like Zeppelin?" Nathan asked, and Tom responded by placing the head phones back into his ears, once again cranking up Kashmir. Nathan smirked and simply headed towards his desk as Tom sat back down in order to add the finishing touches to his drawing. Nathan planted his ass down in his seat, and while rubbing the newly-acquired bruise on his noggin, Mr. Biggles re-entered the room smelling of stale coffee and cigarettes. Both he and Tom looked at each other and smiled ever so slightly. Right then and there, Nathan knew he had found his partner-in-crime.

Through the window, the moon supplied ample light for Nathan as he stared into space. He rubbed his fingers across that part of his forehead and thought he may still have a bump where Tommy's fist made impact so many years ago. It was like the late-late show airing in Nathan's brain, and while he lay in bed, his old room seemed to trigger one memory after another. In no relative order, he again thought about his parents, the Doors and the 27 Club. However, he was beginning to second guess his plans at being a member, probably because he was now in his mid-twenties and twenty-seven didn't seem so unattainable after all. He resumed looking at his posters, and cracked up when he remembered his and Tom's earliest big plans of rock-and-roll world domination.

After that infamous day when Tom laid Nathan out, they became the best of friends, spending the long, boring hours at school fantasizing. Nathan would dream it, and Tom would draw it, everything from gold records and mansions, to expensive cars and fully-equipped tour busses loaded with willing chicks. And this was long before Tom could even play a lick, but Nathan was gifted at making the unobtainable seem attainable, even for a guy like Thomas Len Taylor. Sure he loved music, especially rock, but how could this quiet kid with low self-esteem ever abandon the seclusion of his made-up world? How could he trade it in for the real deal? Quite simply, Tom was full of fear, and the act of transferring the dream from the basement to the stage was going to be a feat within itself. Nathan however, was that life-changing friend. You know, the one who boldly introduces you to your up-and-coming self, the one who shows you what you could be with a little snip here and a little tuck there. He was truly an evil blend of Henry Higgins and P.T. Barnum with a dash of Tony Robbins on the side to close the deal. Nathan Fox was the kid who could front your band, write lyrics and wrap rubber bands around a coffee can for your first guitar (at least until you could get a real one). He was the kid who your parents warned you about, the kid who reached puberty well before anybody else. He was also the kid who showed you just how unfulfilled your meaningless, little life had been … at least up until now.

WATCH!
NOTING THAT AT NO TIME DO THE AMAZING NATHAN'S FINGERS EVER LEAVE HIS HAND!

SEE!
WITH YOUR OWN EYES AS HE BREATHES THE VERY LIFE INTO TOM LEN TAYLOR, A DULL AND LIFELESS LOSER!

BE AMAZED!
AS A DUMB KID WHOSE LIFE CONSISTED PRIMARILY OF VIDEO GAMES, TV AND SELF-DOUBT TRANSFORMS!

SCREAM!
AS NATHAN MOLDS HIS CREATION INTO A FREAKISH, GUITAR-PLAYING, ROCK-AND-ROLL GOD!

Yup, that was Nathan Fox, the little Jim Morrison wannabe, quick-witted and super-fast with a comeback. A front man from the beginning, the one with the big plans whose first order of business was to help Tom convince his mom and stepdad, Phil, that he needed a *real* guitar. The empty, rubber-banded coffee tin was fine for the basement. Hell, it was even good for writing songs. But let's face it, Ace Frehley would've looked pretty damn stupid rocking out on stage with a freakin' Folgers can. Tom and Nathan had a well-thought-out strategy about how their music was good for the economy, world peace and global warming as well as keeping young children off the streets. So, like two young Perry Masons, they presented their case and frankly were quite shocked that Tom's parents bought it. It was pretty easy though as Tom's mom was excited for the fact alone that her son had finally made a friend. Like Nathan, Tom didn't have too many friends either, but for polar opposite reasons. She knew Nathan was kind of a little shit, and she never fell for his Eddie Haskellisms, but she also knew that deep down he was an all right kid. Plus, they had decided a few days earlier to get him a guitar anyhow.

As Tom and Nathan filed into the back of his parent's car, a feeling of first-time excitement and triumph coursed through their veins. Tom was actually on his way to get a guitar, a *real* guitar, and there was no doubt about it that Nathan was the one who made it possible. Tom, overwhelmed with feelings, "bro-punched" his best friend on the arm and thanked him. Nathan simply stated that there was no need and proceeded to mumble something about Tom changing his stupid name, then smiled at him … like the Grinch.

It was official, Nathan couldn't sleep, and he figured if he was going to just lay there as his life piano-rolled on by, he might as well get up. The notion of "just one drink to help him sleep" crossed his mind, but the thought of letting his dad down carried more weight than the urge. Besides, there wasn't any booze in the house, not anymore. But the spider had patience, years if not decade's worth, and it knew that sooner or later it would once again come face to face with Nathan Fox.

Tommy found his ultimate "great escape," and if he wasn't practicing in his bedroom, he was at Nathan's house writing hit songs. Well, at least *they* thought they were hit songs. In a time-elapsed montage, complete with bad, uplifting 80's music, Tommy got pretty damn good, while Nathan continued to craft his writing skills.

Like Lennon and McCartney or Simmons and Stanley, Fox and Taylor where pumping out their own three-minute masterpieces: little gems such as, "Pants Full of Love," "I Hate Your Face," and who could ever forget the 27-Club inspired...

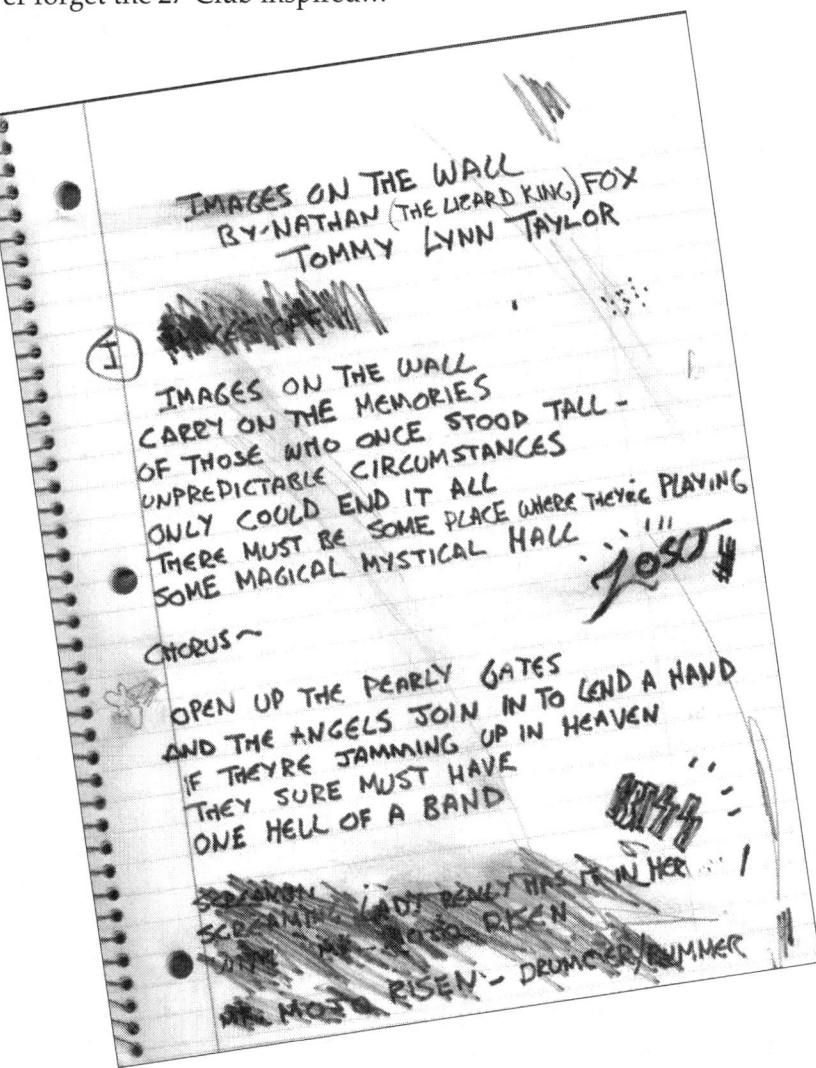

Nathan sat up, placed his feet upon the floor and reached down into the cooler he had placed next to his bed. He cracked open an ice-cold root beer and walked over to his dresser (the one he'd had since he was about eight). It was still loaded with shirts and underwear as well as socks and junk, but in the second drawer, buried beneath his high school treasures, was an old photo album. He pulled out the aging binder of memories, and upon opening it, an old, yellowing piece of paper floated to the floor. It was a drawing of a fierce, fire-breathing dragon wearing shades, a baseball cap and a Led Zeppelin T-shirt. He cracked up and placed the drawing in the back of the album for safekeeping. He then sat Indian style on the floor and began thumbing through the pages. Nathan'd probably never let on that he kept mementos from the past, because that kinda' stuff was for drama queens like Tommy, but he did manage to stockpile quite a few pictures from those formidable high school years.

He often missed those wonderful, younger days when everything was so new and unexplored: things like drinking, partying and, as always, the girls. From the very first day of ninth grade, Nathan and Tommy acted like little rock stars, because in their minds, they already were. They made it clear that this was merely that time-killing period, the one just before the golden goose showered you with a big-time record deal. Nathan loved that period of his life. It was indeed glorious, from his and Tommy's first gig at their pal, Keith's house, to kegs in the woods complete with a homemade stage and a freakin' power generator! And who could forget those sweet, summer nights playing air guitar to a room full of buzzed, giggling girls! Tommy was always the undisputed air-guitar champion back in the day, and Nathan laughed out loud when he remembered that nobody, but nobody, could air-shred like Tommy could! Simply throw on Van Halen I, sit back, then watch as Tommy and a gaggle of drunk bro's from school rocked out to the entire freakin' album! Nathan also remembered puking his guts out at those same parties, because drinking like a rock star was just as important as pretending to be one. But hey, it just added to the whole "mystique" of the thing, and he figured that getting freakin' wasted (like playing air guitar) was simply part of the training. Yup, both Tommy and Nathan were on their way, rock stars long before they ever were.

Nathan loved visiting the past, and as he thumbed through the photo album, he, for the most part, only remembered the good things. However, he definitely didn't miss that whole "puking his guts out" stuff, something that went on long after school and continued up to just a few short months ago. Nope, he didn't miss that at all, nor did he miss the ongoing occurrence of hurling all over his bed, thanks to a bad case of the night spins. Clearly something Nathan had hoped he could forget, but he was finding it difficult, especially when his whole damn room started shaking!

Nathan hadn't even noticed that his precious photo album had secretly slipped between his fingers when he sprang up from the floor. It took him roughly two seconds to gather his bearings and realize what was happening. "Shit," he sighed, "it's another one of those stupid earthquakes," and unfortunately he couldn't escape this one by simply switching to satellite radio. The house moaned in pain, and it sounded like the freakin' end of the world as its wood foundation began to give way while the walls started to crumble. Nathan stumbled over the splinters of his bedroom's collapsing hardwood floor and made his way into the tilted hallway. Brandon Fox was already there, having wrapped each of his brawny arms around the necks of Tommy and Olivia, pretty much dragging them by their heads towards the front door.

"C'mon, Nathan!" he yelled, "It's a big one!" Nathan took up the rear and pushed from behind, and even though it didn't really help much they soon found their way outside.

People from around the hood filed out of their homes to the supposed sanctuary of the great outdoors. But their feeling of relief was very short lived, sort of like surviving a massive shipwreck only to find yourself treading water in a shark-infested sea. The street cracked wide open and began to swallow cars while tall telephone poles toppled to the ground. Transformers blew, sending showers of sparks and debris onto the panicking crowd below. There was nowhere to run to, nowhere to hide. A few of the neighbors jumped in their cars and just began to drive. It may not have been the thing to do, but at least it was something in the midst of a crisis where you're, for the most part, helpless. Tommy motioned everybody towards the Tahoe, and it looked as though they would do the same by trying to out-drive the quake. Fire climbed to the sky in all directions, and as gas mains merged with the flames, the shit hit the fan.

BOOOOSH!!!

In an instant, the kindling that had once been the Fox house erupted into an impenetrable, two-story bonfire. Nathan and Brandon Fox watched on as all of their memories (some good and some, not so

43

much) went up in a massive ball of flames. Nathan was relieved he had saved one of the only things that he ever gave a shit about, his photo album. The one that had slipped between his fingers when he hauled ass out of his bedroom. Time stopped, and Nathan felt sick to his stomach as he and his dad stared on in disbelief. However, shock was a luxury they just couldn't afford at the moment. They needed to move, and the Tahoe was dangerously close to the burning home. If they had any chance of making a break for it, now was the time.

"Let's go!" Tommy yelled, and they gathered around the SUV, watching as the black, high-gloss paint of the vehicle reflected the fire that raged from behind them. Tommy frantically patted his body in search of his stupid keys. He took a deep breath then looked up. "Shit," he sighed ... "They're in there." And he pointed to the blazing inferno.

Steam, heat and fire spewed from within the earth, and the temperature didn't just skyrocket, it freakin' exploded! The streets began to melt, and tar seeped into the lit-up crevices of what was once Lockheed Way. Nathan looked at his rent-a-car, and the rims were already flush with the ground. Black smoke rose as the tires burned into a rubbery goo and ... KABAM!! The convertible exploded, lousy stock stereo and all! Soon the neighbors' cars followed suit, blowing up one after another as the planet's surface turned into a gigantic, red-hot oven top!

They shifted over to the grass, but even the ground from beneath it was beginning to heat up. Nathan began to think to himself that *this* was definitely no ordinary earthquake. He looked around at the surrounding fire, then over to Olivia, who still managed to push her glasses up and give him that ever-so-special, "I told you so" glance.

The few remaining neighbors from across the street, next door and down the block found their way onto the Foxes' lawn, where everybody seemed to be gathering. It wasn't at all safer in Nathan's front yard, not in the least, and the grass certainly wasn't any greener (or cooler), but nonetheless, there they stood. Brandon Fox was thinking that maybe they could haul ass to the train tracks, but that possibility was probably long gone, and even still, the tracks were no safe haven.

A wall of smoke climbed to the sky, and when the grass caught fire, the earth began to crumble from beneath their feet. Brandon grabbed Nathan's hand and pulled him close. Tommy and Olivia moved in as well, along with a few of the Foxes' neighbors from next door and across the street. The flames closed in and their beaded skin began to expand, and as the heat seared through their clothes, the yard erupted in a blazing white inferno.

Chapter VI

Nathan thought he was dead, travelling that long road up to the great beyond as he floated weightless from within an ascending, white sphere. He struggled to open his eyes, only the piercing light was far too intense, so he decided to keep them shut for now. A warm pressure soon closed in and around his hand, and Nathan didn't have to see to know who it was, because he knew Brandon Fox's massive meat-hook-like grip when he felt it. It comforted Nathan. He also couldn't think of any better way to leave this stinkin' planet than with his pop by his side. A little something broke through one of the layers of rock that housed Nathan's brain. Suddenly he was grateful, grateful that if he were actually dead, at least he and his dad were both given a very rare opportunity, the chance to reconcile.

Nathan forced one eye open so he could see what the hell was going on. After the sharp sting of the bright light wore off, he saw not only his dad, but everybody else who had gathered in his yard. He couldn't figure out exactly what was going on, but while his eyes adjusted, he looked past the illuminated bubble they were somehow floating in and glanced down at Palmdale … as it went up in flames.

The horrific sight sucked him in as the fire from the homes below lit up both the hood and the entire night sky. It took him a second to get the logistics right, but as soon as he locked in on his house, he could make out the entire neighborhood, or what was left of it. After that, his eyes instinctively found Tommy's abode a few blocks away, and he watched it burn. Nathan felt a little like Charlie Bucket as he peered down from the great, glass elevator hovering from above, watching his quaint, little town while it baked to a crisp. He looked over at Tommy and almost got sick, thinking he may have just lost his mom and stepdad, Phil. Hovering from the opposite end of the bubble, Tommy glanced over at Nathan with a look of disgust and disbelief. He shook his head, then turned back in order to look down on Palmdale again.

Nathan knew what he was thinking, because he was thinking it

too. This was where Tommy and Nathan grew up, where they met, where they made music together as kids. This "godforsaken place," as Nathan once called it, was where there was family and familiarity. It was hard to imagine just how somebody could feel as they watched their town evaporate in front of their very eyes. Then, in the midst of it all, something dawned on Nathan, and he realized he *did* know someone who had seen this, Olivia.

For the first time, Nathan now had a microscopic glimpse of how Olivia must have felt when she lost her family in the great Salt Lake City blast. His stomach rose into his neck and he swallowed hard. The pain he suddenly felt for her transferred to the grip he had on his own father's hand. He didn't say a word and desperately tried not to show in his face what he felt in his heart. He couldn't help but feel sorry for Olivia as she peered out of the illuminated orb (or whatever the hell it was they were floating in). Her hands were cupped around her eyes, but it was hard for her to get a better look below because her glasses kept slipping down her nose. A strong emotion overtook Nathan and he thought that maybe he had finally seen Olivia for who she really was, a frail, broken woman. The lump in Nathan's throat came back, and he held back the tears. He decided right then and there that from now on, things would be different between him and Olivia. He decided that he would try to practice more patience with her, maybe try to understand where she was coming from. Which (like Palmdale below) must be some sort of living hell.

Nobody seemed to realize or even think twice about being suspended high above the earth in an oversized, illuminated beach ball. Not even the Foxes' neighbors who knew absolutely nothing of the E.I.O. and whose knowledge of kaiju attacks went only as far as the internet would let them. But in this case, it was pretty hard to deny that something was going on, and even if it was just an ordinary earthquake (which of course it wasn't), it had to be hard to stomach. The intense heat continued to rise from below and even though they were high above the earth, it must've been a hundred-and-some freakin' degrees. However, the heat seemed to be the last thing on everybody's mind as they peered out of the transparent, floating force field. Maybe they were just in shock. Or maybe in this post-Rikoku era, nothing really surprised anybody anymore.

The glowing sphere cleared the topside of the clouds and Nathan spied the bottom of an insanely huge, hovering craft. Damned if it wasn't the blasted E.I.O. coming to the rescue with the biggest danged contraption to ever fly the friendly skies. It was the *Tomoyuki*, the metal mother hen that housed squadrons of F.U. fighter jets designed to intercept and, if at all possible, eliminate even the nastiest of daikaiju. The fighters were also as big as freakin busses, and the bottom of the carrier that housed and transported them around the globe was drawing nearer. Through the smoke and haze, Nathan could see the blinking red lights from beneath the hull but couldn't tell where one end started and the other end finished. Yeah, it was that freakin' huge.

It was a magnificent sight, there was no denying it, and Nathan had never seen, let alone been in, an F.U. carrier before. For a brief second, he couldn't help but think that, due to the craft's tremendous size, Jacky boy and the E.I.O. were obviously trying to overcompensate for something, or lack thereof. Either way, Nathan preferred the smaller, sleeker F.U. fighters to this giant, flying albatross, and gathered there must be at least twelve or so of them stowed in the belly of this mammoth beast.

Funny, how you'd never think that two guys like Nathan and Tommy were each capable of flying something as sophisticated as an F.U. fighter. You'd also never think that they were both accredited officers in this secret agency known as the E.I.O. (or the E.I.E.I.O. as Nathan called it). Hell, you'd probably never believe it, but at one time Nathan and Tommy even saved the entire freakin' planet, possibly the whole damn universe! But *that*, however, is another story for another time. Needless to say there they were, both captains in one of the most secret syndicates that the world never had the privilege of knowing about, the Earth Intelligence Organization. But, captains or not, it only took one drunken escapade in Tokyo and Nathaniel James Fox was busted down to second lieutenant. Which basically meant he would remain an officer and a pilot, but now made less money than Tommy. Of course, that pissed him off to no end. It wasn't so much about the money, as both Tommy and Nathan were now kabillionaires due to their rock-star, secret-agent fronts and triple-platinum debut album (also courtesy of the E.I.E.I.O.), it was more the principle of the thing. Or maybe it was just the fact that Nathan wasn't ever happy, unless he was *un*happy, or doing something really stupid.

"We gotta go back down there," Nathan thought to himself. "This is wrong, people are dying. We need to get off of this freakin', floating merry-go-round and do something about it." Nathan couldn't believe what was going on in his head, couldn't believe that he was actually contemplating the idea of putting other people's needs before his. "This can't be at all good," he thought, as this threw a monster-sized monkey-wrench into Nathan's normal way of thinking. And as for his so-called brilliant "Plan B" involving a shitload of tequila, the Keys and his own private harem? Well, it just didn't sound so appealing, at least not at the moment.

Something clicked in the Lizard King, a subtle gift of thought many refer to as a *moment of clarity*: an elusive feeling that, in the midst of the madness, gives you a clear vision of your worthless existence. It also shows you what may happen should you not heed its warning. For some, it's the best thing to ever happen to them, while for others it's more like a messenger of death. It looked like one had just walloped Nathan upside the head, but that's usually the way it goes. You never know when it'll happen, and if your life's a massive piece of shit, like Nathan's was, you'll greet it with wide-open arms.

Over the last twenty-four hours something had changed for Nathan Fox, and as the bitterness seeped from his body, he felt more empowered and less like a victim. Even while the world seemed to burn down around him, he still felt good, not to mention hopeful. He felt as though he could change, not the world, but himself, and maybe that was enough to make a difference. He was floating on that proverbial pink cloud, even if it was just a stupid, glowing force field. Then as fast as the feeling came, it was gone, reduced to nothing but a memory and a vision of a glorious what if …

Nathan welcomed his newfound serenity by pounding frantically on the gel-like bubble. He wanted to make a difference damn it, and he wanted to make it now! However, it only seemed to conform to each hit and then immediately bounce right back. Brandon Fox put his large hand on Nathan's shoulder and gently smiled. All they could do was "keep their hands inside and wait for the ride to come to a complete stop." Nathan calmed down a bit. He didn't like the idea, but came to grips with it as there was nothing they could do while they were still in this stupid bubble thingy. At least he was no stranger to this (not the stupid bubble thingy, the waiting part), as during their world tour he found himself impatiently awaiting test results from local free clinics on more than one occasion. He was just having a hard time shaking that look on Tommy's face, the look he made as he peered down onto Palmdale. He was also having a hard time digesting what must have been going on in Olivia's head. As they drifted up to safety from their floating lifeboat, mammoth gears churned in order to spread apart double steel doors from the bottom of the mothership. "Finally," Nathan grumbled in a serene sort of way.

The gates widened and the force field, along with its guests, floated lightly into the carrier's F.U. fighter jet bay. The massive floor came together from underneath them, and as soon as the all-clear siren wailed, the bubble dissipated. Of course, when this happened everybody fell, slamming about six feet to the deck. Brandon Fox hit first and hardest, unintentionally softening the fall for everyone else. He pushed Tommy off of him, sat up and gripped his elbow in pain. "What the f—"

"DUDES!!"

Nathan grimaced and felt like he'd been run over by the damn Vinyl Crush tour bus. He shook his head, and as everybody lay there piled on top of each other, he sighed out the words, "Freakin' aliens." This wasn't solely due to being dropped either, but because he knew who was behind their little bubble-voyage long before he heard the indigenous call of the Intergalactic Surfasaurus. Nathan's neighbor, Old Man Wilson, didn't move and had lodged his armpit directly into the Lizard King's face, or, to be more precise, just below his nostrils. Nathan twitched his nose, looking as though he had come across a dead skunk in the road, and his eyes teared up. He struggled to see between the cracks of arms, legs, bodies and stuff when he finally saw what he was looking for. He pushed Old Man Wilson's elbow away from his cheek, then attempted to return the call of the Surfasaurus with a broken ...

"Dude?"

Nathan crawled, clawing his way out from underneath his large, immobile neighbor, and as he did he saw exactly what he already knew. There, a few feet above them, Michael was standing behind a security railing that separated the large bay of fighters from the elevator that led to it. His twin extraterrestrial sister, Liberty, stood just to his right with her arms folded.

"Sorry about the harsh landing compadres! Libs and I must've let go of each other's hand just a nano-tad too soon," Michael announced to the clueless crowd.

"No problem, brah," Nathan exclaimed, as he pulled his dad (who wasn't looking too good) to his feet while he bitched about not wanting any help.

Then, before Tommy could say it Nathan blurted out, "We need to get back down there!"

Tommy, who was a little shocked hearing this from Nathan, wondered if he hit his head when the alien-bubble burst, surprised that he actually gave a shit about something other than himself. Tommy, deciding not to question a good thing, jumped to his feet because time was short and he couldn't have agreed more.

"I've gotta get to my parents. I have to see if they're all right!" Tommy yelled.

He began to panic and hightailed it towards the stationary F.U. fighters. Nathan and Olivia followed, leaving Brandon Fox and his neighbors in the dust. There were sixteen F.U.'s stowed in the bay, eight to each side parked in numerical order, ready, armed and fueled to launch at a moment's notice. Michael yelled at Tommy as they ran down the aisle that separated the two rows.

"Tommy, I know what you're thinking dude!" he shouted through the bay.

"Your mother parental-unit and stepdad, Phil, are par-do-in in Mexico!"

Tommy stopped dead in his tracks looking beyond confused, but figured out what must have happened just as Michael screamed it at the top of his lungs.

"They're getting *wasted* in Cabo, dude, thanks to a bogus magazine contest put together by the E.I.O."

Tommy covered his mouth, closed his eyes and sighed in relief. "Thanks man!" he shouted back.

Michael and Liberty dematerialized and reappeared just in front of Tommy, Nathan and Olivia and simply answered him as any alien would,

"No prah-blem-o, dude, me and the Libster's got your back."

Liberty confirmed with a slight nod and then spoke in her alien, matter-of-fact voice, "Yes we do. Now we need to exit the bay as you and Olivia are wanted on the bridge."

Tommy wasn't budging. He had no plans whatsoever of going to the bridge to discuss anything with anybody. And it wasn't because he and Olivia went AWOL from the FUJI over a week ago, gallivanting across the planet on some private endeavor to hunt down the ornery beast known as the Lizard King. Nope, that had nothing to do with it (even if it did). It was because there were a ton of people down there who could probably use their help (even if there weren't). In all reality though, Tommy was relieved his parents were safe in Mexico. But not everybody was, and he'd made up his mind. He was going back down to Palmdale to look for survivors, even if he had to steal an F.U. fighter in order to do so. Tommy looked at Nathan. He had a feeling, but still hadn't established if the captured Lizard King was on board or not. Nathan though (as you already knew) had made up his mind back in the bubble.

"Well?" Tommy inquired, "still thinking about 'Plan B'?"

"What's 'Plan B'?" Nathan asked, and Tommy replied,

"Exactly … Let's go."

Liberty wasn't excited about Tommy and Nathan's plan, to say the least, thinking of it as nothing but an act of defiance towards the direct orders of the E.I.O. She turned to express her dismay to her brother, Michael, only to see him climbing up into the ship (right behind Nathan, Tommy and Olivia). Liberty closed her alien eyes and sighed, probably because she knew better, then followed suit.

It was suddenly like old times. Nathan and Tommy took up the captains' chairs in front, and Olivia took up the seat directly behind them. The Twins sat together at the ship's computer system and proceeded to ready the jet for takeoff. Tommy hit the comm. system announcing to the bridge that FUJI Unit Jet, F.U.2, will be lifting off from the bay area in T minus one minute and to please access the exit point.

Sir Jack barked back through the carrier's radio forbidding them to leave. "Damn it!" he yelled. "We are not cleared for these kinds of ruddy heroics! Nathan Fox, at this point, isn't even an E.I.O. agent! Abort takeoff and get your asses up to the bridge! NOW!"

Nathan swung his chair in Olivia's direction. "What the hell is Walrus Boy doing here?"

Olivia widened her eyes giving him the international look of "Duh!" that no doubt implied what she had already told him freakin' eleven-hundred times, that something big was coming.

Tommy had already backed the craft out of formation and was facing the closed exit point. Sirens went off, and the elevator that led to the bay opened up spitting out a gaggle of FUJI Flunkies. They were armed to the teeth and dashed towards the ship with their guns leading the way.

Nathan laughed, "Like that's gonna help. Let's freakin' go!"

Tommy proceeded to make one more announcement to the bridge.

"Open the damn doors, or I'll make my own!"

He then gave the Lizard King the nod of approval, and Nathan flipped up the concealed-weapons computer from the dash of the fighter, running through a sequence of switches. He wasn't sure if they had changed the codes, but after a series of beeps and clicks, Nathan grinned.

"Target locked and missile loaded, Captain."

The countdown continued ... "T minus 10 seconds ..."

Sir Jack slammed his fist down on one of the operating consoles from the bridge and bellowed, "Damn it! Open the ruddy exit point, get those guards out of there and authorize launch!"

A smaller voice came through the comm. system telling them that they were cleared for takeoff. While the FUJI Flunkie granted them clearance, you could hear Jack in the background bitching about the codes not being changed. The mighty door that led to the skies outside creaked, let out a burst of steam and began to open.

Nathan flipped one more switch above his head and hailed the bridge one final time before takeoff.

"F.U.2 ..." then there was a seemingly long pause, "over and out."

The ship erupted out the side bay of the Tomoyuki and descended back towards Earth, cutting its way through the red-tinted haze. Sir Jack collapsed into his chair and began to rub his temples with his thumb and index finger. "Bleeding hell, not this again," he thought to himself, and as he did, he smiled ever so slightly.

Chapter VII

The F.U.2 descended towards Earth, more like a submarine prowling the murky sea as opposed to an aircraft cutting through the thick night sky. The smoky haze, combined with the early morning mist, created a drizzly, tomato-soup atmosphere that peppered the windshield of the craft, and the closer they approached from above, the harder it was to see. Nathan figured it was somewhere around four in the morning and pulled his cell phone out of his back pocket to verify the time. It was 4:45 am and the light was fast consuming the black. But for now, everything was a bright red-grey due to the fire-lit smoldering remains and darkness. Sweat seemed to flow from every possible pore on Nathan's body, and he wondered if it was his nerves. After all, it'd been a while since his last mission, the one he couldn't remember. He wiped his moist forehead and asked that age old query, "Is it freakin' hot in here or is it just me?" Nathan looked behind him at Olivia and the Twins, then discovered it *wasn't* just him, but before he could say anything, the F.U.2 computer system answered his question out loud.

"Ship's internal temperature is one hundred two degrees. Temperature outside of FUJI Unit Aircraft Number Two is one hundred thirty degrees and rising."

Tommy's cheeks expanded when he blew out a sigh that confirmed he was burning up as well. He clicked off the ship's "voice" option and growled a, "Shut up, Hal," a nickname he had given to the lame FUJI computer system that seemed to know your every move and nark on you whenever you did something wrong. At first he didn't mind it and thought it was actually kind of cool, that was until Hal forbade Tommy from smoking on the Vinyl Crush tour bus. From then on, all the pre-programmed, synthesized computer voice did was irritate the crap out of him. But what Tommy hated most about Hal was that every time he heard it, (which if you were at any E.I.O. facility you couldn't help but hear the damn thing) it reminded him of someone who spoke with a similar inflection, his friend SCOTT.

"No wonder everything is going up in flames down there," Olivia stated while peering through the thick of the window. "I have never been in an actual earthquake situation before, but I do know that tar melting and cars exploding due to an extreme rise in heat is something quite out of the ordinary."

Nathan groaned to himself, because sometimes Olivia's know-it-all tone grated on him like nails on a chalkboard. "Good lord," he thought, "she's like a freakin Gilmore Girl. How many words can that woman fit into one damn sentence?" Funny thing was, she didn't even say anything wrong. However, Nathan had been in a quake once when he was a little kid, which of course made him more of an authority than Miss Prissy Pants here. He turned to Olivia and opened his mouth, but before any venom could escape from between his lips, her glasses slipped down her nose, reminding him of the promise he had made to himself.

"Yes, Olivia, you are absolutely right," he stated with a sappy smile that made him look as though he had some sort of weird stomach issues.

Olivia looked shocked, "Uhm ... Yeah ...," she said back as she examined him closely. The last time Olivia said something about earthquakes to Nathan, he nearly bit her head off. She looked at him and wondered what the hell he was up to, but decided now was the perfect time to practice a bit of that Nathan Fox patience she had been meaning to try.

As they approached, Tommy activated the mobile aircraft lights that spread out all along the bottom of the ship. Beams bright enough to turn midnight into high noon formed long, thin pyramids of light beneath the F.U.2. While they rotated in order to scan the surface, Tommy accessed the HD monitor viewing system. The entire front windshield transformed into a screen, but it was still next to impossible to make anything out through the smoke. Not thinking, he hit the craft's heat sensor to see if it could pick up any signs of life, and the whole damn thing shorted out!

ZZZZPPPTTTTT!!!

The first thing to cross Nathan's mind was, "What are you freakin' nuts? It's a hundred and sixty effing degrees out there!" Instead, he tried some more of that *a-little-less-out-of-the-ordinary* junk, and held his tongue. That didn't stop Olivia though, because it was Nathan she was trying to be nicer to, not Tommy.

"What are you freakin' nuts? It's a hundred and sixty effing degrees out there!" she yelled.

Tommy ignored both the heat sensor shorting out and Olivia's apparently new talent for stating the obvious. He then decided to hover away from the beaten path of ground zero as a few things were becoming pretty damn clear to him. First, there was no way anybody or anything was still alive down there, and second, the F.U. couldn't take the heat as it was now approaching two hundred degrees.

Tommy radioed the Tomoyuki above, requesting they use *their* heat sensor to see if *they* could locate any regions of Palmdale that didn't resemble downtown Hades. He couldn't help but think that this was becoming a colossal waste of time, but still asked the freakin', floating apartment complex above to scan for any possible survivors. Plus, being 10,500 feet in the sky, maybe they wouldn't have the same issue with the sensors as the F.U.2 did. Tommy turned the ship and they headed north ever so slowly. As they pushed on, they continued to access the craft's windshield viewing monitor scouring the surface for life. Nobody really knew just what was going on, but it definitely had that feeling of "The shit's about to hit the fan" written all over it.

The F.U. carrier responded and stated that using the heat sensor was a "no go" for them as well, at least when it came to scanning for life. However, in the attempt, they discovered something very interesting, very scary and very troubling. Sir Jack cut in overriding the HD windshield feed replacing their surface view with his giant head.

"As you all know, we've been discussing the nature of these quakes with Dr. Takarada. Well it bloody looks like he was right again … as usual."

A mutual chill ran down everybody's back. They didn't know exactly what Sir Jack meant or what new information Takarada had discovered, but they knew it couldn't be at all good. Tommy, Olivia and The Twins just sort of stared straight ahead, processing their worst fears, and Nathan, of course, was clueless.

"What is it?" he asked, and neither Tommy nor Olivia replied. He looked at Michael and Liberty, "What the hell is it?" but everybody was a bit too freaked to really pay attention to Nathan and were only listening to Sir Jack as he continued.

"It so bloody simple, I don't know why we didn't discover it earlier."

Nathan, being irritated that nobody was answering his questions, forgot all about the whole "new and improved" thing and blurted out, "Cuz you're idiots." As soon as he said it, he wished he hadn't and gathered that remaining grateful, holding his tongue and being consistently pleasant was gonna be harder than battling daikaiju.

Sir Jack grumbled something about Nathan and a tall bridge, then went on. "Instead of just tracking the seismic activity, we traced out the locations of the quakes. We then micro-scanned those areas for anything underground that read over one hundred thirty degrees."

The F.U.2's windshield screen that occupied Jack's giant head was suddenly replaced with a map of the western United States. The map looked normal, except for a long thin red line that someone had drawn on it with a marker.

Michael and Liberty let out a "whoa" in unison, followed up with a, "You got that right," from Tommy. Both he and Olivia had mentioned to Nathan back in rehab just how odd these quakes were, but what was happening still hadn't dawned on him yet, probably because one epiphany a day was seriously all that Nathan Fox could handle. He looked at the map, but still the elevator was having a hard time getting to the top floor.

"What?" he demanded. Sir Jack began to explain while the map remained on the viewing monitor.

"All right Nathan, do you see the long red line? The ruddy one that starts from Salt Lake City and goes all the way to California?"

Nathan leaned forward to look closer at the monstrous map that now occupied the ship's entire windshield and nodded out an "Uh-huh."

"Very good," Jack commended. "Now do you see how that little red line travels south from Utah to the northwest tip of Arizona?"

Jack had to wait a second while Nathan processed the information, and as he did, he began to grow impatient.

Then Nathan nodded out another "Uh-huh."

"Now do you see that from Arizona, the little red line enters into California and then begins to travel north once it hits Palm Springs?"

Nathan nodded out another "Uh-huh."

Jack shook his head. "Okay, you're doing great, my boy. Now you do remember that we just scanned for anything above one hundred and thirty degrees?"

Nathan inched his butt a tiny bit further up his chair in order to get an even closer view of the map. He pinched his left eye shut like he was aiming a kaiju assault weapon and contorted his face. While he looked, he tried to spot what seemed to be so damn obvious to everyone else. Nathan continued to make an array of "what the hell am I looking for?" faces and was just about to give up when finally, it came to him. Actually it didn't, he still had no clue, but at least he looked really stupid as he tried to figure it out.

Jack was glad the map was the visual on the HD screen display, so those on the F.U.2 couldn't see him pinch his forehead in the tips of his thumb and index finger, a common state for anybody coming into contact with Nathan Fox. However, he was no longer growing impatient, surpassing that to just flat out irritated.

"God blind me, Nathan, how did you ever pass your pilot's exams?" He then dumbed it up as much as he could tolerate.

"The red line is bloody red because it represents something that is very-hot. Now once the very-hot line starts travelling straight up through California, it begins to follow a fragile fault line. The San ..."

Nathan's elevator finally reached the top floor with a "DING!" and he finished Sir Jack's sentence.

"Andreas Fault."

Nathan was now up to speed and flopped backwards in his seat to show he was as equally concerned as everybody else. He felt kinda' dumb, yet another feeling that was a bit foreign to the mighty Nathan Fox, but figured he could save face (even a stupid, contorted looking one) by asking a seemingly smart question, which he actually did.

"So what the hell kind of earthquake travels in a straight line while emitting that kind of heat?"

The windshield feed crackled and Jack's giant head appeared again, replacing the map on the screen. His thick, white hair was rustled, no doubt from scratching his head in a frustrated state of Nathan. Jack quickly regained his not-so-elegant, commanding-officer composure by nonchalantly palming his stressed-out hair back into place, then proceeded to straighten out his un-straightenable tie.

"As you all know, Dr. Takarada has been tracking these quakes for almost two weeks now due to the seismic activity coming out of old Salt Lake City. It has now been confirmed that the tremors that have been hitting California are also related. Takarada thought they were all connected, but now we know without a ruddy doubt that they indeed are. We are not sure what is creating the flow of the red line that appeared on the map, but we do know this. Like a series of veins from a main artery, it's causing earthquakes in all directions branching from its epicenter, it's hot as bloody hell and, until just a few moments ago, it hasn't shown any signs of slowing down."

"What can we do?" Nathan asked.

Sir Jack sighed, "That's just it my boy, there is nothing we can do, at least not yet. The Salt Lake City quake didn't raise too many eyebrows as the place is now an atomic cesspool, and even though the off-shoot tremors were tracked, their seismic level wasn't anything off the beaten path. However," Jack cleared his throat, "this whole Palmdale catastrophe has opened the floodgates, or shall I say the lava gates, because it's not one hundred sixty degrees beneath the surface, it's bloody almost seven hundred. Anything in the path of this bleeding quake-line is turning to molten lava."

"That's why it's so freakin' hot," Tommy concluded.

Jack nodded and stated, "Exactly. That is precisely why most of the damage to Palmdale was contained to the east side."

Nathan interrupted, "At the fault line."

Jack again nodded and, like Nathan and Tommy, he could never resist an opening. "See my boy, you are not as inept as your teammates seem to think. The local authorities were able to evacuate a good number of people. They must have figured this out at the same time we did as their evac route stayed just west of the fault. But it still doesn't look good."

Olivia interjected, "Sir Jonathon, you mentioned that until a few moments ago, it showed no signs of slowing down. Does that mean it has stopped?"

"Well, my dear, on that subject, there is good news and of course there is bad news," Jack said with a bit of hesitation. "The good news is that it seems to have indeed stopped moving north up the fault line."

Nathan closed his eyes and scratched his forehead. "I know I'm going to regret this, but what's the bad news?"

"We're again scanning the heat source, and it seems to be fast approaching the surface from directly beneath you. It is more than likely a geyser of some sort, probably one of molten lava. So if I were you, I would definitely consider returning to the carrier. There is absolutely nothing you can do. By the way, you have about thirty seconds to impact. Winston out."

Jack's giant head disappeared from the windshield, and the fiery inferno of Palmdale again took his place.

Tommy turned back to Olivia and sighed, "I hate to admit it, but walrus boy is right. Let's get the hell out of here." He flipped the comm. system and reluctantly hailed the Tomoyuki above, "F.U.2 returning home."

Tommy pulled back on the craft's U-shaped steering wheel and told Nathan to fire the boosters in order to push them up and out. Nathan complied with an "Aye Aye, Captain," and initiated countdown.

"And in 3 ... 2 ..."

KA-FREAKIN'-CHOOOOOOOOOOOOOM!!!!!!!!!

"Holy shit!" Nathan screamed. A wall of fire and molten rock blasted from beneath the hovering ship and made its way up into the sky! It indeed looked to be like the geyser of lava that Sir Jack mentioned was coming their way, but clearly his timing was a bit off. It missed the F.U.2, but the ship responded with the shock wave of the eruption. It tilted straight up, rose an additional hundred feet and then tipped backwards. It was like a bad amusement park ride, and Nathan began to feel sick to his talking stomach. The immense heat caused the windshield to slightly crack just enough for them to lose their visual feed with the carrier above. The jet spiraled, and in the spinning chaos everybody was tossed throughout the cockpit. Except for Olivia and Liberty that is, who knew to always buckle in, unlike other people in the craft, the ones of the male persuasion. And of course Olivia chose to remind them at that very moment what idiots they really were.

"Now's not the time, Olivia!" Tommy shouted while he sailed past her.

As Nathan fell back he also screamed, "There's no effing way that was thirty freakin' seconds!"

He then hit his head on the floor that was now the ceiling. The F.U.2 spun like a poorly-lobbed football as it descended back towards

Earth, and in the end, it looked as though only three things could happen. It would, one, spiral into the earth, two, spin into the giant erupting wall of fire, or three, plummet into the pit from whence the lava came. Take your pick, they all pretty much sucked.

"Libs!" Michael yelled as he reached up to take hold of her hand. Their powers were still running on empty, depleted from the bubble they created earlier, and twenty measly minutes wasn't nearly enough time for them to reenergize (however the hell that worked). But Michael thought that maybe they could still generate a force field around the F.U.2, and that'd give them enough time to figure something out. Michael again stretched for Liberty and another abrupt spin of the ship flung him to the other side of the fuselage. When he hit, an explosion of sparks shot in all directions, the cabin went dark and things went from bad to worse.

Hal overrode Tommy's override command and announced to the crew that the F.U.2 had lost all power, that impact was inevitable in less than ten seconds and to abandon ship.

Hal then asked, "Shall I initiate procedure to eject cockpit section from Fuji Unit Aircraft Number 2?"

There was a brief silence and then all you could hear was a deafening, "YES!" There was a glimmer of hope, and even though it was a hundred and some degrees on the surface, the odds of survival were still better down there than simply exploding and burning up in a flaming blaze of glory.

"Very well," Hal answered, "I will initiate ejection procedure."

Everybody waited a second (the one they didn't have), and Hal repeated, "Very well, I shall initiate ejection procedure."

Nothing happened, and as Tommy banged around the cabin, he kicked the side of it sending out another array of hot white electricity.

Hal then asked, "Shall I initiate procedure to eject cockpit section from Fuji Unit Aircraft Number 2?"

Tommy could almost hear the malfunctioning computer laughing at him and he snarled, "Screw you, Hal!"

Nathan turned to Michael and yelled, "C'mon, dude, get some of that freakin', wonder-twin mojo shit going … and I mean now!" As they flopped around the cockpit like three rag dolls, Nathan somehow maneuvered himself under Michael and began to push on his butt with his shoulder. Purple beads of sweat garnished the alien's forehead.

Nathan gnashed his teeth together and pushed off the cockpit door, easing Michael towards his sister. Michael stretched out his arm and went for Liberty's hand all while Hal continued to repeat, "Very well, I shall initiate ejection procedure." Nathan shook his head, and Michael just about extended his arm right out of its socket reaching for Liberty; he missed. But he was able to grab her by the nose, and apparently that was enough.

SHOOOOOMP!

It sounded like some sort of giant vacuum seal packaging them in, and an eerie, bright, puke-green glow began to illuminate throughout the cockpit. They stopped dead in their tracks and floated upside down, suspended in an alien-induced force field about three hundred feet from the ground. It was like being underwater, and in the deafening silence Hal again stated,

"Very well, I shall initiate ejection procedure,"

and of course nothing happened. Liberty grabbed Michael's free hand, scowled at him and removed his other hand from her nose. It was at that moment that the ship spun right-side up from within the aliens' shield, kind of angry-like, kind of Liberty-like, tossing Tommy, Nathan and Michael back into their seats. Well almost, Nathan again clunked his head just before landing on top of Tommy, and Michael missed his seat entirely. But he did make damn sure not to let go of his alien-sister's hand as *that* was the only thing keeping them afloat for the moment.

The geyser of fire sunk back into the earth, and a monstrous, black cloud took its place. Grey flakes of ash created a blizzard that was so thick it was even smothering some of the scattered fires. It was still hot as hell and, as wonderful as the force field was, it didn't have central air, and the heat seeped into the cockpit like hot water. Tommy took off his shirt and wiped his drenched body with it, and Nathan couldn't help but notice the scar that now proudly took up residence in the center of his chest. Seeing it reminded Nathan of the pendant that had charred and outlined "Eternity's Child" in Japanese kanji deep into Tommy's skin. While this ran through Nathan's head, it dawned on him that while they were at his dad's, Tommy never mentioned Akira Akemi (the girl who gave Tommy the necklace) even once. He figured something must have happened with Tommy and Akira while he was in rehab. Nathan felt a little bad for not asking, but as Tommy had said to Olivia, "Now's not the time."

The thought didn't last long though, as the heat quickly became everybody's main concern. Nathan sighed and wiped his damp face with his forearm. He wanted to look all sexy, like Tommy, and take off his shirt to dry the sweat from his body as well, but he felt too fat, so he just left it on. He looked over to the Twins and asked if they were able to either lift them and the force field up to the Tomoyuki or maybe even transport them somewhere else, maybe somewhere a little cooler, like the freakin' North Pole.

Michael shook his head, "Sorry, brah, Libs and I are still pretty cashed from saving your asses earlier." He laughed a little bit. "I'm surprised were even able to do this." Of course Michael was referring to the green protective shell he and Liberty were now generating around the ship.

Liberty then interjected, "Unfortunately we are still limited in what we can and cannot do. I am weak and growing tired. This protective sphere will not last."

Nathan wasn't feeling so grateful anymore and started leaning towards the dark side.

"Great, well at least we didn't die quickly in the lava geyser! Freakin' yippee, now we can all slow-cook to death in this effing, floating crockpot."

Tommy'd had enough. He got pissed off, told Nathan to "Shut the hell up!" and stated that things weren't as bad as they seemed and for once, to please, please try to have some effing faith. Nathan stared at Tommy. He was in that awkward place where he knew Tommy was right, but his pride wasn't gonna let him let it go. He puffed up like a dissed peacock and decided right or wrong, what Tommy needed was a swift kick in the ass. He reared back and Tommy went on the defense, but as soon as he was about to strike, Nathan deflated and sunk back into his chair. "Damn it," he thought, freakin' Tommy's right, now's *not* the time to panic, so he just gave in, yet another first for Nathan Fox. He also figured if they were going to die anyhow, why the hell fight it. Nathan wiped a fresh batch of sweat from his brow, took a deep breath and softly stated,

"Sorry, Tommy, you're right. We'll figure something out. We've been in worse situations than this."

Both Tommy and Olivia looked stunned. As far as either one could remember, the only other time Nathan apologized for anything, Olivia was convinced an evil spirit had possessed his very soul. Tommy was digging this new, improved, sober Nathan and even in a moment as hopeless as this, he echoed what his old friend had just said.

"You're right Nathan, we *will* figure something out. I think this heat's been getting to all of us." Tommy smiled, then put a reassuring hand on Nathan's shoulder. The gesture not only contributed in the easing of the tension between them, it also seemed to say how proud Tommy was of him. Nathan was feeling pretty good as well, and it calmed him to think that if he died now, at least he'd die sober, and that suddenly meant more to him than life itself. Maybe that damn spider wasn't so tough after all. Maybe it had given up on Nathan and decided to retreat to the sanctity of its web, setting its sights on another victim entirely. Maybe this was his defining moment, and when confronted with his demon face to face, Nathan chose his new life and not even for a second did he consider the possibility of a drink. He was often told in rehab that the good Lord would never give him more than he could handle. It seemed true, because instead of licking its pincers in the darkness, Nathan's demon was flat on its back with its legs curled up in the air. This was his shining moment, one little victory, and even if he wouldn't live to see another twenty-four hours, nobody could take it from him.

It was nice Nathan was winning his little battle, however, Liberty was losing hers. She was in and out, and the protective orb flickered like a dying lightbulb every time she'd lose consciousness. Michael squeezed her hand bringing her back, but she was getting a little further away every time he had to do so. Not to mention Michael was on the verge of collapsing him-damn-self.

The heavy smoke was dissipating ever so slightly, and as it did, the early morning sun shone through the cracks. It was majestic, and Nathan took it all in as he stared straight into the mystery of the lingering clouds. Tommy ran his finger over the scar on his chest. He had no idea his last thoughts would be of Akira. Olivia also seemed to be contemplating something of great significance. She looked at Nathan as though she was about to say something of extreme importance. Carefully, Olivia pieced her words together, then opened her mouth …

"Shall I initiate procedure to eject cockpit section from Fuji Unit

Aircraft Number 2?"

Of course it wasn't Olivia, but Hal's malfunctioning message echoing throughout the cabin. It was also at that moment that Liberty passed out, this time for good. When she did, Michael too lost consciousness. The force field disappeared and the F.U.2 went with option number three: plummeting into the pit from whence the lava came.

Chapter VIII

The F.U.2 nosedived towards the massive crater that burrowed deep down into the earth. The circumference of the pit was much larger than you'd think, somewhere around the size of the crater that the quake in Old Salt Lake City had left behind. It looked pretty much the same too, but because all of the witnesses were, well, dead, there was nobody who could tell you that it did. They also couldn't tell you what was coming.

Nathan ignored the hot sting of the wind that blew in through the cracks of the windshield and just stared straight ahead, which was actually straight down. He gazed with a shitty-ass grin as the massive pit became closer and closer. All he could think about was how good an ice-cold root beer would be right about now, but he knew that *that* wouldn't be a problem in a few short seconds.

As the wind pounded against the ship, the web of the windshield channeled streams of smoke deep into the cockpit. Chances were, the heavy-ply, kaiju-proof glass would last for the few moments they had left, but it was making it hard for Nathan to watch his life as it flashed in front of him. He forced his eyes to remain open as much as he could stand, and even though it stung like hell, he was determined to see this through to the end. He didn't want to miss one precious second of his own demise. Nathan glanced at Tommy one last time who was still running his finger over the scar on his chest and Nathan figured he'd gone bye-bye. A hand struggled against the G's in order to grab the top of Nathan's chair and Olivia hoisted herself up and into his seat. She dug her right arm around Nathan's lower back to secure herself in. She then pulled Tommy's hand away from his kanji scar and held it tight.

"The Twins are lucky," Tommy stated while giving a nod in their direction, "they won't know what hit 'em."

Olivia added how she envied them being unconscious, and

Nathan remarked about how overrated passing out was. He then made a comment about Olivia not being strapped in, and before she could either laugh or cry, another geyser of lava erupted from the pit as they fell into it.

FWOOOOOOOM!

Something that looked like black domes of high-gloss death engulfed their entire view. Olivia yelled that whatever it was, it was coming at them just as fast as they were coming at it. As it grew closer, it became apparent that the reflective pools were a pair of relentless eyes and merely the larger two of eight total. From underneath, monstrous, blood-laced fangs, or something that looked like them, rose over and parted from what appeared to be some sort of bearded mouth. At first it was hard to tell, but when the putrid spit stretched and constricted, it became obvious they weren't fangs at all, but a repulsive pair of pincers. A ferocious, high-pitched scream emitted from whatever this thing was, and the waves of the roar cleared the front line of smoke that had originally concealed it.

A bolt of sheer terror shot up Nathan's neck, and his heart pumped so fast it forced him to vomit. This was by far his worst nightmare coming true, and it was climbing out of the darkness to seal the freakin' cap on his worthless, little existence. Nathan felt like a sucker for believing the line he had heard repeatedly in treatment, the one pertaining to God, or whatever you chose as your higher power, about never giving you more than you could handle. Because frankly, this was a whole hell of a lot more than he could. He turned a sickening shade of white and joined Tommy in Neverland, as the thought of this thing devouring him and the only people he ever gave a shit about was too much to bear. Nathan's whole idea of facing the pit of fire head-on like a big man deserted him. He screamed like a little girl, and it was pretty creepy. Because nothing will send a chill up your spine quite like the sound of a grown man screaming like a little girl. However, Nathan was drowned out by the piercing wails of Tommy and Olivia, then all simply went silent.

"Shall I initiate procedure to eject cockpit section from Fuji Unit Aircraft Number 2?" was heard throughout the cabin, followed by a "Very well, I shall initiate ejection procedure."

Only this time, a few clicks readied the craft and a series of small charges ignited, separating the cockpit from the rest of the ship. In one evasive maneuver, two front rocket boosters tilted the escape section upright as four bottom exhausts erupted, and instead of dropping to Earth, the freakin' thing launched straight up into the sky. While it made its getaway, the escape pod left a thick, green-tinted, organic-thorium vapor trail in its wake while it climbed towards the heavens above. The main bulk of the F.U.2, however, descended like a stone towards the hell below, and when it went down, it slammed smack-dab into the face of this new demon daikaiju.

KA-BWASH!

The liberated cabin rocketed up, causing Nathan, Tommy and Olivia to snap back to reality. Nathan pressed his face up against the side of the pod's cracked windshield and yelled, "Shiiiiiiiit! Can't this thing go any faster?"

When the F.U.2 crashed, all of the freakin' nukes on board blew up with it, and the top of a mushroom cloud was fast approaching them from below. Tommy grabbed the steering U with both hands, pressed down on the two, red buttons on top of it with his thumbs, waited and got a whole lotta nada. Clearly Hal had taken over. Obviously even a machine could sense that they'd already done enough damage for one day. Luckily though, the escape pod soon out-climbed the blast, and the explosion retreated back to Earth. They leveled off and the tiny craft began to make its way back towards the nearby F.U. carrier, just like it was programmed to do. Nathan looked at both Tommy and Olivia, then back out the window.

"I don't think we helped much," he calmly stated, and Olivia rolled her eyes.

Olivia didn't swear much, so it was always kind of funny (and a bit disturbing) when she did. She turned from the chaos below, pushed her glasses up, glared at Nathan, and said, "No effing shit, Sherlock."

Nathan decided to give his new and improved self the rest of the day off and promptly told Olivia that she could go f—, when Tommy interrupted the both of them.

"Uhm … Did we see something down there in that crater?" he asked.

Both Nathan and Olivia had seen it as well, but Nathan wanted so hard for it to be his imagination that he flat-out denied it.

"I couldn't see jack-shit down there. Besides I was a little preoccupied with the thought of freakin' dying."

Olivia again shook her head and called Nathan the "Drama Queen of De-Nile." She said she was sure she had seen something, and then reminded a certain somebody about the puke that was hardening just above them.

Nathan defended himself and went on about his sensitive stomach, "You know Olivia, the one you mentioned was getting larger!"

She looked at him as though he had just sprouted another head. She swore again and any thought of her ever getting along with Nathan disappeared right along with that damn mushroom cloud.

"All I said was that you look like you've put on a little weight! Jesus Christ, Nathan! Hold things in much?"

Nathan grabbed about an inch of his stomach and began to make it talk in a high-pitched voice, "My name is Olivia and I'm the most perfect person on the planet, but I'm so effing uptight that I squeak when I walk—" and again Tommy interrupted them.

"Uhm ... Remember when I asked if we had seen anything down there? Well, we did."

The smoke and fire that lingered over the top of the crater both inhaled and exhaled as something forced itself upward from below. Massive bony appendages with six joints each were rising up and attaching themselves around the rim of the gigantic crater. Soon you could see that they were actually legs, tipped with some sort of enormous black claw or nail, each one driving itself into the top circumference of the pit for stability. Once it's limbs seemed to be secured and in place, four to each side, the thick overcast in the center of the hole began to ascend. The layer of fog that blanketed the creature drifted downward as the body of the beast rose upward. Even from above, it became obvious how freakin' huge this horrendous monster was, towering to almost sixty meters once its legs were fully extended.

Just before the F.U.2 escape pod was swallowed up by the Tomoyuki, Tommy, Olivia and Nathan could see the hellish abomination in its entirety, and it wasn't pretty. They peered in shock, staring at the beast through the cracked windshield that surrounded the pod. The bay doors closed from beneath them and Olivia held her hand over her mouth. She blurted out, "Heteropoda Maxima," and Tommy did the same thing whispering,

"That's one big-ass, freakin' spider."

Nathan couldn't even speak; he was beyond terrified. The light grew dim when the carrier's doors came together, and he couldn't keep from looking deep into this thing's lifeless eyes, stopping only when the hatchway closed and the dark of the bay settled in. The faint glow of a red light relieved the black of the bay, and Nathan felt as though he had just died. This creature was like nothing before, something he'd only seen in his nightmares, and it scared the ever-living shit out of him. He also knew, beyond any shadow of any doubt, that this was *his* battle, *his* demon, *his* daikaiju.

The escape pod holding area lit up in a fury of spinning white lights, and Hal's voice could be heard throughout the entire carrier.

"Battle stations, kaiju sighting confirmed. All pilots please report to your designated FUJI Unit jet for immediate liftoff. This is not a drill … REPEAT … This is not a drill."

The wheel of a large, steel hatch door spun, and the door to the pod bay burst open in an explosion of metal echo. Four FUJI personal rushed in, and when they parted to each end of the craft to pull everybody out, Doctor Kyoshi Takarada was left in the wake.

The lumbering spider moved like molasses as it stepped over the mouth of the monstrous pit. It stopped and gazed down upon its surroundings, appearing to make its cold calculations about what to do next. The creature seemed to show intelligence and not functioning on sheer instinct alone, which meant that it was more than likely an "intent," a name the E.I.O. had given to any beastie that seemed to have an agenda or intention. The other class of kaiju were labeled as "rogues," a typical, standard, atomically mutated monster that seemed to be a simple victim of its nuclear environment. They also seemed to be popping up more and more these days. The giant arachnid raised its legs in succession and began to move, probing the ground with its hair sensory receptors as it did. One of its two clawed tarsi found at the tip of its leg came down hard and fast onto one of the few remaining houses in the area.

BOOOOSH!

It was reduced to a pile of rubble in a nanosecond, and the creature didn't even seem aware, or maybe it just couldn't have cared less. It continued to move forward, a little like a massive, hydraulic contraption, still slow like it was making sure all was safe to proceed. It also seemed like it was choosing to travel above ground instead of burrowing below. Maybe it figured the cat was out of the bag, so why the hell not. A slight high-pitched frequency that sounded like your ears ringing after a Who concert emitted through the air; even the Tomoyuki from above was picking up on it. They knew it was coming from the monster arachnid, but at this point they didn't know why. And honestly, they weren't too concerned and figured it'd go away once they blasted this thing back to hell.

Palmdale had been reduced to a ghost town, and luckily, most people had already been evacuated. If not, they were just plain dead. With the exception of the lingering tinnitus-like tone, the little burb was now, for the most part, quiet. However, in nearby towns, the air raid sirens began to bellow in the distance while the rumble of the oncoming F.U. assault jets filled the air with a noble thunder.

Eugene Redshirt, captain of the F.U.3, led a battalion of five F.U.s into action. Like his father before him, and his grandfather before his father, the Redshirt's were of the highest level of E.I.O. military stock, bread for brave deeds indeed. The ships created a flying arrow with Redshirt in the front while the other four crafts followed tight behind in perfect formation. As they closed in from above, Redshirt, a burly, cold man, quite familiar with the concept of casualties, shuddered an unwilling "Good Lord" upon his first visual of the monster. There was no doubt that the sight of this tremendous "thing" far surpassed unsettling, even catching a seasoned soldier like Redshirt off guard. He swallowed hard to get a grip, then proceeded to do what he was trained to do … die. Redshirt pulled down the shield of his helmet, flipped the comm. system of the F.U.3 and channeled his fear to fuel, announcing to the other ships and the carrier above,

"This is FUJI UNIT THREE … Missiles locking in on target. I'm going in."

He descended forward in order to go in first and the other four F.U.'s shot straight up while parting, two to each side. A visual, provided by the inner shield of Redshirt's visor, produced a 3-D grid of what lay ahead of him. A rotating targeting system searched and immediately locked in on the upper abdomen of the beast as he approached from behind.

"Missiles locked … FIRE!"

SHOOOSH! SHOOOSH!

Two rockets, each bearing a silhouette of a rogue kaiju with a red circle and a slash down the center of it, blasted from the wings of the F.U.3. Redshirt pulled hard on the steering U, and the ship ascended and rejoined the formation.

FWOOM! BOOSH!

Captain Redshirt observed from above and watched as both missiles hurled right into the back of the creature's abdomen. The spider staggered amidst the explosions, lost its footing and collapsed to its side, falling flat onto a strip of buildings in the remains of downtown Palmdale. A heavy blanket of smoke rose into the air when the monster hit the ground, and it didn't move a muscle once it had fallen.

Redshirt again spoke into the comm. system, "Okay, boys ... this is going to be easy. Let's finish the job and head back home."

The F.U.s regrouped and all ships descended towards the point where the monster had gone down.

Redshirt again addressed the other jets, "FUJI UNITS FOUR and FIVE, prepare weapons for final assault. SIX and SEVEN stay back and cover from above. This shouldn't take long."

Like the tip of an arrow, the three crafts approached straight and true while the spider began to rise out of the ashes. It turned in a slow, menacing nature to face its enemy, and its black eyes made contact with Redshirt's.

He again announced, "Missiles locking in on target," then asked for confirmation of the same from the other two F.U.s. Each repeated that they were locked in. "Ready ... Fire!"

Six kaiju assault missiles cut through the coarse, dust-laden air straight towards the face of the spider, and as they did, waves began to emit from the giant creature. Heated crests generated off of its body one pulse at a time, in turn causing the temperature to climb at an ungodly rate. It only took a few vibrations of energy from this thing, and it was already three hundred degrees. The extreme heat mixed with the force of the throbbing emissions simply engulfed the missiles causing them to explode prematurely. Captain Redshirt's eyes burst wide open, and as he yanked back on the steering mechanism, he commanded the F.U.s four and five to also "Pull up damn it! Pull up!" But it was too late. The waves had risen to almost six hundred degrees as they pumped and filled the vast open sky. One, two, three. Just like that, each F.U. assault craft exploded into a million falling particles.

In an aggravated display, Sir Jack kicked the base of a FUJI Flunky's workstation, then ordered the other ships to abort the mission and return to the Tomoyuki, (which was hauling ass in the opposite direction). Jack tried to rub the stress off of his face and fell into the nearest empty chair. He, like any good commanding officer or friend, hated losing men, especially if he thought he could have somehow prevented it. "God blind me," Jack thought. "How could I have been so stupid?"

It was obvious this creature was capable of emitting intense heat which it used to turn solid earth into molten rock. It was far beyond their current realm of thinking, but this is what enabled it to swim through the lava, just as easily as a fish swims the sea. The instant this thing reared its ugly-ass, eight-eyed head it should have been apparent to him that this creature was not the result of the extreme heat, but the cause. He also should've known (at least that's what he convinced himself) that the searing temperatures it emitted could be used as a defense mechanism, which it did. This, of course, brought him right back to the beginning of this little, inner battle and again he felt like shit about Redshirt and the other two pilots. Jack was no stranger to making hard decisions in the midst of battle, but it was obvious he was growing weary of wars and monsters. He would've felt horrible, old and incompetent if he had the time, but he didn't.

The spider didn't have as much as a scratch on it. Even the two lucky shots that Redshirt managed to get in did nothing but knock the damn thing over, and maybe irritate the crap out of it. It was without a doubt an intent, and it was making its way to the coast, towards Los Angeles, leveling anything that got in its way. At the speed it was travelling, it wouldn't take long at all for it to reach the Glendale area and the other heavily populated burbs that surrounded L.A. Then, of course, Los Angeles itself.

The F.U. carrier tailed the monster from a few miles behind (so as not to become a flying piece of burning bantha fodder) with Jack scrutinizing its every move. Like the F.U. assault jets, the mammoth, plate-glass windows of the Tomoyuki's bridge were capable of projecting HD video feeds. A checkerboard of 3 X 5 horizontal rectangles surrounded the bridge in a televised semicircle, and various shades of lit-up tints flashed over Jack's face. Also streaming were feeds from local television stations and mainstream news networks from all around the world highlighting the invasion. There wasn't really anything captured of the creature crawling out of the earth, but some hotshot camera guy, or maybe someone fast with their cell phone, caught about ten seconds of the spider emitting its heat waves. They also happened to catch all three of the FUJI Unit jets exploding one by one, and all networks were replaying the short blip over and over like Vinyl Crush's first hit single. But, to be fair, nobody would ever accuse the media of irresponsible journalism in a vain attempt at higher ratings. They were simply doing what they did best in any crisis. And that was to incite fear, panic and large doses of chaos.

Jack groaned as he turned away from the screens and ordered a direct call to be placed to the White House. The HD monitors flashed to black and all security procedures began to initiate as the signal went through. Because they, (they, being the E.I.O.) didn't like it when some nosey Nancy listened in on their private calls. Besides, they liked to be the ones doing the listening anyhow and, make no mistake about it, not even the president of the United States was immune to the bionic ears of the Earth Intelligence Organization.

Most other first-world countries on the planet had always played nicey-nice with the E.I.O., but the United States, well, they were of a different breed. They looked at the E.I.O. like they were nothing but a giant thorn, stuck deep in the left cheek of democracy's proud ass. Congress and the higher U.S. departments and agencies were always questioning their every move, whether they needed to or not. There was even a branch within the C.I.A. that did nothing but try to keep the president "in the know" of their super-secret agenda. But when it came to kaiju and the like, you really couldn't blame the United States, because they had to count on the E.I.O. and their divisions (including the FUJI) to keep the war off of American soil. So when Salt Lake City dematerialized as the result of a nuked Japanese battle-bot, it's not like you can say to a country's president, "Whoops, one must've slipped through."

It was funny though, how America and the United Kingdom seemed to hold this invisible grudge against Japan, not to mention the fact that both had never been too keen on the E.I.O.'s relationship with the Land of the Rising Sun either. Neither would ever admit it, but both definitely had issues when it came to Japan and the world's kaiju crisis. Whenever anything happened, be it a rogue or an intent, all of their fat fingers seemed to point to the east. And this wasn't anything new or even anything old, it was something ancient, something that went much further back than the 20th century and long before the Second World War. The loss of Salt Lake City was a travesty that many Americans still blamed Japan for, probably like many Japanese still hated America for Hiroshima and Nagasaki. But when it comes to the demons of war and the hell-spawns it creates, it can only result in one thing, good people dying at the hands of bad men.

The double elevator doors that led to the bridge parted and Dr. Takarada entered. He immediately walked up and took his place at the side of Sir Jack who was standing with the captain of the Tomoyuki. As they waited for the president, Jack spoke from the corner of his mouth so only Takarada could hear him.

"It's bloody about time Kyoshi, thank God you're here." He looked in both directions and spoke in an even softer tone, "So where are the bleeding Archies?"

Jack, for a brief second, was amused with both himself and his little pun of comparing Vinyl Crush to the Archies. Jack hated the Archies, hated their cartoons and hated their stupid song, but must have thought the comparison to be funny as his mustache rose a little bit to the left. A strange phenomenon that happened whenever Sir Jack smiled. Takarada looked cautiously around, thought about the question for a second and whispered back to Jack,

"Who are the Bleeding Archies?"

Jack rolled his eyes, and as he did, Takarada figured it out.

"Oh yes, I see. The bleeding Archies are really Tommy, Nathan, Olivi—"

Jack cut him off. "Where are they Kyoshi? The last thing we need is for them to ruddy show up while we're talking to the president. We're on shaky ground as it is."

Takarada didn't understand the term "shaky ground" and figured it was English slang having something to do with the earthquakes. He did however agree that Vinyl Crush and, well, let's just say their youthful enthusiasm, were a bad idea at the moment, and he answered Jack, "They are all being tested for radiation."

Jack sighed out a "Good," and as he did, Dr. Takarada informed him that the tests were being held in sick bay and that Brandon Fox had already been admitted. He then asked Jack, (not because he didn't

78

know, but because he didn't know if Jack knew) if he was aware of just how sick Nathan's dad was. Of course he was, but before he could say anything, the words "NETWORK SECURED" scrolled past the bottom of the screen and the oval office appeared.

Both men stood erect with arms to their sides and when the president appeared on screen, Takarada bowed while Jack did nothing. The president, who was already in a foul mood, recognized the obvious signal Jack was sending and got right into the face of the camera.

"What in the name of living hell is this thing, Winston?" Which was the president's little way of firing back by deliberately leaving off the "Sir" title of Jack's name.

Jack puffed out his chest, stuck out his chin and replied, "We are unclear, Mr. President, but we do know it has risen from the atomic ruins of Salt Lake City and it seems to be moving with intent towards Los Angeles. I'm sure you have seen the news, sir, and are well informed of this creature's defense mechanisms."

The president sneered because he had seen both the news *and* the tape of the F.U.s exploding at least a hundred times in the last few minutes alone. What he really wished, though, was that he could somehow blame Jack for this and try, yet again, to shut down the Earth Intelligence Organization. However, the president knew without a doubt that they needed the E.I.O. along with their expertise. He also knew they would (as always) need a political scapegoat.

The president walked away from the camera and back to his desk. He settled in, glared at Takarada and began talking out of his ass.

"Dr. Takarada, do you believe this abomination to be a product of the Japanese?"

Takarada looked stunned, he wasn't sure if he heard the president right, faulting his somewhat bad English.

The president asked again, "Do you believe this … kaiju, as your country calls them, to be a direct result of the Japanese-induced nuclear explosion that devastated Salt Lake City? To be more precise, do you, doctor, believe this to be the fault of the Japanese?"

Takarada's blood began to boil as this was clearly a loaded question to the nth degree. There was no right or wrong answer and this was an issue so complex that it couldn't be equated with a simple yes or no. The implication alone, however, far surpassed unjust and showed that even the president had misgivings towards Takarada's homeland. The doctor's arms remained at his sides and his right index finger began to tap profusely against his hip, something he did whenever he was nervous, or in this case, pissed off beyond belief. Forgetting where he was and who he was talking to, a long list a four-letter words covered in the veil of the Japanese language began a full assault on the president of the United States. Not that that wasn't bad enough, but it was then that the bridge doors again parted and the bleeding Archies stepped in.

Nathan (as usual) was the first to open his big mouth and called the president an effing, pantywaist puppet. He then followed his statement up with a "Crap!" as again he had blown yet another opportunity to practice patience and understanding through sobriety. Tommy, however, was not in the middle of any life-changing revelations and slammed his fist onto the nearest computer workstation. Problem being, Tommy's super-damn hand (ironically the one Takarada had built) smashed the desk to a thousand microbits. Nathan began to crack up and howled, "Whoa dude! I forgot all about your freakin' robot appendage!"

The shattered station, mixed with the frustration of the moment, made Tommy irate and he blew a gasket. He started to inform the president (in a very loud voice with an array of colorful words) that Dr. T was not only the smartest man on the planet but had saved them and the whole damn world on more than one occasion. Tommy then disconnected his rebuilt hand and began waving it up and down in homage to the brilliant man. Even Olivia and the Twins got into the act, because the question presented to Takarada was not only absurd, but most uncalled for. Olivia reminded the president of how the E.I.O. and the FUJI had saved both San Francisco and London. She then asked where his scrawny-butt would be if not for the help and sacrifice of the Japanese and the technology of the FUJI, more so of Takarada. Olivia then turned to Nathan as she yelled at the president, driving home the fact that he *was* an effing, pantywaist puppet! And as Jack ordered FUJI Flunkies to remove Vinyl Crush, or the bleeding Archies, or whoever the hell they were, from the bridge, Michael flipped the president the bird.

"Get them out of here!" Jack barked, and as they were escorted from the bridge, the president made a remark in regards to this being typical of the E.I.O. His staff and the secret-service agents who surrounded him all laughed their brown noses off, and as they did, Nathan broke free from the FUJI guard to again defend the honor of Dr. Takarada.

"And another thing!" he yelled, but Jack's plump hand reached in from behind and covered his mouth.

"Shush my boy, I'll handle this." And handle it he did.

"I don't know where you are heading with this, Mr. President. However, if your political agenda has any secret motives moving towards discrediting the Japanese, you'll find yourself at tremendous odds with your best defense against what surely looks to be coming. Not only does this include the Earth Intelligence Organization, but of course it's subsidiaries, such as the FUJI."

The president stopped laughing and quieted his staff in order to ask Sir Jack if he had just threatened the United States of America. Sir Jack replied, "No Sir, not the United States, only you. As you, Mr. President, are exactly what the lad claimed you to be, a pantywaist puppet."

Nathan smiled from beneath Jack's fingers that still covered his mouth and Jack went on.

"Furthermore, by the authority granted to me as commander-in-chief of the E.I.O., I'm ordering that martial law be established in California long enough to evacuate the entire Los Angeles area."

The president scowled as Sir Jack was right on the money. He didn't disagree with the order but did hate where it was coming from. The president, however, knew his place, and being the good, effing, pantywaist puppet he was, piped down. He had no choice though, because the E.I.O. and its administration outranked not only him, but all the other fools in D.C. to which Jack chose to jar his memory on as well.

"I need to remind you, sir, according to the United Nations, the new Geneva Convention and presences who choose to remain anonymous, that in times of crisis I have both the power and the authority to have you removed from office. Should I suspect any foul play, lack of cooperation or believe you to have any motives that our not best-suited to the needs of the people..." Jack walked right up to the edge of the monitor, his giant head engulfing the White House's entire visual, and spoke through his gnashed teeth, "I'll personally drag you and your good-for-nothing ass to Tokyo where you can ask the same question you asked of the good doctor. However, this time I'll have you do it in front of a million or so Japanese, as they, like you, attempt to rebuild their cities. Winston out."

Jack lowered his hand from Nathan's mouth and just stood there for a second. He replayed the online meeting with the president in his head and wondered if it had actually happened. He stopped wondering and realized it did when he surveyed the devastated look on Takarada's face. The bridge was thick and you could cut the tension with a knife, but one thing was for sure, Jack had stunned the crap out of Nathan Fox.

Since day one, Nathan was always cynical of Jack, picturing him as *the man* who was not *of* the people but *of* the high cabal, that big, fat bureaucrat-bastard who didn't give a shit about anything but himself. He started to wonder if he'd been wrong about Jack all this time. Yet another monkey wrench thrown into the spinning head of a sober Nathan Fox. The quiet didn't last long though, and as everybody processed the bullshit, Jack "Harrumphed" and Sir Jonathon Winston surfaced.

"Contact all branches of local military and get those people the hell out of there! I want a full evac to be underway within the next fifteen minutes. Make it clear to the armed services NOT to engage with this thing until we can find out its weaknesses."

A FUJI Flunky gave a loud "Aye" and informed Sir Jonathon that the intent would reach the greater Los Angeles area within the next few hours.

Jack remained undeterred, repeated his orders and added, "Helmsman, chart a course north for San Francisco and the American E.I.O. base."

A billion lights began to flash in sequence as the order was fed to the computer. The HD viewing screens flickered and the red glow of the morning sky reflected on everybody's face when the massive panes of glass returned to simple observation windows. The giant craft began to vibrate while a charging hum of power you could both hear and feel began to fill the bridge.

A snide look overtook Jack's face and once again the giant mustache cloaked his smile, because he had a plan. Not only that, he also had a secret, one that only he and Takarada shared. As Jack forged out the early stages of retaliation in his head, Hal came over the comm. system.

"F.U. Carrier Tomoyuki ready to engage solid rocket boosters for high velocity speed on your mark, Sir Jonathon."

Jack pulled the chained pocket watch from his vest, clicked the top of it and it sprung open. He glanced at the face of the beautiful gold piece and figured the carrier could be in San Francisco in less than thirty minutes. He snapped the watch shut with his thumb and it clicked tight.

"Engage boosters … Bloody full speed ahead."

Chapter IX

The Los Angeles-area authorities and local branches of the military swept through L.A. and its surrounding burbs with the ferocity of a hurricane. Direct orders that came from the Earth Intelligence Organization were quite clear regarding this by-any-means-necessary, no-nonsense evacuation. Time, something they did not have, was of the essence, and in these cases you could always expect resistance from the people who believed they were smarter than the disaster itself. Residents started fleeing the area as soon as the blips of the oncoming threat started showing up on local stations and the internet. Almost every main road heading north out of the greater Los Angeles area was already at a complete standstill, of course making the process that much more difficult. The problem being that most of the vehicles that were trying to hightail it out of town only consisted of the driver and that was about it. Too many cars but not enough evacuees, and unfortunately that scenario seemed to be the dominating factor from all parts of the city.

A multitude of both E.I.O. and local National Guard choppers hovered over the highways and freeways of heaviest congestion announcing to motorists to vacate their cars immediately. Some people responded by following the orders from the sky, while others just simply did not. Some even retaliated by hanging out of their car-door windows while waving their middle finger in the air and shouting the FUJI Unit acronym at the helicopters above. This attitude seemed to be the overwhelming consensus on all roads, and in the end, nobody was going to go anywhere. Although the same commands could have come from any one of the copters (as they were all faced with the same dilemma), it came first from the National Guard chopper hovering over Interstate 405.

"Evacuate your vehicles immediately. Busses are coming for you. Shut off your engines and move as far to the side of the freeway as possible. Repeat … Move as far away from the freeway as you can. We will be sweeping the roads to make room for the busses. You have two minutes to do so."

Still nobody moved, either they were too petrified, didn't think anything of the order or just thought they were too damn smart for all of this "leave your car" nonsense. The National Guard again issued the order, but this time sweetened the deal with a barrage of machine gun fire directly over the motorists, along with a "MOVE!"

Doors began to fly open and people started flooding the freeway and running over cars to get to the side of the interstate. From above, it resembled a kicked-over anthill as thousands of insects cowered towards safety.

The ground started to vibrate as it did earlier in Palmdale, trailed by a series of explosions, crashing metal and the rumble of some monstrous machine. The Los Angelinos who had scurried to the sides of the freeway began to panic and started looking over the buildings and treetops in order to see the tip of the gigantic spider. The siege, however, was almost upon them and still nobody could see anything in the skies except for the swarm of helicopters. Cars began flying into the air as though they were being hurled by some sort of great beast. The metallic bursts were horrendous, and the fleeing evacuees hit the deck in order to hide beneath the abandoned automobiles at the side of the road.

The continuous tracks of two enormous military land-crafts moaned in the distance as the dark, steel brutes thundered in closer, crushing the asphalt while black soot spat from their towering stacks. Each burst of smoke propelled them forward, enabling the tremendous tanks to slice their way through the abandoned cars, right down the center of the freeway. Vehicles parted at the mercy of a magnificent, steel plow attached to the front of the iron monster, while its massive treads crushed anything the relentless shovel left behind. The second "death machine" (the nickname the E.I.O. had given these diabolical mechanisms) did the same, getting any and all of the leftover remnants that the first may have missed. Fires ignited and cars exploded, but the haunting, black machines just kept pummeling their way through. As they passed, a long stretch of busses followed like injured ducklings in their wake: greyhounds, a few Winnebago's, a Silver Eagle, quite a few bright-orange school busses and even a cattle trailer or two loaded to the gills with human cargo.

An open-top, rust-colored, double-decker bus sporting "Star Tours" on its side scoured the edge of the road, nice and slow-like. It was one of the first three vehicles designated to pick up the people who had vacated their cars. Behind that followed yet another which was doing the same, a beat up school bus that read "Pacific Tech" on the destination sign above its windshield. Finally, taking up the rear, was a cookie-dough-camouflaged military transport truck hauling a flatbed trailer loaded with passengers. An armed guard (who may or may not have been actual military) was seated next to the driver instructing people to climb onto the flatbed as the truck was completely full. Every time they stopped for a pickup though, waves of people crashed towards the transports in a vain attempt at a guaranteed seat. And really it was almost justifiable, even if it was wrong. Because nobody, but nobody wanted to be vaporized or fused to the cement in the event of another exploding nuke. It wasn't a farfetched thought either, after all, that's what had happened in Salt Lake City. Now compile that with the Facebook images of a monstrous, eight-legged abomination heading your way and you couldn't blame them, not at all. But when calm and cool are replaced with fear and desperation, some bad shit's gonna go down.

Swooshing blades could be heard beneath the echoes of the choppers as pilots instructed the crowds below to, "Please stay calm and don't panic" and that, "There is plenty of room for everybody." However, the maddening instincts of sheer survival took over, and the panicking masses swarmed, gathering around the Pacific Tech bus like a hundred angry bees.

From the rear, the armed soldier seated in the passenger's side of the military truck kicked open the vehicle's door and stood upon its X-plated side step. He waved an AK-47 about in an effort to discourage the angry mob. He even fired a few shots into the air, but it was to no avail. The driver, however, wasn't playing any games, and since there was no telling what a scared mob would do, he simply announced for the people on the trailer to "Hold on!"

The gun-toting man jumped back into the passenger seat just as the truck growled into gear. He rolled down his window and screamed into a bullhorn, "See ya, hate to be ya!" and they took off.

The little yellow bus rocked at the mercy of a large group of stampeding men attempting to claw their way inside in a self-proclaimed right to survive. A few even yanked and pushed women out of their way, sending them to the ground and to the threat of a thousand trampling feet. The grinding of gears permeated the air; the excess weight was far too much for the Pac. Tech. bus's old engine. The driver toggled the long stick shift that protruded from the floor and pushed it forward hoping to God they would move. The bus groaned one last time and hot steam hissed from beneath its hood. It wasn't going anywhere.

The driver of the double-decker watched the whole thing, courtesy of the large, rectangular, rear-view mirror that was bolted to the side of his bus. It was both hypnotizing and numbing, just like a show on the Disney channel, and the driver (just like a zombified, TV-watching child) couldn't help but stare into the light. That was until the images in the mirror started growing larger. It took him a second to realize that the mob was now coming for *his* bus, and when he did, he started to freak out. People were still filing on, but at a much slower rate than the fast approaching hoard. None of them were going to make it if he had to wait for everyone to get on. He gripped the steering wheel as a nervous sweat peppered his forehead, and the tip of his boot teased the top of the gas pedal. "Just a few more seconds," he thought to himself, "and all I have to do is shove this thing into gear, put my foot down and we're gone." He bobbed back and forth as he simultaneously watched the mirror, the door and the last of the trailing evac busses whiz on by.

"C'mon, c'mon!" he yelled. "Hurry it up!"

The smashing of glass took the driver's eyes away from both the front mirror and the oncoming passengers to the back of the bus. The mob that was fast approaching from behind was now upon them, and an array of fists, rocks and tire irons began to assault the vehicle. Crow bars outlined the little square windows and bloodied bodies began to pull themselves in through the sharp shards of glass. Men made their way up the double-decker's rear spiral staircase to the open-top second level, then began hoisting people up from their seats and over the side. The crowd started to overtake the bus, crawling up its outer walls like a horrible case of kudzu. The driver shouted to the passengers, "Sorry, but we need to leave!" and as he yelled, two hands smashed through the driver's side window. That was it, he knew he couldn't wait any longer. He slammed the bus into gear, begged God to forgive him and buried the gas pedal deep into the floor.

Brawling men on the second level lost their battle with gravity and toppled over the edge when the bus jerked forward. The vehicle shook and rose up, then back down and up again as it made its way over the speed bumps of men, women and children. Desperate people waving their hands in the air jumped in front of the bus before it gained speed and pleaded with the driver to "Please, please stop." He mouthed the word, "Sorry," closed his eyes and pushed the pedal down further. Screams permeated the air from within the vehicle making it hard to hear the muffled thumps the bodies made as the bus drove over them. As they moved forward and cleared the mob, the panicking people on the bus became quite silent. Now that they were safe, the passengers were no doubt pondering the last few moments of their lives. Faint cries from a few children created a perfect underscore, but other than that, the silence said it all, "Was it worth it?"

One mother, who touted a lifelong crusade of a nonviolent existence, thought how she, without any hesitation, kicked another young lady right in the face and off the bus. Another kid in his early twenties wondered if he'd ever be able to shake the scarred image out of his mind of beating up an elderly man for his seat. He also wondered if it was "worth it." That's what the silence kept on screaming, and when it was all said and done, it seemed to be the general consensus. Was it worth it? Maybe being dead would have been better than living with those thoughts for the rest of your life. At least the driver was certainly thinking all of this. But in his mind, he could rationalize that he took a few lives in order to save many, and while he thought this, he cried. He wiped the blood and sweat from his face and hightailed it towards the convoy that trailed the big, black death machines. As the driver watched in his mirror, he could see the injured hoard regroup in order to hijack the next slow-moving vehicle. He sighed as he thought, "All they had to do was wait a few more minutes." Because there were still plenty of evac busses, campers and trailers with enough room for everybody. He also knew that after this, nobody would be coming for them now.

A high-pitched ring emitted through the air, and the masses left on the side of the now-abandoned freeway turned towards the sound in both curiosity and concern. The frequency was loud and haunting, but

like a siren luring its prey to the jagged rocks below, they couldn't help but peer towards the beautiful, yet deceptive noise. It was alluring, and with it came the tranquil sound of death, similar to that of a deer staring straight into the white of a pair of hypnotic headlights, just before getting run down. The ringing grew louder, and as it did, something dark began to take shape from within the early morning's blanket of smog and haze. Then, from in between the circling cement bridges of the entwining elevated freeways, it rose up, its long sectional legs lifting its body to almost thirty stories high.

Its two larger eyes radiated through the thick, gray midst like lit-up beacons in a heavy fog. Then, when it stopped moving, it simply stared down upon the still and silent crowd. The monster arched back, raised its front four legs and prepared to strike when the angry howl of a million sirens began to wail from all parts of the city. It was as though somebody had snapped their fingers and awakened the transfixed mob from their pre-ingestive hypnotic state. Because when those sirens went off, everybody exploded in all directions in a sudden burst of screams. The spider, obviously not a fan of fast food, slammed its front legs down and erupted through the tall bridges of expressways that surrounded it.

FWOOOOMP! SMASH!

Huge slabs of concrete and tar laced with steel plummeted to the earth, crashing down onto the empty roadway and vacant vehicles. Its long, skeletal legs moved with speed and precision in a quick and forward succession. But for the arachnid, it was like trying to catch a thousand ants, as tiny, half-crazed people jumped, crawled or fell into any and all available nooks, crannies and crevices.

The monster's high-pitched ring grew to an almost deafening level, far louder than any of the surrounding sirens, and heat once again began to emit from its body. Each pulse was like a gigantic searing wave of destructive power, engulfing everything that surrounded the beast for almost an entire city block. With each vibrating field, everything it came in contact with first exploded, then simply turned to molten rock, metal or bone. However, the heat had no effect whatsoever on the creature as it waded through the flames and remains of searing earth.

The liquid steel and burning concrete was fast to cool, and as it hardened, the aftermath took the shape of twisted, deformed structures, possibly a reminder for future generations (if any) of this towering black nightmare. And maybe it was only a mere show of strength, one letting the world know just who the new "proverbial" king of the hill was. But the message was definitely loud and clear: you can run, but you can't hide, especially from the quick explosion of an incoming atomic bomb, or worse yet, a pissed off daikaiju.

The monster turned and veered from the main road, opting for more of a direct route into the heart of Los Angeles, bringing it straight through the acres of urban dwellings and such that bordered the up-and-coming city. Houses and structures crumbled under each of its horrendous tarsi as they came down hard and fast with the force of eight massive, solid-iron wrecking balls.

BOOOSH! KA-BOOSH!

Cables of two-inch-thick wire snapped and hissed, coiling around the legs of the monster while it marched through a battalion of high tension towers. Standing only about half as tall as the spider itself, the high-voltage transmission steeples blasted gigawatt bursts of electricity directly into the monster with no effect at all.

As it fast approached the outskirts of downtown, it seemed that the president was growing more and more nervous with each gigantic step the monster took. From the other side of the country, he watched and inspected the incoming video feeds from the sanctity of the Oval Office. After seeing what this monster had the ability to do, Sir Jack had ordered that he and the US defense force stand down. Not because he thought the Americans incapable, but because he knew that traditional weapons were no match for this thing. Jack didn't want anybody to make the same mistake he had made, the one that took the lives of three of his best pilots. He knew this thing's heat mechanism was capable of reducing anything that came near it to smoldering ash, including F.U. fighter jets and their incoming missiles alike. He knew because he watched first-hand as they disintegrated into the nothing before they even got near it. Hell, he even witnessed direct hits slam right into the back of the spider's abdomen with zero effect. Not to mention the fact that they were two of the E.I.O.'s most powerful warheads to boot: the infamous FUJI Unit Kaiju Maulers or the FUKM UPs for short.

Even though he wasn't too particularly fond of the president of the United States at the moment, Jack never let personal opinions and thoughts dictate his actions. Besides, who the hell knew what else this freakin' thing may have had hidden up one of its eight sleeves. The president however, didn't look at it that way, at least not after his little run-in with Jack. He had no problem convincing himself and those around him that this was simply another power play perpetrated by the Earth Intelligence Organization, one to not only cover their asses, but Japan's as well. It wasn't any magnificent feat either, as he proceeded to convince a room full of generals and yes-men why Jack was wrong and why the U.S. needed to take charge. In reality though, Jack had already formulated a plan. But putting it into action was going to take another twenty hours easy. He hoped to God that President Ego wouldn't try to take this creature down on his own when he told him how much time they were going to need. He shuttered when he thought about the large number of good men and women who were destined to fall if the U.S. gave the order to attack.

While the Tomoyuki penetrated the dark, dismal skies towards E.I.O. West, Takarada was already hard at work feeding crews of engineers and programmers the information needed for their plan to go into effect. Now that the greater Los Angeles area had been evacuated, Jack hoped the spider would take up permanent residence, or stay for a day or two, maybe take in a few sights, or at least burn them to the ground. He just needed the creature to either remain there or move to any location where there would be a low number of casualties, and since it was already there ... well, you get the picture. However, nobody, not even Jack, had counted on the monster reaching the edge of the city as fast as it did. And it's too bad, because this in turn left the president and his barking generals no choice but to reject the E.I.O.'s direct order and stop this thing by any means necessary.

All Naval border defense ships and battle cruisers along the west coast were ordered to set a course towards the ports of Los Angeles. The USS Gerald Ford was already stationed in Santa Monica Bay and it was decided that the newly commissioned aircraft carrier would lead the attack. Men scampered on the deck of the one-hundred-thousand-ton megastructure as they prepared a squadron of twenty-four navy Harrier jets for immediate takeoff. The fighters were being armed with long-range missiles in an effort to keep them as far away from the spider as possible. While the supercarriers that were still out to sea fed in the proper coordinates in order to launch their attack from an extreme distance. The strategic goal was to overwhelm the creature with an onslaught of firepower while avoiding its heat defense mechanism at all costs. As the first squadron of Harriers blasted off from the Ford, another fleet of fast-moving Hornets appeared on the horizon, rocketing from the edge of the sea towards the banks of the city.

From the aerial view, the mountainous skyscrapers dwarfed the spider, concealing its exact whereabouts. It was nowhere to be seen, and due to its immense temperature any heat-seeking effort was, for the most part, useless. However, it was easy to formulate its location from its flaming trail of destruction that ended with one building after another collapsing in upon itself.

The squadron leader of the Harrier fleet departed and maneuvered in from above to get a better fix on the beast's location. He spoke the monster's longitude and latitude into his oxygen mask and the onboard computer locked in the coordinates, transferring the data to all of the jets' targeting systems. There wasn't a moment of hesitation and he gave the order to launch all missiles.

From the circling swarm of jets, groups consisting of four fighters at a time broke off in the direction of the creature, launching their entire payload. After firing, the sub-squadrons parted to the left and right in twos, making way for the next set of discharging jets. At the same time, missile after missile launched from the deck of the USS Ford in a blazing eruption of fury.

In a second, the sky was littered with innumerable speeding rockets hurling towards the giant, black beast. The monster, sensing the incoming threat, scurried up the side of one of the tallest aqua-colored structures still standing. From about halfway up the monolithic, manmade mountain it stopped, and heat once again began to pulsate from its body in waves of hemispheric bursts. Buildings exploded into violent rages of fire, and both they and any incoming missile simply vaporized. Circling its way around the skyscraper, the spider scampered back to the ground, and the building gave way in a heat-induced blur.

BOOOOSH!

It was then that the monster arched back on its four hind legs and locked in on the remaining jets that still hovered over the ocean. Its infused head lit up and in a neon blast of green, its two larger eyes erupted into beams of searing energy. Slicing through the air like high precision razor blades, the staves of light cut through the aircraft like a hot knife through butter. Jet after jet began to rain down upon the burning ruins of Los Angeles as the arachnid demon took them out one by one.

The beast screamed, then burrowed into the burning earth and began making its way towards the ocean. The temperature beneath the surface jumped to almost five hundred degrees, enabling the arachnid to travel through the liquefied rock and steel. Streets sunk as cement and tar melted, while buildings that stood directly above the spider's underground route collapsed into a river of lava. When it reached the tip of the port, its heat diminished and it again crawled to the surface. In an act of deliberate defiance, it turned towards the dying city and spanned its horizon with another blast of shimmering beams from its eyes. The entire city was aflame with only the skeletons of mighty buildings showing through the blazing inferno.

The USS Gerald Ford, attempting a "let's get the hell out of here" about face, was still in the bay area when the spider turned back

around and set its sights upon it. Horns thundered and emergency sirens screamed as the slow-moving juggernaut attempted its getaway. From the ship's helm, the captain kept a vigilant eye on the monster, hoping it wouldn't do what he thought it was going to do. As he looked on, he stared deep into the creature's eight eyes from the pair of binoculars he was clutching with both hands. He thought about his wife and children one last time, then lowered the powerful field glasses to his bosom and uttered a soft, "Shit."

In a brilliant blast of white, the twin A1B nuclear reactors of the half-mile vessel lit up the entire sky over the coast of L.A. The raging inferno climbed to the edge of space as a toxic atomic wave almost ten square miles wide erupted out of the boiling sea. The heavens churned in a red and black frenzy while poisonous bursts of lightning polluted the atmosphere. Thick flakes of gray ash fell to the earth burying the city while it spread its cancer to anyone or anything that may have been unlucky enough to have survived. Everything was gone, and as a nuclear-laced wind blew the cloud of despair out to sea, the only thing that remained standing amongst the charred ruins was the spider beast.

The president's satellite feed of Los Angeles discontinued, turning to nothing but a flutter of white and gray. The sharp hiss of static crackled, and the horrid noise that said it all was the only sound coming from within the Oval Office. It was the same on the bridge of the Tomoyuki, where everyone was watching in complete disbelief. Reduced to a state of fear and uncertainty, Sir Jack and the president each looked down from the high thrones of their ivory towers, both unsure not only of America's, but the entire planet's future.

The president on one hand was convinced beyond a shadow of a doubt that this disaster (as well as Salt Lake City) was undeniably the fault of both the Earth Intelligence Organization and the Japanese. It had to be, because he sure as hell couldn't blame the opposing political party and he sure as hell couldn't blame Congress. And there was no way he was taking the wrap for two major cities going down on his first (and probably only) term.

Jack on the other hand believed the president to be acting in a manner unsuited to his position as commander-in-chief. It wasn't just because of the catastrophe in California though, but because of his recent treatment of Dr. Takarada and his administration's accusations upon the east. Jack always knew that the president and his cabinet blamed the Japanese for Utah. It was so damn obvious to him, and we're talking long before President Jackass's latest display of blatant stupidity. But now, more than ever, Jack was convinced of this man's inability to lead and that the tragedy of Los Angeles could have been averted, if not for the rash and abrupt response by the leader of the United States.

West of San Francisco, a good ten miles out to sea and from somewhere nearly forty thousand feet high, the Tomoyuki began its slow, secret descent. Even that far north of L.A., the ocean had grown restless as the relentless shock waves caused the Pacific to pound the shores of the entire coastline. A gaze of concern slipped from the captain of the F.U. carrier and he hesitated, just before he gave the orders to, "Batten down the hatches!" and "Prepare for splashdown!"

The monstrous F.U. vessel penetrated the crashing, white-capped waves and was soon atop the uneasy ocean. While violent water entered through designated portals, its great steel chambers filled and the ship submerged into the sea. The hull of the Tomoyuki creaked and rocked, and the captain demanded more ballast for stability. He then added that in order to connect and lock in with the foundation of the towering, undersea base, they needed to level off. However, the Pacific chose not to cooperate, and the magnificent iron giant sunk like a flat, flailing stone. An all-points red alert was issued indicating that all levels needed to secure in, as it was too late to escape the agitated undertow of the briny deep.

Red lights spun throughout the bridge and the crew fought to stabilize the sinking carrier, all while the ship's HD video feed (similar to that of the White House) continued to transmit nothing but a bright static from the lost signal of L.A. On top of that, Hal kept repeating the monotonous message out loud, as the words scrolled from the bottom of all screens,

"SIGNAL TERMINATED ... SIGNAL TERMINATED ... SIGNAL TERMINATED ... "

It was utter chaos, and as the bridge flickered in red, white and gray, the commotion began to mount, which in turn caused Sir Jack to erupt.

"Would someone *please* shut that bloody computer off?" he yelled.

But before anybody could even lift a finger, the HD comm. system went black and Hal stopped mid-sentence, "... SIGNAL TERM ..."

"Thank God," Jack thought, "a bit of ruddy calm in the midst of the storm." The repeating phrase stopped and even though the emergency disco lights continued to dance around the bridge, at least that confounded computer had shut up. He felt a bit of steam escape from his pounding head and Jack straightened out his permanently messed-up tie. "Right," he croaked, and as he thanked whomever it was that shut Hal down, the computer again began to bellow,

"WHITE HOUSE INCOMING TRANSMISSION ... WHITE HOUSE INCOMING TRANSMISSION ... WHITE HOUSE INCOMING TRANSMISSION"

"Bloody hell!" Jack groaned. "Los Angeles is burning, the damn Tomoyuki is sinking uncontrollably and now the White House is on the line! God blind me! Put them on ruddy hold, at least until we've secured the blasted ship!" he ordered.

In true British fashion, Sir Jonathon gripped the outer edges of his jacket's lapel and, amidst the turmoil, adhered to the mounting pressure. Standing proud and with calm conviction, he first harrumphed, then barked out a series of orders almost as though he were defying the elements.

Of course it was at that time that yet another transmission began to come through from one of the bridge's many HD screens. Jack sneered at the monitor, then looked over to Takarada, as they had a feeling this transmission might be coming. However, it's timing could not have been any worse.

The doctor fought the funhouse floor of the unsteady craft into the seat of an empty computer workstation and began typing at a blinding speed. A visual of current seismic activity charts of the western United States, complete with on-the-spot stats, took the place of the empty static-filled monitors. When Takarada stopped, he paused and looked up. He was well aware of what was happening, as was Jack.

"Are you sure Kyoshi?" Sir Jonathon asked, and the doctor ran one more final scan over the upper southwest sections of California. He turned to Jack and shook his head, it was undeniable.

The complex, entangled, underground arteries created by the tremendous spider were giving way. The countless quakes that had hit over the last few weeks, all the way from Utah to Palmdale, were now coming full circle. And thanks to the nuclear nudge of the USS Ford, the biggest and most unstable mac-daddy of the west coast was now caving in, the San Andreas Fault.

All eyes on the bridge stared in horror at the semicircle of HD screens, and Jack had to remind all personnel that, "We are still sinking in an out-of-control manner," and to "Please stay bloody focused!"

But it was hard to gather your bearings as the depth of the upcoming catastrophe was so far beyond comprehension. An animated red grid appeared on Monitor One, enclosing the edge of Palmdale at the fault line. As the 3D grate blanketed the long line of landscape, a digital timer appeared and the countdown began from five. The control center of the Tomoyuki became a vacuum, and not even the smallest of gasps could escape the thunder of the descending numbers.

As four faded to three, a helmsman shouted that he was able to restore ballast to the craft and that they should lock in with the undersea base in less than a minute. When two became one, the screens flashed a pointless warning of the oncoming quake. When one became zero, the frantic beeping of the incoming White House transmission ceased.

Everything on the Pacific side of the fault began to sink, and the biggest earthquake known to North America sifted the earth down like sand through the waist of an hourglass. It was magnificent on an apocalyptic level, and there was no coming back from this one either. No incredible jets of the future, no aliens with almost supernatural abilities and no giant robots were coming to save the day, not this time. Hell, not even Superman could stop this one. Plain and simple, it was all over for Los Angeles and its many surrounding cities. It was all over.

Chapter X

Nathan picked himself up from the floor and gazed back into the small porthole in the center of the steel wall. Before the Tomoyuki tanked into the Pacific, he'd been watching both his dad and the distant horizon that illuminated the edge of the ocean. Nathan didn't know exactly what the brilliant bursts of red and white meant, but knew it couldn't be at all good. He also had a strong suspicion it had something to do with his new spider pal. Nathan hated being in the dark, but figured it was just due to being out of the loop, because after their little joyride down to Palmdale, he decided that being at his dad's side was where he needed to be. "Screw that whole need-to-know-now bullshit," he thought, "*this* is what's important," and Nathan wished he'd been there all along. He wondered though, if Tommy or Olivia had any clue themselves, but like him, they were also in the dark.

It wasn't by any means their choice either. Being the good little agents that they were, Tommy and Olivia always liked to be front and center for every damn thing, even if it was for ordering freakin' lunch. However, this time, it was in fact because of Sir Jonathon and his direct orders. In an effort to keep the bleeding Archies far from operations, Jack had placed guards in front of all entrances to bridge-accessing elevators. He said it was for their own safety, but that of course was a load of crap. Jack just didn't have the time to babysit a bunch of self-righteous, rock-star types as the shit hit the fan. Nathan couldn't have cared less. He had no intentions of going anywhere near the bridge. He was far more concerned about his pop's worsened condition.

He surveyed his silver view of Brandon Fox's cramped quarters within the tiny walls of sick bay. As the ship creaked from the pressure of the water that surrounded the submerging craft, he couldn't help but feel a bit apprehensive. Nathan kept one eye on his father who laid in his bed and the other on the hatch door. It wasn't really necessary, but just in case that fictional tidal wave he created in his mind was to come bursting in, he'd be ready.

After what seemed to last about the length of one of Jack's long-winded speeches, the Tomoyuki slowed down and the emergency lights once again flashed. This, however, was standard protocol, and Hal announced to the entire ship and its crew, "Please take standard docking safety procedures."

Four mighty locking mechanisms that stood high above the base closed in and wrapped themselves around the submerged vessel. Shafts of solid steel penetrated the ship from each tower as a series of massive reverse-flow pumps pushed out the water left behind. The craft's docking lights went from red to yellow, and Hal announced, "Depressurizing in process." Nathan felt his ears get heavy and a quick pain shot through his head as oxygen both escaped and entered the craft at the same time. It didn't take long, and before Nathan could start bitching about his anxious stomach, the yellow light changed to green and the giant vessel became one with the base.

The undersea compound was magnificent, yet another marvel of industry bestowed upon the Earth Intelligence Organization by Dr. Takarada and the Japanese. It was indeed spectacular and Nathan was hating every second of it. He liked dry land and wasn't too fond of being at the mercy of this giant, sunken tin can so far beneath the surface, especially after their pre-docking turbulent floor show. "Nope, I'll take a hollowed out volcano and the FUJI over this any freakin' time," he thought. He then took another look out of his small, round view of the world, which was now nothing but a window that gazed into a vast and restless aquarium. He felt a tad claustrophobic, then pulled his phone out from his rear pocket for some sort of connection to the outside world. But just as he figured, there wasn't a single bar to be seen. With no reassurance whatsoever, he shoved it back into his pants, looked around and reminded himself of where he was, a mile beneath the damned ocean. The Lizard King mumbled something about modern technology and stepped away from the porthole in order to focus on Brandon Fox.

He still didn't know the extent of his dad's sickness, or even how long he'd had "just whatever the hell he had." Nathan, however, did know that it had taken a quick turn in the wrong direction not long after they came aboard the Tomoyuki. He walked over and scanned

his dad's weakening vitals that were displayed on a screen just above his head. Brandon had slept through the whole craziness of the carrier's uneasy descent, probably because he was so hopped up on a wide assortment of pain killers that it made Nathan a tiny bit jealous. It seemed Nathan, in his newfound sobriety, suffered bad cases of bed spins and gyrating rooms now more than ever before. But nonetheless, at least his dad seemed comfortable.

Nathan held on tight to his pop's sleeping hand. Now that they had been reunited, he had so many things he wanted to tell him, along with a billion questions to ask. Hell, he didn't even know exactly *what* was wrong with him. He only knew it was some sort of effing cancer, but that was about it. Nathan just thought they'd have more time to talk about it; Brandon Fox probably thought the same thing. Something about the sudden rise in heat, or maybe the stress of that quake, or that damn bubble-ride up to the carrier, or freakin' whatever, seemed to expedite his condition. Nathan was beating the crap out of himself for choosing to go back down to the burning surface of the planet instead of staying with his dad. He knew they only made things worse, then, after storming the bridge, all they seemed to do was piss Jack off. And for all of his trouble, what'd he get? A lovely one-way ticket to the side of his dad's deathbed.

Nathan was on the verge of a complete and total meltdown. His emotions were as unstable as organic thorium in its earliest of stages. One second he's thinking he's got it, next thing he knows, he's yelling at people just like the old days, except now he feels like crap for doing so. Not to mention those impending feelings of doom, well, he could live with those. After all, at least that was familiar territory. He just couldn't seem to get a grip on his emotions, and in the middle of all of this bullshit, he was convinced he was going to lose it. He looked at his dad and was overwhelmed with both love and despair at the same time. His eyes began to water up, and he wondered if there was any kind of alcohol or Vicodin or freakin' something around to ease the pain. He loosened his grip on his dad's hand, and as he backed away in order to dig through the cupboards of sick bay, his dad pulled him back in.

His dry lips quivered, but Brandon Fox somehow managed to push out a thin, red smile. He stretched the incoming tubes that were attached to his arm and reached over to hold onto Nathan's hand with both of his. Nathan wiped his own wet eyes with his shoulder and begged his dad to be still. Brandon, however, knew it was now or never, then asked his only son to "Please, just listen."

"You've turned into such a fine young man, Nathan. Your mom would be so proud of you."

Brandon Fox's brown eyes widened and scanned the room to emphasize that he knew exactly where they were.

"I've never been in one of these flying elephants before, not exactly sure what to make of it."

Nathan laughed as much as he could, because he felt the same way about the carrier as his dad did. He was about to comment himself, when his father's words seemed to sink in a bit. Nathan stopped, and as he tilted his head, his eyes became tiny little slits of just what in the hell are you talking about?

"I know you've been chosen for something big," Brandon Fox stated. "Both your mother and I loved you so much, son. But what we did, like you, was not at all what we did."

Nathan looked funny at his dad as he wasn't digging this whole stupid, Yoda, "what we did, like you, was not at all what we did" shit.

Brandon started to cough, and when his vitals spiked, a warning alarm screamed throughout sick bay. However, Nathan couldn't hear anything but the deafening truth of his dad's soft, trembling voice.

"After your mom died, I crawled into a bottle and slowly started drinking myself to death. I'm so sorry I forced you out. I had no idea how to deal with it. Please know, I've always loved you. It wasn't long after you left that Jack got me the help I needed." That was it, Nathan pulled his hand out from beneath his dad's and blurted out a profound,

"Wait! What? Jack?"

Nathan's dad hacked and coughed out a little chuckle, "Jack's always commented on how much you remind him of me. Why he used to even bounce you on his knee when you were a baby!"

Brandon coughed again and all the dots in Nathan's blown mind began to connect. He then instructed his son to grab his wallet that was resting on the night stand next to the bed. Nathan, in a complete daze, picked it up and began to peel apart the brown, leather billfold. As he did, a glimmer of "To Protect & Serve" lit up as the badge reflected the dim glow of the light above. He then told his boy to pull the shield out,

103

as well as an old picture of Brandon and Pamela Fox with their young son, Nathaniel.

"I want you to have those," Brandon again smiled. "I love that picture of us; it says it all for me. Take 'em. Oh, and I think there's fifty bucks or so in there also. Take that too, I'm not gonna need it where I'm going."

Nathan never had a clue, none whatsoever, and even though it made sense, he still couldn't believe it. All those years, he thought his dad was just a fool-hearted man, one who somehow believed he could make a difference by keeping the streets safe from the likes of speeders and nasty jaywalkers. Nathan's brain was overflowing, and he didn't know if he should be angry with his pop or impressed. In the onslaught of emotion, however, Nathan forgot about his dad's condition and began to assault his father with a long list a questions.

"Mom?"

Brandon Fox nodded, "Yep, she was part of it, hated field work with a passion though. She wasn't too fond of Jack either." Nathan couldn't help but crack a smile because he sure understood that whole Jack thing. "Actually, your mom coordinated most of my missions right from the house. That way when you got home, she'd be right there waiting. She spent most of her days working from a secret office in the basement."

"What secret office?" Nathan demanded.

Brandon paused and the tips of his front teeth again appeared from behind his stretched-out lip.

"Well, it wouldn't have been a secret if you knew about it!" His smile turned to a laugh, then his laugh turned to a cough.

"The entrance was the large oak shelf, the one where I kept my CD collection. You never found it because you had to pull on 'The Kingston Trio's Greatest Hits' in order to access the secret door."

"No wonder," Nathan quietly acknowledged.

Brandon Fox slipped his large hand around Nathan's wrist.

"Even when you were a kid, I knew you were destined to either be the next Jim Morrison or to follow in my footsteps ... or both. You are part of a long heritage and you'd be surprised at exactly how many agents started off as, well ... let's just say you'd be surprised." Nathan didn't think he would be. "You can do anything you want, son. You've seen you can be both a superstar and save lives at the same time. But remember, there's no shame in either, or choosing one over the other."

Brandon's grip on Nathan's wrist loosened a bit.

"The hardest thing you'll ever do is stay sober, at least it was for me. Quitting was easy, trying to figure out how to live with myself as I decided who the hell I was, *that* was the hard part. Good, bad, honest, an ungrateful ass, whatever … I discovered I was all of them and sometimes I had no idea which one was gonna rear its ugly head. I also learned that that was pretty normal in the beginning. So don't let the little things get to you, you'll figure it out as you go. There were so many times I wanted to contact you, but I didn't. I don't know why, I guess I was afraid of you telling me you never wanted to see me. I had Jack keep me in the loop though, and I'm sorry, but the intervention was my idea. So don't be too hard on anybody, especially Jack. He was profoundly worried about you, more so than I'd ever seen before. He truly cares for you, son."

Nathan still didn't have a clue about how to react to any of this, not just to that whole Jack thing, but also to his parents being freakin' E.I.O. agents and all. When Nathan was young, he thought (like any kid would) how cool it would have been to have secret-agent parents. Of course now that he was hearing all of this shit about his dead mother from his dying father, it was nothing more than a steaming pile of suck.

"Anyway, Nathan, the only part of being clean that I've done perfectly is not take a drink. At times I've been a basket case, but the longer you do it, the easier it gets, and the more things will start to make sense. You just need to figure out who you are, or better yet, who you aren't. And be sure to forgive yourself for anything that may be eating you up on the inside. That can be a killer. Hopefully this will help you to remember."

Brandon struggled and reached his arm beneath the covers for something he had placed there for safekeeping. It wasn't an easy task, but he somehow managed to find the strength to hand Nathan his three-year recovery medallion.

"I want you to have this too, it may help ease the pain sometimes. Remember, Nathan, to thine own self be true."

Nathan folded his fingers around the bronze coin and held it next to his heart, just before putting it into his pocket.

He saw his dad was slipping and knew that this was it. Brandon

Fox closed his eyes. It sounded like he had said (and made) his peace with himself as well as Nathan. He started to get heavy in the bed, and just before he passed, Brandon's eyes shot open and in his final breath he burst out a name, Dr. Iscariot.

The lines of the EKG monitor settled, and Nathan's eyes burst into a wave a water. He felt himself turning into that six-year-old boy, the very one who was hiding behind the railings of the staircase so many years ago. He hugged Brandon and said, "I love you too, Pop," and the blinking beep morphed into one solid sound.

The doors to sick bay parted, and in walked a flustered Sir Jonathon. Then as they came together, Tommy slipped in sideways. Jack stood next to the bed, let out a loud walrus sigh, then placed his hand on Nathan's back who was leaning over his dad. Tommy did pretty much the same by placing his palm on his best friend's shoulder from the other side. They stood for a few moments, giving Nathan all the time he needed. Sir Jack shut the droning EKG machine off, and in the silence whispered what a fine man Brandon Fox was, noting the countless number of lives he had saved in twenty-some years of dedicated service to the Earth Intelligence Organization. Nathan took a deep breath and straightened out his bent back. He glared at Jack, and his eyes turned to a look that begged him for help in understanding all of this bullshit. Jack then did something he may never had done before, he pulled Nathan in, almost suffocating him in a long, caring embrace. Jack, too, was crying, and as he regained his composure he backed up, cleared his throat and straightened out his permanently messed-up tie. He then let Nathan know that his door was always open, when and if he ever wanted to talk.

Chapter XI

An influx of refugees from the inland borders of Los Angeles seeped into the surrounding regions like a fast-moving brush fire. Once again, north- and east-bound traffic flooded the long stretches of dormant freeways that, not long ago, had been swept clean by the great, black evac machines. Countless thousands, homeless and just plain scared, flowed over the lands on foot, marching towards the safety and sanctity of anywhere else (as though such a place even existed). California still quivered, and with the slightest rumble of each aftershock, evacuees sped up to a frenzied state, which in turn only slowed them down. It may have been over, but it was far from done. And as far as that mile-high mushroom cloud (the one that still lingered off in the distance) went, it wasn't letting anybody forget the fact that they needed to keep moving to stay as far ahead of the oncoming cancer as possible.

The sea that bordered the new coast of California boiled in a heated fury, and the Pacific had turned to a sickening shade of red. The only things that still remained above the churning water were the tops of the twisted steel frames of L. A.'s tallest buildings. The giant, demon arachnid was also gone, presumed to be buried underneath what had been previously known as downtown, which was now the freakin' bottom of the sea. So all in all, it was a pretty safe assumption that the intent had been defeated.

Most of the affected areas had gone dark, while all other airwaves had ceased communication entirely. Even from space, all satellite feeds fixed on ground zero were nothing but a flurry of black and gray dots due to the raging nuclear storm. It was also unclear to the rest of the world just exactly what had happened, but within a matter of seconds the internet was inundated with speculation. This ranged from a variety of statements claiming that the current tragedy in California had been highly exaggerated, to the other end of the spectrum in which

107

the entire western half of the United States had been wiped clean off the map. Either way, the country, as well as the whole damn planet, was in a complete state of panic.

The entire band had congregated to Nathan's quarters and was gathered around his bed. He bobbed a bit as he sat planted on top of the covers with his arms wrapped around each of his folded knees. It was a somber get-together and very reminiscent of his intervention. In other words, it pretty much blew. But like before, they were again worried about him and wanted to be by his side, to show him love, friendship and support. They also wanted to make damn sure his silly ass didn't go for a cough syrup cocktail, because a lot of times when nothing else's available, it'll do. After all, Tommy thought, if Nathan was gonna slip up and have a drink, chances are it'd be now. He knew this because after he left him a few hours ago, he needed a drink or two him-damn-self. Which he had, along with three or four cigarettes in the garbage holding area of the submerged base. Thank God Olivia had joined them in sick bay and had been with Nathan the entire time after he left. It seemed she and Tommy were thinking along the same lines.

Tommy could also tell that Olivia had started developing the hots for Nathan, even if she wouldn't admit it. He had no freakin' idea why as all they did was fight, but chalked it up to that whole dang, lead-singer thing. He also thought she was going to pucker up and plant a big, wet one on him back in the F.U.2, you know, thinking they were going to die and all. But maybe that was solely due to the Grim Reaper pounding down the front door of the ship at the time. So at this point he still wasn't 100% positive, but figured the next time they were about to burn up in a fiery death, he'd know for sure. It probably wouldn't be too long of a wait either.

Tommy had been around Nathan long enough to know when he liked somebody, because it was the only time he was ever at a loss for words. He saw before how Nathan had fallen for this chick, Ramsay, an E.I.O. co-agent and all-around "Q"-type who fronted as soundperson for the band. It almost made Tommy squeamish to even think about it, because the whole Nathan-and-Ramsay thing went horribly wrong before it ever started. It was somewhere in Australia in the midst of the Vinyl Crush world tour that in a drunken stupor, Nathan stumbled into Ramsay's hotel room to find her batting for the other team. Not that there's anything wrong with that, but upon trying to join the party, Nathan quickly discovered that she didn't swing in both directions. After that, Nathan kept any feelings he had about her to himself, and though he'd never admit it, Tommy knew it put a slight tear in the Lizard-King's heart. But of late, Tommy was starting to notice Nathan getting a little tongue-tied (just like he used to do with Ramsay) with Olivia, so it was pretty damn obvious. For a while Tommy thought Olivia had a thing for (or with) Takarada, but who the hell really knew, and right now he didn't really care. He did know that Nathan was in good hands with Olivia and that was very reassuring to him, especially when he slipped out to go have another smoke.

In D.C. a quick crowd of reporters and high ranking officials amassed at the White House. A tech crew prepped the Oval Office in order to go live as soon as possible, all while an array of hands presented the president with a few versions of well-written speeches. The staging manager molded the president like clay as he configured the perfect position for the broadcast. He went back and forth between either a modern stance from the edge of his desk or that more traditional pose from behind the podium. He had the commander-in-chief lean backwards, his butt on the edge of his desk with his hands folded together in front of him. The producer felt this showed confidence along with determination, but also conveyed the magnitude of what had just happened, melded into a calm resolve. "Perfect," he thought to himself and decided to go with it. When the stage lights illuminated the room, a pretty, little blonde rushed in and powdered the president's nose and forehead to reduce the glare. And as the cameraman counted down, the ol' prez still found the time to give her a little wink, a smile and spill his coffee just to the right of the zipper of his presidential pants. In a mad fury, the producer raced to shuffle him in front of the podium. He wasn't too thrilled about it, but it did manage to cover up the newly-acquired round circle on his pants, the one that didn't look a thing like coffee.

"All right, Mr. President, we go live in … three … two …," and he mouthed the one and pointed.

At the same time on the floor of the Pacific, the weight of the world lay heavy on Sir Jack's shoulders. He only had a few short moments, and all he wanted to do was escape to his quarters and have a quick drink, maybe unwind for twenty minutes before facing the inevitable. He felt this was justified. Jack poured himself a scotch on the rocks and plopped down into a rather large recliner in his small, stately abode. He barked, "Television," and the flat-screen TV on the wall came to life.

It was tuned to the BBC (the real one from Britain, not the BBC America channel) which wasn't surprising as when Jack did watch TV, this was all he watched. Even in this crappy-ass time of death and uncertainty, Jack's mustache lifted and he smiled a bit when John Cleese appeared on his tele, stretching his long legs up to the sky with a stout Big Ben in the background. It was one of Jack's favorite television shows, one he rarely saw nowadays, and it had been years since he had seen "The Ministry of Silly Walks" sketch. He took a sip of his drink, and a branding bug faded into the corner of his TV indicating that he had just stumbled upon the BBC's 24-hour Monty Python Marathon. Jack decided he would watch the end of the skit, then get to cracking the whip, giving him about three wonderful minutes to gather his bearings. However, even from the seclusion of his room, buried deep in the E.I.O. underwater base, the president (whom Jack felt a nerve-calming drink was in order before engaging) found him.

The BBC promptly interrupted the show and announced that they were about to broadcast the president's address to the United States. Jack sighed out a "Bloody hell." It was no use, there was no escape, not even for a moment to catch his breath. He started to fix himself another scotch on the rocks to sip while he watched the address. He then wondered if having another drink was the right thing to do at this particular moment, which it wasn't. So instead of having one more, Jack grabbed the whole damn bottle and leaned forward in his recliner to watch the president's speech.

"My fellow Americans … It is with great dismay and heartfelt regret that I inform you of the most recent attack on American soil. At 5:21 am Pacific Standard Time, a large mutation climbed to the surface from within a crater of its own making in Palmdale California. Sources inform us that this creature had been burrowing its way beneath the earth all the way from Salt Lake City, Utah over the last few weeks. It was also confirmed that the subterranean catacombs created by this monster were indeed the cause of the many earthquakes in that region. Our response was swift, and our plan to drive this thing into the sea was a complete success. We were indeed victorious, but many brave men and women gave their lives in the effort. However, due to the unstable conditions created by the endless underground tunnels dug by this ... this monster, we have suffered severe loss and casualties."

The president was getting a bit emotional, probably due to his bad acting, and stopped to moisten his throat with a sip of water. Usually in these brief pauses, the press would ignite into a series of endless questions, but not this time, as they only sat in a stunned silence, waiting.

"Fault lines in California, ones that we know to be fragile, primarily the San Andreas Fault, have given way. We can only assume that once these hundreds and hundreds of miles of giant, interlocking boroughs began caving in, a rippling effect was created. An effect so overwhelmingly devastating that it has caused the biggest earthquake in the history of the modern world."

He stopped again to gather his thoughts, failing to mention the twin reactors of the Ford that exploded with the force of a two-hundred-megaton nuclear bomb, sealing the fate of Los Angeles and sending it to its watery grave. Yup, it seemed that was one little detail he decided to leave out. He went on to state that,

"Many parts of California, including the greater Los Angeles area, are now underwater."

And with that, the press jumped up, bombarding the president with one query after another to the chirps of a hundred cameras and the bursts of a billion white flashes. The president raised his hands, assuring the press that he would answer all questions after the address, and continued,

"As I said, many parts of the Los Angeles greater metro area have succumbed to the tremendous earthquake caused by this creature."

Two guys in black suits wheeled out an old-fashioned, freestanding, wooden frame that housed a map of California, then disappeared behind the drapes. The president extended a pointer and placed the tip on the map. He dragged it north from Huntington Beach, up to Palmdale, then from Palmdale southwest to just a bit above Malibu.

"As far as we can tell, this is the effected region, so any theories of California being completely annihilated are false. But I won't lie either, we now are faced with the greatest disaster in U.S. history. Just to be clear, all of this ...," he again outlined the same part of the map with his pointer, "is gone."

A fleet of hands shot into the air, followed by an onslaught of screams demanding answers. The president again waived his arms in order to calm the press, and as they sat back down, he attempted to answer their questions one at a time.

"Mr. President, the footage of this creature is scarce, and there is still only a minimal number of credible pictures. But stories coming in, and even the almost intangible photos, indicate that this was some sort of ... gigantic spider."

"Yes, the video footage you have seen is accurate. It was, in fact, a sixty-meter arachnid, and the reason you haven't seen more footage is solely due to the creature's defense mechanisms. Any unfortunate persons who were close enough to film or video this thing were immediately wiped out by the tremendous heat it emitted. We did, however, manage to capture this picture."

The president stepped aside, and the secret service men wheeled the archaic map out of the camera's eye. A large screen then lowered behind him and lit up with a long-range image of the massive eight-legged abomination. It was extracted from the cellphone video that someone had captured of Captain Redshirt's encounter with the beast. It was also the best shot available at the moment, and even though the reporters knew what it was, they still weren't quite ready for it. The entire room gasped at once, and when the initial shock wore off, they started taking pictures of the picture. It was beyond surreal and looked more like one of those old-school monster models than an actual giant spider. The president waited a moment, then stepped back up to the podium with the image of the arachnid hovering above his left shoulder.

"Let us call this creature Notawni Nonaashi, according to the Navajo legend, which will forever translate in the English textbooks as ... King Taraxian. Surviving Native Americans on the Utah plain have already claimed that this thing, this Indian god of some sort, was sent to the surface to punish the planet. They also insist that its awakening was a direct result of the great, Salt-Lake-City nuclear explosion. Now,

whether this story holds merit or not, the White House, just today, has already been flooded by many concerned American-Native Navajos claiming the legitimacy of the legend. And frankly, nothing really surprises me in this day and age anymore."

The president paused, as even he couldn't really grasp how farfetched this tale sounded. However, it didn't really matter if he, they (or anybody else) believed the legend or not. Because either way, L.A. was gone, all thanks to a giant, freaky-ass spider. So why not? As everybody processed the story, another hand lifted in an attempt to keep the ball rolling, but maybe in a different direction.

"Mr. President, we have seen and heard the reports of the countless refugees swarming the freeways and of many more on foot. It seems quite a few are heading north, but the majority appear to be moving east into Nevada. How do you plan to deal with this?"

"FEMA is placing temporary shelters and first aid stations on the borders of California and Nevada. Refugees are still moving in an orderly fashion, and we would like them to keep doing so. The good news is, we were able to evacuate almost ninety percent of the area before the quake. Those who wanted help, received it. Those who chose to stay or complicate the process, unfortunately did not survive."

The reporters, not exactly digging the answer to the last question, burst into a whole new series of inquiries based on his response. The president, however, moved forward with a, "Next question please."

"Mr. President, Navajo legend or not, we do know that this thing did develop in the ruins of Salt Lake City. We also know that due to the nuclear explosion caused by the Japanese mech, the ground has been contaminated with ... with ..." The reporter struggled with his notes and pulled a small tablet from his pocket, looked at it, then finished his sentence, "strontium 90."

The president tapped the pages he held in his hands on the lid of the podium in front of him. It was go time.

"Once again, we are not sure of the validity to the Navajo's claim as now we are faced with exploring many possibilities. However, we are certain that this thing was created as a result of, first, the explosion caused by the Japanese in Salt Lake City Utah, and second, by the highly contaminated ground that was left in the wake of the atomic blast." He then added that *this* is where the high levels of strontium 90 were discovered. The president then opened his hatch bay doors in order to drop his own bomb on the reporters.

"And yes, we hold the Japanese responsible, responsible for the cause that ultimately led to the creation of this monster in America and the devastation of Los Angeles. I must also note that to our knowledge it is the first one to be spawned outside of Japan, but we don't believe it will be the last. The daikaiju epidemic has spread like a disease, and this, above all, is what we tried to avoid. The plain and simple fact is that over the last 70 years, the world's kaiju problem has stemmed primarily from Japan, so we decided to offer aid and support. We did this by means of modern weaponry a few years back, immediately following the Utah incident. This was an alternative to another American occupation of Japan in order to combat the problem from the source. As most of you know, we gave to the Japanese, and may I remind you, at the cost of billions of U.S. tax dollars, the U.S.S. Duke in an effort to contain the situation within the borders of Japan. Of course it failed, and the mega-defense system was destroyed in its last confrontation. The U.K. stands with America, and as soon as we get this current catastrophe contained, we, along with the United

Kingdom, will be taking action on Japanese soil. I have already spoken with the prime minister, and together we shall end this kaiju dilemma once and for all. Thank you and God bless America."

The president turned and exited the Oval Office, and as the reporters advanced, the dark-suited gorillas again appeared from behind the drapes to contain them.

Jack's screen quickly shifted and returned back to the BBC's regularly scheduled programming of the Monty Python marathon. It dropped him about halfway into the "Upper Class Twit of the Year" sketch, and Jack couldn't help but think how appropriate this was. He looked down at the bottle that he was still gripping tight from the neck. Sir Jack was surprised to notice that he was too stunned to have even taken as much as a sip off of it during the entire address. This was so far off base it was complete lunacy, even for the good ol' U.S. of A. Something wasn't right; something about this whole American-British occupation of Japan stunk to high heaven. Jack figured he needed to contact the prime minister, maybe check in with MI6 and get the real rundown since the U.S. wasn't squawking.

You see, Jack loved America and its people. He had loved it since first setting foot on her shores way back in 1964, when he was but a young man full of piss and vinegar. Hell, he even lived in New York City for a while when he was a damn, peace-loving, hippy musician, somewhere around the late seventies. So it wasn't about hating it, even though he was at odds with the president, it was about protecting it and all she stood for. And as much as Jack loved the United States, it was only surpassed by his feelings for Jolly Old England. Even though he claimed to never play favorites, he did, a little. He knew if he were to get the runaround from the prime minister, something indeed would be "off." Jack was always of the thought that if it barked like a duck, it was a bloody duck. But he couldn't figure out just what the hell was going on here.

While he sat and pondered, the sounds of laughter that emitted from the television were barely audible. The only thing that seemed to snap him back was the sound of his door chime as it ascended in thirds, followed by Hal's voice telling him, "Dr. Kyoshi Takarada and the agents of Vinyl Crush to see you, sir."

His television turned to a visual just outside his door, and it was indeed Takarada and the band. He was stunned to see that even Nathan was with them. Jack whispered out a "shit" and decided his first order of business was to take a healthy swig from the bottle of scotch. After that, he cleared them for entry.

Chapter XII

The door to Sir Jack's quarters swished open, and six slow-moving figures slumped in, one after the other. Dr. Takarada (who looked far worse than anybody else) led the way, with Tommy taking up the rear in order to keep a watchful eye on the Lizard King. He really didn't need to though, as Nathan was actually becoming stronger than the people around him realized. Still, nobody wanted to chance it, and strong or not, he did have a lot of shit dumped on him over the last few days.

Sir Jack stood up and held the bottle of scotch behind his back as they filed in, to conceal it from Nathan. It's funny how people who drink, think that people who don't drink are so preoccupied with the fact that people who do, do. "They need to get over it," Nathan thought to himself as he glared at both the floor and Jack from the tips of his eyelids, watching him back up to maneuver the bottle and its remaining contents onto the desk behind him. Nathan shook his head, but pretended not to notice as Jack's intentions were good, stupid and a bit demeaning, but nonetheless good.

"This had better be bloody quick. I'm overdue for a conference call with the president of the United States," Jack stated before anybody could even say a word. Which of course was the truth, because he was indeed late on the all-important call. But it was also a lie, because in Jack's opinion, he wasn't primed enough to deal with the commander-in-chief, not yet. It was a solid case of the *luth*, that dreaded act of mixing a lie with the truth so it seems more believable. All the same, everyone in the room knew how Sir Jonathon felt about President Jackass (probably because they felt the same way he did). So E.I.O. commander or not, Jack could save his little-white-luth for someone who was ready to buy into his bullshit.

This was also the first time Takarada sided with the band by openly disregarding Sir Jonathon's wishes. He had no intentions of making his visit, as Jack called it, "bloody quick." He, like Jack, knew something was amiss, and he feared for his beloved homeland. As everyone scattered to different areas of the tight quarters to find a place to sit, Jack's eyes widened at the complete audacity of it all. Tommy and Nathan took the two guest chairs and Michael stole Jack's recliner. Olivia and Liberty planted their butts on the edge of Sir Jonathon's bed and Takarada remained standing. "Bollocks," Jack mumbled, and no longer caring what Nathan or anybody else thought for that matter, grabbed the bottle of scotch and proceeded to kick Michael out of his chair. Michael sat Indian style on the floor next to Nathan, and as Jack sunk into his seat, he demanded to know what this intrusion was all about. Takarada, getting a bit nervous, began tapping his right index finger against his hip as he cleared his throat.

"Sir Jonathon, we have all just watched the presidential address."

Jack set the bottle on the floor, leaned back and stared straight through the good doctor. It was one of those glares that spoke a thousand angry words as it penetrated deep into your very soul. Jack still hadn't decided if he wanted to include the bleeding Archies in this mess or not. This mission was of a different color and wouldn't call for any undercover world tours or mega-rock-concert fronts. He didn't know if he needed to put them in harm's way or not. But it seemed that Takarada had acted without Sir Jonathon's knowledge or approval, something you never do. Dr. Takarada saw the strong look of betrayal coming from the other side of Jack's round spectacles. Takarada's finger picked up speed as his forehead moistened. He knew exactly what Sir Jonathon was thinking, but knew he needed to continue.

"Yesterday I was asked by Tommy and Olivia to join Nathan Fox and the Twins in his quarters. Regardless of the invitation, I was planning on paying my respects to Mr. Fox as to his father's passing anyhow, so I believe that *this* was of the inevitable." Takarada looked directly at Nathan. "Both Brandon and Pamela Fox were fine agents, and as I told Nathan-san, I am very sorry. I must also commend him on his behavior over the last few days. This is not the same young man I knew from a short time ago. I know firsthand the struggles of having to reinvent yourself. It is an incredible load and Nathan Fox has borne it with great honor."

Nathan couldn't help but smile a bit as he believed Kyoshi

Takarada to be a no-nonsense man. If he said it, he damn well meant it. Takarada bowed to him, and Nathan, again feeling overwhelmed by emotions, wiped his eyes and sighed.

"Yes, yes," Sir Jack groaned, "Nathan Fox is indeed an inspiration to us all. Now, what is it you bloody wanted to say, Takarada?" Jack held up his gold pocket watch and tapped the glass to indicate that even though the passing of Brandon was a sad occasion, this was not the time for the Nathan Fox Celebrity Roast.

"I am unsure of the demise of the spider daikaiju the United States is calling, King Taraxian. I must also note that the Native American legend the president spoke of may be complete ..." Takarada stopped in order to pick the correct word, "*unchi*."

Nobody was sure what "unchi" meant, but gathered it was Japanese for bullshit, which it was.

"I am still unclear, but regardless if the legend bears any truth or not, it is like the president stated, it is of no matter. It is the facts we must focus on, and one fact I am certain of is that King Taraxian is still alive. I do not know, however, if *alive* is the proper word."

It was obvious that Takarada had evoked Sir Jack's attention. It was easy to tell as his eyes had shrunk to curious slits and he began to stroke his giant mustache. Because the one thing Sir Jonathon Winston knew was that Takarada's track record for being spot on was still at a glimmering one hundred percent.

"I have been watching the video logs over and over. I am convinced by its movements that it is in fact a cyborg, a creature of organic nature held together by a steel infrastructure. But what has convinced me the most is King Taraxian's heat mechanism. There is only one power great enough on this planet," he glanced at Michael, "and possibly others to wield that kind of energy ... organic thorium."

The bottle of Scotch slipped between Jack's fingers and fell the short distance to the floor from the arm of his recliner. "God blind me!" he shouted as he jumped up. "Of course ... the stolen organic thorium!" and Takarada echoed him.

"Yes, Sir Jonathon, the stolen organic thorium."

At that point (to Sir Jack's disliking), Tommy chimed in to describe his take on what Takarada had already discussed with him and the others.

"Dr. T believes this kaiju is a ploy to force the United Kingdom and

America into a war against Japan, but not for the reasons you'd think! Dr. T believes whoever is behind King Taraxicab is manipulating these countries into fighting a ghost enemy to drain their resources. He also thinks this is only the beginning and soon other countries will be lured in to deplete their fuel supplies too!"

Sir Jack looked irritated at Tommy and looked to Takarada for reassurance.

"It is not how I would have stated it, sir, but Tommy-san is correct. Even with the current abundance of nuclear energy, the act of war is not only financially devastating, but will eventually swallow up whatever sources of power you have. That is, of course, unless it is regenerating and infinite."

Sir Jack interrupted Dr. Takarada, "Like bleeding organic thorium."

Again Takarada echoed Sir Jack, "Yes sir, like bleeding organic thorium. I have not even mentioned the millions of lives that are at stake. Los Angeles may have only been the beginning. We must note that this daikaiju is exactly what we had thought, an intent, because its intentions to me seem deliberate and clear. This is all about power and control of the planet. The tragedy in California was all the proof I needed, proof that this will escalate into nothing more than an extermination. The thought of this thing, or whatever is behind it, gaining access to the E.I.O.'s remaining organic thorium, or even worse, the refinery plant, is … well, I just pray it does not happen."

Olivia shuddered as she remembered Dr. Takarada's early concerns and worries over the stolen radioactive element. It was almost as if he prophesied this whole damn thing. She flashed to her and Nathan's heated discussion, the one they had while he was still in rehab. She remembered telling him all of this junk before any of it happened. Olivia, of course, knew something was up, but never did she believe it would get as bad as Takarada feared. She just thought it made for a good argument when trying to convince Nathan to come back. For a split second, she wished they would've just left him alone, but quickly changed her mind when she thought about the look on his and Brandon Fox's faces after they reunited. She felt a bit reassured in her and Tommy's decision to go after him. But maybe it was indeed like Nathan used to always say before he quit drinking, "The day I go back to Palmdale is the day California tumbles into the sea." Because

on the day he did, it did. She shuddered again. It forced her back to the now and Takarada's sucky envisions of what may be coming next.

"I don't believe either the U.K. or the United States have figured this out, or I think they would be going to war over an entirely different reason, to stop this common enemy. As much as I dislike the president and his absurd questioning of me in regards to my country being the cause of this disaster, I cannot hold him responsible. I believe this to be the motive of the mastermind behind this diabolical plan. Both countries are mere pawns and have been deceived in the highest order. We must convince them of what is happening before it is too late. We must also convince them without making this a race for power, or it very easily may turn to that of a full scale war over energy."

Jack had gained ground on his face, moving from stroking his walrus 'stache to his chin as well. He looked at the band of what he considered misfit agents scattered about his quarters. He'd never admit it, but out of all the E.I.O. rock-star types he'd dealt with over the past forty years or so, these idiots were his favorites. Jack made an old-man noise when he bent his body to pick up the sideways bottle from the floor. He screwed the cap back on and again placed it on his desk.

"So, what about them?" he asked Takarada.

"Well sir, we need to invoke our original plan. The one we had organized before the Americans launched their attack on King Taraxian in Los Angeles. I believe I am correct in thinking it was the reason we came to E.I.O. West in the first place."

Jack put his arms behind his back, clasped his hands together and puffed out his chest. He paced the floor as he gazed at his agents with one eye.

"Are you up to the challenge?" he asked to a less than receptive audience. He waited, but instead of asking for a second time, he now demanded,

"Are you up to the challenge? Because if you are not, I need to bloody know right now!"

Tommy, Olivia and the Twins jumped to their feet with a resounding, "Yes, Sir!"

Jack gazed at Nathan who was still sitting. "What about you, Mr. Fox? I completely understand if you need to bow out of this one."

Nathan looked around the room at Jack, Dr. T and his bandmates, all of whom had stuck with him through thick and thin, all who had been his family, even when he had none. Of course he was saddened over his father dying, but he was also grateful for the fact that he was able to spend his remaining days with him. He was so happy that they had the opportunity to make up and that Brandon Fox could leave this world knowing his son loved him very much. It's a lot more than some people will ever get and that made Nathan feel pretty damn good, and he hadn't felt that way in a long, long time. But there was something Nathan couldn't shake, something his dad said to him just before he died. Actually there were two things he said, and they kind of contradicted each other. That's why this choice was not an easy one for Nathan Fox.

The first point being for Nathan to figure out who he was and what he wanted to do with his life. A few years ago that would have been an easy choice, a no-brainer so to speak. Plain and simple, he wanted to be a rock star of the highest order. It was true that the E.I.O. granted him that very wish and fulfilled his wildest dreams, but how real was it? Really, what were all of those world tours for anyhow? Were they merely undercover missions for agents posing as rock stars to get into places the Earth Intelligence Organization couldn't have otherwise? Maybe, but for Nathan it was more than that, much more. It had to be for the other guys too, cuz they were such damn good musicians! Nathan knew you can't be that good at music unless its real, flowing through your bloodstream, making up the very fibers of your existence. That's the way music has to be, because she's a fickle bitch and it takes everything you have to endure her stubborn ways. Nathan wondered about Tommy, the guy who at one time practiced until his fingers bled, the guy who stayed home from parties to rehearse one lame scale after another even last picked up a guitar. It seemed the E.I.O. had become his life and he was trading in his career in rock and roll for that of his new day job. Not that there was anything wrong with being an agent, and if that's what freakin' Tommy wanted, then that's what he should do. But for Nathan, it was hard for him to play James Bond when in reality he knew he was born to be Jim Morrison.

The second point being what his dad had muttered in his final breath, Dr. Iscariot, or something like that. Iscariot? What did it mean? If he gathered right, it was a name, and this clown may have killed his mother. He wasn't sure, but that's how it sounded. He knew he should ask Sir Jack about it, because if this guy did indeed murder Nathan's mom, he would know. But at this point he didn't want to say anything to anybody. Should the opportunity ever arise that he could kill this bastard, the less said the better. And what better way of finding this guy was there than the E.I.O.? None, there was probably no better way, Nathan thought. Even if he could somehow find the strength to let this whole *Iscariot* thing go (which at this point was impossible), how could he make music in the midst of World War III? The answer was, he couldn't.

"Crap," he thought to himself. "Okay, I'll save the freakin' planet one last time, then I-Am-Out-Of-Here, even if it means pursuing a damn solo career when this is all said and done."

"Oh, and one more thing," he thought to himself, "I don't freakin' care what that thing is, or how long it's been waiting in the shadows for me or anybody else. Machine, cyborg or simply a lousy overgrown house spider, I'm gonna kick that thing's ass." And with that, Nathan had made his decision. He looked Sir Jonathon square in the eye, "I need to do this. I told Tommy I was all in, and I am. I also think my dad would've wanted it this way. Yeah … count me in, Jacky Boy, count me in."

Sir Jack all of a sudden wondered if he was doing the right thing as a countless number of second thoughts ran through his head. He gazed at Nathan with a questionable look, still not quite sure if he was up to the task. But he knew at this point they didn't have too many options. He also knew that Nathan was right, Brandon would have wanted it this way.

"Right then!" he said, and he pounded his intercom with the side of his fist. "Patch me in to the prime minister and the president of the United States for a conference visual in ten minutes." He shook his head at Dr. Takarada. "I need to bloody see if I can persuade these knuckleheads to abort their police action on Japan before it escalades into a full-blown war." With that, a quick thought hit him of how his procrastination, and a stiff belt, may have just saved the world. It made him smile ever so slightly from beneath his mustache, and he was glad nobody noticed. "However, before I do that," Jack added, "you need to follow me."

Chapter XIII

It was hard for Nathan to grasp the enormity of E.I.O. West. The undersea base was truly a marvel and beyond magnificent. In some ways it reminded him of the FUJI, the Earth Intelligence Organization's Japanese compound buried deep within the mighty Mount Fuji-san. The architecture was similar in many aspects, but yet unique within itself. It had Kyoshi Takarada's insignia written all over it. You'd never even know you were on the bottom of the Pacific, if not for the illuminated flicker of green and blue as it danced on the tubeway walls. Tommy complimented Dr. T on the base, and Takarada gave an appreciative nod towards Michael and Liberty. He stated he could not have done it without the help of their alien friends' advanced technology. Michael saluted the doctor with his raised thumb, acknowledging both Takarada and the compliment with his highest of praise, "Dude."

Nathan admired the ocean while they passed through a row of large portholes that were cast into the walls on both sides of them. He fell behind a bit as he peered through them one by one, amazed at the stories of the sea each window told. He also noticed he wasn't the only one doing so. Olivia had placed her hand on one of the thick pains of round glass, and a number of freaky-looking, deep-water fish were attracted to it. She turned and smiled at Nathan as the playful, undersea life followed her hand's every move. Nathan grinned on the inside. He liked it when Olivia was nice to him, and ever since that crazy ride in the Twin's floating hamster ball, he liked it even more. It was funny, though, as the harder he tried, the easier it became. It was one of those stupid paradox thingies he'd learned about in rehab, sort of like that whole, "To get it, you gotta give it away" garbage. But one thing was for sure, he loved it when he got those rare glimpses of Olivia, you know, when she wasn't trying to be a freakin' Little Miss Know-It-All, the one who chewed him a new one so many times before. But thanks to a little thinking outside of himself, he now knew that was a front for the most part. He'd just never dare bring it up to her face, that is if he wanted to go on living. Anyway, Nathan couldn't help but smile back, and as that lame, warm-fuzzy feeling began to overtake his insides, Sir Jack deliberately cleared his throat.

"AHEM! No lollygagging, Mr. Fox. We have much work to do. This isn't a ruddy tea party."

Just before Nathan could become irritated, both Sir Jonathon and Takarada stopped at an elevator protected by two armed guards. Jack and the doctor each raised their right hands and placed them on two separate scanners on either sides of the parting doors. A bright line of light scrolled from the top of each scanner to the bottom of it, and upon completion, Hal acknowledged them both.

"Access Granted. Welcome Sir Jonathon. Welcome Doctor Takarada. Guards, please step aside."

Each of the gun-toting gentlemen raised and lowered his right foot hard and fast onto the floor with a clack of his heels, then sidestepped to his right, clearing the entrance to the elevator. The doors opened and all seven squeezed into the small space that was about to descend even further beneath the floor of the sea.

"Please take a deep breath and hold it as I pressurize the cabin for an additional one hundred meters," Hal suggested over the comm. system of the lift.

Everybody sucked in the limited oxygen, and Nathan's ears bubbled as another layer of thick air poured in. The elevator dropped quickly and Nathan thought about the last time he rode in a small, rickety box of this nature. He remembered it was the morning after mixing massive quantities of scotch and champagne with both Sir Jack and Tommy the night before. He also couldn't forget hurling through the diamond-shaped links of the chain fence that kept them secured in. Nathan, all of a sudden, had one of those moments and was suddenly grateful he wasn't going to puke his guts out this time. Jack, on the other hand, wasn't looking too good and was beginning to take on the color of the sea.

Nathan nudged Tommy just below the ribs and whispered, "I think walrus boy is gonna be sick," and Tommy made a sound like a grunting pig when he tried not to laugh out loud. Nathan didn't really think it was funny, that is until Tommy thought it was, so with that fuel, he decided to push it.

"Sir Jack, you're turning green, sir, are you going to be all right?"

Jack scowled at Nathan. "Stow it, Fox!" he ordered, then went back to feeling sick. Tommy then started naming all of the stuff he was going to have for dinner, including a few new concoctions such as a peanut butter and pus sandwich. Nathan, attempting to hide his laughter, covered his mouth with his palm, only to snort out a rather large dollop of snot through his unconcealed nose.

"EEEWWWWW!" Olivia shrieked, and when Jack noticed the glistening worm of phlegm dangling from Nathan's schnoz, it was too much. Sir Jonathon tried desperately to bend over and face the floor, but due to the tight fit of the lift (and his giant body) he just couldn't.

"AAAAAAAAH!"

"Oh My God!" Olivia howled, "You dumbasses! What the ... Why the hell?"

She was at a complete loss for words, but everybody's screams were making up for her lack of speech quite nicely. Michael began fearing for his alien life as Liberty wiped the remnants of Jack's lunch (bangers and mash mixed with a stale scotch sauce) from the breast of her shirt. Even Takarada was screaming something about "chikisho baka gaijins" as he patted the ooze from the cuffs of his jacket. Tommy and Nathan still had no idea what the hell "vodka guy jeans" meant, but they had heard it many, many times whenever they were in Japan. Once Liberty had wiped most of it from her clothes, she realized there was a better way and grabbed Michael's hand. In a burst of white, every trace of the vile fluid disappeared, just as the doors to the elevator opened. In an instant, everybody was clean, really clean, clothes and all, and there was no trace of anything that would have said otherwise. Tommy twitched his nose and said he could still kinda' smell it, and Liberty shut him up with one of her scary-ass glares. Jack shoved both Tommy and Nathan out of the lift. He was furious but contained his rage, probably because after puking, he felt a whole hell of a lot better.

Nathan gathered his fumbling feet, then stopped dead in his tracks to avoid being run in by the razor-sharp edges of a giant, golden spur. It was twice as tall as he was and resembled the spinning blade of a circular saw, each tip as devastating as that of a newly sharpened sword. He ran his finger along the edge of one of the gleaming points and whistled in that manner that would indicate sheer amazement. Nathan backed up, then placed his hand over his brow in a saluting manner as to shadow the glare of the falling sparks of steel. His eyes then climbed the length of the massive, metallic frame while he processed what he believed he already knew. He wondered how it was possible, but there it stood, in all of its ridiculous glory. From the tip of its cowboy boots to the top of its massive one-hundred-gallon hat, towering over sixty meters tall …

The Duke!

Tommy walked up and joined Nathan by his side.

"Ho-ly shit," he whispered, and as they both strained their necks looking straight up, Nathan responded with a soft growl,

"Yeah … holy shit".

There really wasn't anything else to say, holy shit pretty much covered it. For a few seconds, though, they both stood hypnotized, each one running the instant replay in their mind of their last encounter with the giant cowbot. Tommy overflowed with pride as Nathan drowned in regret, each one at different ends of the spectrum with a completely different take on the same damn memory. Nathan snapped himself back, because there was no time for him to dwell on what happened before (even if he couldn't remember much of it). Then, when the initial shock wore off, he wrapped his arms around himself complaining that "It's freakin' freezing in here!"

Sir Jack chuckled, "Oh that's nothing, my boy, this is merely the chilly remains of a test we ran yesterday. We are only passing through in order to gain entrance to the safe room. It's time for the final test."

Sir Jonathon and Dr. Takarada led them around the bustling pathway that circled the floor of the giant bay. As the band followed, Nathan gazed back up at the bursts of plummeting electricity that had caught his eye. He noticed a dozen or so figures attached to various parts of the Duke, all donning fuzzy-hooded parkas and welding at the speed of light. Not that there was anything odd about *that*, because there wasn't, but what *was* odd was what they were working on. Nathan couldn't figure it out, so he asked Tommy what he thought they were doing.

"I dunno, seems they're giving the Duke a much-needed new look, but I don't know if the Bon Jovi cowboy coat was the way to go."

"Well, it *is* freakin' freezing in here," Nathan stated, and Tommy

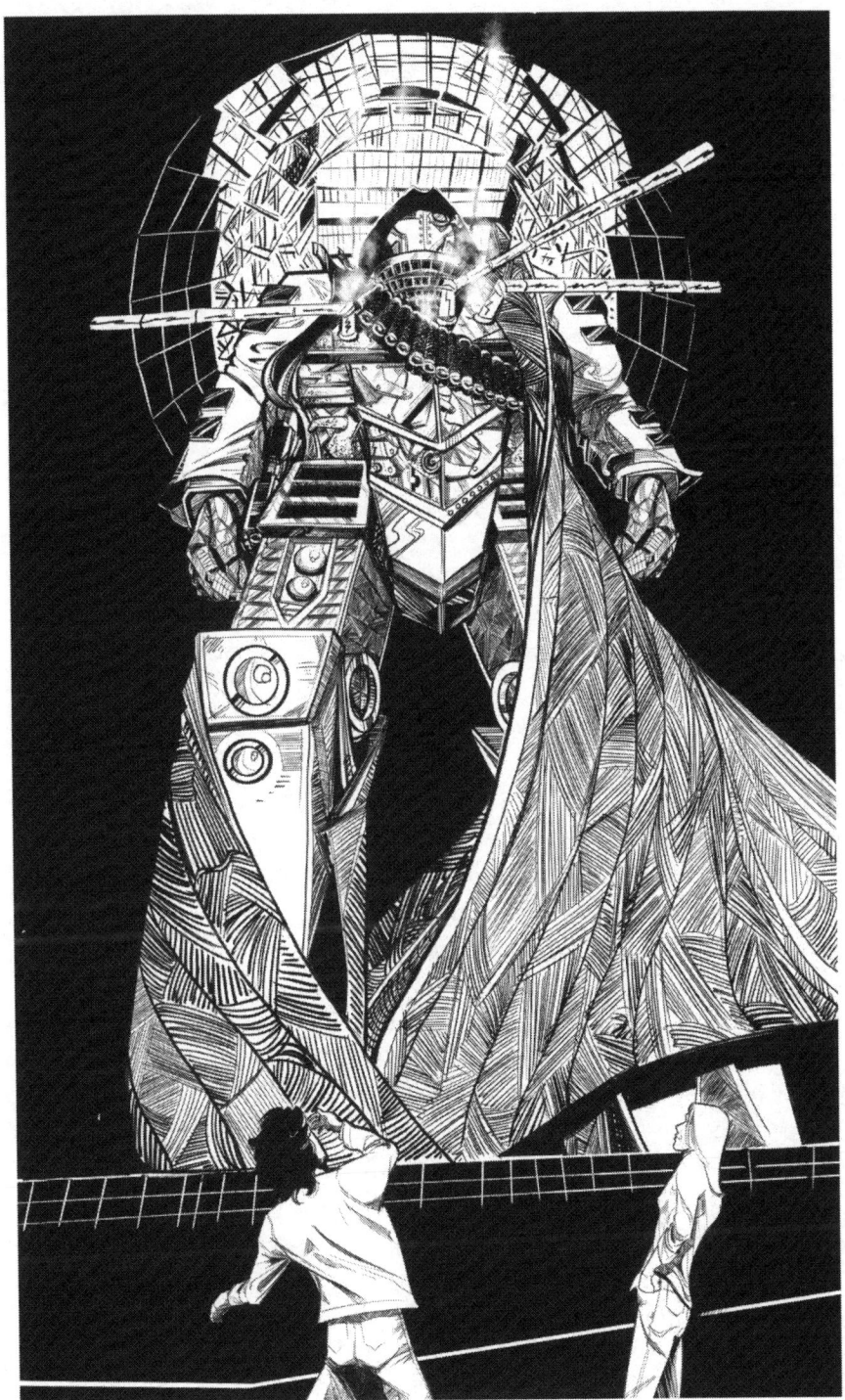

replied,

"Awww, maybe the big, bad Dukey-Wukey was getting a coldy-woldy."

"Maybe," Nathan answered, even though he knew that wasn't the reason. Still, he couldn't help but admire the cowbot's new apparel, regardless if Tommy thought it looked stupid or not. Nathan looked at the long jacket of chromium steel plates. It was pretty damn cool, and as he admired it, he considered getting one for himself, only in black leather.

When they reached the opposite side of the hangar there was another lift, and Nathan could see an enclosed observation deck about halfway up. Upon entering the elevator, Jack warned Tommy and Nathan that if they got any funny ideas, he'd personally shoot them into the Pacific from one of the base's mini-sub launches. Tommy and Nathan giggled like a couple of giddy schoolgirls, and even Michael had to hide his face when he started to laugh. However, all three of them shut the hell right up when both Olivia and Liberty scared them into submission with another terrifying look. Both women were in no mood to see Jack blow chunks again and would more than likely have joined him in escorting the boys into the briny deep. Yeah, Jack carried a lot a weight, but he was nothing compared to Olivia and Liberty when they were pissed off. Nathan was going to comment on how this overgrown freezer was the perfect place for a couple of ice queens, but opted to practice that paradox thingy: the being-nicer-to-people-so-they're-nicer-to-you one. Not to mention, she scared the hell out of him, and he didn't want to push it.

When the elevator shut, it sealed tight with a SHOOOMP, and the lift was warm and comfortable. The ride was quick and quiet (just how Jack wanted it), and when it stopped, it opened to a short hallway that led to another vacuum-tight, air-sealing entrance. Takarada explained how the double set of doors at each end of the hall worked on the same principal as that of a watertight portal leading into the sea. Only this system worked with warm air filling the small space in between the hatches as opposed to water.

Even as slow as Nathan could be sometimes, he began to figure out where all of this was going. That damn spider emitted way too much heat for anybody (or anything) to get anywhere near it, so the Duke was getting some sort of winterized makeover. Takarada and Sir Jack's plan wasn't to fight fire with fire, it was to freakin' freeze it. It was about to get cold in here ... real cold, and not just a normal real cold, but a "kill you dead in a heartbeat" for real kinda' cold.

The doors to the safe room sealed behind them, and Nathan found himself face to face with a two-foot-thick pane of indestructible, diamond-particle glass. It was the only thing that separated them from the bay that housed the Duke and the oncoming ice age. He hoped it was more indestructible than the diamond-particle glass they originally used for the Duke's windshield, the one that shattered.

From the observation deck of the safe room, they we're almost level with the cowbot's chest, just below his right breastplate. Nathan could see where it had been modified. And even though he couldn't remember what had happened, Tommy must've told him at least a billion times, told him the tale of almost being tossed from the hole that was blown into the Duke's chest by Zargatron. Now, three sets of thick pipes filled with some kind of coolant flowed straight into the heart of the mech from beneath his new overcoat. Some of the white, frozen liquid sneaked out, escaping through the tiny crevices that locked the pipes into the chest of the robot. It took Nathan back, reminding him of the dry ice machines that pumped thick layers of fog onto the stage of the Vinyl Crush concerts.

A warning siren wailed, and the welders donning the Eskimo jackets began to scamper down the scaffolding. HAL's synthesized voice then echoed throughout the bay,

"Two minutes and counting. All personnel please exit the area to surrounding safe rooms. REPEAT ... All personnel please exit immediately to surrounding safe rooms."

The siren continued to bap, and Nathan could feel a burst of heated air filling the confines of their observation platform.

"One minute and counting ..."

Everything began to shake and Nathan freaked, as for a second he thought the whole dang glass-encased shack was about to crash to the bottom of the bay. But instead of falling down, their entire box-shaped room followed a track up the side of the wall, bringing it right to the face of the Duke.

"Thirty seconds and counting ... All personnel have vacated testing area."

From the other side of the glass, a thundering electronic hum rose

131

up in pitch, filling the vast hangar with noise and the observation room with hope.

"Ten ... Nine ... Eight ..."

Tommy gazed about the room a bit like Chicken Little, then shrugged a "what's going on" with his shoulders in Nathan's direction. Nathan, waiting for the sky to fall him-damn-self, mimicked Tommy's shoulder statement right back at him, topped with a funny look of "How the hell should I know?"

"Two ... One ... Zero ..."

The beeping siren outside stopped on a dime, and the fluorescent, bright yellow of the observation deck flickered to a cool blue. Then that obnoxious electronic tone that had engulfed the hangar went silent, as it seemed to get sucked up and out of existence.

FWOOOOMP!

The long rectangles of glass outlining the deck creaked as a thick layer of ice encased them in a time-elapsed sort of motion. Even with the high-tech heating system, the observation room still dropped about sixty degrees in less than a second. Blowers kicked in, and heated air began to take the place of the cold. The elevated room shook again, but instead of going up or down this time, Nathan could feel it moving to the left of the tremendous, tube-shaped hangar.

Computers in the room began chattering as results of the test started appearing on various screens. Takarada took a seat at one of the empty stations, and Jack pulled up a chair next to him while the band gathered around.

"So far it seems to have been a complete success."

He continued to type at an ungodly speed, and as more results filtered in, he turned to Jack.

"Sir Jonathon, the Kelvin Duster worked, we have reached negative four hundred degrees Fahrenheit. We have done it!"

Sir Jack observed the screen for a good three minutes, reading and scrutinizing the test results while stroking his giant mustache. His reaction was of both excitement and hope, as was everybody else's who stood within the safety of their observation room. Sir Jonathon reached his hand over the table to offer the doctor congratulations on a job well done. Just before breaking out the celebratory cigars though, a warning sign began flashing on the computer. Jack's extended hand closed, leaving him with his index finger pointed at the screen.

"What's happening Kyoshi?" he asked.

Takarada, at a complete loss, stated the Kelvin Duster was losing power and that the Duke was resuming normal temperatures. The good doctor began to panic, and like a proud parent, he defended his invention, "This should not be an issue, considering organic thorium is the main source of energy." He also noted that all freezing systems were still operational, and because the computer showed no signs of malfunctioning, everything should be working. Takarada started tapping his finger against the desk while he searched his mind for the answer. There was no time for this, no time for a setback of this monumental nature. Plain and simple ... there was no time, period.

Chapter XIV

Jack let out a walrus-sized "harrumph" and walked over to a wall panel that lay level with the observation room's floor. He sighed, then gave it a swift, hard kick with the tip of his Baba boot. The flimsy, tin cover popped open, exposing a tangle of extension cords and a power strip, all held into place by a few strategically placed rows of duct tape. He groaned as he bent over to get a better look, and upon further inspection saw where all of the wires were leading to, one lone, little outlet. Jack wrapped his big mitts around the cord and began yanking on the plug to the computer.

Takarada screamed, "No, Sir Jonathon, don't!" but it was too late, and the black cable separated from the wall. The computers crackled, and circles closed in on each of the screens leaving them all blank. Takarada was beyond stunned, and couldn't say a word because his mouth was stuck in the wide-open position. After waiting a second or two, Jack got down on his knees and fumbled around, looking for the empty outlet. He couldn't see very well as he searched the wall with the tips of the three pronged plug that he held in his hand. After another second or two, along with a few harsh words, he found the empty socket, plugged the computer system back in and the room again lit up.

"*Computers returning to normal. REPEAT, computers returning to normal.*"

Still next to the outlet, Sir Jonathon looked up from his seated position on the floor.

"Bloody piece of shit," he complained.

Takarada was at a complete loss and continued to sit in a stunned silence. Jack winked at the good doctor in reference to pulling the plug.

"Something I learned from my ruddy cable box," he admitted just as the Kelvin Duster began to charge itself all over again. "Right," he softly stated. "We'll plan on reinitiating the system when, or if, it fails by simply creating an internal mechanism that will reboot, and again charge the coat."

Jack hoisted his large body up, straightened out his unstraightenable tie and patted the wrinkles from his jacket. "Can we do that Kyoshi?" he asked.

Takarada, who was still in shock, concurred with a series of quick nods.

"All right then," Sir Jonathon said, trying not to show his many doubts, "We make the best of it and move forward with the reboot modifications."

It wasn't the greatest of ideas, but the Kelvin Duster would be functional, at least for a few minutes at a time. Takarada would need to figure out the problem, but for right now this was all they had and it would have to work. Because as Jack had stated, they needed to keep moving forward, while they still could.

It was pretty easy for everybody to see what was unfolding in front of them. Hell, even Nathan had figured it out, so it wasn't too much of a stretch to guess Jack and Takarada's super-secret plan. But a few questions still occupied Nathan's brain. Could all of this nonsense possibly work? Could the Kelvin Duster withstand 700° temperatures with a protective coating of a measly negative four hundred? A reasonable question, because even as bad at math as Nathan was, he knew that 700 minus 400 still equaled a pretty big number. Then there was that whole stupid reboot thing, you know, just in case the heat issue wasn't quite enough. Nathan groaned, and as he imagined the worst possible case scenarios ever, the mobile safe room began to move sideways. It was smooth and silent, but it was still enough to pull Nathan from his own mind. While still elevated, it eased itself to the other side of the cylindrical bay, stopping at the back of the Duke's neck. The ice on the glass had begun to melt, and when Nathan peered through the window, he saw the all-too-familiar entrance portal located at the base of the cowbot's steel-reinforced skull. It reminded him of yet another small detail he'd almost forgotten about, that *they'd* be the ones in this contraption fighting old, creepy eight-legs.

It didn't take long before the Kelvin Duster was again charged and ready to be activated. Takarada initiated the procedure, repeated the freezing process, and just like before, it lasted five minutes' tops. It still wasn't the best of news, but they now knew for sure of the suit's limitations; they also knew what they needed to do to make it work. Takarada calculated the mods necessary on the spot, and all further testing ceased in order to resume workable conditions.

After the overgrown icebox had defrosted, Hal gave the "all clear," indicating that the hanger was now safe to enter. Nathan had no clue as to what Hal meant by "safe to enter." Hell, he was still trying to process this whole "Kevin frozen TV dinner jacket thingamajig." But as his brain wrapped itself around everything, there's nothing quite like a vibrating floor to snap you back to what's right in front of you. Even if what's right in front of you is directly below your feet.

Nathan barked out a startled, "Whoa," as the two front panes of glass from the observation room extended out and over the 30-story bay.

"Holy crap!" Tommy yelled as the walkway grew into an enclosed passage that led from the safe room to the back of the Duke's head. "Now *this* is what I call the freakin' red-carpet treatment."

Nathan agreed, remembering the old days of having to swing into this thing from a roll-bar above the newly enlarged entrance. Yeah, it was tight, but now they could just stroll right on in. He also figured the easy-access mod would accommodate big-fat Jack if he ever wanted to enter the mech for any reason, like right now.

When the extended section of the observation room locked into place, two of the thick plates of diamond-particle glass opened inward in a brilliant burst of steam. As the air rushed in, Tommy commented on how he thought it would have been much colder, and Doctor Takarada indicated that this was one of the reasons they were going into the robot. They had to make sure the temperature within the Duke remained at a life-supporting level. Previous tests had played havoc with many of the controls, and up until now, they were still unclear about one thing: if the robotonauts piloting the Duke would wind up a freakin' pack of fudgsicles or not. It seemed they were still unclear about many things.

Everybody crossed the enclosed bridge into the Duke and, once inside, scanned the metal catwalk that circled the cockpit of the giant bot. It was hard not to be reminded of that final battle with Zargatron that took place just a few short years ago. Upon remembering, one couldn't help thinking of the fall of Salt Lake City, Tokyo, London and now even Los Angeles. It was surreal, and the reality of it all began to hit even harder for Nathan. This was one sight he thought he'd never see again. But then again, he never thought he could go three months without a drink either. It was funny though, how this all felt "kinda' right" to Nathan, it had a weird, awkward familiarity about it. But now, since his dad had let him in on the family secret, maybe he wasn't so out of place here after all. Nathan liked that idea, for about a second, then shuddered as he felt himself giving in to the power of the dark side.

"Freakin' E.I.O.," he cursed internally, "Tommy may have succumbed to your evil, day-job whims, but you'll never get me!" He thought all of this to himself except for the reassuring, "Never!" that he boldly shouted so loud it echoed throughout the entire cranium of the Duke.

Tommy looked at him, "You all right?" he asked.

Nathan gave him a sinister glare and whispered, "never."

"What-ever" was the only rational explanation to enter Tommy's head, and as he shook it off, he turned to Doctor Takarada.

"So, Dr. T, you mentioned the whole temperature thing was one of the reasons we were in here. Was there anything else?" he asked.

"Oh yes, Tommy-san," he responded, and with a big grin as well. "I think you'll like this in particular."

Takarada keyed in a code on a small control panel mounted to the Duke's wall and stepped back. A series of flashes ignited and steam hissed up from beneath the metal walkway of the round cockpit. Everybody turned at once, being immediately drawn to the center of the cowbot's control room, as a large, illuminated cylinder of neon green rose up from the floor. Tommy tried to focus in on what appeared to be a figure standing inside of it. He wasn't quite sure, but whatever it was, it was attached to a billion or so wires. When the glowing haze that filled the inside of the tube diminished, he could plainly see the silhouette of a man. The rising conduit stopped when the tip of it made contact with the ceiling, and when it did, the black shadow broke free from its harness of twisting cables. The glass door to the cylinder clicked, and as the green mist escaped, the figure stepped out of it. Tommy had to do a double-take. He couldn't believe it and, for a second, thought the smoke was playing tricks on his eyes. He didn't know how it was even possible, and frankly he didn't care. Because right now, he could only think of how happy he was to see someone he thought he'd never see again, his old friend, SCOTT.

Even though Tommy knew SCOTT was a cyborg, for a brief period of his life he was probably his closest friend, even more so than Nathan. As back then, Tommy couldn't stand to be anywhere near the Lizard King. Without a doubt, one of Tommy's greatest regrets was letting SCOTT give up his life, or existence, or whatever you'd say for a damn robot, to save their scrawny, little butts. It truly was the only way though, and if he hadn't, none of them would be standing there now. The planet would be a whole lot different too, if it was still here that is. But that's the thing about regret. It takes all logic and throws it out the window, making sure you'll always be able to beat yourself up over making the wrong decision, even if it was the right one.

SCOTT approached everyone and went straight up to Tommy. Then with his arms at his sides, he bowed to him.

"Hello my boss, it is very good to see you."

Tommy smirked and tugged on the giant, disco collar of SCOTT's new robot-wear.

"Nice suit," he lied. "You look like a Martian, or some sort of alien from the underground world of Planet X or something."

Tommy's smirk turned to an outright laugh, if not he probably would have burst into tears he was so damn happy. SCOTT just stood and stared at him in complete confusion, attempting to decipher what the hell Tommy meant about being from Planet X. But it didn't matter and before SCOTT could make any sense of what the odd human was saying, Tommy buried his chin deep into his friend's chest and hugged him. Funny thing was, SCOTT hugged him back.

The cyborg of Takarada's creation broke away from the embrace, reporting that all systems remained a stable 70° throughout the entire freezing process.

"Very good, SCOTT," Takarada commended and SCOTT added that all additional data was downloading to the doctor's main hard drive. With much work to do, Takarada was about to dismiss himself, when Tommy cut him off.

"Whoa, wait a minute, Doc, Entertainment Now minds want to know! How the hell did Lazarus here return from the dead?"

Takarada apologized and admitted that it was in fact quite simple.

"You see, Tommy-san, SCOTT's processing systems and thought waves were always being transmitted and fed to my computer banks. As long as he was functioning, the data stream would automatically save. So really, his mind never in fact died, and it was as simple as recreating the platform to support the super computer SCOTT uses as his brain. Of course I worked off of my original plans to build his second body. The only difference being that I am trying a new fireproof fabric for obvious reasons. Other than that, Tommy, he is the same SCOTT."

Tommy knocked on the side of the android's head and joked, "SCOTT 2.0, better, stronger, faster."

SCOTT smiled and repeated Tommy's sentiments.

"Yes, better, faster, stronger and extremely good looking."

Tommy cracked up, "Extremely good looking huh?" he asked and SCOTT stated that this was input he had learned from Michael whenever the alien spoke in regards to himself. Michael confessed he had been working with SCOTT and it wasn't his fault that he picked up on every damn word he said. SCOTT then asked Michael if he would like him to repeat what he had heard him say many times about Nathan Fox's singing abilities.

Michael cut him off, "No, no, robot-dude, not necessary!"

Nathan gave Michael a fowl look and before any more could be said, Tommy (to the delight of Michael) interrupted,

"So how come me and Olivia weren't informed? I'd like to think you'd tell us something as important as this."

The more Tommy thought about it, the more he interpreted this as a blatant lack of trust, and he began to get angry.

"It was bad enough we weren't told about the Duke, but why in the hell didn't you tell me about SCOTT?"

But before Takarada could answer, Sir Jack took over.

"Simple my boy, it was none of your damn business. Plus, we weren't even sure if the Duke would ever work again, most of it was scattered from here to ruddy Timbuktu. Personally, I would have scrapped this piece of junk and started from scratch, but the good doctor was convinced we could rebuild it. And as far as the terminator goes, worrying about sentimental agents who want to spend their bloody free time playing paddy-cake with E.I.O. tackle is the last thing I need. That's why!"

Tommy backed down, and Nathan minimized Jack's words by making his best hoity-toity face from behind the commander's back. While Sir Jonathon continued on about secrecy and some other bullshit, Nathan pounded his palm repeatedly with his fist as he tried to lip-sync Jack's every word. Tommy had to look down and shadow his face, but when Jack saw what he was doing, he turned around and busted Nathan in the middle of a silent "harrumph."

"Having fun are we, Mr. Fox? Well, I can guarantee you'll have a jolly-good time when you come face to face with bloody King Taraxian. Then we'll see exactly how much of a smartass you really are. I look forward to the day when Takarada figures out a way to fly this stupid thing without the likes of damn rock stars at the helm. So you all laugh it up, but be sure to get plenty of sleep, because you launch at 0500 hours."

Jack was no doubt at his wits end, plus he still hadn't called the president. He turned in a huff, asked the doctor if he was coming and stomped down the thin hall that led back to the mobile observation platform. Then, as the enclosed walkway retracted, Jack shouted one last thing.

"Let's not have any drinking and driving this time, Mr. Fox, shall we?"

And with that, the glass doors sealed shut and the safe room began its trip to the opposite side of the hangar, leaving Nathan, Tommy and everybody else behind.

Chapter XV

For the most part it had been an uneventful evening, and as night slipped into the early hours of morning, the low bellow of a lonesome freighter echoed throughout the Port of Yokohama. Monstrous shipyard cranes towering to the skies awaited the great vessel and prepared to pick the metal storage bins from its loaded-down deck. As the floating behemoth eased in to dock, another series of sirens alerted both the ship and the harbor patrol that it was safe to proceed. A gentle rain began to fall, and the tiny drops melded with the moist air, blurring the bright circles of the street lamps that outlined the pier. With one final blast of the ship's horn, the captain slowly eased the freighter in and began to bring her to berth. It was at that moment that an immense rogue wave rose up from out of nowhere, jerking the freighter out and away from the dock.

FWOOOOSH!

When the large crest of water subsided, the freighter rocked a bit, but regained her balance and returned to an upright position. The captain shouted, "Nani kore?" as he looked around the bridge, having no idea what had just happened. He peered out of the observation windows, then down at the water below. The only thing that seemed odd was a faint, high-pitched ring that may or may not have been coming from just under the surface. The captain didn't think much of it, and since he saw nothing, he simply decided to try again.

The ship prepared to moor for a second time, and while it did, another wave (even larger than the first) ascended from the depths, pulverizing them from the opposite bow. The thick hull of the vessel tore like a sheet of paper, and a violent jet of water started filling its hold. Men scurried about the deck in an effort to secure the great lines that held the mighty cargo bins into place. But when the vessel tilted towards the sea, the steel cables that secured the semi-trailer-sized containers began to snap like thin thread. The stacks of steel boxes that spread across the deck started tumbling down as one followed the other into the cold black water. It was then that the ocean roared and began tossing the ship about as though it was a child's play toy. Sailors, foregoing their sea-bound duties, started to jump into the bay and swim towards the pier while the angry sea continued to slap the freighter silly. Almost appearing to lift the mighty vessel up, the wall of water reared the ship back and slammed it hard against the dock.

FWOOOOSH!

The wharf burst into a million pieces of wood and cement, then crumbled into the bay, followed by the massive cranes that stood upon it. It was as if a great rug had been pulled out from beneath them as they, and anything else that was on top of it, plummeted into the bay.

The captain gave the order, "Abandon ship!" just as a dark, lumbering form began to take shape, rising up from the black of the water. As it ascended, it grew taller than the ship's bridge that resided high atop the freighter's superstructure. A helmsman clutched the radio transmitter and started to repeat the Japanese equivalent of "Mayday!" over and over again, but when someone finally answered, nobody was there to respond. The crew inside the bridge screamed when it ignited with the brilliant, green glow of eight illuminating eyes. Men of mountainous stature were reduced to little boys crying for their mommies at the sight of the giant, lifeless orbs that peered in through the drenched windows. When they ran for the exit, one of the monster's clawed tarsi slammed down in front of the door blocking their escape. It did this maliciously and with absolute intent. This was not a simple case of an overgrown, hungry and out of place animal that needed your sympathy. This was genocide, plain and simple, and the extermination of the human race had begun. Its tremendous pincers ripped through the steel-reinforced tower of the freighter like a can opener, and as men started falling (and jumping) to their deaths, the superstructure exploded.

BOOOOSH!!!!!!

The beast reared back, lifting its long legs out of the water one by one, casually stepping over the flames of the freighter and twisted steel of the collapsed cranes. It was taking to shore, and the massive fires of the Yokohama shipyards were casting an eerie glow upon its silhouette. It was, without a doubt, your worst nightmare personified, with its gargantuan, black body, eight legs and glowing green eyes.

Towering high above the destruction, proud and conquering like some great war machine, King Taraxian had landed in Japan.

Takarada was indeed correct, probably the one time he wished he hadn't been. Of course the beast had not been slain by the Americans, nor was it buried in the debris of the now submerged Los Angeles. As the E.I.O. received reports from Yokohama, Takarada gathered this thing must be just as functional underwater as it was on dry land. Since the quakes, he had been monitoring all levels of extreme underground heat from all over the planet. After intense scanning, there wasn't anything out of the norm, so if it was still alive, or functioning, he knew it wasn't burrowing beneath the earth this time. Takarada caught himself imagining this giant monstrosity creeping silently along the floor of the Pacific and couldn't help but marvel at its technology.

The doctor and Sir Jack stared at the HD viewing screens from E.I.O. West, watching as many parts of Yokohama burned. King Taraxian had not used its heat mechanism in any way yet, and more visuals than they ever would have wanted were flooding both the base and the world. Jack cursed the kaiju spider for always being able to stay one step ahead of them. However, after having a little chat with both the U.S. and Great Britain some hours ago, both countries had already deployed battleships to Japan. So it had left Jack no choice but to send them a soldier to defend the shores of Takarada's homeland.

Out of the smoke-laden skies, the Duke burst through a large, lingering cloud of smoldering black that still hovered high above the shipyards. Where, from an electronically induced coma, Nathan, along with Tommy and the other robotonauts, piloted the cowbot, manipulating his every thought and move. Each band member was fast asleep within their own cubicle outlining the inner cranium of the towering mech. This, next to sold-out concert arenas, was where all five of them shined the most. It was one of the proven aspects as to *why* the Earth Intelligence Organization favored musicians for their agents: their natural processing skills when it came to math and time itself, their ability to function as a team, but most of all, their creative skills. But there were downfalls, a few flies in the ointment so to speak. First off, no human is immune to indecision, and that extra second you may need to figure something out may be the one that kills you, along with everybody on board. And second, there is a high level of risk when utilizing the conscious brains from a bunch of spoiled-brat rockers. So in order to avoid all of that mindless BS (and arguments over who gets the last green M&M), Takarada had decided early on that tapping directly into their subconscious was the only way to control a weapon of this magnitude, hence the sleep-state.

A little reassurance never hurt either, so SCOTT was stationed on the inside of the mega cowbot, overseeing and monitoring every final action of the giant mech. He was also the computer within the computer, the big enchilada needed to hold all operations together. Placed in the center of the circling cubicles, he stood attached to an array of wires from his reinforced, diamond-particle protection tube, watching. He oversaw each band member (according to his or her character and individual talents) as they controlled one of four lobes. Each dictated the Duke's moves by emitting their own brain impulses directly to the bot's overgrown, supercomputing cerebral cortex, giving bona fide evidence that we (along with stupid cowboy robots) are but mere slaves to the committees that reside in our heads.

After decimating the docks, King Taraxian beat the warehouse district to a fine pulp and was now upon the foot of downtown. The twin rockets of the bot's massive boots erupted when he locked in on the spider and bulleted towards the heart of the city. The cavalry was coming and the trumpets rang out in the form of the Duke's thunderous steam whistle. It shook the very foundations of the planet itself as it blew loud and proud throughout Japan's morning sky.

BWWWWWOMP!

King Taraxian, hearing the battle cry, hauled ass inland and scurried up the side of the city's tallest building, the Yokohama Landmark Tower. About halfway up, the razor tips of the spiders eight claws penetrated the structure locking itself into place. The eerie tone the beast emitted grew in volume, and its abdomen began to pulse as it prepared its heat weapon. Knowing the creature's defense mechanism, it took the Duke less than a microsecond to process the incoming information from the five sets of individual brain waves, leading the giant robot to the quickest course of action.

CHOOM! CHOOM! CHOOM!

One photon burst after the other blazed from the massive chrome barrels of the cowbot's dual-plated six shooters. Each one exploded in a flash of silver upon both the rear of the beast's brawny exoskeleton and the building itself. King Taraxian gripped tight to the skyscraper, but due to the barrage of explosions, and of course the extreme weight of the monster, the tower itself crumbled from the center and both fell backwards.

KARAM! BOOSH!

A thick, white cloud expanded and swallowed up the maze of city blocks, while dust and debris climbed to the heavens. The Duke circled from above, watching the array of buildings that tumbled down, burying the demon daikaiju in a massive grave of steel and stone.

The rising sun began to consume the dark, and as the light grew brighter, the air-raid sirens grew louder. A brigade of Japanese AX-1 fighter jets advanced, but were warned to keep their distance in the event of King Taraxian turning up the heat. They readied their missiles and kept a watchful eye from what they hoped was outside of the monster's seven-hundred-degree shield.

Two thick streams of propulsion kept the Duke upright and he lowered in for a closer look. His computer locked in on the mountain of rubble, and when the cowbot touched down, the massive pile of decimated concrete began to breathe. The mech stepped back and his great spurs spun as they lowered, locking the lofty chrome bot into the asphalt. Waves of refraction pulsated from the buried spider, and the air distorted into a series of bursts as an expanding dome of energy rippled into the sky.

Takarada and Sir Jack watched the various computer readouts that overlapped their screens from the control center of the undersea base. Timing was of the essence. Aspects such as velocity, motion and position all had to be considered, right down to the precise second. Ever-changing digital calculations ran the patterns of numbers searching for zero, the magic number in which the Kelvin Duster would be administered. But not only would the chilled, armor-plated jacket protect the cowbot from the high temperatures of the beast, the burst of sub-frozen air would actually contradict its effect. Two officers each administered a key and turned them in perfect sync, activating the ability to fire the weapon at hand. Jack's lips pressed tight together as he peered through his thin, round glasses, scrutinizing the monitors, waiting for the golden goose egg.

The ruins of the Yokohama Landmark Tower crumbled to all sides with the rising of the great, black monster. The pulsing waves increased in speed as it ascended, and the eerie, high-pitched tone it produced screamed throughout the air.

A thin bead of sweat broke through the skin of Sir Jonathon's forehead, as every calculation was nothing but a digital blur. His hand trembled while he held his fingertip the width of a thin sheet of paper above the big red button. Takarada, staring at the circling numbers spinning on the HD feed, began tapping his pencil at the rate of Jack's heartbeat on the council of levers, switches and lights. Sir Jonathon shook his head in fast, tense, tiny movements and whispered through his teeth, "Not now, Kyoshi."

Takarada, made aware of his nervous tick, stopped when Jack pointed it out, and it was at that very second that the spinning digits, containing three numbers each, stopped. We're talking a "so fast it would have thrown you from the windshield upon impact" kind of stop. Then, before anybody could even blink, the semicircle of screens that surrounded the control room lit up in a parade of zeros.

"FIRE!"

Sir Jonathon's pudgy fingertip bent outward as the button that activated the Kelvin Duster went inward. The screen erupted in a veil of white, and all visuals (courtesy of the Japanese news and a few well-placed satellites) turned to black.

The combined bursts of both the Duke and King Taraxian lit up greater Yokohama as the double explosions blew each backwards to the outer edges of the downtown region.

WA-BOOOOSH!!!!

In the time it took for the blasts to subside, the temperature jumped to a blistering 130 degrees. Yeah, it was hot, but not hot enough. It worked, the Kelvin Duster freakin' worked! Not only did it work though, it also reduced most of the spider's heat and covered the Duke in a shimmering coat of frozen, armor-plated goodness. However, it was still unclear just how long the colossal freezing systems would work until they shut down. But for now, a proud, steady stream of liquid helium pumped through the chambered, steel sheets within the long jacket of the mech. His ice-cold chrome panels glistened, while each square of metal turned into a blue, wintery work of frost-covered art filled with frozen gas.

The inside of the Duke's cockpit dropped to below freezing with the initial burst, but then climbed and stopped at a comfortable 70°. From the sanctity of cube number two, Nathan dreamed his dreamy little dreams. From there, he operated both the motor and sensory cortexes of the mech, while the others, also in a controlled sleep-state, took on the additional lobes of the cowbot's computerized brain.

As Nathan slept, he saw himself singing to a sold-out venue of 50,000 screaming fans. The chants and cheers far surpassed the deafening music as head bangers proudly displayed their "Fox Rox" banners while Nathan-obsessed girls lifted up their shirts. He looked in either direction of the stage, and though the tunes were both thundering and familiar, none of the band members took on any distinct image. It wasn't Tommy, Olivia or the Twins, and even though the music was Vinyl Crush, his bandmates were nothing but faceless forms. While the stage exploded in a rainbow of lights and flash pots, the three-story jumbotron boldly displayed one name, lit up in illuminated red neon, climbing high above the drum riser to the ceiling of the arena … NATHAN FOX.

Even from his electronically-induced coma he smiled, and as Nathan "The Lizard King" raised the microphone to his lips, the concert was cut short, stopped dead in its tracks, cancelled by the promoter. The wonderful dream turned to a horrible nightmare starring everybody's favorite, that overgrown, eight-legged abomination, King Taraxian. From the inside of his mind, Nathan watched in horror as the spider descended upon the floor seats, crushing thousands of terrified concert-goers while consuming many loyal members of Nathan's fan club, the Fox Army. The lights dimmed, then casted the long shadow of Nathan's silhouette over the rising fog that blanketed the stage. He placed the microphone into the clip that secured it to the stand, stepped back, then looked up into his abyss. With the exception of a subtle sneer, Nathan didn't even flinch, not once. He stood his ground upon gazing into the fisheye images of himself, mirrored by each one of the monster's round, soul-draining pools of black. Dream or no dream, it was funny how he wasn't scared, not at all. Maybe because there comes a time in a man's life when you either run away or look the problem straight in the eye (even if there's eight of them). Now was not the time for insecurity or fear, now was the time to kick some ass.

Chapter XVI

The Duke lay waste to the smaller structures of the city, trampling all beneath his steel boots while gaining momentum as he charged upon King Taraxian. The thin layer of ice that coated his jacket creaked and crackled like the fragile glass of a frozen pond with the cowbot's every move. Everything was working, from the initial freezing blast of the Duke's new jacket, to the sole purpose of the Kelvin Duster: to protect the robot from the spider creature's devastating heat mechanism. Things were going 100% according to plan, but there was no telling just how long they would continue to do so. The bot needed to gain the higher ground and quick-like, so immediately the Duke commenced to opening a can of ice-cold whoopass. He had to, before he lost his refrigerated overcoat and before King Taraxian had a chance to charge up, or re-energize, or whatever the hell it did.

The hissing spider arched back and rocked from side to side, bearing its monstrous pincers, readying itself for battle. It was now obvious that when the giant creature used its extreme heat pulse as an isolated weapon, it (like the Duke) was also left drained and defenseless. Well, as defenseless as a 12,000-metric-ton spider could be.

BWAM!

The cowboy mech rammed into King Taraxian, forcing his mighty shoulder deep into the monster, smack between its jaw and wavering pedipalp.

KRAM!

Upon contact, air turned to steam when the chill of the frozen bot combined with the extreme heat of the arachnid creature. The metal joints of the Duke echoed, akin to the sound of twisting girders, and the bot pushed harder against the demon daikaiju. It tried to hold its ground, but began to teeter when a pair of back thrusters from beneath the Duke's coat ignited in an eruption of propelling power!

FWOOOSH!

That little extra burst was all it took and King Taraxian lost its footing (all eight of them) and made contact with the planet when it fell backwards.

KA-BOOSH!

The Duke turned his head, and upon locking in on one of the city's massive high-tension towers, began ripping the spear-shaped structure from the ground. Tar and cement fell away as trillion-watt bolts of electricity escaped the snapping wires. When it broke free of the earth, the cowboy mech held it tight with both hands and lifted off. King Taraxian struggled, it's legs flailing about while it lay helpless on its back, and at that moment the Duke began his ascent.

E.I.O. West resumed visual and a cloudy image of the cowbot swooping down from the burning skies engulfed all of the screens. This seemed to be it, and the entire control room cheered as the Duke advanced like hell from above, readying to plunge his 100-foot, sterling-chrome lance into the stomach of the monster spider. But of everybody, it was probably Jack who was hoping the most, hoping that this would indeed be *it*, the ruddy end for God's sake. Not saying a word as he looked forward, both of his hands gripped the edges of the workstation as he waited in quiet desperation. Jack was growing weary. He was far more than ready to close this bloody chapter of his life.

The Duke rocketed with the piercing tip of the tower aimed at the underbelly of the beast, and everybody held their breath. It was then that a thick stream of web ejected straight up from two pairs of spinnerets located at the business end of the spider. Its four, finger-like organs worked in accordance with each other, somehow maneuvering the continuous flow.

The external sensory mechanism of the bot locked in on the oncoming freight-train-of-steel webbing, sending an internal warning to the slumbering crew. Each of the robotonauts winced as a bolt of pain shot through their wiring when the great mech immediately changed direction in midair. But even so, the determined beam of silky super glue still managed to lock tight when it connected with the chest of the Duke. As the cowbot rocketed towards the heavens, the umbilical cord that now joined the behemoths together drew tight, flipping King Taraxian right-side up. In one great motion, the spider beast came about, yanking the thick cable in a downward fashion. The Duke lost his grip, and his high-tension javelin pierced the edge of a building, just before the bot slammed into the earth.

KRAAAASH!

Before anybody even knew what was happening, the arachnid pushed itself into the air with its eight tremendous legs, landing on top of the Duke. Instantly, it began slamming the tips of its mighty two front claws into the ground with the ferocity of giant, twin jackhammers. The cowbot, now on *his* back, jerked his head to the left and right in an effort to dodge each of the skull-crushing impacts.

KRAM! KRAM! KRAM!

The emergency cherries that donned the walls of the mech's inner cranium began to spin in a fury of red light. The freezing effects of the Kelvin Duster were wearing off. It needed to be recharged and, if necessary, fired again.

Trapped beneath the tremendous creature, the Duke struggled to move, as the crushing weight of the beast was holding him prisoner. In a desperate attempt, he eased his long chrome arm through the assembly line of attacking legs, reaching for one of his photon six-shooters. While his metal arm stretched, the other pushed hard on the sunken head of the spider, trying to avoid its flapping, fang-tipped chelicera that closed in on the robot's face. The Duke's powerful fingers wrapped tight around the chrome-steel handle of the massive shooting iron. He raised it up to fire and just before the photon blast could escape the barrel of the cannon, King Taraxian's front talon pierced the armor of the mech's wrist! His hand sprung open and the magnificent pistol fell to the ground. The spider's front two palp-like arms began moving at a rapid rate, taking on the image of two giant knitting needles. A flow of silk as strong as liquid steel protruded from the beast's abdomen, and it began covering the Duke in a cocoon of web.

While Jack watched, a haunting vision interrupted his thoughts, and he had to pause. In an instant, he was transported to a cobblestone path that stretched alongside a beautiful, green garden. While he walked he inhaled the fresh air, basking in the sweet aroma of an assortment of flowers. When he stopped to whistle along to the catchy melody of a plump red robin, he noticed a magnificent web glistening in the midday sun. Its beauty drew him in and Jack went down upon bended knee when he saw five tiny flies scattered about the sticky weave. Each one wrapped up in their own silken package, waiting as the purveyor of the web moved in for the kill. He stopped whistling when the tune of the bird faded off into the distance. But he listened hard, because he could have sworn he heard an altogether different chorus, one of faint cries, almost as if the doomed insects were calling out to him. From his kneeling position, Jack nudged himself in for an even closer look and gasped aloud when he thought he saw five familiar faces. He slammed his eyes shut in complete disbelief, then covered his ears to muffle the loud shrieks of the little flies, the ones bearing the faces of Nathan, Tommy, Olivia and the Twins as they each screamed,

"HEEEEELP ME! PLEASE HEEEEELP ME!"

Jack wiped the condensation from his forehead while doing his best to conceal the fact that fear would be dictating his next maneuver. He interlocked his fingers from behind his back, stood erect, watched the screen and gave the order, demanding they reboot the Kelvin Duster to fire simultaneously with the ROT beam. Takarada grimaced. He hated that damn thing, probably along the same lines that Einstein hated the atomic bomb. Yes, he had invented it, but it was so freakin' powerful that the hands of mere mortals shouldn't be allowed to tamper with it … ever. The heat ray that fired from the cowbot's monocle was a concentrated stream of pure organic thorium, capable of taking out an entire city block. This fear wasn't speculation on

Takarada's part either, because in a previous misfire, that's exactly what happened. Upon activating the beam, the robotonauts missed their target and did just that, took out an entire city block. After witnessing the complete and total devastation caused by the weapon, Takarada would now only allow it to be fired by himself from the control center and not from the cockpit. Now Jack wanted to fire the ROT beam and activate the Kelvin Duster at the same time? Takarada did not like the idea. But desperate times called for desperate measures and, confident they wouldn't make the same mistake (and also not being one to argue with Sir Jonathon), he agreed.

Dr. T spoke loud and clear from within the control center of the underwater base. It seemed he was losing his mind as he gave the direct order into the thin of the air. But in fact, his directions were being transmitted, traveling thousands upon thousands of miles from E.I.O. West directly to the cockpit of the Duke and into SCOTT's computer.

"Please initiate ROT beam procedures, SCOTT. I will fire on Sir Jonathon's mark." The doctor ordered in a very non-ordering kind of way. "All failing freezing systems also tell me that we are a go for initiating the ... the ..."

Takarada paused, being a man of calculated science he hated even speaking such a word as foul as this. The jury-rig implication of its title alone was enough to make him feel as though all were being left to chance. He sighed a bit and forced the words out of his mouth, "Are all systems a go for initiating ... reboot?"

From the other side of the planet, SCOTT's voice rang out through the control center of the submerged base, "Yes sir, all systems are indeed a go. Both will be operating at 100% capability upon regeneration."

"Good," Takarada replied, then he went on to ask, "How are our young pilots doing?"

SCOTT answered, "Well sir, considering we are being spun into a sixty-meter cocoon of arachnid webbing stronger than steel, I would say other than that, they are fine sir."

Takarada didn't dare smile, and Jack wailed, "Good Lord! Even the bloody robot is a sarcastic son of a bitch! Please refrain from your remarks, SCOTT, and gentlemen, you can chat later. Now, charge the ruddy beam if you please!"

A great impulse of power climbed in a succession of pitches when SCOTT initiated the energizing procedure. With the addition of the Kelvin Duster, it would take more than twice as long to charge both weapons. So while the Duke got fitted for his brand new silk threads, all they could do was wait.

Sir Jonathon couldn't look away as he watched the giant arachnid from the satellite relay. He was both amazed and terrified at the speed and precision of the large beast. He also knew that if the Duke were to go down, King Taraxian would be heading straight for the FUJI. He placed his hands on his hips and ordered the remaining squadron of F.U. fighters to deploy from the compound hidden within the inactive volcano. His plan being to aid the Duke if necessary, but more important, to defend the mountain. Jack knew what was coming, this was all too familiar, it was London all over again. Right down to the FUJI's new refinery plant and its protected supply of the most powerful element on planet Earth. He had a hunch this blasted, eight-eyed freak of nature would head to Japan. He figured that out the second Takarada mentioned the amount of energy needed to drive this thing's internal heating system. And now with both the Yanks and Great Britain already in Japanese waters, the E.I.O. would have their hands full just trying to keep the damn peace.

"Weapon systems at 20% and counting."

It was as though time itself had come to a complete stop. Jack's thoughts raced a million miles a second as both the ROT beam and the Kelvin Duster seemed to charge at a freakin' snail's pace. With no signs of the spider's blistering heat to distort their digital feed, the shocking image was crystal clear, creepy as all get out and next to impossible to look at. But Jack couldn't turn away, and he watched the thick strands of silk eject from the monster's spinnerets in a grotesque discharge of liquid yellow. Being the longest any kind of visual had been able to hold a fix on the monster, Takarada and Jack were both noticing things neither man had seen before. The Doctor tapped the table with his index finger while Sir Jonathon stroked his mammoth mustache as they watched ... and waited.

"Weapon systems at 30% and counting."

Jack turned to Dr. Takarada.

"Kyoshi, I believe there is much more here than meets the eye. That thing," Jack stated as he pointed to the control center's middle screen with a trembling finger, "is more than just a bloody mechanical daikaiju. It is without a doubt, alive and breathing, not the mere machine we once thought. That thing," he repeated, "is more than a soulless monster fueled by stolen organic thorium."

Takarada nodded, because it was becoming just as apparent to him.

"We know King Taraxian is being controlled by an outside entity."

Takarada again nodded.

"We just don't know by who … or by what. However, there is one final element we are not accounting for. The bloody black magic that is either holding this half spider, half mechanical contraption together," Jack paused, "or giving it life."

"Weapon systems at 50% and counting."

Jack cursed the time it was taking to charge the beam. Then, trying to somehow get an idea of who was behind all of this nonsense, frantically replayed the succession of events through his mind.

With both the Americans and the Brits stationed inside of Japanese waters, he knew they were readying themselves to execute a non-peaceful police action. Jack was confident this show-of-force was a mere effort to contain the ongoing kaiju crisis. He did not believe the United States and England to have any ulterior motives as he once thought. At this point, he reminded himself, they were nothing but stubborn and pig-headed pawns in this whole fiasco. So, in order to stop the big kids on the playground from beating up the little kids, Jack sent an even bigger kid to protect them, the Duke. Which in fact worked out quite well when spider-boy reared its infused head out of Yokohama Bay. He also knew, without a shadow of a doubt, there was one reason King Taraxian was in Japan, to steal the remaining organic thorium that had been transferred from London. That, and according to Takarada, to lure two of the world's largest superpowers there to start a ghost war. He and Dr. Takarada had deciphered this knowing the two western countries would indeed trigger a large-scale action. This was obvious, due to Japan's unfortunate involvement with the United States and the losses of Salt Lake City and Los Angeles. Then, as Japan and her allies were forced to retaliate, the true nemesis, this invisible enemy, would advance on the FUJI. As World War III started, he or she, or it, or they, would bloody slip in, steal the organic thorium and gain control of the planet.

Jack stood and began to pace, and while he did he grew impatient, which led him to pull out his pocket watch. He looked at the face of the gold timepiece, then up at the viewing monitor screen and gave it a sour glare.

"How are we coming with that weapon system, SCOTT?" he demanded.

"We are at 75%, Sir Jonathon."

He turned from the screen, then resumed both his pacing and thinking. It was funny how this chain of well-instigated events, that at one time seemed so coincidental, were in fact part of an elaborate scheme. Everything from chasing that proverbial carrot across the deserts of Utah, to the Tomoyuki showing up over Palmdale, then finally the Duke winding up in Japan. Jack racked his brain as he tried to figure out every crazy nuance of this dastardly plan. He wanted to know who was behind all of it, because he dreaded what might be coming next. Of course his mind fixed in on the possibility of Oko Rikoku, but anonymity wasn't her style. She'd be making damn sure that everybody knew exactly who was pulling the strings of the daikaiju puppet. Besides, Jack shot Rikoku in the head, so that ruled her out. He tugged at his white, wavy hair, trying to force the already established connections into place: the stolen organic thorium, a bloody giant spider and someone, or something, with an insatiable appetite for power.

"Weapon systems at 90% and counting."

It was then Jack added one final element to the equation, one factor he hadn't considered, the person who could've tied all of this together, had she not been killed in a freak accident only days after making a startling discovery. It was funny how Jack hadn't thought about her in years. Now, over the past few days he must have heard her name at least a hundred times. It's odd how it always seems to be like that, but just the mere thought of Pamela Fox was enough to trigger Jack's neurons into igniting the light bulb that illuminated above his head.

"Blimey!" he yelled. Because he knew, he connected all of the dots and by God, he knew, knew who was behind it all! It was so obvious, Jack thought, and it couldn't have been any more so if the whole bloody scheme had been tattooed to his ass.

It was none other than his old arch enemy, that international Judas … Iscariot.

Jack, just about to let Takarada in on his little epiphany, opened his mouth and SCOTT's voice came out of it.

"Regenerating organic thorium weapon system at 100%. Kelvin Duster at 100%. We are now fully armed and awaiting your mark Sir Jonathon."

The two men placed their fingers on the awaiting buttons. It was pretty obvious to assume that if the Duke was charged, King Taraxian was also fully energized. Still looming over the cowbot that now lay in a silken tomb, the creature prepared to insert its monstrous fangs into the vacuum-packed mech. The high-pitched tone of the spider increased in sound, rising to a deafening crescendo as it prepared to strike. It, like the cowbot, seemed to be going for that dreaded double-whammy, cremating the Duke, while simultaneously plunging its pincers deep into his head.

And on tonight's menu … a lovely, flame-broiled Duke, with a silken side of roasted robotonauts.

The maddening numbers on the HD monitors again counted down, searching for that illusive zero. But time had clearly run out, and as King Taraxian's front pincers descended like two swift daggers, Sir Jack hollered, "We can't wait anymore Kyoshi! Fire the blasted thing, NOW!"

In that second, a great sphere of ice and snow burst from the Duke in a blinding fury of white upon the activation of the Kelvin Duster. The impacting waves launched the giant spider into the sky, also freeing the mech from beneath it, along with the webbing that held him captive. But if that wasn't enough, the freezing blast was accompanied by the thick, blistering ray of the ROT beam firing from the cowbot's monocle!

BWAM!

It was like a left hook from hell, and when it connected with King Taraxian in midair, the lethal light blasted him back into the bay!

KRAM! SPLOOOSH!

The Duke pulled himself to his feet and tore the remaining shards of web from his chassis. He then pounded his fist into his open palm and his chrome boots thundered in bursts of metal as he made his way towards the pier.

The water churned in a circle of steel, stone and blood and the monstrous spider was nowhere to be seen. The cowboy mech stepped from the city into the sea and the Pacific hissed when it made contact with the freezing metal of the bot. Ocean turned to ice and slush, immediately breaking as the frozen mech waded out into the rough waters, searching for the submerged beast. As he scanned, two F.U. fighters from the FUJI joined from above, while twin squadrons of both American and British jets roared in from the not so distant edge of the horizon. The ocean was climbing to the cowboy's waste while the swarm of planes (from all sides of the war) circled about him like hungry vultures. An array of tracking beams gleamed from the hulls of the F.U. jets as they hovered just over the top of the water, still finding nothing. The Duke trudged through the murky deep, even surpassing Yokohama Bay to the tip of the sea where the fleet of U.S. ships had weighed anchor.

The Kelvin Duster that wrapped around the mighty robot began to creak, due to the waters of the ocean counteracting its cold effect of liquid-helium coolant. The massive engines of his internal freezers groaned as great cogs spun faster trying to accommodate. A mighty wave crashed upon the side of one of the American battleships when the Duke waded up alongside the vessel. Some men ran while others stopped to lay witness to the awesome sight of the world's greatest weapon as it splashed by. The ship's bosun's whistle chirped throughout the decks while the captain ordered all topside hands to retreat below. An emergency horn soon followed, but for a different purpose altogether, and two large turrets housing three cannons each began to turn towards the sea. The lumbering mech paused beside the

ship, only the guns didn't and their thick barrels raised up. The Duke turned in accordance with the spinning metal citadels that housed the Navy persuaders and stopped when they did. It was then, not even a quarter nautical mile away from the stern, that the angry ocean started rippling in all directions. White-capped water slammed into the air and the sea began to boil. Then, as the cannons locked into place, the gigantic spider rose up from the deep.

From the digital feed, both Sir Jack and Takarada "ewwwwed" in teenage unison at the sight of the messed-up arachnid. The ROT beam had not killed the beast, but it did manage to blow one of its front legs clean off. It also succeeded in melting one of its two larger eyes, leaving nothing but a black dripping ooze in its space. But what was far worse was that the ray had charred a good portion of the monster's skin and hair fibers, revealing most of the burnt skull of the creature's exoskeleton, as though spiders weren't freakin' creepy enough.

The guns on the battleship exploded into a full assault, and every last fighter jet (be it Japanese, American, British or E.I.O.) started pummeling King Taraxian with an onslaught of missiles. The Duke didn't hesitate either, pulling one photon grenade after the other from the massive bandolier that wrapped around his chest! He chucked them at the monster, creating a smokescreen on the surface of the ocean as the jets closed in. Jack again gripped the edge of the table that supported the computers from E.I.O. West. His knuckles turned white while he watched the injured beast succumb to the endless barrage of firepower. He clenched his teeth as the words, "Die you bloody thing, just die damn it," overtook his thoughts. Was this the "it" that Jack had been waiting for? While he watched, he envisioned the superpowers humbly apologizing to both he and the E.I.O. for ever doubting him. Then he'd bloody retire and get back to doing what he loved most, which was, believe it or not, writing music. As the towering creature's remaining seven legs withered, Jack's mustache rose a bit when he smiled.

"We've got the bloody thing, Kyoshi, we've got it right where we want it, and I want it dead!" he yelled.

As the spider burned, its loud shrieks were being drowned out by the sound of a piercing, high-pitched tone. It was the same one it seemed to emit just before the repeating pulses of heated waves began to swell from its body. Jack's eyes widened, and he pulled his round spectacles from his face.

"Abort!" he screamed. "Repeat, everybody abort mission! Get your asses out of there! The monster has not yet fired its primary weapon! Move!"

It was assumed that when the Duke activated both the ROT beam and the Kelvin Duster, that King Taraxian had fired its devastating heat mechanism as well. Sir Jonathon's nails dug deep into the wood of the desk, only removing them to cover both his heart and his mouth when he let out a loud gasp of,

"Oh my God."

The atmosphere expanded in a wave of devastating fury as King Taraxian emitted his pulsating heat mechanism. Remnants of circling jets that couldn't escape in time spiraled to the earth after melting in midair. In an effort to shield the American battleship, the Duke turned and arched over the vessel. His back lit up in a flash of silver and red while he attempted to block the oncoming blast. The Pacific erupted in a spectacle of fire, and as hell itself consumed the waters, the viewing screens of E.I.O. West crackled to white and gray, the color of nothing, because that's all that was left … nothing.

Chapter XVII

Nathan pried his eyes open and winced from the series of sharp pains that ran from one end of his skull to the other. He knew he wasn't hung over, but that didn't stop his head from pounding like John Bonham's kick drum after a twelve freakin' hour rendition of Moby Dick. He may have been concerned too, if not for the textbook headache, upset stomach and bad case of the Zactly's. (You may remember the Zactly's, that dreaded condition when your mouth tastes zactly like your ass.) So he knew not to worry too much, because this was nothing, just that sucky process you have to go through after taking a ride in the Duke.

It was odd though, as he seemed to remember much of what had happened this time. Something that, at least to his knowledge, wasn't very common whilst under the influence of the robo-coma. It was sketchy in the form of a hazy dream, but nonetheless he remembered most of it. The end, however, was a big fat blur, so he figured something must have gone horribly wrong. Or maybe he didn't make it at all, and this was his last stop before heading to that great concert in the sky. Oh well, so much for the 27 Club, he thought.

While he lay there contemplating one thing after another, his mind shifted from being one of the dearly departed to the thought that he'd been here before. Nathan massaged his temples, and as he cleared the mist of his foggy mind, he was almost certain of it. Only when the soft melody of a sad cello began to seep in through the walls did he know for sure. He wasn't dead after all; he was deep within the rock of the mighty mountain. Hell, he was even in his old quarters, and the dump hadn't changed a bit, right down to the emergency bottle of champagne that he stashed above the tile of his suspended ceiling, so long ago. Yeah, he knew exactly where he was, the FUJI.

After pulling the bottle down from its hiding place, he maneuvered the tips of his thumbs at the base of the cork, pushed and it burst open. A little spilt in the process, but not much, and since it was Dom Perignon he felt obligated to at least sniff the cork. As he poured the contents down the drain of his old sink, he looked about the dismal flat. Even from the confines of his closed room, he could tell that something was different on the other side. It wasn't the bright, white, bustling, hospital-type ward he remembered it to be. It was dark and barren, and with the exception of the cello's wavering moan, it was quiet, way too quiet. It occurred to him to try contacting the control center from the comm. system within his room, not caring if ol' Walrusaurus himself answered on the other end. But even that was wishful thinking as all he heard was static. Nathan opened his door a bit and peered through the crack that ran the length of it. He widened his view and stuck his head into the hallway, scanning the row of doors that ran down both sides, all the way to the only exit he knew to exist in the barracks' wing of the FUJI, the elevator. With Olivia only a few feet away, he figured everybody must be here, and he slipped out of his room to go find them.

Nathan stopped and leaned up against the inside frame of Olivia's open door. Yeah, he was a bit concerned about what had happened and *why* they were where they were, but that didn't prevent him from taking a few minutes to listen. Because Olivia Olivetti was the only person on Earth that he knew who could play a cello like she did (not that he knew anybody else who could). Nathan stood there and let the music sink deep into his soul, forgetting all about robots, spiders and secret missions. But it was easy, because Olivia played like an angel. He soon found himself lost, entwined within the delicate parade of soft notes, following them all the way to the song's end.

"That was beautiful," he whispered, his soft voice giving her a slight start.

Olivia's head sunk a little bit and she blushed out an honest "Thank you." She turned the cello towards her and admired its spruce top, then admitted she was glad she hadn't found the time to have it

shipped back to the states yet. Olivia sighed, "As a matter of fact, most of my instruments are still here, somewhere." She loved playing, but like Tommy, it was something she did less and less of nowadays.

Nathan asked her what the piece of music was.

"It was Bach's Cello Suite Number 2 in D minor," she replied.

Nathan, trying to impress her, commented that D minor, in his humble opinion, was the saddest of all keys. Olivia didn't agree, nor did she disagree, chances are she didn't make the Spinal Tap connection either. She then asked Nathan the question she was sure he already knew the answer to.

"You know where we are, right?"

He replied with half of a nod.

"Do you think everybody else is here?"

This time he replied with the other half, but also added that they were probably still out cold from that freakin' Duke coma. Twelve hours of continuous sleep was the standard length of time it took to recover from the electronically-induced nap. Sometimes Michael and

Liberty would even be down for an entire day, depending on how much robot, inner-cranium, alien crap was necessary.

Olivia seemed to require the least amount of rest after the sleep-state, never needing (or wanting) more than eight hours. Nathan didn't think he'd been out for too long, but it always seemed to work like that. He'd probably still be sawing logs too, had he not been awakened by Olivia's concert from across the hall. So with all points considered, Nathan figured he must've been out for nine to ten hours, give or take a cello suite or two.

As the music wore off, their situation wore in, and Nathan looked around, trying to figure out the hows and whys of the FUJI mystery. Normally if he woke up here, it wouldn't be such a big deal. He'd roll out of bed, get himself a sandwich and go harass Jack. But this wasn't right, something was definitely wrong. He told Olivia he was going to go try the elevator to see if he could figure out what the hell was going on.

"Don't bother," she said, "it was the first thing I did after I woke up."

Nathan acknowledged her efforts with a skeptical, "Hmmmm," then meandered down the hallway towards the lift anyway to see for himself. Olivia stood in her doorway, shaking her cello bow at Nathan's back. As he walked away, he rolled his eyes and she yelled,

"I'm quite certain I know how to check an elevator to see if it works or not, thank you very much."

Her angry voice followed Nathan down the empty hall and while it did, he could only think of one thing, the joy on Olivia's face as she played with the aquatic life from the other side of a great glass porthole. He knew that was the real Olivia, the brilliant, cello-playing beauty who resided under the skin of the angry agent. Just the mere thought of that moment in time made Nathan feel all tingly on the inside. She then screamed something else, something about kicking his butt if he didn't wait for her. So he did.

Nathan could smell the stale stench of cigarette smoke, indicating one thing, that Tommy must be awake as well. He snuck up and kicked the door to Tommy's room in three quick intervals. *BAP! BAP! BAP!*

Of course Tommy knew who it was, as this was the signature knock of Nathan Fox. He eased the handle and slipped out through the long, thin crack, trying to prevent the cigarette smoke from escaping the confines of his room. Tommy didn't really care what anybody thought about his smoking, because frankly he was quite used to it. He just didn't feel like listening to Nathan go on and on about it, because he too knew something was amiss.

"What's rup Raggy?" Tommy asked, and Nathan answered him with a concerned,

"I don't know, Scoobs ol' pal, but we should try to find out."

Tommy thought about it for a second, concurring with a, "Ro-Kay."

Olivia had no clue whatsoever as to what these idiots were talking about and just stood there perplexed. Tommy and Nathan began to make their way down the hall, and when she still didn't move they shouted, "C'mon Velma!"

Olivia looked around for this Velma person, but when she didn't see anybody else, she pushed her slipping glasses up the bridge of her nose and scurried to catch up.

Tommy walked up to Michael and Liberty's door. It only made sense that if they were all in their old quarters, the Twins would also be in theirs. He knew they were probably still sleeping, so he started with a nice, subtle Nathan knock. *BAM! BAM! BAM!* He waited a second, got nothing and tried again. *BAM! BAM! BAM!* Still nothing, which was odd because even though Michael could sleep through a full-scale kaiju invasion, Liberty could not. As they waited a few seconds longer, Tommy asked Nathan if he thought it was kind of weird that the Twins slept in the same bed. Nathan said he never really thought about it, and after spending countless years on the road, he'd seen things a lot freakier than that. Hell, he'd taken place in things a lot freakier than that. Of course for the brother and sister aliens this was simply the norm, because they were more like one entity split up into two bodies. So what appeared to be Appalachian, extraterrestrial incest to most, was in fact how this race survived, two acting as one. For Michael and Liberty, it was as natural as breathing. But it still eeeked Tommy out a bit, and he shook his head while sighing out a disconcerted, "Freakin' aliens."

Nathan jiggled the handle and was surprised to find that their room was unlocked. They weren't there, and from the looks of the empty flat, they never were. Nathan began to wonder if he was still asleep in the Duke. Maybe this was nothing but a weird dream, and in reality they were still in the heat of battle with King Taraxian, some sort of nasty side effect from being placed into one too many electronically-induced comas.

He shut the door and suggested they try the elevator. Olivia, still irritated and holding to her claim of, "I already did and it doesn't work," agreed in a beautiful tone of sarcastic loveliness. Nathan pressed the button, and when nothing happened, Olivia folded her arms in a smug, "See, I told you so" manner. But before she had a chance to let out a big, Jack-sized "harrumph," the small circle of the lift dinged into a tiny glow of red. Of course it was probably a good thing that it was working, but nonetheless the fact that it did made Olivia furious. Nathan gave her a quick wink, and she pushed her glasses up with her middle finger.

Nathan placed himself in front of Olivia just in case he'd need to protect her from whatever was coming their way on the elevator. Tommy groaned, while Olivia (who was still irritated) softened a bit as she thought the gesture was kind of sweet, even though in reality she could kick his ass from here 'til Tuesday. Nathan went into his best Kung-Fu stance, and when the doors opened he was prepared for anything, except for what he saw, nothing.

While still in karate-kid mode, Nathan blurted out, "It's empty!" and Tommy pushed him, causing Nathan to lose his balance and stumble into the lift.

"No shit, Bruce Lee," he said, "let's see where it goes."

The FUJI's internal elevator system not only traveled up and down, but sideways as well, making it accessible to most parts of the compound. Nathan's stomach rose up to his chest, letting him know without reservation that they were going deep and at an increased level of speed. Which could only mean they were on their way to the

FUJI's massive, underground hangar from where the F.U. fighters launched. It was basically a damn underground airport, and Tommy could never forget the first time he saw the magnificent bay, one of his greatest and earliest memories of his new life with the E.I.O. Plus, the thought of it always reminded him of when he met Michael.

Both of them were plunging straight down within two chutes of the world's biggest crazy straw, one that lowered from the ceiling of the hangar, placing them into the cockpit of an F.U. jet. Tommy was terrified as they plummeted at freakin' light speed from what seemed to be a mile up, while Michael simply played air drums on the wall of his clear, thermoplastic pipe. It was then that he realized how much he liked Michael, watching him jam along to (what Tommy figured had to be) either Led Zeppelin or Rush, drummers from two of Michael's favorite bands.

The elevator stopped and Nathan went from Chuck Norris to Shirley Temple upon the parting of its doors. All three backed up against the lift's furthest wall into a tight huddle, staring at the black tip of a giant talon that blocked their exit.

"No, no my frenz … do not be afraid. My little das liebchen is sleeping, he cannot hurt you."

A lanky fellow, escorted by a few photon-rifle-toting cronies walked up and put his palm against the long, black nail that stood as tall as him. His hand ran up and down it, and as he stroked it, he added a sinister, "Only I can do zat. Unt I vill, unless you tell me vut I vant to know."

All three eased out of the elevator, and Tommy's eyes widened at the sight of this weird guy in a lengthy lab coat. He turned to Nathan and even though neither one could place him, they both thought he looked familiar. Tommy then snapped his finger, and when he did, both he and Nathan seemed to figure out exactly who he was. They were silent for a second, but then burst into an explosion of uncontrollable laughter. Olivia, once again, just stood there clueless. Nathan had to wipe the tears from his eyes and he could barely speak.

"Oh my God! he cried, "he looks just like the evil scientist dude from that Robot Chicken show!"

Tommy laughed harder and screamed, "Oh no ... it's evil Doctor Chicken! Run Away! Run Away!"

"Good Lord," Olivia thought to herself, "That's right you morons, piss the bad guy off even more."

She looked at the poor bastard as he gazed down upon himself, trying to figure out what was so damn funny. It became apparent that Evil Doctor Chicken had never tuned in to Adult Swim, and he shouted, "ZILENCE!"

He shot his hand into the air and all weapons lifted, aimed directly at their faces. Nathan and Tommy turned into two statues upon shutting the hell right up and Doctor Chicken (or whatever this guy's name was), curled his lip and hissed, "Good, unt now zat I have your attention, please observe."

All three gazed through the massive legs of the dormant spider, following the tip of their host's finger that led their eyes straight to Michael and Liberty. They had been shackled to some archaic-looking contraption by their hands and feet, each mounted in an "X" formation, one just out of reach of the other. Michael lifted his heavy head and upon seeing Nathan, Tommy and Olivia, still managed to give them two thumbs up from his restrained hands, along with a hearty, "Dudes!"

"I have taken zee liberty of making sure zat your frenz are unt comfortable. I have alzo made sure that zey keep zare distance frum each other, as vee don't vant any alien surprizes now do vee?"

Angered at the sight, Tommy stepped forward.

"Just who the hell are you and what do you want?"

They, unlike Jack, did not know who this person was, this architect of terror, the one behind the latest assault against this very world.

"I am Iscariot, Doctor Leopold Iscariot," he stated, and as Nathan heard this, he could feel a tinge of electricity shoot down his throat disconnecting his heart. Without even thinking (something Nathan was quite good at) he lunged towards Iscariot with his hands aimed straight for the doctor's neck. One of the guards, one that looked to be his main henchman, sidestepped in front of Iscariot to shield him. Just before Nathan could wrap his mitts around the throat of the person who he thought killed his mother, he was judo-chopped on the back of the neck and went down. PAP! Upon seeing this, both Olivia and Tommy sprang into action.

Three guards surrounded Olivia and she back kicked the one that approached from behind, followed by a flawless, spinning-wheel strike to take out the one in front of her. She then spun around, let out a "HIYEEEEE!" and proceeded to pummel the third guard with a Kin Geri to his privates.

FWAP! CRAM! BAP!

Tommy swung around, and the tip of a long rifle edged itself up against his chest. He couldn't help but crack a slight smile when he reached up with his bionic hand, grabbing the barrel then twisting it back towards the face of its bearer. While the crony was busy not believing his eyes, Tommy let him have it with a solid right cross. POW!

Nathan jumped to his feet, and one of the other guards went for his weapon. Nathan, who was on him in a second, kicked the gun out of his hands, protected his face with his clenched fist and began to decimate the guard's jaw with a series of quick jabs. It was fast and relentless, and as the mug went down, he had no idea what just hit him. Tommy, Olivia and Nathan were like a well-oiled fighting machine, working with both speed and precision. There was also no doubt they would have won the scuffle, if not for …

"Zenuff!" cried Iscariot. "You vood not vant anyzing to happen to your frenz!"

As he said this, the doctor pulled out a small remote and pointed it at Michael and Liberty. The four steel bands that had them bound by their wrists and ankles began to pull in four opposing directions. The Twins screamed in pain, but Iscariot didn't stop, proving that he was not effing around. He grinned as he watched, then yelled again,

"Say ven!" and Tommy, who saw no other choice, stopped dead in the middle of a flying foot sweep.

"When."

Iscariot's boney thumb touched the remote and both the stretching device and screams stopped. His guards regrouped, enclosing Nathan,

Tommy and Olivia in a semicircle, only this time with cocked weapons.

Doctor Iscariot approached Tommy and grabbed his wrist. Tommy resisted, and when he did the cold, black tip of a loaded rifle kissed his cheek, forcing him into submission. Iscariot lifted Tommy's arm and observed his hand.

"Very interesting," he stated while he examined it. "Obviously the verk of Kyoshi Takarada, very interesting indeed."

Iscariot reached over with his other arm, grabbing Tommy's wrist in one and his hand in the other. He jerked it a few times and when it clicked, he both sneered and smiled. He pulled as he turned and Tommy's robotic hand slipped off.

"I don't zink you'll be needing this anymore," and the doctor dropped the heavy hand into the deep pocket of his white lab coat. Tommy felt humiliated and helpless and covered up his empty wrist with his other hand. Olivia walked over to him, not giving a shit about the guns that followed her every step, then interlocked her arm in his.

Iscariot sniggered, "How touching. Let's get down to bizness shall vee? Vare iz zee organic thorium?"

Olivia turned her head to Nathan, who didn't know how to react as he truly thought the organic thorium was here at the FUJI. Not that he would have told this clown if it was, but it freakin' wasn't! Nathan had no idea and looked over to Tommy for a little help, who only continued to look down at his barren wrist. Nathan felt bad for Tommy. He was also getting really sick of this new habit he was developing, the one of imagining his friends at their best when they were at their worst. Nathan started thinking of Tommy playing his coffee-can guitar, the one they made when they were kids, and how much that stupid little thing meant to him. He couldn't help but remember the look on Tommy's face as he strummed those rubber bands so long ago. It was priceless, and that alone was well worth the cost of admission.

Nathan sighed upon returning from his flashback and gazed at what Iscariot had done to his pal. An intense anger began to consume him, flowing through every fiber of his being. For a split second,

Nathan wished he was Bruce Banner so he could turn into the Hulk and just smash this Iscariot guy's head in. But as we all know, that's just ridiculous. But what wasn't ridiculous was the fact that the organic thorium was-not-here. Then it hit him.

"DUH!" Nathan face-palmed his forehead from the inside and groaned when he realized why the damn FUJI was a freakin' ghost town. Jack knew this thing was coming all along, so when nobody was looking, he transferred the O.T. the hell out of here. He just kept it real hush-hush, never letting on to anybody or anything. Jack had a hunch King Taraxian was heading towards Japan, so to be safe he removed the element. It made sense, especially after witnessing what had happened in London, and with the gravity of the spider's heat mechanism, he had the base evacuated. That blast in Los Angeles was pretty freakin' bad, no doubt about it. But it would have paled in comparison if Mount Fuji were to explode in a thundering blaze of organic thorium. Jack just kept the whole thing real quiet-like, never letting on to anybody what he was doing. Because loose lips sink ships, and a pretty good number of them, just like the Duke, were already at the bottom of the Pacific.

"It's not here, and we have no idea where it is," Nathan confessed.

Iscariot gazed at the three with a look of icy steel, because this was the only reason he had them pulled from the submerged cockpit of the cowbot … answers. Now, upon hearing this, he contemplated if he even wanted them alive or not. Agents can be quite troublesome, but maybe they could still be useful in one way or another, even if that meant sweeping the floors. He had plans for Michael and Liberty, and as soon as his schedule permitted he would be dissecting them, so that was a no-brainer for the doctor. But if Nathan, Tommy and Olivia had nothing to offer, they were simply extra baggage, and he had plenty of that already. However, if they could tell him anything about the organic thorium, Jack, or even the FUJI itself, of course they could still prove to be invaluable. The doctor knew E.I.O. agents were trained in the art of deception, they had to be for moments such as this. Iscariot conversely was also trained, as it too was part of *his* E.I.O. education. He also had a few other tricks up his lab coat's sleeve.

The doctor commanded his guards to lower their weapons, the very ones that were still aimed at Tommy, Nathan and Olivia's heads. They were a bit reluctant, but did as he ordered. Iscariot then slithered up to Tommy, reached into his pocket and pulled out the detached super-damn hand. Olivia, who was still holding tight to Tommy's forearm, sneered at Iscariot when he grabbed Tommy's handless wrist. He got real close, then forced out a quick grin, one that offered proof that his evil empire was in desperate need of a good dental plan.

"Just to show you I am not all zat bad, here."

Iscariot reattached Tommy's hand, then asked if he could show them what he had done with the place. Nathan demanded he let the Twins go, and the doctor replied,

"I am sorry, but I cannot do zat, not yet, but in zee meantime ..."

Iscariot reached into his other pocket and pulled out the remote for the stretching mechanism, then handed it to Nathan.

"Here you go, zay are now unt in your capable hanz."

Nathan eyed the remote, remembering something that Michael had mentioned, something about him always singing off key. Although he was tempted, he decided now wasn't the time. Besides, if Nathan was correct in his thinking, they were going to need the help of the Twins very soon.

It was pretty obvious Iscariot was changing his tactics, opting for the "good cop" ploy, hoping since they couldn't beat him, maybe they would join him. He turned and started walking beneath the giant spider that still towered above them all, then asked if they would please follow him. He demanded that his guards get their guests some cold water with lemon, a small piece of dark chocolate each, as well as a few ibuprofens. It was odd how he knew this, but it was the exact remedy for battling that dreaded Duke hangover, the same one Takarada had prescribed them way back when. As they walked, the doctor figured he would get zee ball rolling.

"You should know, zat it vas me who pulled you out of the sea from zat zing zey call a robot. I must say, I never liked zee Duke, unt stupid piece of American made scheisse. But I did like zee modifications Takarada had done to it, he is a brilliant man, a brilliant man indeed."

Iscariot didn't need to turn around to know the look that was donning all three of their faces, their stunned silence said it all. It was just enough information to lure them in, followed by little bits and pieces to keep them interested. Because one thing Iscariot knew, was how the human mind worked. He knew the wanting would morph into a desperate need of knowing. He especially knew this to be true of Nathan Fox.

Chapter XVIII

Iscariot led Nathan, Tommy and Olivia through a fleet of insect-like drones to the opposite end of the bay towards a mother-craft taking up the spaces of four evacuated F.U. fighters. The aisles of Iscariot's war machines were almost as vast as the hangar itself, surrounded by the sprawling limbs of a dormant King Taraxian. Nathan looked up at the underbelly of the monster and could see the damage the Duke had instilled upon the great beast. It wasn't much, but it was still better than he thought, and he looked forward to the next opportunity to do even more. Tommy didn't give a shit one way or the other and, sleeping or not, it still gave Olivia the heebie-jeebies as she peered up at it from below.

Minions worked with the proficiency of well-trained ants, tending to every nuance of the king spider, from the fresh appendage right down to its new, Claude-Rains-style, armor-plated, Phantom-of-the-Opera mask. This was needed in order to house the new robotic eye of the monster, replacing the one that the ROT beam had melted into a seeping black ooze. It's front leg, the one that was blown off, was again fully grown and was being infused with a robotic, steel infrastructure, just like the others.

While they walked, the three noticed that the subterranean runway, used as a means for FUJI jets to come and go, had been decimated. Nothing was getting in or out, unless of course it was a colossal, burrowing arachnid. From within the rubble of the caved-in landing strip, Nathan could see the deep, gargantuan pit that more than likely went all the way to the Pacific. It was pretty obvious that this was where King Taraxian had dug its way in, clearing the path not only for itself, but also for the doctor and his army.

The busy hangar seemed to be the only section of the FUJI that Iscariot had confiscated. It looked as though he was regrouping, licking his wounds and preparing to leave ASAP, more than likely due to the lack of organic thorium he thought to be hidden within the base. For the sake of time though, he was hoping for a little cooperation from the threesome on the whereabouts of the new O.T. refinery, but knew that was a long shot at best. Plus, there was the possibility that they honestly did not know where it was. Either way, with or without them, eventually Iscariot would again locate the regenerating element, just like he eventually located the supply he stole from London. But now that the doctor knew that Jack was aware of his plan, time was even more of the essence. He gave Sir Jonathon credit for figuring it out as quickly as he did. It threw a massive monkey-wrench into the spinning cogs of the doctor's scheme. Because now it seemed that both the Brits and the Yanks had been swayed in the opposite direction of war against Japan. Jack, of course, had a hard time trying to convince both countries of Iscariot's plan, not to mention the fact that the president of the United States hated Jack's guts. But when the Duke arched over in Yokohama Bay, shielding the American battleship from King Taraxian's heat weapon (saving the vessel and all on board), the president became a bit more receptive.

Iscariot led the way up the ramp to his hovering vessel, and as Tommy, Nathan and Olivia followed him, the doctor's guards trailed close behind. Nathan was amazed with the craft, but also thought how much it reminded him of a scaled-down version of the Tomoyuki. Its engines ran soft and quiet, while its clean exhaust system emitted a familiar scent, that of organic thorium. It was the same design all right, a blatant rip off, right down to the placement of the six rotating turbines that kept it afloat. The only difference being that it was painted in evil-doctor black, plus it was quite a bit smaller than the E.I.O.'s flying freak-show. But there was no doubt, this had Takarada written all over it. Once they were all aboard the hatch door shut tight, sealing them, Iscariot and the guards in.

SHOOOOMP!

Nathan looked about the control room, then complemented the

doctor on his keen ability to create such a fantastic piece of work, one based off of somebody else's brilliant ideas.

"Just like rap music," Tommy added, and Nathan cracked up. More so because Tommy had been a bit quiet after that whole "hand" thing, so Nathan knew if he was back to being his typical smartass self, he must've felt better.

"Yes, Mr. Fox," the doctor replied, "you are right in zinking zis looks like zee Tomoyuki."

This got Nathan's attention, that and the fact that Doctor Chicken here knew his name. Nathan was still trying to play it cool, but if Iscariot knew who he was, it could only mean trouble. Because if he did indeed kill Pamela Fox, there was no way he didn't know that Nathan knew.

Iscariot ran his long, thin hand along the surface of a large, computer-looking machine that stretched almost the entire length of the ship's inside wall. He had a sinister look on his face, very similar to the one he donned while stroking King Taraxian's giant talon. It was a very odd contraption, and there was no denying he was very proud of it. It wasn't only mechanical though, it was organic as well, with plant-like cables that ran inside and out of the console in a mesh of electrified vines. The computer was living and breathing, containing the elements key to King Taraxian's existence. It also held that final component, the one that made this all possible, what Jack had thought to be the black magic holding it all together.

"Notawni Nonaashi" were the words that seeped through Iscariot's clenched teeth and, convinced the doctor was casting an evil spell of some sort, Nathan and Tommy hit the deck. After their share of Yokai witches, they would both agree that one tends to get a bit jumpy when questionable types start lobbing peculiar phrases in your direction.

"No you boneheads!" Olivia shrieked, "Notawni Nonaashi is the actual name given to King Taraxian by Native Americans. Remember when the president spoke in his address of the Navajo legend?"

"Very good, Olivia, you are indeed zee smart one of zee group," Iscariot noted, "But it is no legend, unt zee spirit of Notawni Nonaashi is very much a fact. It was freed upon zee same nuclear explosion zat killed your entire family."

"That's ridiculous!" Olivia snarled, and the doctor sneered back at her. "Unt like Yokai are ridiculous, unt like zee daikaiju are ridiculous, unt like your family being vaporized is ridiculous. It seems zat ridiculous is zee new norm in zis day unt age. Zee legend is true, unt King Taraxian lives!"

Olivia didn't hate hearing the truth about the legend as much as she hated this twisted man speaking her name. It was also obvious Iscariot knew who they were far beyond that of normal nemesis protocol. Most evil, bad-guy types wouldn't take the time to get to know their victims, that is unless it was crucial to their plan, which in this case it was.

"Okay then," Tommy fired back, "you seem to know a lot about this Indian spirit-god, Natalie No-Tushie, or whatever its name is. You also seem to know a lot about us. So why don't you tell us a little about you. I mean that's only fair, right?"

"Absolutely, Mr. Taylor, you are indeed correct," and Iscariot acknowledged Tommy with a humble nod. Even though this was all part of his plan.

"At one time, I vas zee vorld's most gifted neurologist. Zat is unt why Sir Jonathon recruited me in zee first place. He convinced me zat my talents unt superior abilities in encephalon studies made me a perfect choice for zee Earth Intelligence Organization. He alzo offered me endless resources, recognition, unt zee opportunity to work with zee greatest scientific minds of our time. He said it vas a vunce in a lifetime opportunity and it would not be offered again."

Tommy snuck a peek at Nathan from the corner of his eye, as they both had heard a similar recruitment spiel from ol' Jack them-damn-selves. Sir Jonathon was good, a real master when it came to getting what he wanted. He also had a keen sense of knowing just what that person needed as he dangled it right in front of their face. It was quite unsettling how Iscariot's story sounded a little like their own.

"Sir Jonathon chose me to head up zee team for his advanced neuro-computer program, unt zat is where I met a very young Kyoshi

Takarada. We verked together for many years on unt many zings, including zee subconscious mind operational system zat eventually vas used in zee Duke. Takarada unt I alzo created—"

"So speaking of the Duke, where is tall, dank and ugly anyhow?"

The doctor wasn't used to being interrupted and almost lost it on Tommy for cutting him off, but instead leveraged the question to his advantage.

"Zee robot is in pieces at zee bottom of Yokohama Bay, along with every vessel unt aircraft zat dared to go up against me, unt my Notawni Nonaashi."

Of course that wasn't quite accurate, as the Duke had saved at least one ship, not to mention a few fighters, from all sides of the war. He wasn't going to tell them that though, because he knew that wouldn't gain their allegiance.

"You know, I zaved all of your lives. You would have surely died had I not pulled all of you out of zat tin can, zat piece of shit zey call a robot."

Tommy thanked Iscariot for being such a damn good Samaritan, you know, for saving their lives and all. Obviously he did it out of the sheer goodness of his heart, it's not like he wanted anything in return. Tommy then agreed that the Duke wasn't the best idea, and that maybe the Americans could have come up with a better plan. He knew that their intentions were good even though he disliked the president at the moment. They were only pawns in Iscariot's plan of turning country against country in order to exhaust their resources. Then when they were beaten down, Iscariot would step in with the only supply of regenerating power left on Planet Earth, the organic thorium. But Tommy still had hope, as he knew at least one thing that the doctor did not.

Iscariot forced out his best fake grin (which wasn't fooling anybody) and asked if Tommy would like to hear zee rest of his story.

"By all means Doc, don't let me interrupt you," Tommy stated, and Iscariot mentioned that he already had.

Then Tommy asked, "Had what?" and Iscariot said,

"Interrupted me," and Tommy inquired,

"When?" and the doctor said,

"just now."

Tommy responded with a, "No, I don't think so Doc," and Nathan then jumped in saying,

"I think you did, Tommy," then Tommy said,

"What?"

"Interrupted him," Nathan replied.

"About what?" Tommy asked, and Nathan looked over to Iscariot, "Yeah, about what, Doc?"

The doctor was getting flat worn out and started contemplating killing them on the spot and finding the new organic thorium refinery on his own. He probably would have too, just when the very thought of the element jarred his memory.

"Zee Duke!" Iscariot shouted with a big smile, "Vee were talking about zee Duke!"

Tommy looked confused and gazed at Iscariot, "What about the Duke?"

The doctor began shouting something or another in German, then pushed his palms towards the floor in an effort to calm himself. Olivia, like Iscariot, wanted to punch both Tommy and Nathan in the head, but at the same time was glad she wasn't the only one they drove crazy. She looked at Iscariot, seeing what a few minutes with these idiots had reduced him to, and for a second she almost felt sorry for him … almost.

"Unt as I vas saying. Along with zee neuro-computer program, I alzo spent many years with Takarada on zee creation of organic thorium. Unt zis is why it is as much mine, if not more zo zan it is his. But it vas my unt experiments with spiritual entities unt demonic forces zat zese fools did not understand! Zey feared I vas not ready, unt I vas unstable! Unt when I would not stop, zose schweinehuds, Sir Jonathon unt Kyoshi Takarada, had me abolished!"

It was becoming pretty obvious to everybody just why the hell the E.I.O. had ousted Doctor Fun here. Olivia then asked him that if he did indeed know the secret to developing organic thorium, why did he go through all the trouble of stealing it? Iscariot, again complimented her on being the smart one and answered her question with one of his own.

"Tell me, my dear, what is zee most valuable component of organic thorium?"

It didn't take but a second and Olivia knew, even though she didn't answer.

"Yes, both you unt I know, we both know zat zee Glaucusidious cells are zee key! We also know zay aren't too easy to come by, unt vithout them, it is useless. But soon zat vill not be zee problem either! Unt soon I vill show zem, I vill show zem all!"

Nobody knew where the doctor was going with all of this Glaucusidious jazz, but it seemed that while he was talking, they were safe. What was obvious was his distaste for Jack, Takarada and anything to do with the E.I.O. At least that's what Nathan was gathering, and if he could play on that assumption, maybe they could buy some more time.

"So doc, speaking of stolen organic thorium, how did you lift the O.T. from London anyhow? Whatever you did, it was freakin' genius.

I'll bet big, fat Jack and Takarada still have no idea how you did it."

Iscariot's eyes shrunk into two curious clefts and he glared at Nathan, weighing out the pros and cons were he to tell the hows and whys. After a bit of consideration, the doctor figured he had nothing to lose. Besides, he was either going to force Nathan, Tommy and Olivia along with the Twins to join him, or he would eliminate them all, that simple. Plus, he was dying to tell someone.

"I am zo glad you asked zat my boy, unt I vould love to tell you. While you unt zee E.I.O. were preoccupied vith Oko Rikoku unt her demons, I had already assumed control of zee giant spider-god. I verked right under everybody's noses in zee desert wasteland of Zalt Lake Zitty. With zee exception of a handful of survivors it vas completely barren, even your government made it a point to stay away. As vee dug deep into zee earth, I found out zat zee Navajo myth was, in fact, real. Zare, far beneath zee rotting desert, I found what zee Natives had named Notawni Nonaashi. Unt even zoe it vas still dormant, it had been freed, unt vas feeding off of zee poisoned land, readying itself."

"Readying itself for what?" Tommy asked. The doctor scowled at him for again interrupting his story. He then asked Tommy what he thought an angry Navajo god, one that was buried deep in an atomic-laden desert in the form of a colossal spider, would be readying itself for. Tommy figured it out.

"Anyvay," he continued, "zis gave me a unique opportunity to test my new machine, to zee if I could extract the spiritual essence of an entity, one zat resided in any kind of host. Unt vith zis beautiful machine, I not only succeeded, but I found I could alzo control zee spirit with my neuro-computer. Unt after a few large doses of strontium 90, zee beast mutated at an abnormal rate. Unt even zo it was of a spiritual nature, it's body vas not, unt I had to construct its titanium robotic infrastructure zo it could support its own weight. Zee unt obstacle however, vas zat of powering zee great creature. It could verk on nuclear fusion, but I needed somezing with a bigger oomf, I needed zee organic thorium. It vas upon zat thought alone zat my plan came full circle. My vision of power unt world domination came to me in zat fleeting zecond."

Olivia balked. She wasn't buying any of this crap, or at least she was pretending not to, which of course only fueled Iscariot's need to prove his genius. So he promised her a demonstration, just as soon as he was done with his freakin' long-ass monologue.

"Zee spider had innate burrowing capabilities, unt I tested my machine's capacity to control zee beast by having it tunnel its vay to Europe. It caused a few quakes, but I had it dig deep enough not to arouse suspicion. Upon reaching zee secret refinery under zee palace in London, I claimed my portion of O.T. from beneath the earth. Unt vile I did zat, Zargatron came from above to retrieve his. I vould have taken all of it too, but needed to leave some behind for Oko Rikoku as to not make her, or Sir Jonathon, suspicious. It was an unfortunate must, but I knew I needed to keep the world's focus on Rikoku's ploy of intergalactic domination. Zen when her plan failed, as I knew it would, I could execute mine, showing zose fools at zee Earth Intelligence Organization, unt zat goody-goody, Kyoshi Takarada, just who zee real genius was."

Iscariot started to go all mad-scientist like and began laughing maniacally.

"Whoa," Tommy stated, and Olivia, not skeptical but curious, asked him about King Taraxian's heat mechanism.

"Ah yes," he said as he nodded, "zee heat mechanism. Zis vas always part of Notawni Nonaashi's supernatural abilities. I hate to admit it, but I did not create zee monster's heat pulse or ray. I did, however, turn it up substantially upon powering zee arachnid vith organic thorium. I did not expect zis to happen, a fortunate zide effect, unt he who controls zee spider, controls zee ray. Vun zat is quite handy ven it comes to destroying zittys, unt zer millions of inhabitants."

Iscariot then dragged his index finger down the front of his freaky computer, stopping at three adjacent toggle-type switches. He flipped them, one after the other, and a panel on his machine lifted exposing a glass container. It wasn't very big, not at all; you could hold it between your two hands at a shoulders width. Even though the capsule was small, it looked like it held something similar to our galaxy itself, and the doctor grinned as he admired it.

"Now, as promised, a demonstration of zee greatest neuro-discovery known to man. Inside zis container is Notawni Nonaashi, zee very spirit of zee god itself! Unt I control it!"

He asked his guests to gather around the craft's viewing portholes and to please look into the hangar where the sleeping spider stood. Iscariot pressed a few buttons, flipped a couple more switches and spoke towards the machine.

"Nay-Nih-Jih!"

Both Tommy and Nathan again started getting a little nervous, and Olivia reassured them he was speaking Navajo and not casting ancient Yokai spells. King Taraxian all of a sudden gave the impression that a great switch had been flipped, and the monster came to life. The eye of its new faceplate flickered twice, then glowed in bright red and it awaited its orders.

"Na-Na-O-Nalth!"

The beast lifted its new leg and slammed the claw of its tarsus deep into the steel cast flooring of the hanger.

KRAM!

"Very good," the doctor hissed.

Then the spider lowered its modified, metal skull down towards Iscariot's craft, just outside the windows that everybody was watching from. Its sharp pincers spread apart, and as a cream-colored swill dripped from its jaw, the horrible thing screamed, "GRAAAAAAAAAAP!"

They shrieked and jumped back from the portholes, and this made Iscariot giggle.

"You zee, it does vatever I tell it." He picked up an oval microphone and stretched its coiled cord in order to also look out one of the ship's round, glass windows. When he spoke into it, his voice thundered throughout the giant hangar. "Unt very good, gentlemen. Unt be ready to disembark on my zay-zo."

Iscariot hung the mic back up and bellowed one more command.

"Tah-Ah-Kwo-Dih!"

The spider stretched its long legs and again propelled up with its back against the ceiling of the colossal bay. Its eye flickered twice, then went black and the beast was still. Olivia gasped. She couldn't get a grip on the concept and was sticking to her claim of ridiculous, this time adding a, "That's impossible!"

His sideways smile grew longer, "Yes, zat is vut everybody said, my dear, but I, Doctor Leopold Iscariot, vound zee secret to zyphoning a spirit's very essence!" He rubbed his palm down the side of his computer again. "Unt, zis is it, unt I discovered it, vile verking on zee electronically-induced, sleep-state technology."

"No way, Doc," Nathan said, more so in an effort to keep Iscariot yacking. He didn't doubt the doctor's claim. He was just hoping for more time to figure something out.

"Oh, but it is true, Mr Fox, unt soon I von't even need zis large computer to operate it either." The doctor pulled a small, velvet, flip-top case from his side pocket, opened it and showed them the next evolution of his great machine. "In zis syringe is zee fully operational microchip needed for me to control everyzing from right here." As he said this, Iscariot tapped the side of his head with one finger, then put the needle to his temple with the other.

"Are you nuts?" Tommy yelled, followed by a, "Wait, let me rephrase that. Are you nuts?"

Olivia shook her head and told Iscariot to, "Please go right ahead, and don't let any of us stop you."

"I know vut you are zinking, Ms. Olivetti, you are hoping zis vill kill me. Vell, vee shall zee in a moment, won't we? But I must add it is unt similar to zee chips zat were alzo implanted in all of you."

They all stared at Iscariot after his claim, mostly in complete disbelief, even though a bit of suspicion couldn't help but show itself.

"What a load of shit," Olivia shouted, adding it to her previous list of "ridiculous" and "that's impossible."

The doctor again laughed, "Unt why is zat zo impossible? Zare is no vay zee sleep-state can work without zee microchip implants, zat is vat is impossible. You zink you know zee E.I.O. so well, my little liebchens, zare is probably unt tracking devices in your chips as vell. Unt let's not forget zee standard static charge either. At any unt time, your frenz, Sir Jonathon unt Takarada, can turn your brains to jelly vith zee mere press of a button. Zis is standard E.I.O. protocol." Iscariot stopped, "Zey may have failed to mention zis to you." He then plunged the needle deep into his skull.

Chapter XIX

Mount Terror towered to the frostbitten heavens of Antarctica, casting its lumbering shadow across the frozen island fortress from which it stood. Both Jack and Takarada had agreed early on that the dormant volcano was the only logical choice. Not only had Mother Nature surrounded it with ice and rock a hundred miles wide and almost two miles deep, she had also provided them with the coldest spot on planet Earth. It truly was a chilling tundra of death where temperatures sometimes fell to 200° below zero. Pretty horrible living conditions indeed, but the setting was perfect for battling giant spiders that emitted heat so extreme it could melt your face off. Not to mention it was remote and uninhabited, as most weren't stupid enough to go anywhere near the foul place, nobody but the Earth Intelligence Organization that is.

Sir Jonathon and Doctor Takarada had vacated E.I.O. West and were scheduled to arrive in Japan in just a few short hours. From there they would transfer to an F.U. fighter, then head straight to the new Mount Terror base, and to where Jack had relocated the organic thorium. And with a little luck the frozen fortress would be ready, or at least functional enough for what Sir Jonathon thought was sure to be the last stand. But first they had to make a slight detour to Yokohama to meet with the president of the United States and the prime ministers of both Japan and England.

As they flew, Takarada kept a watchful eye on the blinking five blips of life that appeared on his laptop. This proved to him that Nathan, Tommy, Olivia and the Twins were not only at the FUJI, but were still alive. It also proved that Iscariot was telling the truth about those microchips implanted in their heads. Takarada tapped the computer's keyboard as the index finger of his other hand percussed nervously against the side of his seat. He, like Jack, knowing Iscariot had assumed control of the FUJI, knew the mountainous base didn't have much longer. But that was always part of the plan, only neither had ever counted on Iscariot getting his hands on their agents.

Jack placed his hand on Takarada's shoulder as he knew what he was thinking.

"Don't worry Kyoshi, they'll be fine. This is what they have been trained for." Then he added, "It's Iscariot I'd be worried about. Ten minutes alone with Nathan Fox is enough to make even the most insane go bloody mad."

Takarada didn't even flinch, then asked, "Do you believe Leopold will take the bait, Sir Jonathon?"

"I have no ruddy idea, Kyoshi, but the organic thorium beacon we sent should have reached his intel by now. He'll know it's a trap, but at least in that frozen cesspool we'll have a bloody chance against that blasted spider of his. Kyoshi," he added, "Iscariot was coming for the organic thorium, no matter where it was or how many people he would need to kill to get it. This *was* the absolute best plan possible."

Takarada concurred, but was still worried. He couldn't help it. While he watched the pulsating blips from his laptop, Takarada wished they could have recovered the Duke from Yokohama Bay before Iscariot had gotten to it. At least that way they could have retrieved not only the cowbot, but all on board. But that was a fallacy at best, as no living thing (other than that godforsaken spider) could have come within a mile of the boiling waters that saturated the Pacific. Takarada was certain that this was when Iscariot must have transported the agents to the FUJI, no doubt utilizing the half-spider, half … whatever it was to do so. Once again, he caught himself drifting on the spectacular design of the giant arachnid, when the thought of its robotic infrastructure brought his mind back to the Duke. He was almost sure the mech was not at all operational after being blasted by King Taraxian's heat mechanism. But still, he could not say he was 100% positive, because in the past, he had witnessed firsthand what this so-called, subpar, cowboy robot was capable of. That may also be why he had grown quite fond of the American's towering heap (after he had modified the hell out of it of course). But still, the giant, lanky bot seemed to have something very special indeed, heart. Because as Takarada knew, when the chips were down and when all else failed, that was your best option. But even if the Duke was inoperable, he knew, in the same way he knew about Nathan, Tommy and everybody else, that SCOTT was not.

Playtime had come to an end for Iscariot. He was getting nowhere with Tommy, Nathan and Olivia and was growing weary of the FUJI. He needed answers, and if they weren't going to give them to him, he wanted them dead, plain and simple.

"Vare is zee organic thorium?" He exploded. "Sir Jonathon unt zee E.I.O. are telling you lies! It is zey who vant a world run by a totalitarian cabal! Vith zee organic thorium, unt my machine, vee can persuade all countries to live in peace, or not to live at all!" He waited for a response, but got nothing. "Tell me vare zee organic thorium is! Tell me now, unt tomorrow vee march on Tokyo, then zee world!"

A twisted vein shot down Iscariot's frustrated forehead, he then staggered and placed his palm over his feverish brow. He was burning up, and his heated skin moistened the inside of his hand when he attempted to wipe his face dry. The microchip was settling, lodging itself deep within his skull as a thousand fiber tracts merged with it, making it one with his brain. His pupils dilated then his eyes rolled back into his head. He felt faint, and the syringe he was holding slipped between his fingers and dropped to the floor. Iscariot struggled to stand, but clung to his neuro-computing machine, thus preventing him from completely falling. Nathan, Tommy and Olivia stared at him, not saying so much as a word. Iscariot could feel their condescending glares upon him. They had no intentions of joining him and only looked at the doctor as a fool gone mad. One of his guards rushed to his aid, and while the crony helped straighten out the discombobulated doctor, he whispered something into his ear. Iscariot sneered out a busted-up smile. This was what he was waiting for and he had no more need to even pretend anymore. He wasn't going to get anything from the agents anyhow, so the mad doctor let the son-of-a-bitching snake he really was rear its bad self. He wiped the condensation from his damp head, then peered at Nathan.

"I am zo zorry about your father. By zee way, did you ever find out vut kind of cancer it vas zat took his unt life?"

Nathan didn't answer and only stared back.

"You didn't? Vell I know! It's a new strain, one I am led to understand zat slowly destroys all of your internal organs over zee course of a few years. Did you know it vas your father zat convinced

Sir Jonathon zat I vus crazy? Vell, it vas, it was alzo he who led zee commission zat got me abolished from zee E.I.O."

Nathan still didn't say a word, but stated a proud, "Way to go pop!" from the inside of his head.

"Unt did you alzo know zat Pamela, your mother, vas my assistant even before meeting your father? And did you know zat it vas your father who talked her into testifying against me unt my methods? I'll bet you didn't! Unt zat is probably why she spent zo much time at home after zee hearings, because she vas terrified! Terrified because on zee last day, as zey escorted me out, I unt whispered a soft promise in her ear. I said I vas coming for her, zen I was coming for you. Zee stress must have been unbearable on your dad. It may even have caused him to take zee drink or two. It's too bad, especially about your mother. Pamela was a good woman, at least she vas before she met your father. But isn't it unt funny, Nathan, how accidents happen?"

Nathan couldn't handle it and that calm-demeanor cover he was trying so hard to hold onto exploded. And call it a coincidence, but it was also at that moment that (thanks to the precious few minutes he had stolen while Iscariot babbled on) he was able to come up with an idea. It was truly a brilliant scheme, the perfect plan, and Nathan erupted from where he stood and lunged fists-first at Iscariot for a second time. Tommy and Olivia didn't even move, as they were still a few moments back in time, trying to decipher the doctor's story about Nathan's mom and dad. They honestly had no clue to what Iscariot was talking about, but both let out a resounding, "Oh" when Nathan shouted,

"You killed my parents you bastard!"

Nathan connected to the doctor's chin with a powerful right hook, and Iscariot, already lightheaded from the shot, fell to the floor. Every weapon from every guard that was stationed in the craft encircled Nathan, and the photon rifles pulsed as they readied to fire. Two guards reached down and yanked Nathan up while the others grabbed Tommy and Olivia by their elbows holding them into place.

"I have been vatching you for a long time Nathan, you unt your frenz. I am sure zee last few months have not been easy. It is unt hard to live life on life's terms ven you have never known how to do zo. Zumtime's zee emotions are too much to handle, unt zumtimes a little pick-me-up is in order."

The doctor grinned at Nathan and snapped his fingers in the air. One of the doctor's cronies entered the cabin. He was carrying an elegant platter supporting a glass filled with ice, and next to that stood a bottle of Jack. Iscariot picked the crystal container from the silver dish and filled it with bourbon. He swirled the glass in his hand and the ice made that tinkling sound, the one Nathan loved oh so much. He put the edge to his nose and took in the aroma, then he even took a small sip.

"Aaaah," he proclaimed. "Zee reward of a long day's toil."

The guards held Nathan, and Iscariot circled the glass and its contents right under his nose.

"C'mon, my boy," he teased, "no one can fault you if I unt force you."

"You're effing sick!" Olivia yelled, and both she and Tommy struggled to get free. Nathan backed up and winced when the alluring smell of his favorite Kentucky bourbon flowed into his nostrils. It was that familiar scent, sweet, yet poisonous, and more terrifying to him than a thousand King Taraxians. Nathan licked his lips, pushed back on the guard who held him captive and kicked the glass out of Iscariot's hand, right into his machine.

ZEEEEEP!

Sparks shot out of it as the liquid infiltrated its circuit boards, then the bolts of electricity turned to smoke. The doctor watched his computer hack and cough, then Nathan reminded him that even the smoothest of whiskeys can kick like a mule.

When Iscariot turned towards him, Nathan thought he was a goner for sure after busting up his machine with the lethal cocktail. He prepared himself for impact, but the doctor only smiled, then the smile grew back into that creepy maniacal laugh of his. Nathan thought about all of the bullshit emotions he'd been going through since he quit drinking. He suddenly felt quite calm, taking comfort in the fact that he wasn't even half as crazy as this freakin' ass-hat, Iscariot.

The irritating laughter subsided and the doctor stood erect. He folded his arms, then eased his eyes shut. Nathan looked about the cabin, trying to figure out what the hell Iscariot was doing, hoping it wasn't what he thought. But when an intense high-pitched ring began to emit throughout the hangar, Nathan knew it was *exactly* what he had hoped it wasn't.

King Taraxian's red-jeweled eye flickered twice, and it stood in a receptive state, awaiting its commands. Iscariot twitched, then the beast turned about and lumbered into what remained of the runway tunnel towards the great pit from whence it had come. It climbed in and as it descended, Iscariot's army of insect-shaped ships began to lift off in sequence, following the spider one after the other into the deep, dark shaft. The crafts were quiet and over them you could hear King Taraxian's high-pitched frequency, decreasing in sound the further away it got, until it couldn't be heard at all.

Nathan and Tommy stood in sheer amazement. Even Olivia was blown away by the complexity of the doctor's brilliant achievements. He was quite mad, there was no doubt about it, but it did prove one thing. If he did get his hands on the organic thorium, he would indeed be more powerful than any country on the planet, even more so than the Earth Intelligence Organization.

Nathan started to freak out a little the more Iscariot's plan began to unfold. Obviously through the chain of catastrophic events that had taken place Nathan knew, but that didn't mean he really "knew." It was sort of like listening to a song for twenty-some years until one day you finally realize just how fantastic, or maybe how horrible, it really is. He could feel the old butterflies in his stomach flutter, and the more he got it, the less he liked understanding just what the hell was happening. After all, there was a long list of earthbound spirits just chomping at the bit for the chance to again walk the planet. It scared him to know that this one man, this insane doctor, was able to control the essence of a god such as Notawni Nonaashi. He didn't get the details of course, but that's probably one of the elements that drove Iscariot mad, so Nathan didn't want to know. But seeing that he could now control them simply from his mind sent a cold chill down the back of his spine. Upon King Taraxian's departure, he also figured out that the doctor's army of flying insectoid machines were pilotless drones, and like the giant spider, it seemed he was able to control them as well. At least that's what it looked like. It was unsettling to him just how bats this Iscariot guy was, and there was no telling how many times he had stuck needles into his head either. Nathan was pretty sure this wasn't the first time. But even while being blanketed in his little veil of self-epiphanies, there was still something that puzzled Nathan, something far more than anything else, and he peered at Iscariot.

"Where the hell did you get the scratch to build all of this cool shit? I mean, are you kidding me? I know the E.I.O. is funded by the governments of every free country on the planet in exchange for protection, so that's a no-brainer. But I don't think anybody even really likes you, let alone would give you the cash to outfit such an organization. And there is no way, no way your mad-scientist, neurosurgeon pension comes even close to covering a fraction of all the stuff you've got!"

Iscariot squirmed up to Nathan. He wanted the Lizard King to feel the heat of his hideous breath as he hissed the answer into his ear,

"Kickstarter."

"Take zem avay! Unt lock zem in one of zee steel storage garages, we are unt leaving. Plot a course for Antarctica, unt zet zee charges to go off in twenty minutes, zat vill be enough time for us to get unt far away."

Iscariot's top gorilla pointed into the now vacant hangar at Michael and Liberty, who were still shackled to the doctor's iron stretching apparatus.

"What about the two aliens' sir?" he asked.

Iscariot rubbed his chin.

"Leave zem. I won't have time for such nonsense now. If zey stay separated, zare is nothing zey can do. Zey will die here, with zee rest of zem."

Iscariot began to exit the cabin when something occurred to him. He slithered up to Tommy and made that face of "ooops, I almost forgot," then reached behind Tommy's two captors and again pried his super-damn-hand back off.

"You won't be needing zis," he snarled, and the guards hauled them out of the craft.

Iscariot's remaining men placed explosives throughout the base, while another team of guards escorted Tommy, Olivia and Nathan towards one of the installation's storage facilities: massive garages within the hangar that had been excavated into the walls. Some stored various FUJI vehicles, and some were designated maintenance areas for jets and such. One even held all of Vinyl Crush's giant, arena-sized staging, along with all of their touring equipment. Now just to give you a better idea of the size of these stalls, it took four semi-trucks and trailers to transport all of their gear. Yeah, they were pretty big. Each sporting its own three-story, accordion-style, steel-reinforced garage door with nothing but a two-inch-thick iron entry adjacent to each one. There were no additional exits, and once you were locked inside, you weren't going anywhere. They all knew it had to be now or never, because once they were imprisoned inside one of these giant metal boxes within the mountain, there would be no escape.

Of course Olivia could see what was happening in front of her, but at the moment she was more concerned about what was going on from behind. She eased her head about halfway around, and as she did, she ran the scenario in her mind, because it was nothing more than a simple matter of math. There were four guards total leading them in a straight line, a line that (from front to back) went, Tommy, guard, Olivia, guard, Nathan, guard, plus an additional guard taking up the outer rear. She crunched the numbers and it didn't take long at all to formulate a solution, one that would solve the equation they were in.

Olivia stopped, then proceeded to bend over right in front of one of the armed guards. He must have liked what he saw and that's probably why it took an extra second for him to lodge the tip of his rifle deep into her spine.

She, without so much as looking up and in her sultriest of voices asked, "Can't a girl even tie her shoe?"

The guard, obviously enamored, smiled and pointed out that her boots didn't have any laces.

"Oh, my bad," she said, and she back-kicked the photon weapon out of his hands and right into Nathan's. Nathan, who was enjoying the scenery him-damn-self, was just as surprised as Iscariot's guard, and the gun almost slipped through his fingers. As he fumbled trying to get a grip on it, Olivia rolled her eyes as he looked more like Jerry Lewis than a suave secret agent. He reached underneath the barrel and (unintentionally of course) pulled back on what appeared to be a safety mechanism, and it began to fire in all directions.

"Holy shit!" Tommy yelled and he and Olivia hit the deck.

FWAP! FWAP! FWAP!

When Nathan finally got a grip on the rifle, the shots of bursting energy subsided, and everybody was lying on the floor. Well, everybody except him. Still a bit shaky and a little freaked out, Nathan surveyed the scene and both Tommy and Olivia sat up.

"That was some heap a fine shootin' there, Tex," Tommy

complimented from the side of his mouth. "I don't know how partner, but ya seemed to get ever' last one of them varmints."

Nathan gave a self-approving nod, then stuck out his lower lip to commemorate himself on a job well done, when the wail of the evac sirens pulled him out of the moment.

Iscariot's craft began to blast its "Let's get the hell out of here" horns, and his remaining men filed onto the ship as it prepared to leave. Tommy, Nathan and Olivia looked across the vast distance, the one that spanned between them, the Twins and the elevator that brought them down. Maybe they'd have enough time to rescue Michael and Liberty, then haul ass to the lift and to one of the upper exit points. While they ran, Nathan felt a pain in his pocket as something pushed up against his skin. He put his hand over his thigh and felt a plastic bulge. "Ha!" he thought, Iscariot may have remembered Tommy's hand, but he had indeed forgotten about the remote for the device that held the Twins captive! Nathan pulled the device out and aimed it at Michael, who was bound ten feet up in an "X" position, just like Liberty next to him. He pressed one of the buttons and Michael screamed when the machine stretched his body in four different directions.

"Sorry!" Nathan yelled, "wrong button."

He pressed another and both Liberty and Michael were set free from the contraption and they fell to the floor. Tommy and Nathan lifted Michael up, resting each of his arms on their shoulders while Olivia helped Liberty to her feet. Even though they were awake, they were in pretty bad shape, and Nathan knew there wouldn't be any alien miracles saving the day.

The jet turbines on Iscariot's craft whined, and its thrusters exploded from beneath it.

SHOOOOM!

The ship then rose up and began to lower into the long tunnel King Taraxian had dug from the sea.

Tommy looked over and yelled, "You jerk! I want my freakin' hand back!" and he raised his arm and gave the descending craft the wrist, which would have been the finger, had he had any.

As the craft descended, a series of well-placed charges that outlined the massive hole exploded one after the other, sealing the spider's giant pit.

BOOSH! BOOSH! KABOOSH!

All five watched Iscariot make his getaway. Nathan screamed "C'MON!" and they made their way to their last chance, the elevator, the one that blew up before they could even get anywhere near it!

BOOOOSH!

Both Tommy and Nathan shouted, "Shit!" in unison, just as all of the other charges started going off.

Various parts of the tremendous bay went up, and when they did, the top of it started coming down. They huddled close, trying to shield the tired Twins from the falling rock and metal. There was no way out, and if the mighty hangar caved in, that no doubt meant the end of the FUJI. Tommy and Nathan dragged Michael and Liberty close to one of the giant garage doors, as the upper frame that encased it offered a bit of temporary protection from the collapsing base. A small shard of tin mixed with broken cement found its way to Nathan's forehead, and a stream of blood ran down the side of his face. Olivia knelt down beside him and wiped it away the best she could with the tip of her sleeve. Nathan grabbed her hand, and as he looked at Olivia, her glasses slipped down the bridge of her nose. He smiled and before she could nudge them up, he took them off and pulled her face to his.

It was one of those memorable kisses, not just another ordinary, run-of-the-mill-type kiss either. It was an "it's about time" kind of kiss, and all it took was the freakin' collapse of the mighty Mount Fujisan to make it happen. It was the longest Nathan had ever kissed a girl without opening his mouth, and at that moment he knew he was in love with Olivia. Both saw the fireworks and each could feel the earth move beneath them while everything exploded and the planet tumbled down around them. Michael, with what little strength he had, tapped Tommy on the shoulder and tilted his head toward Nathan and Olivia.

"I freakin' knew it," Tommy yelled, and he and Michael cracked up, as a matter of fact, they all did. What else could they do?

It was then that from the opposite side of one of the storage facility's steel-reinforced doors, something was coming to life, something that wanted "out" in the worst way. And due to the collapsing of the FUJI, nobody could hear its low-throated growl, giving them no clue whatsoever to its fast approach. Nor could they feel the vibration of the megaton monster as its treads brought its giant

197

silver plow up to ramming speed. That is until it smashed through the enormous door of the garage in which it, and three more, were kept.

SMASH!

With its two-tone horn blasting, the death-machine burst from within, ripping through the center of the massive wall of metal that held it captive!

FWOMP! FWOMP!

Other than pictures or videos, it was the first time Nathan or Tommy had ever laid eyes on one of the agency's horrid evac-vehicles. Nathan couldn't believe the size of it and figured out why other members of the Earth Intelligence Organization had dubbed these demons, "The Death Machines."

The giant behemoth thundered up on its four sets of treads, and upon its abrasive stop, its armored chassis rocked back and forth until it stabilized. It was then that the driver's door kicked open and SCOTT jumped down from the machine. He didn't say a word and went right to picking Michael and Liberty up, carrying one in each of his arms before placing them into the cab of the vehicle. Tommy was of course happy, but at the same time, wasn't surprised at all about the arrival of his android friend, he knew damn well he'd be there. The fact being that amidst Iscariot's rambling, Tommy had figured out that he had no clue that SCOTT was onboard the Duke when they were pulled from it. Hell, he wondered if Doctor Chicken knew if Takarada's creation even existed, he very well may not have. Either way though, it didn't really matter if he knew or not, Tommy thought to himself. All that mattered was that this was going to come back to bite Iscariot right in his hasty, arrogant ass.

Tommy and Nathan filed into the front next to SCOTT, while Olivia climbed into the back with the Twins. As soon as everybody was in, they all began to bombard him with an array of "what the hell took you so longs?" But the android only grinned, not wanting to bother anybody with the drawn out, boring details. He then pointed out that with the compound caving in and all, maybe they should be less concerned about that and more concerned about leaving.

Tommy agreed, he even smiled because he liked this new SCOTT, then announced in his best game-show-host voice, "SCOTT 2.0, better, stronger, faster and quite the smartass."

SCOTT nodded, he liked it too. He then shoved the long stick-shift into gear, followed by another couple blasts of its thundering horn.

FWOMP! FWOMP!

In one massive thrust, the death machine charged forward towards the mouth of the cave and the remains of the FUJI's tunneling runway. The ground still smoked, and tremendous chunks of earth were still falling from where the explosions had sealed King Taraxian's exit point. But it was the only way out, and while this was indeed a concern for SCOTT, there simply was no other way. It was also impossible for the android to calculate the outcome, so all he could do was hope (as much as an artificial lifeform could) that the weight of the vehicle wouldn't cause it to collapse into the deep pit of the spider. The top of the hole was still smoldering, and the fresh dirt and debris that now covered it was pretty damn flimsy. But there was really no way around it, and going back wasn't an option, because the FUJI was doomed.

KARAAAAAAM!

The iron beams that spanned the entire length of the fifty-story hangar's ceiling snapped in succession, while the massive girders that supported everything came crashing down. This was immediately followed by a downpour of earth that fell like the granules of a magnificent hourglass, one that had run out of time. This was it, the end of the FUJI.

"Oh my God!" Tommy shouted as boulders of flaming rock reigned down upon them, both denting and penetrating the thick armor of the death machine.

"Hold on please," SCOTT said in a very calm fashion and he pushed the pedal to the metal. The beast moaned and spewed thick bursts of black clouds from its twin smokestacks, screaming with its great silver shovel leading the way! Nathan reached his arm to the back seat so he could hold Olivia's hand, with the plan of gazing deep into her eyes until impact. Olivia thought it was quite romantic, but it only grew awkward as they stared and stared, then stared some more, but there was still no blistering crash. Nathan pulled his hand back, then looked through the windshield. It seemed as though they were taking off and into the air from within the damn tunnel, right over the freakin' spider pit of doom! SCOTT didn't go through it, hell, he didn't even go around it, he went over the damn thing while everything caved in from behind!

SHOOOOOOOOOM!

Both Nathan and Tommy screamed, "YEEEEEEHAW!" and they rocketed in slow motion right over the spider's buried pit to loud banjo music playing in the background.

They collided with the other side, clearing King Taraxian's deep shaft, (one that surely would have sent them to their deaths) but were now faced with having to plow their way through the debris of the decimated runway tunnel. Asphalt, dirt and rock ricocheted in all directions as the great plow of the death machine cleared the way, the same way they did on the congested freeways. Its mighty treads pummeled the earth into powder while they made their getaway. The tunnel was pitch dark and at least two miles long, lit only by the dim glow that reflected in the veins of the vehicle's cracking glass.

SCOTT told Olivia to pull the Twins to the floor and get both her and them behind the seat. He also advised Tommy and Nathan to stay as low as possible and get beneath the dash. Nathan was about to ask "Why?" when the thick windshield shattered into a billion pieces.

SPEEEESH!

Rubble came hurling into the cab, and SCOTT reached up and bent the roof inward to act as a protective shield. He lowered himself in order to see through the gap in the barrier he had created, when a light the size of a needle's point began to expand over his eyes. It was the edge of the great runway, and the massive door that hid it from the rest of the world was collapsing, right along with everything else. SCOTT pushed even further down on the accelerator, and they broke through the crumbling earth and into the sunlight. The injured vehicle began its descent down the steep slope of Fujisan towards safety, and while it did the mighty mountain collapsed into itself from behind.

Chapter XX

The brilliant rays of the rising sun broke through the scattered clouds, spreading out far and wide to the vast edges of the horizon. Takarada smiled. It was breathtaking, and as he and Jack circled high above Yokohama Bay, he believed the magnificent view to be a good sign. Both men gazed from E.I.O. One, witnessing the fleets of Japanese and American battleships that surrounded the HMS Queen Elizabeth. The sight was truly spectacular, and nothing shy of a miracle either, as all three countries were working together in order to guard England's largest maritime vessel. Not only were they protecting the carrier, but also the precious cargo that lay atop her deck, with his massive steel leg dangling over its side.

Takarada could see the smoke of Mount Fuji off in the distance and stepped over Jack to get a better look from the other side. Heavy ash and soot climbed to the sky, and the mighty mountain now sported a gigantic, crater-like sinkhole from its waist. Yeah, it was gonna leave a mark, but she still stood tall and proud, and the new basin would forever remind Takarada of this victory. It also gave the impression that maybe the docile volcano really wasn't so meek after all, proving that the wrath of Mother Nature was never more than a mere heartbeat away. At least that was the story they'd be sticking to when the world wanted answers. Takarada was devastated over the loss of the FUJI, but that was always part of the plan and saving lives was always his first and foremost objective. Because there was no doubt that evacuating the installation probably saved countless thousands, and aside from a few of Iscariot's men, there were no casualties whatsoever. No FUJI personnel or Japanese lives had been lost. It was indeed a shining moment, as bittersweet as it was.

Sir Jonathon stood up to stretch and Takarada, having had enough of the scenery, pulled down the oval-shaped window shade. He sunk into his leather seat, entwined his fingers behind his neck and exhaled out a daikaiju-sized sigh of relief. Jack was feeling a bit of the same way, and even though this escapade was far from over, they had made some monumental strides. This was primarily due to the fact that Britain and the U.S. were now wise to Iscariot's plan, knowing they'd been played like a freakin' bad fiddle.

Of course it was pretty hard for the superpowers to believe a single word of what Jack had told them after the Los Angeles incident. It probably seemed as though this whole "Iscariot thing" was nothing more than a contrived and convenient excuse, one perpetrated by the E.I.O. to get Japan off the hook with America. With poor relations between the United States and the Earth Intelligence Organization, more so between Jack and the president, Iscariot knew the E.I.O.'s pleas would fall on deaf ears. But everything changed when the Duke's heroic actions saved the American battleship and its entire crew, which included the son of an affluent campaign contributor. So in the end, after killing a number of innocent people, it seemed that all Iscariot had done was create a united alliance against himself. After all of his plotting and planning, there would be no war, no war against countries who were victims of the kaiju struggle and no war over power, or lack thereof. The only war that was coming now was the one against him.

Takarada was elated for another reason as well, and after he folded his laptop shut, he reached into his jacket's side pocket for his cell phone. Sir Jack chuckled,

"Sending a limo for the bleeding Archies are we?" he asked, and Takarada said,

"No, Sir Jonathon, we'll need a helicopter."

Jack's chuckle turned to an outright laugh, and as he tried to straighten out his un-straightenable tie, he reminded Kyoshi to please attend to the Duke immediately upon landing. Takarada nodded and Jack added,

"And while you do that, I'll handle the bloody top brass."

From within the center of E.I.O. One's trapezoidal wings, twin thrusters rotated to face in a downward fashion. As the jet slowed, streams of propulsion ignited from the bottom of each side, enabling it to descend straight down towards the deck of the HMS Queen Elizabeth. While it hovered, double metal cylinders, each the height and width of the fuselage, lowered like landing gear from the main hull, one from the back of the craft and one from the front. Then, as its engines decreased, it lowered upon them. But they didn't only support the craft once it landed, as each column was equipped with a lift system. When the smoke dissipated and the all-clear was given, the rear cylinder opened and Sir Jonathon and Doctor Takarada stepped out.

Both men were met by the commodore of the carrier and the two sets of officers that accompanied him. He raised his hand to salute Jack and Takarada, then offered loud greetings above the declining whine of the aircraft's turbines.

"Gentlemen, welcome aboard Her Majesty's ship, the Queen Elizabeth."

Jack acknowledged the captain with a handshake because he didn't feel like screaming over the noise, and Takarada placed his arms at his side and bowed.

"Looks like we've bagged a bloody, big one!" the commodore shouted as he pointed towards the Duke.

Jack laughed in a "that's not very funny and I'm in a blasted hurry," kind of way, then asked if he could please be directed to the prime minister.

"By all means," the commodore conceded, and he ordered his men to escort Sir Jonathan below deck.

Takarada watched Jack disappear into the bowels of the floating city, and an oncoming thunder, one even louder than the cooling engines of E.I.O. One, demanded his attention. He looked up to see the aircraft carrier's helicopter high above the ocean, approaching straight and fast after its quick trip to Mount Fuji. Once in range, a group of sailors gathered on deck, while a ramp rat in a stunning orange vest waved the chopper in for a landing.

Two seamen leaned forward and scurried up from beneath the spinning blades while they slowed, followed by another who yanked the copter's sliding door wide open. He looked in, then as he asked if everybody was all right, Takarada's smiling face rose up from behind the sailor's shoulder. The copilot of the craft helped everybody up, and when Tommy stepped out, Dr. T immediately noticed his robotic hand was missing.

"I see that you met Leopold Iscariot," he sighed, and Tommy didn't say a word. The doctor lifted Tommy's arm, giving his empty wrist a good once-over and stated that he could fix him a temporary if he could come to his mobile lab. When they came upon the two black tubes that acted as landing gear for E.I.O. One, Nathan asked the doctor if he always "just so happened" to keep a spare lab on hand for such an occasion. Takarada pushed in a code from the black cylinder's indented keyboard. I ts door swooshed open revealing the craft's elevator, and he simply said, "Yes."

Nathan felt himself getting a bit "squirrely," a term he had learned in rehab, usually referring to a state of irritability associated with the throes of early (and sometimes not so early) sobriety. It was an uncomfortable feeling he knew all too well, and when Dr. T and the gang took the lift up into E.I.O. One, Nathan slipped away.

He had no idea where he was going, or what he was looking for, something that was becoming all too familiar to Nathan Fox. But there was one thing he knew for sure, he was freakin' starving. He stopped a crewman and asked where a guy could get a cheeseburger and was steered downward into the great vessel, towards what he had called the mess deck. Nathan thanked him, and by the time the crewman had disappeared, he still had no clue to where he was going. Looking confused, Nathan peered all around and saw nothing but an assortment of long, thin hallways, hatchway doors and more stairs. Famished, angry and tired, he was about to give up and go back to E.I.O. One to get Olivia, when he latched onto a line of men and women who were filing past him. Obviously Nathan didn't know where they were going, but figured they looked pretty hungry them-damn-selves and hoped they were heading to dinner, or breakfast, or whatever.

They went even deeper into the carrier and finally came to a lower deck hanger, that, to Nathan's surprise was gearing up for some kind of celebration. Planes were lined up against the walls, replaced by white-clothed tables and a long bar (one that would allow crew members two drinks each) stationed just at the entrance. Balloons were strung from the metal beam rafters and there was even going to be live music. He walked up to the small, sectional stage that had been assembled and gazed at the limited assortment of backline equipment. It made him think of those days before Vinyl Crush when you got by with what you had. Not that the onboard band was lacking in gear, because they weren't, but when you get used to playing for 30,000 people, you tend to get spoiled. You take for granted a billion-watt P.A. system, seventy stacks of amplifiers and a freakin' George Lucas light show.

Nathan then found himself remembering when he and Tommy first came to Japan, hoping to place them and their band, F-BOMB, smack dab into the heart of Tokyo's ever-growing music scene. "Yeah, that didn't work out too well," he thought as he reminisced about their last gig at a dive called the Flooid Zoo. It was the last stop on their little live house tour, and they were about to get the axe for repeatedly filling the place with a total of maybe six people. Oh, and they would've been fired for sure had it not been for a giant, Japanese mech destroying the bar as it got its ass kicked all over the Yoyogi District.

Nathan spotted an acoustic guitar hanging on a stand and was chomping at the bit to pick it up, something he would not have had a problem doing in the not-so-distant past. Nathan knew touching another man's instrument without permission was taboo, an act that was along the same lines as inviting yourself on stage to play with the band. It was just something you simply did not do, not to mention a sure sign of an amateur.

A soft voice came up from behind and stated to Nathan, "Ah, she's a beaut, ain't she mate?" of course referring to the guitar.

Nathan responded with a, "Sure is."

"It's mine. Go pick her up, Nathan, tell me what you think."

Nathan looked at the man in a sideways manner and the guy knew just what he was thinking.

"I may have been puddle-jumping from one bloody tin can to another over the last few years, but of course I know who Nathan Fox ruddy is."

Nathan smiled, it'd been a while and he really hadn't given much thought lately to the fact that he was famous. He didn't really like to even think about it, as in treatment it did nothing but haunt him, not because people liked it, but because they hated him for it.

The gentleman reached out his hand and introduced himself, feeling it was only right since he already knew who Nathan was.

"I'm Paul, it's bloody great to meet you."

Nathan grinned, then gripped the man's hand and said, "It's bloody great to meet *you*, Paul," and they shook.

"What the hell are you doing here anyhow?" he asked.

Nathan simply replied with a, "I have no freakin' idea."

It seemed Vinyl Crush's agent status was still somehow top secret, and figuring Nathan didn't want to discuss the reasons, Paul changed the subject.

"Go try it," he said, and he nudged Nathan onto the stage. The Lizard King wasn't a great guitar player, but he was good enough to play rhythm and even a simple solo here and there. He also liked to strum chords and pluck out a melody (something he learned from Jack, believe it or not) to aid in the whole song-writing process. He sat down on the edge of the stage and began humming the lyrics to a tune that had been floating around in his head for a couple of weeks. It'd been a while since he even last picked up a guitar, maybe not as long as Tommy, but still it'd been quite some time. As he found the flow of words, he played an accompaniment of chords, and they melded together in harmonious perfection. He only had one verse and the chorus, but it was definitely suited to Nathan and his life-changing events of the last few months. When he finished, his new friend sat down next to him on the edge of the stage. He noted that was one of

the best things he'd ever heard, and as Nathan handed him the guitar back, Paul said that it reminded him of the Beatles.

Nathan thanked him, then looked about the converted hangar, asking Paul if he thought this celebration was a bit premature. After all, he'd seen firsthand what King Taraxian was capable of.

"Blimey," Paul choked out. "This is more of a going away party. I don't think anybody thinks they're going to bloody well live past tomorrow. We're uppin' anchor in a few minutes and while we're 'edding to Antarctica, they're gonna live it up for a few hours. Commodore's orders!"

"Sounds like a great plan," Nathan sighed, and he nodded in the direction of the long strip of bar that had been assembled in the hangar. "I didn't know they could serve booze on these things," and Paul let on that they usually don't. But then stated that this had been deemed a special occasion.

"They do it once in a while, even sometimes on the eve of war. It's not like anybody can get shit-faced, attending crewmembers only get tickets for two bleeding drinks." Paul laughed, "And that's for beer and wine only, nothing strong. Hell, why even bother, it used to take me at least six pints just to get sober!"

Nathan agreed without even knowing he did. Then in the small fraction of silence, Paul slipped in the fact that it had been almost seven years since his last drink.

Nathan gagged out a, "No way!"

Paul responded with a, "Way!"

Getting a bit suspicious, Nathan looked at him with a questionable glare, wondering if Paul was an undercover reporter for *Entertainment! Now* or something. (Sure it sounds far-fetched, but as Nathan would tell you, those rats at *E!N* were always striving to reach new lows of scumdom.) But rather than getting all paranoid decided he liked this guy for some reason. He wasn't sure why, he just knew that he did. Nathan then stated that it must be hard not to drink in the armed forces, and this time Paul gagged.

"I'm not in the ruddy armed forces, I'm just a guitar-playing bloke for the CSE."

Nathan didn't know what he was talking about and asked him, "What the hell is the STD?"

"The C-S-E," Paul explained, "is the British equivalent of your USO. I travel all over the world playing vessels like this, military installations and the such. I'm no sailor, don't have the ruddy discipline."

That's when it occurred to Nathan why Paul was dressed in civilian clothes. At first Nathan wasn't going to say anything about being sober himself. But he liked the idea of talking to somebody who was going (or had gone) through some of the same BS as him, figuring that it made them kindred spirits in a sense. He pulled out the medallion his dad had given him and showed it to Paul.

"Whoa! You too?"

Nathan nodded, and as Paul held the coin, he read "To Thine Self Be True" out loud and said, "Now *that's* a line that packs a bleeding wallop, mate."

Paul complimented him on three years clean and handed the medallion back.

"No," Nathan admitted, "I wish it'd been three years. I think I'd be done with most of this inner freakin' crap I seem to be going through."

"Yeah," Paul stated, "It's not for the bloody faint of heart, that's for sure," and he asked Nathan how much time he had accumulated.

Nathan looked at his watch and Paul cracked up.

"No, really," he said, and Nathan then told him he almost had four months.

"Wow, that's bleeding fantastic! Do you have a sponsor?" he asked, and again Nathan, not quite sure what he meant, stated that when they toured they had tons of sponsors.

Paul told him, "not that kind of sponsor! Somebody to bleeding talk to when you feel like taking a drink or ruddy slitting your throat."

Nathan didn't have one, but he definitely liked the idea.

"Look, here's my number. I'm just outside of London, call me anytime you need to. But don't call collect, I know you can afford it."

Nathan looked at the card. It was wrinkled and the edges were worn. On the front it said, "I'm not yet the person I want to be, but I'm not the person I used to be."

Nathan flipped the card over and saw where Paul had written his number on the back of it. He then placed it and the medallion back into his pocket.

"Hey, I gotta great idea!" Paul barked out of nowhere. "You should join us, get up and sing a few tunes! Consider this your cordial invitation!"

"That sounds like a freakin' great idea! You bet your ass I'll get up and belt out a couple!"

They started naming a few songs off, ones they thought the other might know, when Tommy and Olivia made their way into the hanger. Nathan could see Tommy was already sporting a new hand, compliments of Dr. T, and figured that this may be the perfect time for him to try it out!

"Check it out, Tommy!" Nathan yelled, and his new friend held up the guitar. "This is Paul, and he asked if I could sing a few tunes with them, maybe ..." Nathan paused so as not to invite members of his own band onto another man's stage. Paul, however, catching Nathan's vibe grinned, then insisted that they ALL join in for a song or two.

"Wow," he said, "I can't believe you guys are here." Paul looked at Tommy and again held up the acoustic. "Tommy, would you sign the back of my guitar? I've got a marker right here."

He hesitated and Nathan could sense something was up, because Tommy loved to sign autographs, but for some reason he seemed a bit apprehensive.

"Ah, sure" he said, "but quickly, 'cuz we need to go."

Paul handed the guitar to Tommy, and he scribbled "Keep the faith" on the back of it with his perfectly working robo-hand. Paul lit up and then asked Tommy if he would like to play it.

"No, I wouldn't, I mean, no, I can't, I mean …" Tommy looked at Nathan. "We need to go, now!"

Nathan rolled his eyes and told Paul he'd see him in a little bit, and Tommy stated, "No, he won't," and started walking back towards the exit.

Nathan was perplexed and looked at Olivia, who only shrugged her shoulders in regards to Tommy acting like such a douche, when Nathan realized he hadn't introduced her.

"Paul, this is …," and Paul interrupted him,

"I know, Olivia Olivetti," and they shook hands.

"Very nice to meet you," he told her, and after they broke their grip, Olivia's palm fell into Nathan's and they walked out together.

"Thanks, Paul!" Nathan yelled as they turned towards the door, "I'll call ya!"

"Wow, seems like a nice guy," Olivia stated, and Nathan replied in a very bad British accent,

"Yeah, 'ee seems to be a bit of the okay."

Nathan looked ahead to Tommy, who was a good ten feet in front of them, and asked what the hell his problem was. He stopped, turning to Nathan.

"Whaddya mean?" he demanded.

"I mean, he was a nice guy and you were a major jerk, bro. You cut him off and almost chewed his head off for inviting us to play. I mean, what gives? You're a lot of things, but I've never seen you act like that, and I've NEVER seen you turn down an opportunity to play a guitar!" Nathan wondered if his hand wasn't quite up to par and asked him if that was the problem.

"Uhm, yeah, that's the problem," Tommy lied, forgetting Olivia was there, who then reminded him that she watched him pop a tennis ball and ace every one of Dr. T's dexterity tests. Nathan, having known Tommy for a billion years, then figured it out.

"Dude, when was the last time you even held a guitar?" he asked, and Tommy proudly stated about a minute ago.

"Jesus," Nathan said out loud, "freakin before that."

Tommy turned and began to walk away, and Nathan yelled at his back that he shouldn't worry about it, that he hadn't really sung in a long-ass time himself. He assured Tommy it was no big deal and Tommy stopped.

"It is a big deal!" he screamed, "And I don't plan on picking up a guitar ever again!"

Nathan was floored and stopped dead in his tracks. He knew Tommy had given in to the evil whims of his day job at the E.I.O., but he thought he still picked a bit, maybe a little, a weekend warrior in the very least. But he was wrong, Tommy had quit entirely, and it seemed he had no intentions of ever touring or playing again.

"Why?" Nathan asked.

Tommy sighed, "Look Nathan, I think I've just grown up a bit since you went to rehab. Yeah man, I still like to goof around and have fun. I still even enjoy getting ol' Walrus-boy worked up, but I just feel that what I do for the Earth Intelligence Organization is far more important. I think with the problems in the world and with the degree of our responsibilities, it makes playing kind of dumb and senseless."

Nathan paused and thought about his words, careful not to blurt out the first thing that came to his mind, which he did.

"So what are we fighting for then? A cold world with no music or art? A world where we just survive, live in the gray and fight monsters? I can't believe you're even saying this."

Nathan looked at the ground and Tommy fired back,

"Me? You're the effing idiot who destroyed half a city! You're the one who drank himself into a freakin' liquid stupor! And you seem to forget that BOTH of your parents are dead and all you want to do is play music? Grow up man!"

This obviously had been brewing in Tommy's head for quite some time. Something, somewhere changed in him, and Nathan, though pissed, was now smart enough to know it wasn't because of him. All that guitar thing seemed to do was open the floodgates, and Nathan wanted to know why. He thought he might have known the cause, he also figured he had nothing to lose.

"What happened between you and Akira, Tommy?"

Olivia, still holding Nathan's hand, squeezed it in a covert manner, telling him to shut the hell up, which made Nathan realize that she too must have known, and he repeated the question.

211

"What happened, dude, she dump you?"

Olivia squeezed even tighter.

"She leave you for a Yokai prince or something? She get sick of the mighty Tom—"

POW!

Nathan went down breaking his grip with Olivia when Tommy's super-damn-hand connected with his face. Nathan just sat there as the birds and stars encircled his head, and he pointed out that there was clearly nothing wrong with the temporary hand.

Tommy knelt down and put his face right up to Nathan's. "No dude, she's freakin' dead!" and before he had a chance to pull away, Nathan grabbed him and pulled him in. He put his arms around Tommy and held him tight, and even though he tried to pull back at first, Nathan wasn't letting go. Both men began to weep, and Olivia sat down next to them on the cold floor of the carrier and the three embraced.

Olivia (like most people) of course knew about Akira but had decided to let Tommy tell Nathan in his own time, which apparently was right now. He wiped his eyes and apologized to Nathan for not telling him earlier. He was afraid of laying more bad news on him, not wanting to break the back of his newfound sobriety, especially with his dad being so sick.

Nathan thanked Tommy, telling him how much he appreciated the sentiment and told him to never freakin' do it again, to which he agreed. With that being said, Tommy explained to Nathan how Akira's body couldn't survive after the death of her sister, Oko Rikoku. They knew they were physically connected by Yokai forces. They also knew that one could not kill the other. What they didn't know was that neither one could survive very long after the other had passed.

"For some reason," Tommy stated, "the doctors think she lived longer than expected after Rikoku's death due to how happy she was."

Tommy started crying harder. "She was happy with ME! She was the only one who EVER made me feel like I've always wanted to feel."

Nathan thought how he once accused Tommy of being incapable of seeing just what he had with Akira, even calling him a little dink in the process. Nathan also realized he had said all that shit to him *after* she was gone, and Tommy hadn't said a damn word. Nathan looked through the locks of Tommy's long, blonde hair and into Olivia's eyes.

He now knew what he had with her, and maybe Tommy's decision wasn't so ridiculous after all.

Tommy broke free, and as he wiped his eyes dry, he stood up. "I haven't picked up a guitar since."

Both Nathan and Olivia joined him vertically, and the Lizard King wrapped his arm around Tommy's neck. "I'm really sorry about Akira, bro. I had no idea."

Tommy eked out a smile. He appreciated the words. He also felt a tremendous release, as he never really talked about it with anyone. "It's okay," he assured Nathan, "I actually feel a hell of a lot better now that you know."

Tommy then felt compelled to apologize to Nathan once more, this time for being a jerk back in the hangar.

"Dude, I would've loved to have seen you get up and sing, and you know what, after this I probably would have joined you, but we're pulling out. We're leaving immediately for Mount Terror with Sir Jonathon on E.I.O. One. I guess we need to be briefed on a bunch of garbage."

Nathan was familiar with the drill. It wasn't anything new, and he asked, "What about the Duke?"

Tommy said that according to Takarada, the Duke was fully operational, and even though he went down, he was never out.

"However," he added, "the Kelvin Duster is toast. Takarada has to remove it from the Duke, but I think he has a plan for it, or something." He paused, then added, "I don't think Dr. T ever liked that freakin' thing."

Nathan cracked up then moaned in pain, placing his hand on the spot where Tommy had punched him. Funny, but it was the exact same place where he had hit him all those years ago.

Nathan decided, right then and right there, that he didn't care what the hell Tommy chose to do with his life. After all, it was *his* and "To Thine Own Self Be True" applied to everybody, not just Nathan. Little Tom Len Taylor would always be his best friend ... always, whether he played freakin' guitar or not.

Nathan then stood in between Tommy and Olivia, and they made their way to the flight deck. He placed his arms around their outer shoulders, and as they walked, he asked if anybody else was hungry.

Chapter XXI

Aurora Australis frolicked throughout the black of the great wide open, shining down upon one of the most devastating regions on planet Earth, Antarctica. Being the only light source for almost a thousand square miles, it flickered across the frozen wasteland of Ross Island, illuminating Mount Terror in an eerie glow of green and purple. It was winter within the winter, the coldest season of the year, and the sun had already set, not scheduled to make its next appearance until October.

Within the dark of day, magnificent beacons of light cast thick beams upon the seaward-facing side of the mountain as crews worked at a frantic pace. The preparation was almost complete, and they engaged the labor with extreme ferocity, almost as though their very lives depended on it, because maybe they did. Not just theirs though, but everybody's, and the next few hours would determine the future fate of the entire world.

The Tomoyuki hovered from high above, keeping a watchful eye from the ever-changing sky while aiding in the delivery of the arctic base's remaining tackle. Twin-blade helicopters transporting men, freight and necessary equipment descended from the massive flying machine's cargo hold, lowering themselves and their content deep into the mouth of the docile volcano. From the bay of the surrounding sea, the HMS Queen Elizabeth prepared, arming squadrons of jets from three different countries.

F.U. fighters armed to the teeth waited in twin rows from a landing strip carved of thick, white ice that stretched as far as the eye could see.

In the new mountain control center, Jack made last minute preparations. From there, he could dictate the flow of the battle, observing through the double-story row of diamond-particle glass that extended from the side of Mount Terror. It wasn't anything fancy, it was only sufficient, because there simply wasn't enough time for

214

anything else. They couldn't even install the traditional wall of HD viewing monitors and instead had to use two big-screen televisions with direct digital feeds to the Tomoyuki.

Jack stood in front of the semicircular wall of windows with his hands folded behind his back, looking through the fresh falling snow to the lights of the busy army below. Even from halfway up the mountain and past the dark of the shimmering green, he could still see the HMS Queen Elizabeth. He admired her noble beauty as she waited at the edge of the island, just a bit out to sea. Her deck lit up in a brilliance of white, and he stared at the long line of jets that were eager to launch. In the midst of its majesty, Jack simply imagined boarding the great vessel and sailing back with her to England. Sir Jonathon sighed, then peered up to the glistening diamonds in the sky. He thought about his old life, the one he left behind so many years ago and wondered if he could ever go home. Once there was a way, but that was a long, long time ago. There were still so many things he wanted to do, and even if they were things he had done before, he wanted to do them again, before it was too late.

Meanwhile, from the foot of the mountain, Takarada yelled orders above the roar of a tremendous crane that lowered the final iron girder into place. He pulled out a pair of binoculars and put them between the thick fur that outlined the hood of his parka. The snow grew heavy and as the light powder turned to a cold flurry, he hollered for the welders to "Hurry it up!" Sparks of molten steel ignited and rode the howling winds as they put the finishing touches to the last of the giant, freestanding, screen-like structures.

During the course of the Queen Elizabeth's long journey to the arctic fortress, Takarada and his team worked around the clock from the deck of the carrier. The Kelvin Duster needed to be removed, and at first it was solely for the purpose of returning the cowbot to an operable condition. But as they torched the tremendous plates of hollowed steel from the mech and dismantled the freezing system from his chest, Takarada came up with an idea. Instead of just scrapping the chambered metal sheets, crews of men, led by SCOTT, now detached the jacket for a different purpose, a new weapon. Takarada had the thought of building monolith screens at the base of Mount Terror, each one capable of a freakin' -400° blast. Something to even the score if necessary, but only in the worst-case scenario, as the chilling devices would have no way of deciphering the good guys from the bad. The oncoming storm was approaching, and Takarada ordered everybody back into the mountain. Just before leaving, his eyes followed the snow-laden beams from the spotlights that illuminated the front of the fourth and final screen. He took one last look at the team's accomplishment, and frankly, he was quite impressed.

Then finally, towering against the inside wall of the volcano's barren magma chamber, stationed just above the remaining organic thorium and the refinery that processed it, stood the Duke himself. Spit-shined to perfection, standing tall and looking quite cranky, he anticipated round two of his match with the spider god. His forearm where King Taraxian had pierced his armor had to be repaired, and, thanks to his brief engagement as a boat anchor, some of his electrical equipment had to be replaced. But all in all, it didn't take much to get the injured bot back up to speed, and from the cranium of the mech, Nathan and everybody else waited. Then, once that transmission came through and SCOTT rose up from the center of the Duke's cockpit, it'd be time. From there, the five robotonauts would slip on their headgear, get the all-clear from Jack, lean back and go into the electronically-induced coma. And when it was all over, they'd wake up, hopefully.

So far the odds had been in their favor, but with each roll of the dice you push fate a bit further, probably one of the reasons the payoff was so effing big. Tommy and Nathan made pathetic gobs of money, but the funny thing was hardly any of it came from the E.I.O. These Earth Intelligence Organization bastards were so freakin' brilliant, they barely paid their agents minimum wage. They didn't have to as guys like Tommy and Nathan made their money from album sales and touring. It was yet another reason why the E.I.O. used agents posing as rock stars, because it came with a built-in paycheck, a freakin' huge one at that! And there was no use complaining to Sir Jack about it, as it worked the same way for him, always had. But over the course of the last few years, Nathan was beginning to think this nonsense wasn't all it was cracked up to be.

He used to think that this little arrangement with the E.I.O. was a pretty fair swap. He helps pilot some dumb robot, and in return they give him fame and fortune. Sounds good, no problem, and in the beginning he thought it was the greatest opportunity to ever be

216

bestowed upon a mere mortal. Maybe because that's how he looked at this whole freakin' rock-star thing sometimes. It was like some sort of delusional quest, one as difficult as finding the Golden Fleece or even the Holy Grail itself. So of course he jumped on the opportunity, figuring if he didn't make it to the top, he'd rather be dead anyhow. He, however, didn't think it was so great anymore. Nathan now believed this whole secret-spy, kaiju-fighting, bot-flying junk was more bullshit than anything else, as the agent end of it now far exceeded the rock star part. God forbid you take five stupid minutes out of your busy day to write a hit song. He knew it sounded selfish, but it's what he wanted to do. He'd done his time, he'd paid his dues and don't forget, he'd already saved the planet once, thank you very much. Nathan started stewing on the thought that someone else could step up to the damn plate for a freakin' change. He felt himself getting a bit angry as he thought, "But yet here I am, *again*, and instead of playing music, I'm waiting to die in the skull of this stupid, cowboy robot."

The more he dwelled, the more a fierce heat set a course straight for his head. Nathan then decided he'd better chill, and since now wasn't the time to get all pissy, that's just what he did. Chances are, though, everybody was thinking along the same lines. The wait to launch always freakin' sucked, and even though none of this was anything new, it still didn't make it any easier. It was also hard to talk in the cockpit once those cubic walls ascended up, cutting you off from the world, leaving you to your lone thoughts. Well, except for Liberty and Michael, since they shared a cubicle. Plus, they could carry on conversations for hours without so much as opening their mouths even once. But this was always, without a doubt, one of the worst things about war, the waiting. All hoped for the best, but that still didn't stop the old mind from meandering as you imagined dying in the most horrible ways possible, like at the fangs of a freakin' daikaiju spider. At first this didn't really bother Nathan, but for some reason it did now.

Before getting bounced into rehab, Nathan thought his life was nothing but a giant piece of shit. He figured he was nothing but a mere victim, the rich, world-traveling, worshipped-by-all, rock-star kind, but nevertheless a victim. His mom was dead, he hadn't seen his dad in years, the band sucked, Tommy was a dink, Olivia was a bitch and as far as the Twins went, well you didn't even want to get him freakin' started. Yup, that was pretty much the everyday consensus for the Lizard King. It was always somebody else's fault, and if they'd just come around to his way of thinking, everything would be all right. But it never happened, and he soon discovered that living a life of isolation, especially while surrounded by a million people, was pretty hard to do. Even now in recovery, he still had brief encounters with that way of thinking, and he wished that the Nathan that wasn't afraid of the big, nasty spider would show up, because he was scared. It was kind of funny though, how not so long ago he didn't think he had anything to lose. And when you feel that way, it seems to make everything easier, probably because you just don't care. But now, he felt as though he had *everything* to lose, and even if it was only his dreams, it was still too much.

He reached into his pocket and pulled out the business card that Paul had given him, then went a little deeper for his pop's medallion. Nathan clutched the coin in one hand while reading the writing on the small piece of paper he held in the other,

I'M NOT YET THE PERSON I WANT TO BE

BUT I'M NOT THE PERSON I USED TO BE

He repeated the words over and over, then glanced at the bronze coin, *"To Thine Own Self Be True."* Both phrases swirled throughout his head, and when he squeezed his eyes shut, the water was forced out and down the sides of his face. In silence, Nathan asked his folks to be with him during the battle. He then reminded God (whom he had chosen as his higher power) to not give him more than he could handle, a promise he accused the Big Guy of welching on not too long ago. In retrospect though and after looking back at everything that had happened, something dawned on Nathan. It was peculiar, but in some way, shape or form, everything *had* worked out, at least so far.

He rummaged through his pants for a piece of paper or freakin' anything he could write on. He had a great idea for a song and since the thoughts were usually fleeting, and because cell phones weren't allowed on the Duke, his search became quite frantic. It was funny how that lame lyrical muse worked, always seeming to show up at the worst possible times. He reached down between his legs as he thought he might have a pen in his satchel, the one he kept hidden under his seat. It was an emergency-type nylon pouch with a black shoestring sewn into the top to tie it shut. Usually it was reserved for emergency kits or medical aids, but for Nathan it held a peanut butter sandwich, old deodorant, a spare pair of underwear and some other junk he had accumulated. But it was still freakin' nothing compared to Tommy who kept like six rolls of duct tape, his old Walkman (complete with a decaying cassette copy of Deep Purple's *Machine Head*) and a reserve pack of smokes in his. Nathan pulled the bag up, fumbled through its contents and not only did he find a pen, but a small notebook as well. He figured he must've had this idea before, and just as he put pen to paper, the signal came in.

Various treble-laced, tin murmurs began echoing over the comm. system, confirming massive increases in seismic activity from the floor of the ocean. Yes, they were only men reading reports, but the oncoming threat seemed to exaggerate their tone, giving their voices a terrifying, Cylon-like quality. They also reported that the epicenter, the very heart of the quake, was also in motion. Nathan was pretty sure that the wait was over, and he crammed everything into his pocket. Then, when the steam rose from beneath the steel-laced floor, and SCOTT ascended from within the Duke's control cylinder, he knew for sure. SCOTT smiled, offered greetings to all of the robotonauts and asked if they would please put on their helmets and prepare themselves for the sleep-state.

Chapter XXII

In the vast and black emptiness, the million or so stars that floated high above the surrounding sea began to multiply. First one became two, then two became four, the cycle repeating itself over and over until it was impossible to tell one from another. That is, until the mass of illuminated specks descended upon the tip of the infinite horizon and closed in.

From behind the great wall of curved, two-story, diamond-particle glass, both Sir Jonathon and Takarada observed, laying witness to the beginning, and the possible end. Jack stroked his giant, white mustache and the men and women in the new arctic control center awaited his orders with bated breath. He watched while a mass of lights rode the crest of the ocean on course towards the mountainous base, devouring any unfortunates in the way, like the HMS Queen Elizabeth.

"Launch first wave!" Jack barked, and the words echoed twice, followed by the deck of the Queen Elizabeth erupting as the jets took off in screaming succession.

SHOOSH! SHOOSH! SHOOOOSH!

Fighters, not only from Britain, but also the U.S. and Japan, formed a wall of immense force and began pummeling the oncoming threat in a barrage of rapid fire! Fierce, dotted lines of red rocketed over the surface of the sea, and upon impact, the neon glow of the southern lights melded with the explosions, causing the perpetual darkness to ignite. The flickering light gave identity to the thousands of small attack drones that approached, one hundred ships thick. Then, rising up from behind the multitude of crafts was Iscariot's mother vessel. From within the center of its bridge, he sat perched in the chair of his mobile ivory tower, a seat that looked more like a throne than that of a noble captain. His boney hands rested on the arms with his long fingers draping over the sides. He looked at the screen in front of him that projected the image of what was happening below, then simply closed his eyes.

Like a swarm of loyal offspring eager to please their father, the mass of black, insectival crafts lit up in a dull glow and began to return fire. Violent beams of green (the color of organic thorium) erupted from the abdomens of the sleek ships and, like rays cast from the sun, expanded in every direction. The brilliant bursts were fantastic, spreading like the many gleams of angry disco balls, relentlessly taking out any jet that happened to be in its trajectory.

BOOSH! KA-BOOSH!

A line of Japanese fighters rocketed down to just above the surface of the water and beneath the attacking horde. Then, from below, they pulled straight up, pulverizing a group of Iscariot's drones with rocket upon rocket! The explosions were swift, and the small vessels left a blazing trail of fire as they plummeted, exploding when they collided with the surface of the sea.

Iscariot smiled through the tinge of pain that shot through his head when the crafts ignited, while servicemen and women from the HMS Queen Elizabeth cheered! Just like Jack did, when he bellowed out an abrupt, "RIGHT! Take that Iscariot, you bleeding wanker!" from amidst the control center. "Launch second wave!" he commanded. "Send in the Tomoyuki."

The massive vessel broke its position and burst through the overcast of thick clouds with a full onslaught of long, thin photon blasts. The deadly streaming staves of red fired from her tremendous metal skin as she descended towards the Queen Elizabeth in order to fight by her side.

Iscariot tightened his grip on the arms of the chair, and a group of crafts broke away from his large battalion of fighters. They dropped like they were crashing, but upon splashing into the icy sea, they began cutting their way through the black water towards the hull of the Queen Elizabeth. While more of Iscariot's drones followed suit, the Tomoyuki's photon beams began picking them off one by one, and upon each direct hit, they exploded two times.

An eager squad of F.U. fighters erupted from the belly of the E.I.O.'s giant, hovering ship, almost smashing through the hangar doors as they launched!

FWOOOSH!

When they exploded into battle, some rocketed to just above the surface of the sea while the others plunged into it! After entering the water, jets of streamlined air took the place of rocket boosters, propelling the multi-faceted crafts towards the immersed drones.

Iscariot's submerged ships irradiated the surface of the water with their blasts from below, causing the Queen Elizabeth to rock as parts of her steel exterior ripped. The F.U.s that pursued from behind closed in, taking out each and every one of Iscariots immersed insects in an underwater shower of deadly sparks. The drones were fast and agile, but they were no match for the sum total of weaponry between the jets of the Queen Elizabeth, the F.U.s and the Tomoyuki.

Jack had a feeling of hope, albeit a small one, as he watched the three countries coming together to fight this common enemy. Accompanied by the tiniest swell of fear-masking pride, he lay witness to the biggest freakin' dogfight the world would never see. Jack tried to overlook the total amount of firepower needed to battle this army, because he knew how Iscariot worked. It was his hope that they could at least take out the swarm of drones before having to bring in the big guns. If they could hold out that long.

Both Jack and Takarada kept a firm fix on the fight, gazing from the long row of windows within the control center of Mount Terror. There they watched the war unfold as though it was merely a video game on a tremendous screen. The stress was brutal, and Takarada tapped his index finger against his outer thigh while Jack stroked his giant stache. Sir Jonathon's eyebrow rose above the rim of his round spectacles, and he let out a little sigh of relief. Iscariot's insect-like crafts started to drop, falling like a thousand decimated flies under the relentless show of force. But as the steam released from Jack's full head, the valve was quickly spun hard to the right, trapping the remaining pressure before it had a chance to escape. Yes, the drones were indeed falling ... falling smack into the mighty iron hull of the Tomoyuki, then down even further to the deck of the Queen Elizabeth.

BOOSH! BOOSH! FWAM!

Sections of each floating vessel exploded upon impact while Iscariot's falling crafts dropped like bombs from the war-laden skies. The Tomoyuki was able to withstand the blasts throughout its vast surface, not to mention their expanding green bursts. However, the Queen Elizabeth wasn't, and jets and F.U. fighters alike began firing upon the drones while they fell, trying to force them to explode from the air. As soon as they began raining down on the deck of the aircraft carrier, one caused an American jet to blow, setting off a chain reaction and taking out the second squadron even before it could take off.

Jack's worry returned, only tenfold, as Iscariot's diabolical attack was clearly working. It was obvious he was simply depleting their resources, and though old hat for the mad doctor, it was nonetheless proving to be successful. During the early cheers of the battle, Jack bit his lip thinking that maybe this wasn't going to be so tough after all. This is probably just what Iscariot wanted him to think, a little hope before ripping his heart out. Because now the drones kept coming and coming, and they were having to take them out even after taking them out! It was like watching a massive army of flying cannons, Jack thought to himself, cannons that upon outliving their usefulness, simply turned to another weapon, a bleeding projectile that would explode upon impact. He watched the fighting crafts of the allied forces exhaust their ammunition, but in no way could he tell them to limit their firepower, as they then wouldn't even have a chance in hell. Sir Jonathon knew what it was time to do, their first and second lines of defense were almost completely wiped out and still with no sign of King Taraxian. But Jack, and everybody else, knew the monster spider was coming, if it wasn't already there.

"Launch the bloody Duke."

The countdown commenced and Nathan awaited the oncoming coma of the electronically-induced sleep-state. His head was swimming, but amidst it all, his biggest concern was Olivia. He wished he'd kissed her goodbye, because he wasn't too sure if they'd be waking up this time. He knew this was to be a battle like no other, and even though every battle was like no other, this truly was to be a battle like no other. Nathan lay there and caught himself trying to process the nonsense of his last thought, then just as he almost had it all figured out …

The Duke erupted up and out of the mouth of Mount Terror leaving two thick streams of white smoke in his wake. All eyes fighting the blazes from the Queen Elizabeth below suddenly gazed up to the heavens above. The majesty of it all was undeniable, making it impossible for the ship *not* to erupt into a flood of applause when the sky ignited into a shimmer of brilliant steel. The Duke then leveled off and rocketed towards the army of drones and the heart of the war. His fist extended straight ahead, while his other hand gripped the handle of one of his photon six-shooters that waited to be drawn.

He plunged boots first into the sea, and along with the explosion of water, the cowbot forced great waves of ocean to the decks of the burning carrier. Men and women held tight as the influx of spray doused much of the fire. The Duke, who stood about as tall as the carrier's deck, began to yank on the torn flaps of the monstrous vessel's damaged hull. The giant bot pushed and pulled, folding the torn sheets of protruding steel inward, sealing the rip. It was crude, there was no doubt about it, but it would hold for the time being.

Iscariot's insect crafts swarmed about like moths to a flame, and even though blasting them would've been nothing shy of shooting fish in a barrel, it couldn't be done. Because even the slumbering robotonauts knew that this would only fill the skies with an endless flurry of falling bombs, something nobody (maybe with the exception of Iscariot) wanted. Besides, there was nothing the carrier could do anyhow, at least not until her planes were ready to land, because from here, she was nothing but a sitting duck.

The cowbot forced his cast-iron legs through the water, and as the drones buzzed around him, he waded alongside of the magnificent ship towards her rear. He pulled the vessel's anchor up from the floor of the ocean and only caused minimal damage when he set it gently upon the flight deck. From there he lowered down, turned his back towards her stern and heaved. After a few great strides to build up momentum, he stopped pushing and the HMS Queen Elizabeth began her solo drift towards the blackened edge of the horizon. Jack, seeing what the Duke was doing, ordered the Tomoyuki to ascend straight up to the exosphere and (like the drifting carrier) out of harm's way.

Iscariot, of course, was no idiot and could see what was happening, even if his eyes were shut, but it left him in a bit of a conundrum. He couldn't pursue the Tomoyuki because his drones weren't capable of space travel, and with the Queen Elizabeth pretty much down for the count, why bother. So he figured he only had one option, and with that set his sights upon the Duke.

The swarm of drones surrounded the cowbot in a dense cloud of fury, and like a million mosquitos coming to feed, began to attach themselves to his chassis. It made it damned near impossible to even see the mech from beneath the garment of small attacking crafts, that is until they started exploding!

BOOSH! BOOSH-BOOSH!

The Duke teetered a bit from the blasts, but stood firm while yet another group of tiny attacking ships lowered from the sky. From above they began to pummel the towering bot from all sides with an array of their expanding explosions. The Duke bent his arms from the shafts of his titanium elbows, then pulled the photon six-shooters from his sides, twirling the weapons around and around from the tips of his fingers as he did.

SWOOSH! SWOOSH! SWOOSH!

Jack ordered the remaining jets and F.U. fighters to get their asses out of there and take cover from the other side of the mountain. He then demanded that the control center, from where he, Takarada and a small team of FUJI Flunkies dictated the battle, be shielded. He also stated that it was time to batten down the bloody hatches on the entire base as well.

The observation platform that extended out of Mount Terror in a semicircle of glass began to vibrate just before it was sucked into the side of the mountain. Once completely in, a great wall of rock and ice covered up any trace of the base. While atop the docile volcano, a large barrier of reinforced titanium closed in from four ends of its big mouth, meeting in the middle and sealing it shut. "Right then!" Jack bellowed. "Switch to a digital feed from the Tomoyuki and fire these blasted things up!" Jack pointed to the twin flat-screen televisions and the satellite image from the hovering ship crackled into existence.

Towering above the surface of the ocean, his boots planted on its rocky floor, the Duke spread his arms out wide and began to rotate from the waist. Still gripping a six-shooter in each hand, his upper torso spun faster and faster like a turbulent cyclone, until he was nothing but a blur. The latching crafts tried but couldn't hang on and were being launched in every direction! As they flew, rapid fire-blasts from his photon six-shooters filled the surrounding sky!

BAM! BAM! BAM! BAM!

The drones exploded, then exploded again, threatening a whole lot of nothing because the Tomoyuki was a good fifty miles up and the Queen Elizabeth was already a good ten miles out. Iscariot clenched his head each time one of his little insects blew into a kabillion microbits, cursing the Duke and the stupid robotonauts who piloted him with each ping of pain. The spinning bot slowed, and once again the smoking guns twirled one time around before returning to their holsters.

The giant robot turned and faced Iscariot's hovering ship, sending a message that was quite clear. "If you want to get to the mountain and the toy surprise inside, you'll have to get through me first." But just in case it wasn't clear enough, the mighty machine saluted Iscariot's floating craft with the steel shaft of his middle finger. Jack sighed and lowered his forehead into his palm, expressing his annoyance with the bleeding Archies for such a blatant display of vulgarity. He found it hard to believe that they, or at least a few, or probably just Nathan Fox, could still retain such a smartass persona even from a blasted coma. Sir Jonathon turned to Takarada, and before he could condemn their actions, both men cracked up. At that moment, Jack envisioned the ROT beam firing from the monocle of the Duke and blowing Iscariot *and* his pint-sized Tomoyuki out of bloody existence. "If only" he imagined, because he knew if he could take him out now, it would in fact sever Iscariot's link with Notawni Nonaashi. Jack thought how nice it would be to end this ruddy ordeal right now. He could take out Doctor Crazy, his ship and his overgrown pet spider in one fell swoop, saving a mass of lives even before the wretched, eight-legged beastie had a chance to attack. It was a nice thought indeed, but Sir Jonathon knew it wasn't going to be that easy, not to mention it was too late.

From within the control center, the ever-present display of the heightened seismic monitor spiked, and the entire mountain trembled. Jack retained his balance by holding on to the corner of a workstation, while Takarada chased the readings on his computer. "Seismic activity has now progressed to a full earthquake scenario. Temperatures are rising and the epicenter is closing in!" Takarada stopped typing and looked up to Sir Jonathon. "It is here."

The tundra that surrounded Mount Terror shook profusely as King Taraxian dug up from within the bowels of the planet. The violent tremors caused towering steeples of ice and earth to shatter to the ground, while the excess heat began to play havoc on the great white blanket that covered the land. Rock and snow tumbled into the massive sinkholes that were spreading at the foot of the mountain, causing the awaiting F.U. fighters to fall into the crumbling void.

"God blind me! The damn thing is coming up from below the new airstrip!" Jack hollered, just before ordering all crafts to bloody launch! The large FUJI Unit jets rocketed straight up in a chaotic getaway, and as they did, the many sinkholes from beneath them collapsed creating one magnificent crater. Most of the ships managed to escape, while others were pulled down deep into the pit of the monster arachnid. It was just like Palmdale, right before the molten rock spewed up from within the earth in a towering geyser of relentless fire. Jack waited for the tremendous rise in heat, then glared at their two big-screen monitors from the sanctity of the buried base. He knew that if the projected images remained, they at least made the right decision picking this godforsaken place, and if not, this could very well be the end. Because if the deadly, mind-numbing cold didn't do the trick, everything within a ten-mile radius would become nothing but a charred wasteland surrounded by a boiling sea.

Jack and Takarada watched while the liquid rock caused by the tunneling spider's heat mechanism rose up from within the depths of the crater. But as the upward stream of fire came in contact with the twenty-story layer of ice (not to mention the ass-freezing temperature), the majority of the face-melting magna merely fizzled into an eruption of steam.

SPSSSSSSHHHH!

The extreme cold, for the most part, was doing just as they had planned, at least for now. Takarada jumped up from his seat and shook his clenched fist at the image on the big-screen monitor. "Hai!" he proclaimed. "It seems to be working!" Sir Jack was surprised at Takarada's reaction, because it was a bit out of character for the doctor. But he indeed understood, as he felt the same way. Jack nodded in approval, then demanded that everybody stay bloody focused, reminding all within the control center that this was only the beginning.

The black talons of King Taraxian's eight claws attached to the rim of the newly-formed crater, while beams from an array of searchlights ascended with the creature as it hoisted itself out of the hole.

The monster's new jeweled eye lit up in bright red and it assessed the mountain, giving Iscariot a crimson-tinted view within his head. The spider from inside the cage of spotlights lumbered forward, and the mad doctor readied it to climb to the top of Mount Terror. It was unfortunate that this time the beast could not come up directly from beneath the base as it did in London. The core of the docile volcano was a mile-thick shield of petrified stone. And even though it was quite capable of digging through, the effort would take hours, hours that in most attacks could not be afforded, something Jack had counted on.

As the demon creature creeped to the foot of the mountain, it stopped, and Iscariot scrutinized Takarada's row of massive frost barriers. Courtesy of a visual from the colossal spider, he saw everything it saw and, seeing what the screens were capable of, determined that they could indeed prove to be problematic. The red glow of the arachnid's new visual prosthesis dimmed and as it did, the other of its two larger eyes illuminated into a blinding flash.

SHOOOOM!

A thick blast erupted from the beast's eye, destroying the first of Takarada's line of frozen defense in one mighty display of force!

KA-BOOOOSH!

The explosion shook the foundation of the volcano and the steel sheets of the frost barrier crashed to the ground when the weapon's massive girders melted. The spider shuffled its enormous legs, moving its entire body so it could focus the eight eyes of its chrome-plated head on the next screen. King Taraxian began ripping the second screen down with its bare claws, fine tuning the damage with its two smaller pedipalps and trampling over whatever remained.

While Jack watched the spider decimate the giant frost screens from the viewing monitors, he began to wonder. They had discovered in Yokohama that King Taraxian's organic thorium power source may be infinite, but like the Duke, its internal firing systems still needed to recharge once exhausted. Jack stroked his mustache and thought, "This thing just dug itself halfway around the world to bloody get here." He also knew for a fact, it couldn't have done so without its burrowing heat mechanism, which was the spider's primary weapon. He then pondered, "Why the hell is it manually pulling down the screens after so effortlessly blasting the first one apart with its devastating ray?" Jack suddenly gasped, as this was the tipoff. Because over the years, he had learned quite a bit about daikaiju, and there was one thing he knew for bloody certain. One thing he knew to be 100% true and that was that kaiju positively loved their lasers, lightning bolts and atomic heat beams. This was a plain and simple fact, especially when any of the aforementioned nasties could do the majority of the dirty work for them. Jack slammed his fist down onto the nearest flat surface. "God blind me!" he wailed. "That thing's weapons systems are depleted. It's recharging right now! Let's give 'er everything we've bloody got! Prepare the ROT beam!"

The Tomoyuki descended swiftly from the heavens above, while beams of devastating energy blasted straight down from her enormous hull. The F.U.s also joined the battle, pelting the creature on both sides with one FUKM UP after another. The monster's back erupted, sending thick chunks of spider blood and flesh into the air, exposing much of its steel exoskeleton. The beating commenced, and parts of the earth expanded as the onslaught of explosions sent the ice, rock and debris into the smoke-laden air. Then from behind, the Duke rocketed fist-first on a collision course with the rear of the spider.

BWAM!

The force spun the arachnid around in a complete 180, and it tried desperately to force the tips of its razor-sharp claws into the slippery surface of ice. Of course it was having a hard time, but the Duke was happy to lend a hand, more so a fist, stopping the spinning monster with the cracking metal of a fierce right hook!

CHING!

Iscariot felt the steel impact against his cheek, and the hit must have left him a bit loopy, because he began mimicking his thoughts that controlled the spider. He jumped onto his chair and raised his arms as he lifted one leg that bent at the knee. Then, from a Ralph-Macchio-like stance he shouted, "AL-TAH-JE-JAY!" which was Navajo for "ATTACK!"

King Taraxian reared back on its four hind legs and just as the Duke advanced, it pushed off, wrapping itself around the cowbot's entire body. The mech tried to move his arms, but the titanium limbs of constricting metal were much too strong. His chassis moaned the tighter it squeezed, while great bursts of steam escaped through his iron joints like oxygen leaving the body. The Duke fought to retain his upright stance, but the clinging spider forced itself forward, causing them both to go down in a thunderous blur of exploding rock and snow.

KRAM!!!

King Taraxian's claws began slamming into the earth like the pistons of a great wrecking machine, trapping the Duke within the cage of its tremendous eight legs. But before the demon daikaiju was able to gift wrap him in a cloak of impenetrable web, the bot (a tad wiser for the wear) had other plans. He pushed his boots straight up, right into the spider's unprotected underbelly, and his golden spurs began to spin. Chunks of arachnid showered down on the cowbot as the mighty revolving blades dug deep into its stomach.

RRRRRRRRRRRRRRRR!

The spirit of Notawni Nonaashi shrieked from within its spider host, causing the giant beast to scream, while Iscariot fell to his knees and vomited.

The creature responded to the excruciating pain by flinging itself backward. But before it could one-up the Duke, it met with the opening of the giant pit (the one of its own design) that lay behind it and fell in.

BOOOSH!

Everybody in the control center applauded, then applauded again as the Duke pulled himself to his boots and advanced! The last of the F.U.s then closed in from behind, trailing the sleek, red lines of their firing missiles, devastating the edges of the crater.

FWOOOSH BOOOSH!

The remaining jets of the Queen Elizabeth unloaded the rest of their payload as well, then hightailed it back to the carrier that (thanks to the Duke) was now safely out to sea. Jack complimented the commodore on a job well done and ordered them back to England, because there was nothing more they could do but survive. The same went for the outside world as well as there was nothing anybody else could do either. This battle was now between Iscariot and the Earth Intelligence Organization.

The Tomoyuki brought itself in closer, bombarding the beast with another round of isolated laser strikes. The assault rocked the frozen surface as earth and ancient glaciers alike collapsed amidst the explosions, turning towering titans of ice thousands of years old into monstrous puddles of weeping tears. It was coming down to this, and Jack both hoped and prayed (something quite rare for Sir Jonathon) that they could bury this thing in its own hole and send it back to hell. The Duke, from the edge of the giant crater, began yanking the plasma

grenades attached to his steel bolero, then dropping them down into
the hole.

BOOSH! KA-BOOSH!

Jack watched and waited while Takarada's fingertip hovered over
the switch to engage the ROT beam. It was time, time to finish this once
and for all and freakin' go home. The visual from above provided the
control center an aerial view of King Taraxian's spider ass, trying to
hide within its pit to escape the series of explosions. The Duke dug the
points of his mighty steel-toed boots into the thick layer of ice, and
Takarada prepared to fire the weapon.

"In 3 ... 2 ... --"

SWAAAAAAAAP!

In less than the final second of the countdown, King Taraxian shot
a bolt of sticky steel webbing into the air that attached to the bottom of
the Tomoyuki! Then, from inside its own pit, the spider dropped
within its walls, pulling the gigantic carrier down to the surface of the
earth, right on top of the Duke. The mammoth vessel not only sealed
the opening of the monstrous hole, but took the full impact of the ROT
beam, blasting the ship from the inside as the Duke's head breached
the bottom of its hull!

KA-FREAKIN' CHOOM!

The fierce explosion shook the planet, and a good part of Mount
Terror collapsed inward. The entire compound convulsed as rocks and
debris broke through the ceiling of the control center. "Get down!"
Jack yelled and he pushed Takarada out of the way while half of the
room began to cave in. It's steel-plated doors crumbled like aluminum
foil from the extreme weight of the above earth as it pushed down
upon them. Sir Jonathon fell to the floor and looked up to see the
digital feed from the Tomoyuki dissolve. The base went dark for a brief
second, then the yellow of the emergency lights illuminated their new
prison cell. Nobody was going anywhere. Sir Jonathon pulled himself
to his feet and in the aftermath of the great explosion, the Tomoyuki
blew for the third and final time.

BOOOOOSH!

The mighty mountain again rocked, and rubble continued to
shower down from within the control center. With his palms firmly
placed on the edge of a workstation, Jack wobbled, but never fell,
propped up by sheer defiance alone. Pissed off didn't even begin to

cover it, and he sneered from beneath his giant mustache. He didn't need a bloody screen either to tell him what had just happened, because he knew, visual or not.

Chapter XXIII

The fires of the downed Tomoyuki raged, turning the shifting green lights of Aurora Australis to a flickering orange and red. Even without the spider's heat mechanism, the great blaze from the war and the Tomoyuki combined were enough to raise the temperature to a dangerous level. What was once a land of towering glaciers atop great layers of ice was fast becoming a sea of thick, gray slush and smoldering ash. Iscariot let out a triumphant yell and closed in from the edge of his kept distance. Even Doctor Psycho knew not to get too close, knowing he had no real protection either should he have to use the monster's heat weapon. Just like you really don't want to be anywhere near your ground zero when you decide to drop an atomic bomb on it. His visual was dark, but soon the red-tinted view within Iscariot's head opened up as King Taraxian rose above the wreckage. He gazed forward through the eyes of the creature and steered the eight-legged monster towards Mount Terror. From there it would climb the peak in order to tunnel in to the magma chamber, where the organic thorium was waiting, destroying the new base and burying all inside in the process.

Beginning its ascent up the mountain, Iscariot scoffed at the final frost barrier that stood amidst the burning rubble of the other three. Apparently he no longer viewed the freeze screens as any kind of threat, and King Taraxian simply ignored it. The last of the F.U. fighters came about, swarming around the beast hoping to distract it or lure it away somehow. Because they sure as hell knew they couldn't stop it, but still, nobody was giving up, lost cause or not. Then, as they merely annoyed it with the remains of their dwindling payload, the monster turned to face them from the side of the mountain. Its eye ignited to an eerie shade, similar to the southern lights that surrounded the wretched tundra, and it blasted the ships out of existence.

FWOOM! CHOOM! BAM!

Now proving it was not only the king of the freakin' hill, but also fully charged.

Small bursts of sparks escaped through the wilting panels that spanned the inner confines of the Duke's circular cockpit. Thanks to the Tomoyuki freakin' crashing right on top of him, the bot's systems were either failing, or just flat-out destroyed. This included the diamond-particle cylinder from which SCOTT stood, summing up all of the robot's controlling thoughts. Yeah, that was gone, having been blown into a million pieces, along with much of the Duke's chrome-steel head. From beneath the mass of the burning ship, waves of heat and smoke began to seep in through the cracks of the mech's riddled face. While one lone beacon rotated in bright flashes of red, the robotonauts were being pulled out of the electronically-induced sleep-state (something that was standard protocol with technical issues of this magnitude). Then, as Nathan came to, he could hear the faint sound of Jack through the crackling comm. system.

"Duke … Do you bloody read? Come in, Duke. SCOTT … Do you read?"

The partition walls that separated each of the bot's cubicles had already lowered, and as Jack's voice filled the cockpit, nobody heard a word he was saying. Nathan pulled off his headgear in order to assess the damage and sighed, "What a freakin' mess." He then glanced over his left shoulder to check on Olivia, and she removed her helmet. "Thank God," he thought, and Nathan stood up to look behind him to see the Twins were doing the same. He looked to his left at Tommy who was still sleeping and began knocking on top of his E.I.O.-issued hardhat.

"Hey Scoobs, get up."

Tommy groaned and put his hands over his shielded face, blocking out the orange of the sun that lit up the inside of his closed eyelids. After a long stretch he noticed the rank taste in his mouth and smacked his lips a few times. It was a horrible case of the Zactly's and Tommy knew immediately he was returning from that damn Duke coma. He laughed aloud remembering a similar time when he thought he was home waking up from the sleep-state, but was actually in the Duke, still in the throes of battle with Zargatron. "Man, that sucked," he thought, and while he yawned, he was thankful … for about a second.

The smoke and heated toxic fumes were fast filling up the Duke's inner cranium. Tommy yelled that they needed to go to manual, then looked up to the giant switch that lowered from the ceiling between him and Nathan. His mind again slipped into the past, to the last time he had to activate the Duke's manual mode. It took all of his 134 pounds and Michaels 100 or so to engage the damn thing. Tommy let out an irritated groan and, not wasting a second, jumped up and again hung from the red and yellow striped bar of the massive lever. Michael then climbed over the twisted metal within the cockpit to join in. When they were forced to engage the switch before, their combined weight was enough, but this time it wasn't budging. Nathan looked down at his stomach and decided the give the extra poundage he had put on the chance to actually earn its keep. When all three men hung from the lever, they shook and jerked their bodies in an effort to trigger it. It was no use though, because it wasn't a matter of weight this time, the stupid lever was stuck, plain and simple.

While Tommy, Nathan and Michael hung with their heads squeezed between their upward-stretching arms, Tommy looked behind him and asked Liberty or Olivia if they had any bright ideas. Olivia thought for a second, pushed her glasses up, and hadn't a clue, maybe for the first time ever. She then reached down beneath her seat and pulled out her copy of the Duke's *Easy Steps User's Guide* and began thumbing through its pages. Liberty suggested that she and Michael could create an orb and before she even finished her sentence, Michael (getting tired of hanging around) agreed with a quick, "Shyeah, sounds like a plan sis." Nobody really had any idea as to what they were actually going to do, but the soft, monotone voice that resonated from behind them did.

"Or, you could activate the manual mode of the Duke from this button right here."

Olivia and Liberty turned around (as did Nathan, Tommy and Michael while still dangling from their pull-up position) to see SCOTT standing at the rear of the cockpit.

"Dude!" Tommy shouted into the sleeve of his shirt, "Glad to see you! Are you all right? And what the hell are you talking about?"

SCOTT twitched when he felt something that may or may not have been a tinge of computer concern. He did not feel it was he that Tommy should be worried about, as he observed the dumb humans while they hung from the ceiling. But SCOTT knew there were a lot of things he didn't understand (and this was clearly one of them), so he simply answered all of Tommy's questions in the order they came.

"I am glad to see you, too. I am all right also, and *this* is what the hell I am talking about."

SCOTT pointed to the little, red, insignificant button that was right beside him on the wall, just to the left of the exit hatch. It was a tiny thing, one that sat shyly underneath the big, bold letters that read, "PRESS FOR MANUAL MODE." The button was bordered by a metal frame, a frame donning the same damn red and yellow stripes as the massive lever, the one that they, at this very moment were hanging from. Nathan, quite a bit irritated, asked the android if he planned on mentioning this, and SCOTT, giving him another confused glare, simply stated, "I just did." SCOTT then suggested in that smartass, not-trying-to-be-a-smartass tone of his, that they could also let go of the large lever at any time, but only if they felt inclined to do so. Nathan and Tommy dropped into their chairs that were still flat to accommodate the sleep-state position, followed by Michael who fell down on top of them.

Nathan growled and suggested that maybe robot-boy needed a tune-up, when SCOTT reminded him, as well as everybody onboard, that they had learned of the manual switch at the very beginning of their training. This was something even Olivia had failed to remember, something that must have seemed to be of no significance to all at that time. SCOTT then remarked how strange he thought it was that they did not use the small switch to activate the manual mode during the last battle either, adding that he now knew why. After pointing out that the hefty lever that hung from the ceiling was for use *only* if the electronic initiation failed, SCOTT then pressed the small button, with absolutely no effort at all.

The Duke vibrated to the sputtering, electronic pulse of the manual mode, attempting the initiating process.

RRR ... RR ... RRRR ... RRRR!

SCOTT stepped above the circle of sharp shards of the control cylinder from where he once stood. He looked down, then surveyed the billion or so wires that were usually connected to him. It seemed an impossible task, maybe for a human that is, but not for SCOTT. His hands became a mere blur as he reattached many of the severed cables back to his body, working at a tremendous speed in order to aid in the possible resurgence of the robot.

Fumes continued to seep in from the new torn-steel windows of the Duke's face. Some would need to remain simple gateways to the world, while others needed to be covered. Tommy pulled out his trusty satchel and … *SKEEEEETCH! SKEEEEETCH!* … began adhering duct tape to the wilted panels after bending them back into place with his super-damn-hand. The Twins then took it one step further, sealing the deal with a glowing, purple ooze over the strips of wonder-adhesive.

RRR … RRRR … RRRRR!

However, nothing seemed to be working. Olivia, with her face still buried deep in the manual, then discovered yet another process within the mech that could be used in emergency situations. It would redirect energy from the bot's failing systems and convert power to his *still* functioning components, such as his main engines and weapons. Both of which they were going to need, especially since the ROT beam was now freakin' toast. Olivia read from the instructions aloud, and Nathan followed them to a T, typing in the commands on the keyboard within the circular dash in front of him.

The cockpit flashed in a strobe of bright transparency a few times and the front windshield of the Duke flickered, finally erupting into what appeared to be a giant, furry caterpillar. Tommy let out a startled scream along with both Olivia and Liberty upon the gruesome sight of the upper-lipped beast. They stared in horror as the hideous, harry creature began to speak as though nobody knew it even existed, demanding to know if they had a bloody connection or not. Only you couldn't hear any kind of response, because the size of the mighty, white walrus monster was far too vast, depriving anybody on the reverse end of the screen anything but the sight or sound of itself. The monitor again flashed, and Sir Jack backed up into full view from within the shaky camera's frame.

"Come in, Duke," he uttered, placing his palm to his bandaged head, then repeating the words again. "Come in, Duke, do you read?"

On the other side, the flat screen from within the buried Mount Terror control center also flickered, and jagged, gray lines straightened out to the image of Tommy's face.

"Yes, we read and see you Jack!"

237

The cheers of the personnel trapped in the entombed base rang through, because if the Duke was functioning, there was hope for everybody. Even Jack muttered a soft, "Bloody thank God."

Nathan stuck his big face in front of Tommy's, right into the Duke's screen that projected a fuzzy image to the compound and said, "What was that Jack?"

Where Sir Jonathon responded with an angry, "Stow it, Fox, we have bleeding work to do. This isn't —" and Nathan interrupted him, "Yeah, we know … a ruddy tea party, rumph, rumph!"

Jack almost smiled, but instead got right to the point. "Are you mobile?" he asked, neglecting to mention that they were in a bit of a sticky wicket them-damn-selves. Because the last thing Sir Jonathon wanted was for the bleeding Archies to worry about him and Takarada, especially when they had an entire world to save.

Tommy glanced over to Olivia, who looked about the cranial cabin, waiting for both the manual mode and the redirection of power to kick in. The wait was not a long one. In less than a new heartbeat of the Duke, the cockpit fired up in a series of blinking lights, and the robot began its journey back from the dead. Olivia gave Jack a nice, evil kind of grin and replied, "Not yet Sir, but we will be in about two seconds."

Jack allowed himself a brief moment to show his appreciation by extending a quick nod to Olivia, then to the others, "Jolly good, jolly good indeed!" Then he quickly changed his tone. "You are all we bloody have left. If Iscariot's monster gets to the organic thorium," Jack paused, "well, I don't need to tell you, now do I? Your orders are clear and concise. Stop King Taraxian at ALL costs. Because if you don't … I'll bloody have to. Winston out."

The energy transfer linked with the activation of the mech's manual systems and the organic thorium that flowed throughout the cowbot's veins surged! The seats from which Nathan and Tommy slept upon during the sleep-state swiveled, then faced forward. Two U-shaped steering mechanisms, lined with various buttons and switches, ascended up from the floor and Tommy and Nathan wrapped their hands around them. Hal welcomed them to the Duke's manual mode, which was followed by great blasts of power, transforming the spattering of the initiating systems to a full-blown burst of adrenalin!

RRRRRRRRRRRRRRRRRRRRR! CRASH!!!

The Duke broke through the twisted debris of the Tomoyuki that held him captive and towered up to the sky! Great twin plates of chrome steel that covered the upper visual region of the mech's head parted, revealing the diamond particle windshield that protected the robotonauts on the other side. The giant robot slammed his boot down, pounded his titanium fist into his open palm and stole the silence with a thundering blast of his battle horn!

FWAAAAAAAAAAAAMP!

The cowbot launched towards King Taraxian, searing his way through the flurries of smoke-filled snow with Nathan and Tommy gallantly at his helm. Even through the black of the white storm, the sight of the tremendous monster sent a cold chill straight down Nathan's spine. Of course it wasn't the first time he'd physically laid eyes on the beast, but that still didn't make it any easier. Nathan could only stare at it, watching it grow larger in the windshield the closer it came with each passing second.

Upon the oncoming rumble of the mighty Duke's rockets, Iscariot managed to reach a whole new level of complete irritation. He was beyond fed up with the robotonauts and the blasted cowboy mech's never-ending will and determination, two honorable characteristics he truly despised. Time was growing short. He knew he needed to do away with the bot and these meddling E.I.O. punks, once and for all.

The all-too-familiar high-pitched frequency of King Taraxian began to grow louder, which was the surefire tip-off that meant only one thing: Iscariot was preparing the monster's primary weapon for firing. From the side of the mountain, the demon kaiju's abdomen began to throb, and the first pulse of its heat waves radiated into the sky. Nathan signaled the control center within the mountain, telling Takarada to get ready. But before the good doctor could ask exactly what he was getting ready for, the Duke went into action.

The searing heat began to encompass the entire area in a steady flow of distorted vibrations, and the temperature skyrocketed. The outer wave expanded, but just before it could connect with the Duke, Michael grabbed Liberty's hand and the cowbot lit up in a blinding purple force field!

SHOOOOOMP!

The oncoming cowbot didn't even flinch when the extreme pulses of heat, meant to turn it into molten metal, were simply absorbed into the Twin's gel-like orb. What's more (and thanks to a bit of alien knowhow), the molecules within the blistering waves were somehow being forced to slow down. When coming into contact with the force field, the searing vibrations were turned to a mere simmer, offering the robotonauts even more protection from the rising heat.

"Hell, yes!" Nathan yelled, not having the slightest clue to the "hows" but taking full advantage of the "whys."

SCOTT also concurred with a subtle, "Impressive," as flows of Duke-dictating electricity coursed through his body. However, they had to hurry, because everybody could see what a tremendous load it was for the brother and sister aliens to bear. They could only take so much, and unfortunately their limited powers didn't work like the freakin' Force. Size and duration made an incredible difference, and too much of either would extinguish Michael and Liberty's life forces. In other words, they'd cease to exist, probably why Jack didn't have them teleport Iscariot *and* his dumb spider to the farthest reaches of the galaxy in the first place.

Tommy and Nathan rocketed the Duke up the slope parallel to the side of the mountain and closed in on the beast from behind. They were racing with time on all levels, because even though the heat wasn't penetrating the alien's orb of protection, it was still doing a number on the arctic remains. Plus, the Twins were beginning to fade.

The bot came up fast and eased himself beneath the legs of the mammoth spider, then pushed off from underneath. It forced the creature up, then sent it sliding upon its back, knocking the proverbial king of the hill down to the bottom of the summit, right to the base of the remaining frost barrier. The wind left both Iscariot's and the arachnid's lungs when it hit with a colossal, *THUD!* which in turn cued Nathan.

"NOW!" he screamed, and Takarada knew just what to do!

ZZZZZZZZZZZZZZZZZZZZZZZZZZZZZZZSPSHHH!

The screen erupted in a frostbitten flash of white brilliance, not only counteracting, but cancelling out the fierce heat of the spider! As soon as the air returned to Iscariot's chest, he shouted an array of colorful four-letter words into the emptiness of his ship's bridge. He cursed the Duke, Jack and Takarada, but mostly Nathan, because he could see his face on the other side of the cowbot's diamond-particle windshield. It was plain as day, and Iscariot could make him out sneering through the glass from behind the tips of the mech's twin six-shooters. The ones that were aimed directly at the undercarriage of the huge beast, right between its curling legs that were reaching for the sky.

Nathan glared at the monster while they rocketed straight down towards it at mach 1 from a freakin' 90-degree descent. Only this time it wasn't a dream, this time he was wide awake. Nathan could feel his blood boil. He hated this thing and Iscariot both with every freakin' fiber of his being, almost as much as he hated himself, well, at least his former self. Because the clearer his mind became, the only thing Nathan despised as much as Iscariot was that drunk, self-absorbed womanizing son of a bitch he himself used to be. Not too long ago, Nathan honestly couldn't see what the stupid big deal was. Yeah he drank a bit, so freakin' what. It wasn't hurting anybody and it was harmless enough. Only now Nathan knew, knew what a bastard that guy was, kind of like Iscariot. The guy that would sure as shit step all over you in order to get exactly what he wanted, even if he had to use a damn giant spider to do it. Nope, Nathan didn't even like the shadow of his old self anymore and didn't want anything to do with him. Not unless it was to help him or somebody in remembering just what he was capable of becoming. And as far as those confusing inner conflicts of figuring out who he was went, shit, they were nothing compared to the misery of his past life. After all, it's not so bad to screw up if you're sincerely trying. Like his pop said, he'd figure it all out if he'd just give himself half the chance.

Nathan reached his hand into his pocket and without removing the three-year medallion, clutched it tight. He then did the one thing he had yet to do, admitted to himself what he had known all along, that he was indeed an alcoholic.

The Lizard King placed his thumbs on the little red buttons atop both sides of the steering U, then looked over to Tommy and he did the same. A general feeling of "lets kick some effing ass" overtook Nathan, and he gazed into the eyes of himself from within the head of the beast. Because he now got it, he now knew that his monster, like Notawni Nonaashi or any other spirit, would always be there and could never die. It would forever be in the darkness, sharpening its pincers, waiting for the chance to arise from the bowels of the earth. He now understood, knowing he'd have to be on his toes every damn day in order to send the vile thing back to hell should it rear its ugly face. Nathan pressed forward and shouted throughout the cockpit, "Let him have it!"

BOOSH! KRAM! BOOSH BOOSH! BWAM!

The iron shafts of the bot's magnificent pistols erupted in a series of bursts, pummeling the creature with an onslaught of photon lead! Great searing chunks of roasted arachnid projected straight up, blinding Nathan and Tommy for a second, when a burning piece of brown flesh splattered smack into the windshield. The searing aroma was sweet and totally disgusting, but just before Nathan had the chance to puke his guts out, it disappeared with the great gusts of wind. Then, just before colliding into the downed monster, the Duke arched his steel spine, raised his chin and shot right back up into the sky. He also made damn sure to blast the beast with the raging trail of fire that poured from his ascending boots as he did!

"That's bloody it!" Jack screamed from the control center. "The underbelly! Keep hitting the wretched thing in its ruddy bread basket! Don't let it flip over, this may be our only bleeding chance!"

The Duke leveled off amidst the smoke-filled clouds and hovered while pulling the remaining plasma grenades from his glimmering bolero. Hurling them down one after the other, he watched from the sky as each emitted an explosion of fire, spider flesh and bone upon impact. King Taraxian fought repeatedly to flip itself over in order to regain the high ground, but each intense blast from the bot was telling it otherwise. The Duke was hitting it hard, pounding it right where it seemed to count the most with everything he had. Then, as the cowbot tossed its final grenade, it went for its last two pieces of hope.

He aimed his iron fists down towards the creature, and steel panels slid open from atop of the bot's plated arms, revealing two FUKM UP missiles in each. It wasn't in the hopes that the same devastating warheads, the very ones that proved so damn worthless on the beast from its upside, would prove more effective on its underside. Nope, that wasn't it at all, it was because they were all the Duke had left. The two rockets, spanning the tips of his wrists all the way to his elbows, rose up from within his chambered forearms and launched in a smoke-filled fury.

SHOOOM! SHOOOOM! BWOOOOOOOSH!

Yup, that seemed to be doing the trick and the FUKM UPs were indeed living up to their not-so-official title. Because that was just what they were doing. It also proved to Jack that attacking the soft underbelly of a kaiju, rather than the heavily-protected shielding of its massive exoskeleton, just may be the better option.

King Taraxian wasn't moving. A combination of blood and organic thorium poured heavily out of the demon daikaiju's wounds, turning the earth-riddled slush of the arctic landscape into thick, chunky pools of spider guts and ooze.

"Holy shit!" Tommy yelled, "Old eight-eyes is down for the count! He's freakin' down!"

Olivia and the Twins jumped up, then stood behind Nathan and Tommy watching the finale from behind the windshield of the Duke. SCOTT even ripped the attached wires from his body in order to be by their sides. The great fire flickered through the glass, and they gazed at the flesh and muscle of the spider-god, observing while it burned to nothing but charred remains. Their battle-worn faces reflected the lives that had been lost, of course due to the beast itself, but primarily due to Leopold Iscariot and his hell-bent crusade for power. Nathan rubbed his chin (in that same damn way Jack rubbed his mustache) pondering the results of the assault. After all, it was *his* metaphor that was lying beneath them in a heaping inferno, so he had every right to be extra cautious. It was probably hard for him to accept that the indestructible creature was actually dying, as he witnessed its layers of skin melting away. However, seeing was believing, and there was no denying that it wouldn't be long until all that remained was the titanium skeleton of Iscariot's design.

The arctic cold was slow to return due to the remaining spike in temperature caused by the final blast of King Taraxian. In addition, the burning piles of rubble that now littered the tundra were still ablaze and emitting large amounts of heat. Great streams of water flowed down from all sides of the mountain, and the spider began to sink through the top layer of the collapsing ice.

The boots of the Duke splashed into the remaining snow, rock and slush next to the towering blaze of the spider. He folded his steel arms, making sure everything was as it seemed, observing the melting ice as it extinguished the inferno of the creature while the earth swallowed it back up. The beast squirmed, discharging one last blast of wavering web into the smoldering emptiness. But it seemed it was just a reflex response, one that signified the death of the giant arachnid.

While the flesh of the spider-god burned, Iscariot found he could no longer contain the great Navajo spirit as it fought to return to the earth, the very spirit held prisoner within the synthetic cage of his eight-legged machine. Searing rods of pain raced through the neurons of his brain as Notawni Nonaashi and his brilliant computer retaliated. Another cog within his twisted mind slipped, and he began clawing at his pounding head, trying in vain to rip out the very microchip he had implanted in his skull not long ago. The agony was excruciating, but worse than that, Iscariot knew that once the essence of Notawni Nonaashi escaped its arachnid host, the chip would heat up and melt. Nothing big mind you, but the searing plastic buried deep between his ears would cause irreversible damage to his perfect brain, something that his bold and silly arrogance had convinced himself could never happen. With Iscariot's hands interlaced behind his neck, the relentless torture pulled him to his knees. Just before he passed out, he called for his minions, demanding they grab a sterol scalpel, a surgical clamp and the remains of the whiskey he had used to taunt Nathan.

The Duke stood tall like a protective parent with its hands upon its steel hips and his chin protruding far beyond his face. If he had a cape, the frosty arctic wind would surely have been blowing it from behind him in a proud display of robotic triumph. He watched as King Taraxian gazed up from beneath the melting ice that flowed over its infused head, while the black water sucked it below the surface.

Jack interrupted, causing the display of the healing earth projected upon the Duke's windshield to be consumed by his big, fat face. He reminded them that they still needed to apprehend Iscariot (or what was left of him) before breaking out the bubbly. Nathan was about to comment on Sir Buzz-Kill's impeccable timing and as he—

FWOOOOOOSH!!!

Ice and ocean erupted into a watery fury of blue steel, and the tremendous force shoved the Duke backwards into the mountain, right onto his robot ass. He immediately drew his six-shooters, (the ones that hadn't recharged) sending nothing but echoing clicks in the direction of the freakish sight that broke through the wet explosions. Its razor-sharp, titanium claws from the tips of its tarsi plunged into the ice, pulling itself forward one metal leg after the other as it advanced. The synthetic flesh that once wrapped itself around the monster, as well as its cyborg insides, was all but gone, leaving nothing but the metal skeletal remains. In other words, it was the steel, robotic infrastructure Iscariot created due to the increase in size when he served the spirit its organic thorium and strontium 90 cocktail. But now, the proud, Indian spider-god had broken free and had returned to the earth, as Notawni Nonaashi wasn't about destroying the planet ... nor had it ever been. It was merely a prisoner held within the bars of Iscariot's neuron computer, just another pawn in his sinister plan, and now, like its insides, it too was gone. As was Iscariot, because he had now become the beast.

Chapter XXIV

The steel spider hissed while organic thorium oozed like molasses through its sinister faceplate, right down to the tip of its alloy pincers. Thick and green, the vile liquid splattered onto the Duke's face, all while the arachnid's metal skeletal legs trampled the downed bot deep into the ground.

The mech's chrome reflected shimmers of red, making it appear as though he was being beaten to a bloody pulp. When in actuality, it was the glow of the creature's only remaining eye. It was shaped like a jewel and the ocular prosthesis within its steel skull resembled Iscariot's own modified seeing appendage. Because his eye (just like the chrome spider's) was gone too, along with a good portion of his head. And it's not because looking like a bloodied zombie was all the rage, but because it was the only way to remove the ticking, time-bomb microchip.

Perched within his captain's chair, cables resembling the snakes of Medusa's hair flowed from the insides of Iscariot's altered head to the banks of his neuro-computer. The small canister that was once filled with the essence of Notawni Nonaashi had now been replaced with chunks of Iscariot's skull and bloodied pieces of his brain. Minions were quick to wipe the carnage up as it fell to the floor, while sparks spit through the gaps that now infiltrated his mutilated melon. It was he, himself, whom Iscariot was now controlling in the form of the gargantuan, eight-legged mechanical skeleton, not some blasted, unworthy spider-god. Not anymore that is, and he shrieked in his new cybertronic, synthesized voice, "If you unt vant something done right, you unt need to do it yourself." He then laughed hysterically as he slipped into that little chasm located within your head, the dark, scary one from which no one ever returns.

Everybody was being thrown about the Duke's cabin each time

one of the arachnid's metal claws came slamming down. The sound was devastating, echoing in their ears like a hundred or so hammers beating on the tin of an enormous garbage can.

BWAM! BWAM! BWAM!

And from the cranial cockpit's windshield, the rampaging legs from above looked almost fake, like the bad special effects of a cheesy, sci-fi monster flick. At least until one of the spider's cast-iron nails punctured the cheek of the cowbot, then things got real pretty damn fast.

BWOOOOOSH!

Olivia fell towards the claw that had busted through the Duke's steel-reinforced face, and Nathan reached fast, grabbing her hand just before the massive, steel nail rescinded.

"Jesus Christ! What the hell is that freaky looking thing?" Nathan screamed and as the bombardment persisted, SCOTT tried to help them back into their seats, telling them above the outside thunder,

"It is the steel infrastructure of King Taraxian created by Leopold Iscariot, the robotic skeleton needed for the arachnid daikaiju to support its own mass."

BAM! BAM!

The pounding was relentless and Nathan lost his footing, falling against the thin railing that outlined the Duke's cockpit cubicles. He groaned, but still managed to pull himself back up.

"Yeah, like that robotic leg we saw him replacing at the abandoned FUJI, only that was surrounded by spider. Not like this freakin' one-eyed, titanium whatchamacallit."

Steam began to hiss through the metal and the Duke's failing systems' alarm again began to wail. Tommy yelled that they needed to try to get to their stations and regroup, but Hal knew better, when he politely informed them that they needed to "Abandon ship."

SCOTT changed his course from getting them to their seats, to just getting them the hell out of the Duke because Iscariot was not stopping, therefore neither was the demon spider-mech. The evil doctor was indeed determined, determined to tear the cowbot apart piece by piece, then do the same with all of those on board.

BAM! BAM! CRACK!

This time SCOTT tumbled with the robotonauts, and they all fell to the rear of the Duke's head, at the base of his skull's back and only door. He reached down and spun the massive iron wheel that opened the Duke's escape hatch, only (and as suspected) nothing was happening. The android began to pull on the door, and Tommy reached down with his super-damn-hand and began to help. Michael grasped for Liberty and Nathan stopped him. Michael gave him a surprising glare and uttered a soft, "Dude?" Nathan stated that SCOTT and Tommy could get it open and that he and Liberty should save their valuable, yet limited powers because he had a hunch they were going to need them.

The metal door burst open, and the cold, arctic air rushed in along with a shot of steam when the hatch depressurized. SCOTT lowered Olivia down first to the slushy ground beneath the Duke's head, and as he was about to help Liberty, Jack's face engulfed the cowbot's windshield.

"Ladies and gentlemen, it is with the deepest regret that I must inform you of our failure on this mission. Many parts of the compound have been compromised to the point where some of us will not be going home. We will, however, be evacuating those who are able from the base, and I also urge you to do the same. We believe Iscariot will be attempting to gain control of the organic thorium immediately upon destroying the Duke."

Sir Jonathon began to slip away from his stuffy commander's status and Jack took over.

"Get your bloody asses out of here if you can. Utilize Michael and Liberty's special powers if need be, but get as far from here as possible. Do not attempt re-entry into the mountain compound. REPEAT … Nathan, Tommy and even you SCOTT, do NOT attempt re-entry into the mountain. It has been my, as well as Kyoshi's, greatest pleasure to serve with you."

Doctor Takarada joined Sir Jonathon by his side, bowed, then ordered SCOTT to save his friends if at all possible. Then he smiled, as did Jack.

"Good luck and God speed. Winston out."

Nathan glared at both Tommy and SCOTT, "What the hell does that mean?" he asked, and Tommy replied with a,

"What the hell do you think it means? They're gonna freakin' nuke the mountain!" he yelled as he climbed out of the bot.

Nathan felt his heart enter his throat and he looked up to SCOTT as he jumped down. "What do *YOU* think it means?" and SCOTT echoed Tommy's reply,

"Yes, they are going to freaking nuclear the mountain."

"They can't do that!" Nathan yelled and not because he was scared, but because he didn't want to leave this world with effing Leopold Iscariot ruling it. Nor did he want to leave Jack and Doctor Takarada behind.

"Whatcha thinking, Raggy?" Tommy asked Nathan, even though he already knew.

"We gotta get them the hell out of there, that's what I'm thinking. I'm tired of people dying on our watch. And how the hell are we supposed to fight Iscariot without Jack and Takarada anyhow? We're not! Besides, I think I have an idea."

Then, just as SCOTT joined them on the ground and the ass-kicking soundtrack was about to start, the great metal chassis of the Duke was whisked away! Pierced through the heart, it was cast aside by one of the eight claws of the steel demon.

SHOOOMPH!

The red-jeweled eye of the creature glared through the flurry of fresh snow, down onto SCOTT and the other robotonauts. They retaliated by being as petrified as possible at the up-close-and-personal sight of the giant titanium skeleton. Frozen with fear, they waited while it moved in to devour them, or smash them, or do whatever the hell a gargantuan robot-spider did.

Michael slowly eased his hand in the direction of Liberty's. She did the same, slipping hers behind Olivia's back, towards his, but before they could make contact, *BWAP!* The mighty, steel tarsi of the monster machine knocked the alien a good ten feet away from his sister. It wasn't in the mood for any surprises. Michael sat up from the puddle he had landed in, and even though he was drenched he was okay, well, except for the cold slush that had soaked through his pants and infiltrated his underwear. That wasn't good at all.

Iscariot wasn't wasting time with funky traps or elaborate schemes to slowly bring forth their demise, not anymore. There would be no more games, only death, plain and simple, swift and deliberate. The titanium skeleton reared back to strike, and SCOTT pulled everybody in and attempted to shield them from the inevitable.

In less than a second, the southern lights dimmed and the scattered fires smothered when the devastating cold returned in an explosion of frozen arctic air. The perpetual darkness then lit up from amidst the glow of one star and one star only, as the surrounding mountains of glaciers erupted into a million flailing shards!

KA-BOOSH!!!!

Flurries of white consumed the sky, and Nathan glanced up. It was hard to tell through the blur, but it appeared to be two magnificent hands tightening around the back of the metal spider-monster. "Everybody freakin' run!" he hollered, and even though the run was more of a trudge, it was a wise move nevertheless. The great claws crammed the infused head of the robotic skeleton into the rock and snow, pushing it down as deep as it would go! It then pulled back on the titanium shoulders of the arachnid and forced its face down again … and again.

Nathan watched the battle from over his shoulder as they attempted to make their way through the tundra. It was a little like watching an old monster movie on an even older television. One of those piece-of-crap, black-and-white specials, complete with tinfoil rabbit ears and snowy reception. Yup, that's just what it looked like as the towering, dinosaur-like brute lifted the steel skeletal frame of the spider high above its head!

"Hit the deck!" Nathan yelled, and the kaiju who had risen from the ice hurled the arachnid into the side of the mountain!

FWAM!

Rock and hardened snow rained down, and everybody covered the backs of their heads with their hands. Not that falling rubble from the sky was a good thing, but Tommy had to stop anyhow because he needed to catch his failing breath. It wasn't because he smoked like a freakin' chimney either, but because the devastating cold was seriously effecting his lungs. The faster you ran, the deeper you inhaled. The deeper you inhaled, the more your insides felt like you were swallowing an angry swarm of bees. It wasn't just him though, it was all of them, with the exception of SCOTT. He, of course, was having no trouble, probably because of the whole not-needing-to-breathe thing. For everybody else, it was a serious problem and cause for great concern. There was absolutely no heat left in the air whatsoever, no remaining remnants of King Taraxian's final blast. Even the tremendous scattered fires of the Tomoyuki had all been extinguished with the coming of this big arctic beastie. It was clear that not becoming spider fodder was a good plan, but running wasn't the answer.

Tommy stood up from the snow and did the "I'm freezing" dance, and as he patted the sides of his arms, the oxygen escaping his lungs became visible in the frozen air.

"Hey Look!" he joked, "I'm a daikaiju!" and he pretended to exhort an atomic heat-ray with his frosty breath. Nathan shook his head as Tommy's God-awful pun was hitting just a little too close to home for right now. He then removed his leather jacket and offered it to Olivia, but before she could refuse it, a warm, purple glow surrounded them.

"This should protect us for a good amount of time," Liberty stated. "It will be sufficient until we decide what our next plan of action is to be."

However, Nathan already knew exactly what they needed to do. It always seemed that whatever they were supposed to do was exactly whatever Jack told them *not* to do. In this case, they needed to get to the compound where Sir Jonathon and Doctor Takarada were. Because if Liberty and Michael could indeed get them far away from here as Jack had suggested, there was no way the bus was leaving without them. Nathan then said out loud exactly what everybody thought he was thinking, that they needed to get into the base and rescue Jack and Takarada. Even though the idea was almost sheer suicide, there was no resistance whatsoever, not even from SCOTT, who, thanks to Tommy and Nathan, was growing accustomed to disobeying direct orders.

The android stated he knew of the base's hidden entrance the transport trucks used to access the landing strip at the foot of the mountain, which really wasn't a shock to anyone. However, he added it was almost a mile away and also in the direction of the battling daikaiju.

Nathan smiled and gave a slight jerk of his head. "Sounds like a plan! Stick close to the mountain, follow SCOTT, catch a show and die a horrible death all at the same time!"

Tommy and Olivia agreed as they looked around, probably trying to figure out another solution, but there really wasn't any other. Liberty then advised that they may want to lose the purple, glowing force-field, as it would more than likely attract unwanted guests.

"Even better!" Nathan said, "Let's go."

SCOTT ripped pieces of fabric from his designer android wear and suggested that people (and aliens alike) cover their mouths to protect their lungs. Any extra clothing like jackets or shirts on top of a shirt were also torn up and used to cover exposed areas of skin, like their faces. The Twins walked everybody the short distance to the foot of the mountain, where they lined up single file to get as close and concealed as possible.

"We ready?" Nathan asked, and before anybody could answer, Liberty loosened her grip on Michael's hand, and the warm orb of protection dissipated.

Chapter XXV

The Twin's protective orb dissipated and the freezing air welcomed everybody with a harsh bitch-slap right to the face. It was a different kind of cold altogether (not that he knew much about it growing up in California) and far surpassed anything Nathan could have ever imagined. God how he hated it, hoping to hell they wouldn't need to endure the freakin' tundra for too long. Nathan was getting quite pissy, then decided it was time for an attitude adjustment and that he needed to remain positive. This was actually pretty easy, because he was absolutely 100% positive that they were going to die a slow and agonizing death in this giant, effing freezer.

The quick thought of how nice a whiskey straight up would be right about now entered his numbed brain. Nathan's mouth trembled when he imagined the fiery liquid warming his insides, from the tip of his tongue all the way down to his cold and empty gut. The idea was fleeting, it came and went, but he still hated himself for even thinking such a thing. He shook it off … he had to. Besides, there wasn't any booze for a billion square miles, so even if he wanted a drink, he couldn't have one. And that was indeed a good thing, because sometimes a lack thereof is all that saves your ass. Nathan looked ahead to his friends while taking up the rear of the single-file line that eased along the cold wall of rock and ice. Even as the winter air chilled him to the bone, he dreamed about all the things he wanted to do when this effing war was over, and it gave him both hope and strength. It was almost like that brief, little bolt of lightning that zapped Nathan's brain, his so-called moment of clarity. The one that made him realize just how good he already had it, or for that matter, could have it. Sometimes though, it shows you the rotten things, sometimes even horrible things, and you either learn to deal or you get pummeled by the falling boulders of life.

FWOOM! CRASH!

Everybody backed up against the sterile volcano as a waterfall of jagged stone, ice and earth came tumbling down around them. The colliding rocks were followed by a tremendous, *WUMP!* when the thick walrus-hide of the arctic kaiju crashed to the ground right in front of them! The beast hoisted itself up and let out a roar, forcing the cowering robotonauts to cover their ears, then dissolved into the snow and star-lit dullness, back into the battle!

Nathan forgot about the cold for a split second, let out an abrupt "Whoa!" and hollered over the distant war, "I don't know where the hell that thing came from, but I'm freakin' glad it's on our side!"

SCOTT pointed out they were almost there, but they again had to stop as the brawling beasts took turns slamming the other into the side of the mountain. The android then noted he could actually see the entrance point. It had been buried a bit, but *that* wouldn't be the problem. The problem was that damn eight-legged mechanical contraption pushed up against the slope of the summit, bracing itself in with its back legs. Tommy mumbled through the strips of shirt that were protecting his face,

"What the hell is that thing doing?" and it was as though the steel creature itself answered his question.

A sharp blinding light forced their forearms over their eyes, and a green ray shot from its red-jeweled eye!

FWEEEEEP!

The spider's heat beam sent the monster backwards, and even though it fell onto its spikey tail, its massive layers of fat absorbed most of the blast.

BOOOSH!

This was followed by a, "Holy Flirkin' Snit!" from both Tommy and Nathan.

"That freakin' spider-thing still has its heat ray!" Nathan shouted. "I hope it doesn't have any other tricks up its sleeves we don't know about!"

The sound of choppers high above cut through the wintery sounds of the arctic when the base started the evacuation process. Black silhouettes of twin-blade helicopters began to rise up and out of the mouth of the volcano, making their hurried escape towards the ocean.

"Unt nine!" Iscariot whispered while the wires that ran from his head into his neuro-computer emitted tiny sparks of processing thoughts. Beams again ignited from the electronic eye of the spider skeleton, and it began picking off the copters one by one with its ray as they attempted their retreat.

BOOSH! BAM!

It then lowered its infused metal skull and again blasted the mighty kaiju, this time sending it off the surrounding volcanic island and into the sea.

KER-SPLOOOOSH!

Both SCOTT and Tommy began pushing away the debris that had blocked the hidden entrance of the base. Like SCOTT had stated it didn't take much, and as soon as they entered, the fierce cold subsided. It wasn't anything tropical mind you, but it was indeed a vast improvement. Nathan asked the Twins how they were holding out, and Michael responded with a quick thumbs up. They knew Nathan had plans for them, or they would have simply teleported themselves right into the buried control center that was holding Jack and Takarada prisoner.

SCOTT tried to use his inner-communication system's link to Takarada to let them know that the cavalry was on its way, only to encounter android static in his head. Something in the frozen air was jamming the signal, either that or it was Iscariot. Much of the compound within the mountain had been destroyed and, like the base's control center, was buried in piles of rock and metal. The good news, however, (and Lord knows they could have used some) was that it was a relatively clear path up the stair shaft that led to Jack and Takarada.

All hands reached down and began pulling away the debris that blocked the iron doors leading to the observation platform. The task would have been impossible too, if not for SCOTT's robotic strength and the power Tommy held within his bionic super-damn-hand. It was also the first time anyone had witnessed the alien Twins physically exert themselves over such a mindless task as moving stone, obviously they were still saving their powers. Olivia stood just behind Nathan, tossing every rock he handed her as far off to the side as she could. He then pulled up a large chunk of cement garnished in sharp steel, and a dim dust-laden glow broke through the cracks beneath it. He sighed and wiped the soot from his forehead. He could see they were almost there. They hauled butt to remove the final rocks, but as they did, the tremendous cogs that pulled the control center into the side of the mountain began to vibrate. Everybody glanced up to the massive iron wheels that trembled above, spitting earth and dust down upon their heads while they struggled to spin. It was obvious Jack and Takarada were trying to return it to its original mountainous perch for a possible means of escape. That, or maybe they just wanted better seats to the show because neither of them had any idea as to what was happening below.

The fabricated wall of ice and rock used to conceal the black windows of the control room growled while it forced itself open. Its steel wheels creaked as they rolled the mobile deck along the damaged tracks to the outside of the slope. But as the hidden room revealed itself and ascended out the side of the summit, the space it had just occupied (the very space Nathan, Tommy and everybody else were rushing to clear) started to give way. It seemed the only thing holding up the earth above the control room *was* the control room, and when it departed, so did the support system.

FWAM!!!!

SCOTT kicked the beaten doors wide open with the base of his booted heel, and the entire band stormed in through the thick of the smoke. They almost looked kinda' cool too, sort of like superheroes donning the cover of a Jack Kirby SPECTACULAR SPECIAL COLOSSAL EDITION comic book!

Well, maybe superhero wasn't quite an accurate description, especially when the rising debris from the floor caused Tommy to stumble over Michael's shoe, which led him to fall on top of Liberty. She in turn reached for Olivia as she fell, pulling her down with her, while SCOTT parted the dust with the palms of his hands attempting to locate the fallen agents. Nathan, amidst the chaos, then stepped over the entanglement of people up to front and center, and as he waved the floating dirt from his face, he coughed out a loud, "Ta-Da!"

Sir Jonathon was pinching his cheeks with his thumb and index finger and looked at everybody as though they had lost their bleeding minds.

"Good Lord! Do you ever listen to a ruddy word I say?" Jack uttered and as he did, Takarada snapped a digital picture with his cell phone.

"Great to see you too, Jacky Boy," Nathan blurted out in a nice tone

of total sarcasm. Even though Jack would never let on, he was actually glad to see them, his anger stemming more out of mere concern than anything else. Sure he was worried about his agents' well-being (probably both physically and mentally), but there was something even bigger that was bothering him.

"Now that we are all ruddy here, just who the hell is going to wage the next battle against Iscariot? Who will protect the planet after we all die like bloody trapped rats in this mobile tin can? Nobody, that's who!"

And it may have been a bit arrogant on Jack's part, but he shuddered when he imagined the E.I.O. trying to hobble along on one leg without himself, Takarada, SCOTT or even the bleeding Archies. Not to mention that the world would be ruled by the likes of Leopold Iscariot, who in a very short time would possess the strongest source of power on the planet and all elements needed to create it. Yup, it was indeed pompous for Sir Jonathon to insinuate this, but it also happened to be true.

Jack, however, did what he always did, he pushed forward. After all, what was he going to do, scold them? Damn right he was!

"Come look at this!" he demanded, and Jack led them to the plate-glass observation windows of the incapacitated mobile control center. "What do you see?" he asked, more in an attempt to demonstrate his point, not really looking for actual answers.

Then, as Nathan began to name each failing element of the E.I.O. (including the Duke) that lay scattered across the tundra, Jack told him to shut the hell up. Nathan then mentioned another small detail, but this was having something to do with Iscariot's spider and the tiny fact that it was climbing up the side of the mountain, right towards them!

Jack turned, then pulled his gold pocket watch out from beneath his wrinkled and dust-covered jacket. He clicked it open and stared at it, then looked at the concerned face of Takarada. Both men shook their heads at the other, tipping off Nathan that they were indeed in a race against time. He then heard SCOTT's voice from within his head, declaring in a flashback doused in way too much reverb, "They are going to freaking nuclear the mountain."

Yeah, Nathan already knew that, but he was hoping to rescue Jack, Takarada and all who were trapped in the control center before the big mountain went boom. He was also hoping that the explosion would take out Iscariot and his blasted spider *after* they were gone, not the other way around. Because even if the damn thing was skipping his lunch of "E.I.O. agents under glass" and going straight for the organic thorium, it didn't really matter. Either way they were dead, be it by a creepy robotic spider or an atomic blast, neither of which were part of Nathan's overall plan. But using the powers of the Twins had always been.

"Damn it!" Nathan shouted. "We have to move now! Screw daddy iron legs, we need to get the hell out of here!"

He hated to have to do this. He knew if they left now, the war with Iscariot would become almost impossible to win. However, they'd still be alive, and that beat the shit out of being dead. Besides, there was no saving the organic thorium now anyhow. Nathan looked to the Twins, then to Tommy who agreed with a quick nod. Liberty told everybody within the control center to gather into a circle and brace themselves.

"We live to fight another day, dudes!" Michael hollered, and when Liberty reached for his hand, a steel claw of the spider crashed through the window!

The immobilized observation deck jerked down, tilting even more from its damaged axis.

CRASH!!!

The freakish, plated face of the spider's skull peered in, it's tremendous weight pulling the mobile platform downward like the sloping deck of a sinking ship. All within the control center fell, sliding towards the shattered windows that opened up to not only the mouth of the steel creature, but also to the plunging summit below!

Michael still gripped Liberty's hand, but now more for the purpose of preventing her from sliding into the metal jaws of the monster. He braced both of his feet beneath one of the heavy workstations and held on by the tips of his black boots. He then latched onto another person with his free hand when she glided down on her butt towards the beast. Veins bulged from Tommy's arm and he gnashed his teeth, because freakin' Jack weighed about a ton and a half, but he had no intention of letting go. He also had no intention of letting go of Takarada's hand either, who was holding on to both of them. SCOTT dug his android fingers deep into the floor, while Nathan, Olivia and one other FUJI staff member held on to his ankles. The spider reached its massive claw in through the frames of the shattered glass, and the

259

room dropped forward even further. The quick jolt snapped SCOTT's body like a wet towel, and Olivia lost her grip. Nathan tried to grab her, but Olivia's fingers slipped through his grasp, so he too let go of SCOTT's hand.

There was far too much chaos and far too many bodies being tossed about for the Twins to safely teleport anybody anywhere. But they were still the only ones who could do anything, and there was absolutely no reason to ration powers any longer. Michael closed his eyes and the woman he was grasping screamed in disbelief when he loosened his grip on her hand.

SHOOOOOMP!

A transparent, glowing purple goo took the place of the shattered windows and followed along the curved archway that lined the crumbling deck. The flexible mass was just what the doctor ordered, and the tumbling people (including Nathan and Olivia) simply bounced off the reflective rubbery substance. Even ol' spider breath, with its mammoth, piercing iron fangs couldn't penetrate the oozing orb of protection. It didn't seem to matter though, and the arachnid simply climbed upward, leaving all inside with nothing but a view from underneath its metal abdomen.

The observation platform again began to shake, and over the hum of the Twins pulsing, purple wall, Nathan, like everybody else, could hear the demon's alloy talons rip into the rock above.

There was no way Michael and Liberty could maintain the flow needed to not only keep the monster out, but also to prevent the deck from crashing down the side of the volcano. They just didn't have the means or the capabilities, at least without dire or deadly consequences.

Nathan remembered a time when they teleported a rogue, daikaiju crab from Tokyo to London, and it damned near killed them both. He also remembered the five-way handshake between them, himself, Tommy and Olivia, pledging to never use their powers if they were ever to put them in danger. He remembered that promise very well, the promise he knew they would break to save everybody if necessary.

The purple glow grew and so did the hum that accompanied it. Nathan wasn't sure what the hell they were going to do, but he, Olivia and Tommy knew they were up to something and screamed, "NOOO!"

The room jerked upwards, like it had a coiled spring beneath it,

260

and the only thing that happened was the orb dissipated when Michael lost his grip with Liberty. Nathan looked about the deck, then over to Michael who only shrugged his shoulders just as the steel torso of the spider was yanked up. The room was momentarily still, and those scattered about the floor stared out the now vacant row of windows, waiting.

BOOOSH! CRASH!

The frame of the titanium arachnid smashed into the slope from below the deck and rolled down the side of the mountain. Nobody had any idea what was going on while they watched the twisted, metal frame of the beast disappear within the haze of its own tumbling body. That is until the chrome-steel heels of the Duke came hurling down from the other side of the shattered windows in front of them. His boots landed full force, crunching deep into the snow, hauling ass after the spider down the slope of the dark mountain, which was actually getting brighter due to the growing light of a flickering star.

Takarada grabbed one of the tilting workstations and pulled himself to his feet, then took inventory of all around him, accounting for SCOTT and all five of the robotonauts. He then turned back to the windows and to the Duke, observing as the charging bot hauled ass down the mountain after the spider. He wasn't quite sure what to make of this new development, but as he glared at the resurrected cowboy mech, he did know that this was impossible.

Chapter XXVI

The North Star cast an eerie glow upon the frozen tundra, finding its way in through the shattered windows of the tilting observation deck. Jack and Takarada eased themselves down to the bent frames that once housed its huge plates of glass, where they held on and peered out. The wind was whipping, and even though it was quite the fall to the summit, they needed to know what the hell was going on. As both men gazed upon the growing battle below, a large circle of green light appeared on the rustling waves that surrounded the volcanic island.

In one mighty thrust of crashing sea, the arctic kaiju emerged from the freezing, white-capped water, back onto the icy shore. It stretched its thick, massive body upwards, clenched its fists, bent its mighty arms at its elbows and flexed. The lone star crackled, and a solid beam of white and blue ice blasted from the middle of the monster's muscular chest!

FWAAAAAAP!

The frozen ray made a mighty, steel ping when it collided with the spider, and the force pushed it backwards, right beneath the Duke's descending boot! This was followed by a multitude of sparks showering the ground from the sudden impact of metal hitting metal!

KERANG!!

"Blimey!" Jack stated, "whatever that thing is, it bloody hates Iscariot's wretched spider just as much as we do!"

Takarada moved in even closer to get a better view and added, "Maybe even more so, Sir Jonathon," watching as the monster's two wide fangs bit right through the metal of one of the spider's robotic legs!

CHOMP!

Takarada took note of the surrounding sky that flickered every time the lumbering beast exerted large amounts of physical energy or any kind of weaponry. He then asked SCOTT to search his databanks for any information pertaining to the myth of the legendary Pangea monsters. Sir Jonathon had never heard of such a thing, but most people hadn't and his eyebrow raised up in curiosity when Takarada mentioned it.

SCOTT's computer searched the entire web in about three seconds, and the results were just about nonexistent. He stated from a few obscure sites that the parting segments of the original continent, Pangea, had been assigned a protector by the spirits of the old world. He added that each guardian was based off of each separate land mass's location on Earth, capable of utilizing the characteristics unique to that particular continent. And that was about it, nothing more could be found, probably because the two-million-year-old legend, for the most part, had died out.

It was beginning to make sense though, and Takarada now knew that it was never the spirit of Notawni Nonaashi laying waste to the planet, but Iscariot himself. Through his neuro-computer, the evil doctor thought he could contain the spirits and demons that occupied this world in order for them to do his bidding. He, of course, found out the hard way that he could not, learning that the flesh (be it of organic or cybernetic nature) would play an important role in holding any spirit, or god, a prisoner. Then, upon the body of the spider burning to a crisp, Notawni Noonashi escaped and again returned back to the earth. "Or did it?" Takarada thought. That had to be it, there was no other possible explanation, especially after learning that the Indian spirit was capable of entering any kind of host, be it a human, an animal, a spider, or even a 60-meter battle bot.

Was Notawni Nonaashi a Pangea monster spirit? Takarada wasn't sure, but he was sure that the Navajo god was now pulling the strings of the Duke. And as far as this other daikaiju went, he figured it was obvious. Because after seeing it in action and witnessing its weapons, dinosaur-like stature and thick walrus hide, he was sure this one was indeed a Pangea monster. Takarada continued to observe the mighty winter-beast's every move, watching as it battled to the ebb and flow of the North Star's flickering light.

Nathan and Tommy slid down to Jack and Dr. T's side on the edge of their mountainous perch, then asked what the hell was going on. Takarada bit his lip, knowing his hypothesis would probably sound like a complete load of unchi, the same word he once used to describe the Navajo legend. But then again, after all of this, what *wouldn't* sound like a bunch of unchi?

He cleared his throat and began with a shaky, "Well ..." Just as Jack turned from the waging war below and towards the doctor, as he was also quite interested in hearing this for himself. Takarada repeated the "well" part and pointed his hand out the windowless window into the cold air towards the cowboy mech. "I believe it is the spirit of Notawni Nonaashi that is now controlling the Duke." He then paused and waited for the wails of disbelief, but only heard a soft, "No way," from Michael who, with Olivia and Liberty, was listening from behind. Nathan nodded and stated that maybe a few days ago he would have found that hard to believe, but after seeing Iscariot's freakin' machine, the one that imprisoned the essence of Notashi Nonan ... Notashi No ... King Taraxian in it, of course it made sense. He could also see how the noble spirit might just be a little pissed off too. Jack interrupted Nathan, the way that people who think whatever they have to say is more important than whatever you're saying and asked, "What about the other one, Kyoshi?"

Takarada lifted his index finger up towards the celestial brilliance that shined in the most northern part of the arctic sky and said, "Please watch the star and the beast at the same time." And with that it became obvious, the monster was indeed one with the flashes of flickering light, moving in sequence to the star's wavering beams cast upon the frozen earth from above. Takarada pulled his hand in from the other side of the broken window and brought it straight down to his warm pocket, then turned and stated,

"It is a Pangea monster, a defender from Gondwana, the most southern part of the tremendous mass that split into the continents of the world. I'm naming it after the northern star from which it derives its power source, Polaris."

Polaris spun around and thwacked his thick tail against a building-sized boulder of solid ice, launching it through the chilled air and sending it crashing down upon the back of the metal spider-monster! *BWAM!*

The weight of the massive slab of hardened water forced the creature down, and its legs shot out in eight directions from beneath

it. Followed by the Duke, who crashed his elbow through the frozen rock, pummeling the spider's titanium cephalothorax (it's freakin' head) into the earth with a flying forearm smash!

CHING!

Iscariot picked himself off the floor, spit out two of his bloodied teeth and reinserted one of the cables that had come loose from his head.

"Zo you unt vant to play rough?" he hissed. "Okay zen ..."

The chrome-steel skeleton of the massive arachnid pushed straight up with its tremendous legs, knocking the Duke backwards into a deep drift of snow. It then disappeared in the gray flurry above. Polaris looked up into the empty haze and waited. From behind the arctic dinosaur protector, the spider dropped, and its iron pincers plunged deep into Polaris' shoulders.

SHOOOMP!

The arachnid robot then attached itself to the back of the daikaiju with its chrome-iron talons and plunged its fangs even deeper into its cartilage. It forced Polaris forward, then down to its stomach into a freezing pool of its own blood.

BOOOOOSH!

The spider's legs flailed about, piercing the thick hide of the arctic guardian, just like the paper-pounding metal bars of an antique typewriter.

STAP! STAP! STAP!

The Duke launched straight up from the mountainous drift and came down hard and fast, smack onto the back of the spider, which, by the way, was still on top of Polaris. The cowbot placed his iron butt down upon the abdomen of the attacking creature and latched onto two of the spider's legs, right where they connected to its chrome skeletal body. The arachnid jumped, bucking like a freakin' titanium, zombie bronco and kicked itself right off of the arctic daikaiju's back! The Duke let go with one of his hands and held onto his 100-gallon hat with the other. The spider tried, but couldn't throw off the cowboy mech, who slammed the heels of his boots onto the covas of the spider's front two legs, followed by the spinning of his massive chrome spurs!

ZWEEEEEEEEEEEP!

The severed appendages fell to the ground, turning the pure-white snow to a toxic green when the steel limbs bled out a stream of organic thorium.

Iscariot pulled a few of the flesh-laden wires from his head and fell to his busted knees. He twisted his back and reached for the remains of the whiskey he had intended for Nathan, first taking a healthy slam, then pouring the rest over his head to sterilize his bloodied wounds. He called for his minions to set him into his chair, then placed his trembling hands back on its arms. He looked at the cracked glass that resided just above the face of his famous mouse watch and knew he was running out of time. A tear of blood streamed down what was left of his cheek, and his glowing red eye pulsed.

The spider scurried towards the mountain, turned around and again reared back as both Polaris and the Duke advanced. Its electronic, jeweled visual prosthesis lit up, then blasted a blinding beam of organic thorium green! Pulverizing the cowbot and the arctic kaiju with such ferocity, it sent them both off the edge of the island and back into the sea in one great explosion!

BOOOOSH!

Jack hollered for everybody to back away from the shattered glass of the tilting observation deck as tall, dark and creepy hauled ass back up the summit, right towards them.

SCOTT had been trying to dig an emergency exit through the fallen rock, but soon discovered it was somewhere around fifty feet deep. Even with his tremendous strength, he had only made a small dent in it. But it was still perfect for a group of humans to cower into as the demon skeleton quickly approached … then passed them right by.

From within their little igloo-sized hole in the wall, Nathan blurted out a confused, "HUH?" as he watched the ass end of the spider disappear.

"I thought we were Taraxian tarantula-chow for sure."

From their cramped quarters, Jack pushed the Lizard King out of the way so he could reach into his vest for his pocket watch.

"That bloody wanker Iscariot isn't going to bother with us anymore. He knows he only has a few precious minutes."

"Until what?" And then Tommy remembered, "Oh yeah … boom."

All could feel the mountain tremble when the steel skeleton began digging its way into the volcano towards the chamber that concealed both the refinery and the O.T.

"We're bleeding right back to where we started from," Jack groaned and he clicked his gold timepiece shut.

Nathan leaned over to Tommy and whispered from the corner of his mouth that he had another idea. Tommy then whispered back, stating he hoped it was better than the last.

"Look, I thought of another way to get us out of here, and I personally don't want to take the time to run it past the freakin' committee. Cuz' we need to do it now while were all crammed in here."

"And go where?" Tommy argued, "Even the Twins can't blast *all* of us to the other end of the planet."

"Nope," Nathan agreed, "but they can blast *all* of us there!"

Tommy looked in the direction of Nathan's nod, past the sloping floor of the tilting observation deck, outside its barren windows, across the tundra to Iscariot's ship that was approaching from above the sea.

Tommy thought the Lizard King's new plan was actually worse than his first, but really didn't see any alternative. Nathan backed up to Michael and Liberty, and as he whispered in between them, they both looked up to the oncoming craft and nodded their heads. Nathan, not wanting to give anybody a heart attack (primarily of the fat, aging, walrussy variety), explained his intentions.

"Okay everybody, hang on, because we're going to surprise Iscariot by having the Twins teleport us to his ship. We then take out the evil doc, let the Duke and Polaris take care of the spider, let the mountain blow up and go home! Everybody got it? GOOD!"

Of course before anybody could even utter a swift word, the entire room (or what was left of it) exploded in a flash of alien purple, and they all disappeared.

SHOOOMP!

The Duke burst through the surface of the sea, rocketing upwards towards the top half of Mount Terror where the spider-mech was digging its way in. The angry cowbot then yanked the screaming creature out of its descending tunnel by its kicking hind legs. And not that it was planned, but as soon as everybody vanished, the steel arachnid came tumbling down the steep slope, flattening the observation deck in the process.

Through the spider's electronic eye, Iscariot could see Polaris at the foot of the mountain, waiting. It dug its iron talons deep into the sloping terrain, but once it slowed, it found itself again gaining speed, being pulled down by Polaris who was somehow manipulating the magnetic poles of Antarctica. Great pulses surrounded its entire body and flowed inward, drawing the steel arachnid closer and closer to the clenched fists of the awaiting daikaiju.

The purple glow dissipated, and Nathan opened his eyes to see that they had teleported into the hovering ship's cargo bay. It was completely empty except for the oncoming charge of Iscariot's men. His reflexes were quick though, and Nathan stuck out his foot and stepped to the side, pulling the crony's photon rifle out of his hands as he fell. He politely thanked the kind gentleman and started blasting guards left and right.

BATTA-SPAP! SPAP!

SCOTT held up two guards, one in each hand, and brought their heads together hard and fast. He then discarded them to the side and reached for two more.

CLUNK!

The Twins, using what little power they had left, sent purple gobs of goop hurling across the room which stuck to the barrels of the bad guys' weapons. It rendered them useless, and some of the men simply threw down their arms and ran away, while the others advanced with their bare hands. Tommy grabbed Olivia's wrists and began to spin her around. As he gained momentum, he let gravity do the rest, taking out a number of guards with the spiked heels of her boots when her feet lifted into the air.

BOOF!

Takarada quietly eased the FUJI personnel towards the back wall, corralling them into a corner, while trying to keep them calm. He felt the cold steel of a photon rifle upon the back of his neck and was ordered to "FREEZE!" He did just the opposite, launching into a triple-spin assault with three kicks to the face of the guard.

WACK! WACK! CRACK!

It seemed they were getting their minion-asses kicked and Iscariot's lead henchman ran to the wall, reaching for the wired radio communicator. However, he stopped rather sudden-like when the click of Sir Jonathon's Walther PPK thundered in his ear.

"I wouldn't even bloody breathe if I were you," Jack advised, then demanded they be brought to the man in charge, Iscariot.

"Zare is no need, Sir Jonathon, I am unt right here."

Two guards wheeled in the doctor (who was now a permanent resident of his captain's chair) through the double doors of the bay. They were moving at a snail's pace so the other two men pushing the machine he was attached to could keep up. He looked a thousand years old. His artificial eye dangled from its socket while an array of clear tubes pumped blood from his head, bubbling back and forth from his skull to what was left of his neuro-computer. He clutched Tommy's bionic hand, the one he had stolen from him at the FUJI, holding it up to his heart like some sort of security blanket. Nathan leaned up to Tommy's ear.

"Thaaaat's a bit creepy," he said beneath his breath, and Tommy didn't even want to know.

Iscariot opened his mouth, no doubt about to say something brilliant, but before anything came out his chin jerked straight up and he fell backwards.

Polaris and the Duke were beating the spider to within an inch of Iscariot's life. The flunkies helped him get his limp body back to its feet, supporting him from beneath each arm. The mad doctor wasn't giving up, he was far to close and far too gone to throw in the towel now. He closed his eyes and looked as though he had just died, when in fact he was retaliating against the behemoths below. There was no way to tell just what Iscariot did in the form of the steel arachnid, but it was still fighting and no doubt would do so as long as Iscariot was still breathing.

"Give it up, Leopold," Jack demanded. "Even if you ruddy get to the organic thorium with that beat-up, tin spider of yours, you won't live long enough to get to use it. Why don't you end this bloody war right now and just die already? Retain an ounce of your dignity man, while you still have an ounce to retain."

Iscariot shook his weakened fist at Jack, "Zats unt good coming from you, Winston, little you know about dignity."

The evil doctor's insides boiled as he replayed his own twisted version of his short career with the Earth Intelligence Organization in his head. He viewed the scratchy black-and-white memories of

270

making fantastic discoveries side by side with Takarada, only to be tossed out on his ass when Sir Jonathon called him mad. Just as the mercury was about to erupt from the tip of his skull though, he could only glare at the ground. Wincing from the pain in his body, he grimaced while his broken mind tightened around the box in his brain, the one that held his past dreams and ideas, but most of all, the hate. Leopold Iscariot returned for a split second, and when he looked about himself and at the others around him, he wept. For that brief moment, he saw that he was insane and also realized what he had become. After all of this bloodshed, all the lives lost, the power he craved was now sifting like ash, right between his brittle and busted fingers. He then knew, beyond a shadow of any doubt, he had truly lost the war he waged, and with that, Iscariot was again gone.

"Unt you are right, I vill be dying soon, unt ven I do, unt so will my little acht-legged-liebchen. But unt before I give you zat satisfaction, I warned you about placing microchips in zee heads of your unt agents. Zey don't like—"

SCOTT knew exactly where Iscariot was going with all this microchip jazz and burst out from behind Tommy and Nathan, straight for evil Dr. Chicken. Even an android could only take so much. Iscariot grinned, letting SCOTT get just close enough and *ZAAAAAP!* White lightning bolts discharged from the barrels of what Nathan and everybody else presumed were simple photon rifles, but they weren't.

SCOTT collapsed, and the guards lowered their smoking weapons.

Iscariot laughed, "You unt like that Kyoshi?" he shouted to Takarada, who by all means could not help but be impressed.

"Zat is the world's first anti-organic-thorium ray! I know you're dying to know how it works, and since you will be, I vill unt tell you. It's a highly-intensified heat ray that electrically stimulates zee Glaucusidious cells within zee thorium ... stimulates zem to death!"

Takarada gasped, it was both horrible and ingenious, because this ray had the acute ability to neutralize the main element within the organic thorium. It could actually take the regenerating component out of the mix, making the O.T., as well as anything that used the infinite source of energy, powerless. The thought of Iscariot not only controlling the world's organic thorium, but also being able to take it away from anybody (like the E.I.O.) who already depended upon it, was mind-numbingly scary.

Iscariot looked at SCOTT who lay defenseless on the floor, his computer mind as flawless and sharp as ever, held in a body that couldn't move. Tommy kneeled down next to his android friend and sat him upright. He then placed his butt on the floor next to SCOTT and held him up by placing his arm around him. Tommy followed it up with a sneer and the raising of his middle finger in the direction of Iscariot.

"How sweet," the mad doctor stated. "You have zee unt little robot friend."

Iscariot tilted his lip in some sort of twisted smile, then stopped when he completely lost his train of thought, his melting mind succumbing to the tremendous demands of the neuro-computer. It was kind of awkward as everybody waited for his next line, only he just sat there, strapped to his electric chair looking far off into space. His crony nudged him and he snapped out of it, mumbling something about schnauzers unt sauerbraten. Tommy, Nathan and even Jack cracked up and Leopold, feeling kind of dumb, shouted,

"Zilence! Now zen … vare ver ve. Oh yes, I remember now … zee microchips."

Iscariot's red-jeweled eye flickered, and all E.I.O. agents within the cargo bay, including Jack, Takarada and even the alien Twins grabbed at their heads. He stuck out his bottom lip and let out a "Hmmm," when he saw even Sir Jonathon and Dr. Takarada do the same, surprised that they too, had the chip implants. His dangling seeing appendage grew in intensity, and with it, so did the excruciating pain. Iscariot laughed,

"Let's ze how you unt like it! I had to pull mine out before it unt melted my brain! You should feel unt lucky, because yours vill not, but zey vill turn your cerebral cortex to unt strudel!" He cackled louder, "Regardless, you vill all be DEAD!"

As he laughed, Iscariot tossed his blood-stained surgical scalpel at Nathan.

"You have unt ten seconds, my boy, to pry it out!"

Nathan cursed Iscariot as small beads of blood began to protrude from his sweat glands. He reached for the scalpel, imagining himself plunging it deep into Iscariot's warped brain, but the pain was too much; he knew he was going to die. So instead he reached for Olivia's hand that was interlocked with her other at the back of her bobbing head. He forced it free and held it tighter than anything he had ever held before. Olivia's head convulsed to the point where her glasses finally fell from her nose, but she still somehow managed to smile at the Lizard King. Nathan even smiled back, then looked deep into her flooding eyes and chose "Thank you" for his last words.

Tommy's disconnected robo-hand, the one Iscariot had been clutching, fell to the floor when the mad doctor's arm shot straight up into the air and bent completely backwards at his elbow!

SNAP!

Iscariot screamed in pain, and from his red-tinted mind's eye, he could see the iron limbs of his steel spider's pedipalp hanging from the mouth of Polaris! He grabbed his arm with the other, and the pain in Nathan's skull subsided as Iscariot's thoughts shifted to his own. Nathan lifted his head, and while everybody else remained in the fetal position on the floor, he grabbed the scalpel Iscariot had so graciously tossed at him. Nathan could barely walk, yet alone take out the guards in two swift kicks and one punch, but somehow he did. He yanked the wires from Doctor Chicken's head and blood spat from the clear tubes all over Nathan's scowling face. He placed his forearm beneath Iscariots brittle chin, pushed up and placed the shiny blade of the surgical knife against the skin of his temple, demanding that the remaining guards "Back the hell off!"

For a moment, Nathan looked as demented as the mad doctor himself, becoming one with a rage he never knew even existed inside of him. A drop of blood dripped down Iscariot's cheek when the tip of the knife penetrated his tissue-paper skin. Nathan sneered, because he liked the idea of carving Iscariot up into small portions. He thought about his parents, and his resentment forced the knife even deeper. But in the midst of his darkest rage and from within this very thought of pure anger, Nathan knew something he didn't know before. He knew that he could no longer afford the luxury of a hatred this intense. Nathan sighed, even getting a bit irritated while he held the knife up to Iscariot's head. Apparently, *this* was the kind of crap his dad was talking about. The junk he'd have to come to terms with, more of that inner-bullshit-turmoil freakin' stuff. However, as much as he hated it, he saw that he ultimately had a choice. He could either forgive the man who took his parents' lives or (like Iscariot) let his sheer hate dictate a life of resentment and bitter frustration. Nathan thought hard but not long, and just as he made his decision, Iscariot smiled. It was then that Nathan, along with his friends, felt the fierce pain return deep within his skull.

"You are an unt fool, Nathan Fox! Just like your father!"

Nathan gnashed his teeth together and, through the immense pain, pushed hard on the scalpel, opting for curtain number two. He figured he could live with it.

Iscariot's body, still seated in an upright position from beneath Nathan, went limp from within his chair and the searing pain subsided. His head, with the scalpel buried into it, slumped, and his chest eased forward, stopped by the constricting wires that were attached to his machine. He was dead.

His minions also fell, because more than likely they were also being controlled by the now-deceased doctor and his neuro-computer. They weren't dead, they just dropped, as did Iscariot's ship that was also no doubt being operated from inside the evil doctor's head. Takarada stated they needed to get to the bridge of the ship, and because it was of his design, they all knew just how to get there.

Michael and Tommy dragged SCOTT by his arms, and Michael wished he and Liberty had a little juice left, because the android weighed about 600 freakin' pounds. Olivia and Takarada even had to help, and while Nathan stood in a stunned silence, Jack placed his arm around him.

"You learn to live with it," he said in a soft voice, "just like you'll learn to live with everything else. It's never easy my boy, nor will it ever be."

Jack cleared his throat, patted Nathan on the back and stated they needed to get to the bridge or quite simply, they were all going to die. Nathan nodded, and while they made their way to the door, Jack added,

"Both your mom and dad would be proud of you, Nathan ... I know I bloody am. And even if we had all gone up in a ruddy blaze of glory, I would still be proud of you. You've slain more than one demon today ... which is far more than I've ever done."

At the base of Mount Terror, Iscariot's demonic, eight-legged skeleton-creature was literally being torn limb from limb. The Duke ripped its last appendage from its torso, while the mighty four-nailed foot of Polaris pounded the broken body of the spider deep into the ground.

BOOOSH! BOOOSH!

The artic kaiju then ripped Takarada's remaining massive frost barrier from its concrete foundation, lifted it high above its head and slammed its plated, steel, corner edge into the back of the spider's legless chrome body.

CHING!

The Duke followed up with a barrage of photon blasts from his twin six-shooters into the side of the mountain, *CHOOM! CHOOM! CHOOM!*, burying the arachnid monster in an avalanche of snow, rock and ice.

KA-BOOOSH!

It, like Iscariot, was dead.

Nathan, Olivia, Tommy, the Twins, Jack and Takarada all watched the finale from the viewing screen within the bridge of Iscariot's ship. It was easy for Takarada to link the craft's mainframe with SCOTT's computer, who was now flying the large vessel. Even though the android couldn't move a synthetic muscle, it didn't matter because the organic thorium only controlled his body, not his brain. Takarada looked back from the screen and asked how he was doing. SCOTT stated,

"I am quite fine thank you, though I look forward to again moving soon."

Takarada agreed and promised him an O.T. transfusion as soon as they returned to the FUJI. He then stopped and had to remind himself it wasn't there anymore. He sighed, and Jack told him not to worry as they had their eyes on a quaint little location in Osaka.

Jack pulled his pocket watch from his vest, clicked it open and held it up to about chest level. He gazed down at it, then back up to the screen.

The Duke circled above Polaris as the mighty beast made its way towards the edge of the island. The arctic kaiju acknowledged its robot friend with a bellowing roar, then jumped from the icy cliff above into the waiting sea below.

SPLOOOOOSH!

After the tremendous splash subsided, the blue and white water

churned into a raging whirlpool and the Pangea monster was gone. The Duke turned and rocketed back towards Mount Terror, then descended from the sky, landing at the foot of its rim.

BOOOSH!

Snow erupted from beneath its gargantuan steel boots and his arms fell to his side.

All watched the bot from the viewing monitor of Iscariot's craft, gazing as it stood tall and proud amidst the scattering flurries of snow. The North Star was fading back to its normal cast and darkness was returning to the tundra. Soon the twilight was upon the Duke's shimmering, steel chassis, and it sparkled with hints of green, reflecting the lights of Aurora Australis. Everyone swallowed hard and swelled up with pride at the sight of the majestic bot that stood tall and victorious. It was almost breathtaking, especially when the arctic winds added to the moment by dancing around the mech in a celebration of sleet and snow.

Funny thing was, it seemed like while they were watching the Duke from within the screen, the cowboy robot looked to be watching them as well. Jack stared at the bot's torn-up body, its battered head and the shattered monocle that sat beneath the metal brim of his cowboy hat. The Duke had done his duty, and Jack raised his hand to his brow from the confines of the bridge, saluting the bot through the screen. Takarada did the same, and everybody slowly followed suit.

The star known as Polaris glistened one final time, and while they stood with their hands to their heads, the Duke collapsed like a marionette whose steel strings had just been severed.

BOOOOSH!

It was odd, but somehow it was no surprise either, not when you consider everything that had happened. Nathan lowered his hand to grab Olivia's, and his brown eyes thinned as he admired the downed bot, that giant piece of scrap known as the Duke. Tommy eased up to Nathan's other side.

"Looks like we've solved another one, Raggy," then blurted out a, "Hey, look at that!" and pointed to the screen.

It was moving yet slightly creepy watching the black and reddish haze seep from the Duke's body and into the frozen ground. Michael asked, "Is that ...?" and when he paused, Dr. T answered his question.

277

"Yes Michael, that is Notawni Nonaashi, returning back to the earth."

Followed by nothing but a slow, "Whoa," from the alien.

Tommy suggested to Jack that he call in a few copters, or a ship, or something and retrieve the chrome-steel carcass of the robot. Jack pulled out his gold pocket watch, clicked it open, shook his head at Tommy and barked,

"SCOTT, get us the bloody hell out of here!"

Iscariot's craft ascended straight up and Mount Terror, the Duke, the smoldering rubble and the surrounding sea grew smaller and smaller on the viewing monitor. Jack sighed, placed his timepiece back into his pocket and suggested that everybody hang on to something and to please turn away from the screen.

KA-FREAKIN-CHOOM!

Chapter XXVII

The jitters were hitting Nathan pretty hard, something he used to combat with a shot or two or twelve of whiskey. Today, however, it was a different story, and the monkey that rode around on his back now seemed to prefer root beer to Tennessee bourbon. He squeezed his hand into the front pocket of his Robert Plant jeans (the ones that left nothing to the imagination), and pulled out two bronze coins. Of course one was the three-year medallion his dad had given him. The other was one he picked up this morning, indicating he had gone nine months without a drink. Nathan clutched them tight, looking for a little luck and a lot of reassurance while trying to keep himself both calm and grounded. Pre-show nerves were pretty normal, but Nathan was feeling anxious, probably because it was his first time performing without being absolutely wasted in quite a few years. But as of late, Nathan was more about facing his monsters head on. It wasn't always easy but, like Sir Jack said, nothing worth it ever was. He now looked his problems square in the eyes (two, eight, whatever) and chose to face each one as opposed to drowning them.

The newly-rebuilt Flooid Zoo in the heart of Tokyo was packed to the gills, and Nathan snuck a peek from his dressing room at the crowd. The manager (who used to hate his guts) spied the Lizard King and gave him a big, brown-nosing smile. It was funny how different things were this time around, because this little live house where he once played to maybe four people was, thanks to him, sold out.

But that's how it goes, and it doesn't matter if you're performing solo or with your triple-platinum band. Once you make it big, people will always remember you, or at least they'll want a piece of you. And that never seems to go away, unless you're that guy from Wham!

Nathan closed the door and sat back down upon the red, crushed-velvet couch, and Paul asked him how he was doing.

"I'm nervous, but I'm good," he simply replied.

Paul was holding his guitar, going over some of the changes in the upcoming songs, and Nathan reached over and picked up his as well.

"You wouldn't believe it Paul, but last time I played here, there were about three people."

Nathan looked around the room, giving it the edgy once-over and from under his breath said, "and a few kaiju."

Paul didn't hear the part about the kaiju. He also had no idea of Nathan's past, had no idea he was a super-freakin' agent for the E.I.O., flew a robot or any damn thing like that. As far as he knew, Nathan was just a recovering rock star who wanted a fresh start, a singer trying to make a go of it on his own. Which was indeed true, even though going solo was scarier to Nathan than any of the demons he'd ever faced. It was also pretty damn scary leaving Vinyl Crush, because there's a certain amount of comfort that comes with staying in a band that's sold 16 trillion albums.

But what Nathan hated the most was not sharing a stage with Tommy. Sure, he always had visions of a solo career, but that didn't mean he wouldn't take Tommy with him. After all, it took Nathan this long to mold him into the guitar-playing freak he was today, or at least was yesterday. It drove him crazy that Tommy had quit playing, but it wasn't his decision to make, it was Tommy's. So he forced himself to be cool with the whole thing. Tommy was still his best friend, would always be regardless if he played guitar, fought daikaiju or flipped freakin' burgers, and Nathan wanted to keep it that way. As a matter of fact, he was going to be there any moment.

The door jerked open and Olivia fought her way into the dressing room. A million hands grabbed and pushed pens and Vinyl Crush CDs at her from behind, while the security guards pulled them back. She plopped down onto the couch in between Paul and Nathan, and laid a big, wet kiss on the Lizard King.

"You look great in those jeans!" she commented and Nathan said he owed it all to Jenny Craig.

Paul laughed too, "Yeah mate, you were easily a good twenty pounds heavier when I met you on the Queen Elizabeth."

Nathan "Yeeeshed" when he remembered, not because of the weight thing, but because that was the day Tommy told him he had quit playing forever. It was also then that he learned about Akira Akemi. Nope, there'd be no forgetting that one.

A repetitive paradiddle played from the opposite end of the door, and Nathan knew Michael had arrived, which of course meant Liberty was there too. They entered to the same grabbing hands and when the door closed, Michael bee lined it straight for the catered spread on the long, white table. He scooped up a handful of green M&Ms, filled his mouth and asked,

"Whaptch blekken dwop oner?"

Nathan looked at his phone and answered, "About ten minutes," and Michael responded with a quick nod. The Lizard King thought some percussion would go great with his unplugged-esque show and knew of nobody better than Michael. He was the only member of Vinyl Crush, other than himself, who would be performing tonight. The original plan was simply Nathan singing his new songs and strumming, while Paul accompanied him on guitar. But like so many things do, it grew and grew. Even a few labels got wind of the event, and that's when Nathan decided to up it with a bit of alien groove.

One of the security guards knocked politely and peeked in through the small crack of the door,

"Anata no tsure to itteiru hito ga kiteimasu ga."

Of course Nathan had no idea what the hell he was saying but could hear Sir Jonathon bitching from the packed room outside and figured it out. For a second, he thought about messing with Jack and not letting him in, then decided he'd better.

"Yes, yes, hai. Let … the … walrus … in."

A wasted Jack flopped into the room, almost falling flat on his face when he burst through the door. Faithfully by his side, or more so behind his shwacked ass, was Takarada, who rarely ventured into the private sector but would not have missed this for the world. Another gentleman of a sleek nature, probably about the same age as Jack, sporting a long, trench coat and a fedora followed in after both men. Jack introduced the man as one of his oldest and dearest friends.

"This is Robert Jones!" Jack announced. "Treat him with bloody respect and dignit … digni … dig … treat him with bloody respect!"

Jack laughed, then kissed Robert on his cheek.

"Bloody hell, Mr. Fox!" he shouted as he sat clumsily next to Nathan on the arm of the red-velvet couch, but still careful not to spill his double-scotch straight-up. He put his arm around Nathan and stated how much he loved this young man, just like his own ruddy son. Nathan knew he was loaded, but also knew he was sincere. He liked Jack now more than ever, which was a giant leap from not liking him at all. Jack got even closer and Nathan fanned Sir Jonathon's nasty-ass breath away from his face.

"Today, my boy, we celebrate! *We* celebrate two bloody milestones in both of our lives."

Nathan smiled as he shook his head.

"And what's that, Jacky boy?" Nathan laughed.

"First my lad, there's this."

Jack reached into his jacket and pulled out a wrinkled envelope and handed it to Nathan.

"What the hell is this?" he asked and Jack giggled,

"Why … why don't you bloody open it and find out."

Nathan opened the envelope and pulled out the card that was in it. In bold letters it stated, "Happy 50th Birthday" and sported the picture of a long-faced mule that was sticking out its tongue. Nathan looked a bit confused while he gazed upon the card, then Jack's friend Robert pointed out that Sir Jonathon just picked it out about 15 minutes ago. Nathan didn't really know what to expect, plus the fact that Jack's handwriting was about 180 proof didn't make it any easier.

Dearest Nathan —

Congratulations my boy on your 90 days clean you are an inspiration to me and many others I'm very proud of you.

Sir Jonathon Winston
Always your friend,

John

A daikaiju-sized lump grew in Nathan's throat, and he was about one second away from bursting into tears when Sir Jack wacked him on the back and burped. Nathan set the card into his empty guitar case that lay at his feet and snapped it shut so it would be safe. At that moment he decided he was going to get another photo album (just like the one he lost when his house went up in flames) with this as his first keepsake. Jack, as well as everybody in the dressing room, sat there for a second in silence, and Olivia reminded Jack that he had mentioned there were two things there were celebrating tonight. Jack snapped his head, hollered and raised his spilling glass into the air,

"Right you are! I'm proud to say, that today I have officially retired from the E.I.O. ..."

However, and before anybody said a word, Takarada put his cupped hand to his mouth and coughed out a loud and deliberate, "AHEM!" And Jack, even as drunk as he was, caught wind of the subtle hint, remembering Nathan's new guitarist was not "in the know" and he backpedaled.

"Right then ... I have officially retired from the E.I.O. ... bloody ... Pancake ... ruddy Emporium."

Yeah, it was stupid, but it worked, and the room broke out into cheers! This was a long time coming and everybody knew it, especially Jack. It was time to move on, even if moving on meant moving backwards towards the thing he truly loved the most. And, like Nathan, it was music.

Another knock came at the door, and whoever was on the other side announced in broken English, "Ten minutes to show time, Mr. Fox."

Paul stood up and said he needed to tune up and was going to head in that general direction. He picked his guitar up and went to the back of the dressing room, to a long hallway that led to just behind the backstage curtains.

Michael yelled, "Wait for me dude, I wanna make sure my congas, bongos and king-sized cajonays are good to go."

"You mean a king-sized cajone, right?" Paul asked, and Michael smirked. Paul didn't even want to bloody know and they both faded into the dark.

Nathan also stood, "Yeah, everybody get the hell out of here. Security will lead you up to the front-row table I reserved for you guys."

This time Nathan knocked on the door, and when it opened a wee bit, he asked for his guests to be escorted to their seats. Olivia gave him another kiss for luck and she and Liberty eased out. Takarada practically had to lift big-fat Jack's drunken ass off the arm of the couch, then pushed him ever-so-gentle-like out the door. He stopped, turned to the Lizard King and bowed. Robert, following close behind, stopped and reached his hand out to Nathan.

"That's quite the accomplishment," he said with a very refined British accent. "They say for some bleeding reason the 90-day medallion is the hardest one to get."

Robert smiled showing his less-than-perfect yellowing teeth adding, "I have absolutely no idea why they say that."

Nathan flexed his eyes on the gentleman. He could tell Robert must've known a thing or two about this sobriety stuff, which he did, because he then stated that he had almost 30 years clean himself. Nathan gripped his extended hand and Robert pulled him close.

"Nathan, should you ever decide you would like to come back, the Earth Intelligence Organization will always ... ALWAYS, have a place for you. You will always be welcome."

The Lizard King, while still holding onto Robert's hand, repelled ever so slightly as it was a bit of a shocker that this friend of Jack's (who he had never seen or heard of) knew of the super-secret agency. Nathan asked Robert what gave him the authority to offer such a thing. Robert moved in even closer, and through the casted shadow of the tip of his fedora, Nathan for the first time could see his mismatched eyes and he whispered,

"Because I'm in charge now."

He squeezed Nathan's hand one final time, breaking his grip as he turned.

Nathan was suddenly glad to be moving onto bigger and better things. Then Tommy showed up, brushing up against Robert's chest as he was leaving. Robert tipped his fedora, and Tommy saw his face just before he vanished into the crowd. He looked at Nathan,

"Whoa, what's the matter with that guy's eyes?"

Nathan said he had no idea, then Tommy asked who he was and the Lizard King said he'd be finding out soon enough.

Tommy stepped into the dressing room and looked around.

"Damn," he said, "this dressing room's freakin' huge."

"Yeah it is," Nathan replied, "holds about a hundred people too."

Tommy continued checking out the room and, while looking in the opposite direction, let Nathan know he was glad he'd decided against joining the 27 Club. Nathan smirked. He'd forgotten all about it and in a soft voice noted that he was kinda' happy about it him-damn-self. Tommy let him know, that if he were ever truly miserable, he could always start the 28 Club. Nathan shook his head and said, "Still too soon," then admitted he liked the idea of a 98 Club better. Tommy laughed, while still nervously looking about the place, the same way Nathan did when he had first arrived.

"Wow, remember what a dump this place used to be? This building collapsing to the ground was the best thing to ever happen to it. This place looks awesome!" Tommy stated.

He looked down and noticed Paul's empty guitar case on the floor and couldn't help but feel a bit like an ex-whatever. It was sort of like going to your old boyfriend or girlfriend's house and seeing somebody else's sexy underwear scattered all over the floor. Yeah, this was nothing like that, but Tommy was still feeling a bit uncomfortable and Nathan could tell.

"Look dude, I love Paul and he's a great guy as well as a great player, but he's no Tommy Lynn Taylor. Trust me man, I'd love to have you up on that stage with me more than anybody else on this whole damn planet."

Nathan then gave Tommy a desperate glance.

"Especially Jack, because he's already invited himself up to play a song or two. He even freakin' asked me if we could play a few tunes by The Beatles.

Tommy shuddered, not because of Jack wanting to play something by The Beatles, but because he too knew the etiquette. He knew that you never asked to play on another man's stage, you had to *be* asked. He also knew how wasted Jack was, which wasn't going to help in the least.

Nathan then put his hands on Tommy's shoulders.

"Whenever you're ready dude, I'll be waiting. You just let me know, and I'll break out the rubber-banded Folgers can and we'll get right back to writing some great music."

He added that Tommy, like himself, needed to do what was right for him, not something that was right for someone else. Nathan revisited his pants and again pulled out his most prized possession, his dad's three-year medallion. He held it up and read the writing forged upon it,

"To thine own self be true."

Nathan then placed the bronze coin into his best friend's hand and said, "Keep it." Tommy knew how much this meant to Nathan and there was absolutely no way he was going to do so. Nathan closed Tommy's fingers around it and said, "Don't worry about it, I have another," then pulled his nine-month coin out and showed it to him. Tommy still balked, so Nathan made him the same promise that Akira made to Tommy a few years ago.

"I'll tell you what, you hold onto it for now, and if you're still hell-bent on giving it back to me," Nathan stopped and grinned, "you can, the first time we get together to jam out some new tunes."

Tommy liked the idea, then hugged his oldest and dearest friend.

Another knock came at the door announcing to Nathan that it was show time. He took a deep breath and looked at Tommy.

"Wish me luck," he said and Tommy of course did.

Nathan slipped out from the back of the dressing room, fading into the long hallway that led to the stage and Tommy called out to him,

"Hey man, I know it's in bad taste to ask this, but ya think I could maybe play a couple tunes with you tonight?"

Nathan yelled back, "What the hell do you think?" He never said anything, but he had a hunch that sooner or later Tommy would come around, and this made him smile … like the Grinch.

He heard the club announce his name to the eagerly awaiting audience, and the Lizard King took a long, deep breath. He then pushed the curtains to one side, eased through the thin veil that separated him from the stage, and Nathan Fox walked back into the light.

Timothy Price is a full time musician and author who hails from Minneapolis, Minnesota. Tim is an honors graduate from the prestigious Atlanta Institute of Music, and other than touring, writing scores and performing solo fingerstyle guitar, has been featured on countless albums as both a guitarist and producer. Since the release of his first novel, Tim has written for *Mad Scientist* magazine, attended conventions nationwide as a panelist and guest author and with this book (the one you're holding in your hands right now) has completed the second installment of his ongoing *Big In Japan* series.

Tim and his lovely wife, Alyce, live with their two kids in a small town south of the city, where he and the boys force mom to watch 8mm monster films, blast tunes and collect kaiju toys.

Timothy Price

Alan OW Barnes

Alan O.W. Barnes is a storyteller from Damascus, Virginia who has just moved to Providence, Rhode Island with his wife, Kim, and their daughter, Keira. Alan draws stories. Some he also writes, some use time (like music and animation), but he loves storytelling in all its forms. Alan is over-educated, with master's degrees from Belmont University in Music Composition, and the Savannah College of Art and Design in Sequential Art (the fancy term for drawing comics).

Alan has made ads for giant companies and the fabulously famous, taught at one of the largest art schools in the country (Ai), has worked for accrediting bodies and designed curriculum for a host of colleges. All the while he has been creating original content, like this book.

Made in the USA
Middletown, DE
20 June 2016